BALAAM'S CURSE

BALAAM'S CURSE

BOOK ONE OF
THE STONES OF GILGAL

C. L. SMITH

MOUNTAIN VIEW PRESS

© 2016 by C. L. Smith. All rights reserved.

Published by Mountain View Press, www.mountainviewpress.com,
Toll Free (855) 946-2555.

ISBN 13: 978-1-63232-371-2 (Print)
        978-1-63232-372-9 (ePub)
        978-1-63232-378-1 (Mobi)

Library of Congress Catalog Card Number: 2015943268

DEDICATION

For J. Paul Stauffer, my major professor at Pacific Union College, with much love and respect. Kind and eloquent, he is a true renaissance man. His gift for reading our creative writing assignments so even the feeblest effort sounded like literature gave me the courage to believe I could write.

CONTENTS

ACKNOWLEDGMENTS

Above all, I am grateful for the exciting stories of Scripture and the God who gave them to us. *Balaam's Curse* is, after all, part of his story from his book. I have a strong sense that God has opened and shut doors for me, holding me back, pushing me in new directions, guiding this project in ways that have proven to be just right. I am humbled and grateful for that guidance. The original inspiration came to me while I was reading the ancient texts, but I am also grateful for the illumination of many commentaries and a wealth of information from other books and websites. And I really should thank the characters themselves—Acsah, Othniel, Salmon, Jonathan, Phinehas, Abihail and Rahab. They have taken things into their own hands more often than not and directed subplots in ways I didn't see coming until my hands were on the keyboard.

I could not have even conceived of doing such a project without the encouragement and support of my husband, Eden, who is truly "the wind beneath my wings."

And then, my wonderful children . . . Thank you to my daughter, Melinda, a far more gifted writer than myself, who read the original first chapter years ago. Through countless hours and many transformations of the story, she has patiently taken time from her own writing career to provide invaluable criticism, encouragement, and (in the inevitable role reversal of life) lots of technical "parenting" of my infantile computer skills. After watching my struggle to sound "Tolkeinesque," my son, Eden III, and my son-in-law, Kem Nicolaysen, both gifted writers and avid readers, provided me with stacks of fantasy novels to bring me up to speed on the genre. Kem, who is a walking encyclopedia with an incredibly broad spectrum of knowledge, has recently developed an interest in ancient bronze weaponry and, just a few months ago, taught me more than I knew there was to know about Canaanite swords. His wife, my daughter Shelly, who teaches comparative religion, has shared many insights and books about ancient Judaism and religion in general. Her wisdom has broadened my thinking in more ways than I can tell. My daughter, Melissa, a busy plastic surgeon, slashes at my work now and then with her quick wit and incisive comments. Being more a doer than a reader, she passed on my manuscript to an Iranian patient, a recent immigrant with many interesting insights from his Middle-Eastern perspective.

I am most grateful for the priceless encouragement and help of many friends. Julie Lewis, Shona Macomber, and Wendy Wheeler read and provided feedback on various early versions of the long manuscript (before I divided *The Stones of Gilgal* into two books and figured out that the story was morphing into a series). My sister-in-law, Heather Smith, shared her family heritage expertise by charting the "Family of Nations." Marjorie Moran created the beautiful map and my sword logo as well as illustrations of the Gilgal. I must mention my informal focus group, the many Facebook friends who responded enthusiastically and helpfully to surveys and questions.

I also want to thank James Rupert, branding consultant, who helped me figure out who I am. And then there is the publishing team at Mountain View Press, a division of Redemption Press. My heartfelt thanks to Athena Dean Holtz for her initial encouragement of my project, Amber for keeping everything on track, Inger for her competent editing, and Brittany for the graphic design that pulled the cover together. Getting the right cover art has been one of the biggest challenges of this past year; so with great relief and joy, I give special thanks to Marcus Park whose artistry so beautifully captured the essence of the book in one image. It is said a picture is worth a thousand words. I say the right picture for a book cover is priceless!

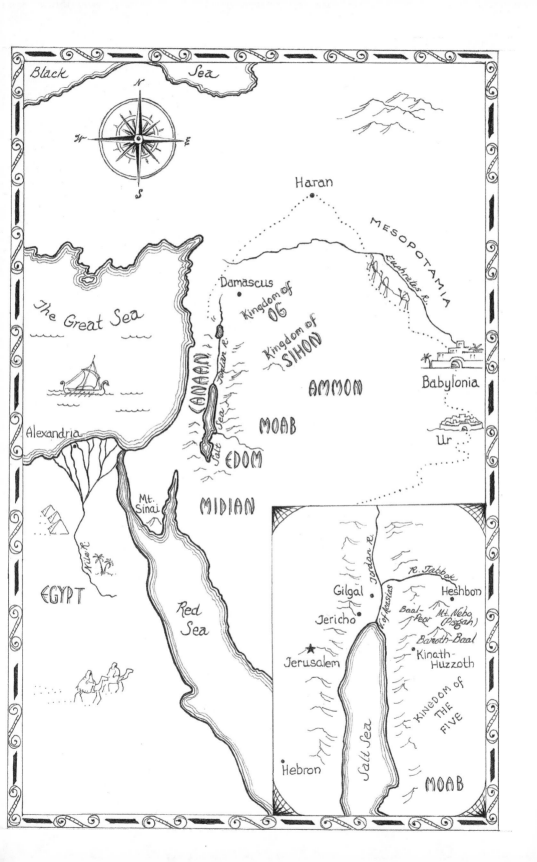

Remember, My people,
how Balak king of Moab plotted to destroy you,
yet I turned the curses of Balaam, son of Beor, into blessings.
Consider your journey from the sorrows of Acacia Grove
to the triumph of Gilgal,
that you may know the perfection of my mighty acts,
and my faithful love toward you.
—Micah 6:5 (KJV, author's paraphrase)

The prophet stormed across the lower courtyard. It was not difficult to divine the disdain here. It diffused through every corner of the temple and it was directed at *him*. Anyone could see the white-robed priests peering at him from every side, watching from shadowy portals, peeking furtively from behind pale sandstone pillars, snickering as he entered their domain. No, it didn't take a seer's eyes, and it didn't take an oracle from the gods to interpret the cloud of whispers billowing around him.

"So much for this Babylonian seer."

"He cannot *see* the gods, and they do not choose to *see* him."

"Perhaps he has power in his own country, with the tamer gods of Mesopotamia, but not here. Not in Moab."

The prophet bristled. Such a thing had never happened to him in Babylonia. Never. Once, twice, yea, thrice, the God of Jacob had flipped him and his incantations turban-over-sandals as if he were a foolish child playing with spells he could not comprehend. This third attempt all the more humiliating because it took place here in full view of these unenlightened "luminaries."

He crossed the portico and started up the broad stairway, his richly embroidered cape swishing and billowing behind him like a purple sail. He was urbane. He was elegant. He lifted his turbaned head high as he approached yet another ignorant Moabite priest, an ancient and shrunken man with a face like a walnut. The gold lightning bolt blazing down the front of this man's turban signaled that he was the high priest here at Baal-Peor, but his words revealed a mind as shriveled as his visage.

"King Balak thought he hired a potent foreign tool," the old man cackled. "He got an impotent foreign fool. Heh, heh. Potent tool. Impotent fool. Get it?"

The others laughed at the simple-minded attempt at humor, all but one who uttered his advice with great seriousness. "King Balak will come crawling to us for help, and when he does, we must make him pay dearly."

"Balak will pay, and this seer . . ." The high priest met the prophet's eyes boldly as they passed one another. "This seer, if he is so foolish as to remain within our borders, will never *see* again." If the old cleric thought his grin was menacing, he needed to think again. He had no teeth.

The prophet clenched his jaw. Any retort would be wasted on the likes of them. Yes, there had been a setback, but he was not finished. He may have been blindsided by a god who refused to play by the rules, but he *was* a seer. These burbling bumpkins never saw anything beyond the verbiage frothing from their muzzles.

The seer marched into the inner chamber to confront Baal himself. The great bronze image towered ominously over the room, the top of its head nearly brushing the ceiling, its entire body luminescent with the light of a thousand olive oil votives. Craning back his neck, defiantly challenging this ineffectual excuse for a god, the prophet bellowed out his anger. "Where was the supposed power of Baal today? You are worse than useless."

There was no answer, but the cold glare of Baal's ruby eyes and the lightning bolt gripped in his bronze fist reflected the seer's own heart perfectly. This was a friend rather than an adversary. All thoughts of the churlish priests vanished as the frustration of the day twisted and knotted the prophet's heart in focused loathing toward the God of Jacob: the God who scorned King Balak's lavish offerings, the God who would not respond to divination and made a mockery of his prophetic words.

The prophet threw himself on the polished pavers before the image. "O Mighty Lord of Peor, arise against these interlopers. I want no more of Yahweh. He has become my enemy. But, in truth, he is *your* enemy. These homeless mongrels leveled your strong-holds—the mighty kingdoms of Sihon and Og. They desecrated the high places and smashed the images of Baal and Asherah throughout this valley. Did you not notice the smoke ascending? Have you not seen the ashy blotches that were your holy sites?

"Now they crouch like ravenous lions on the banks of the Jordan, contemplating their next meal. Listen and you can hear their captains consulting one another: *Shall we roar up into the highlands of Moab, or leap the river and devour Canaan?* Will you, Lord Baal, do nothing? Have you no respect for the fidelity of King Balak? Though he beseeches you daily to stop them, he does not rest on prayers alone. He summoned me from Babylonia. He was willing to empty his coffers in payment. Yet my every effort to curse these people was undone by the power of this Yahweh. Again I ask, where were you when our names were flung onto the dung heap together?"

The air around the prophet crackled with energy. He could sense it sizzling up from the cold pavement into his body. Baal was listening.

The prophet's argument morphed to a prayer. "Hear me, O Baal. Help me. I offer you my life and strength. Together, you and I *will* destroy Israel; we *will* reverse Yahweh's blessing. Our honor will be restored and our names irrevocably linked." He rose to his feet, glancing upward again at the hard lines of Baal's face. For a fleeting moment, he thought he saw the image smile.

At the same instant, a plan, fully-formed, filled his mind, and the seer saw that it was destined to be the ultimate triumph of his life. Direct curses against Israel were doomed. Their defeat would not come through the schemes of King Balak, but through the Baal-blessed allure of the daughters of Midian. The seer was seeing clearly once again. Seeing so very clearly. Laughter surged up from deep inside him, bursting forth uproariously until tears streamed down his cheeks.

A swarm of priests rushed him, gnashing their teeth at such an outburst in the inner sanctum, but the prophet did not care. What could they do to him? He was no fawning servant of this god as they were. He and Lord Baal had just become partners, and he could not contain the glee. Just as the clutching hands of the first priests were nearly on him, a storm of hissing, snapping lightning shot from the image, and they drew back in terror. Even Baal could not resist adding his dazzling touch to the moment of mirth.

"Hah!" the seer scoffed. "Surprised by the fierce flashings of your storm god? Where is your faith?"

The priests vanished like roaches into nearby nooks and crannies, and the prophet left the temple in triumph. He strode down the steps into incense-laden moonlight while beguiling strains from harps, flutes, and silver finger cymbals swirled around him. Pulsing drumbeats thrummed through his body, and the pace of his heart quickened. His mouth went dry at the memory of his night at Baal-Huzoth, his first taste of Canaanite fertility worship. But tonight, nothing must be allowed to divert him. The earthy allure of Baal worship would have to wait until the plan was consummated. His steps were solid with newfound purpose. He must go to the Five and convince them to join him.

So focused was he on the path ahead that he was only vaguely aware of a light footfall pattering down the steps behind him until a hand brushed his shoulder and a low feminine voice murmured, "Come with me."

The prophet steeled himself against temptation and shrugged the woman off, but with remarkable strength, she wheeled him around. Her black eyes burned into his, reducing every thought of resistance to smoke. Her voice was as hard as her grip. "I am Cozbi, daughter of King Zur of Midian."

When she released his shoulder and stepped back, the prophet couldn't move. He could hardly breathe. A goddess stood before him, drenched in moonlight. The gauzy linen of her temple dress floated lightly over her body like a gossamer wisp of cloud over the silver orb of the full moon. But it was not merely her beauty that stirred his senses. A fire burned through his bones, filling him with the certainty that this was his partner, not in love, but in war. Baal was already orchestrating the plan.

She silently turned away, gliding back up the steps of the temple, and the prophet meekly followed. Once they reached the privacy of her quarters, Cozbi faced him again, her chin high and one brow arched arrogantly. "It is no accident that I am currently serving Baal on this mountain. The gods have placed me here for this very time."

"I—"

She silenced him with a quick slice of her hand. "Together we will defeat Yahweh and the children of Jacob the Deceiver. The Lady Asherah showed me your pathetic plight this very afternoon in a midday dream following my prayers; and just now Baal sent me forth to fetch you."

The princess quickly outlined every detail of the plan exactly as it had appeared in the prophet's own mind only moments ago. Even better, she had the means to put it into action. He stared at this creature in astonishment, hardly daring to believe what Baal had provided—a woman wondrously imbued with beauty, intelligence, and power beyond that of any mortal he had ever known. Perhaps the Canaanite goddess Asherah had taken on a body of flesh and blood. The ancient stories spoke of such things.

Cozbi seemed to bask in his look of awe, favoring him with the radiance of a divine smile. "You must go. Find my father and his allies straight away." As she spoke, she slid her hand through the crook of his arm and led him to the door. "We are partners in the destruction of Israel, but when it is over . . . who knows?" She leaned close as she whispered, her breath as sweet in his nostrils as the words that tingled from his ears to his toes. "I look forward to sharing the spoils with you." As she reached around him to grasp the bolt bar, the pressure of her body against his stirred a sudden desire to have this goddess as his partner in love *and* war.

He laid a restraining hand on hers. "Perhaps we could seal our alliance here and now." His voice was thick with a sudden rush of heat.

Instantly the lock bar crashed. Cozbi flung the door wide, drenching the prophet with cool night air and equally frosty words. "It is the victorious who are rewarded. You have just failed miserably."

Nearly blinded by a dazed mix of desire, humiliation, and hope, the seer left the temple, the final words of the Midianite princess ringing in his ears. "Go quickly to my father. Summon the Five and meet me at Kiriath-Huzoth in three days."

He staggered to the edge of the mountain, the site of his defeat only hours earlier, and spat into the air at the sight of the Israelite camp stretched out below him.

"I despise you, O Jacob. You may have defeated King Sihon in a single battle. You may have demolished the armies of that warrior giant, King Og, with one stroke. But I will not be destroyed by a solitary defeat."

Evening fires, tens of thousands of them, were dying across the encampment, but the tabernacle in the center glowed with its own interior light, light that radiated upward, illuminating a towering cloud and bathing the Valley of Acacias with a beauty beyond moonlight. Other peoples had solid images of gods that dwelt in the heavenlies, but this God lived with his people in the form of a mysterious light, a peculiar, mesmerizing fire. It was unnatural, unheard of among the nations. Everything within the prophet raged against it.

"This land belongs to Lord Baal," he thundered.

Suddenly gripped by prophetic vision, the seer saw the plan unfold. He saw the gleeful participation of the people. He saw the consternation of that old man, Moses. He watched deadly bolts of Yahweh's anger flash from the glory of that pillar of cloud, striking the tents of Israel as if they were the enemy. He saw plague and war and death, and then as he watched, the fire sputtered out. The cloud vanished. Yahweh was gone. The children of Jacob were alone and defenseless in the darkness. The irony was hilarious. Curses failed, but the blessings of Baal worship would prove the undoing of Israel. The seer was exhilarated by the revelation. After all his frustration, triumph was certain. He convulsed with laughter again until his sides hurt.

CHAPTER ONE

THE VALLEY OF ACACIAS

Caleb

Shouts of joy shot from tent to tent as dawn brightened to cloudless azure. Since daybreak, snatches of song had been echoing from the surrounding hills across green fields of barley and wheat, rebounding over meadows splashed with a floral rainbow, the sounds of celebration mingling deliciously with the scent of dew-fresh grasses and fragrant flowers. The wilderness wanderings were over. The children of Israel camped on their own land for the first time—and such an Eden! It was not technically the long-promised inheritance, but how could they do other than celebrate when such glorious land had fallen into their hands so miraculously, so unexpectedly?

Caleb tramped wordlessly across the meadow beside his nephew Othniel, crushing two new sets of footprints in the already-trampled wet grass. His eyes swept across the meadow to the hazy plains and hills of Canaan across the river. The shallow fords, the sole barrier separating God's people from the Land of Promise, could not be seen from here. In fact the entire river lay hidden from view, writhing in serpentine twists and turns through the deep green thickets of a deeper depression, the *zor,* a valley within the valley

7

splitting the long, verdant floodplains from north to south. Those hidden fords were the gateway to the inheritance of Jacob. Caleb shivered with a thrill of joy as complex as the journey of his life.

He touched Othniel's arm and pointed west. Othniel met his eyes, grunted, and dipped his head in a nod of understanding. The young man's biceps bulged under the weight of the freshly sacrificed ram on his shoulder, but the spring in his steps affirmed his anticipation. Like the others his age, Othniel was eager to celebrate, but none of these young folk could possibly grasp what this day meant to an old man like him.

Caleb knew he was a hero to them. They relished the tale of Caleb and Joshua, "The Faithful Spies," but what did they comprehend of the cost of that fame? Could they imagine the disappointment of having the taste of milk and honey snatched from one's lips, replaced by the grit of desert dust? It was like Jacob awakening from the ecstasy of his wedding night to discover Leah instead of his beloved Rachel in the bed beside him. Jacob only had to wait one week to claim his dream, but both Caleb and Joshua had been forced to wander in the wilderness for forty years with the faithless. Rebellion carried fearsome consequences, even for the loyal.

Caleb glanced sideways through a wispy lock of white hair at the solid profile of his nephew. Life in the Land of Promise was his future. It was the future of his daughter Acsah and the future awaiting his sons and their families, as well as that entire generation of young people. These children of the wilderness would have the opportunity to carve out a new kind of nation in a bountiful land, to be the chosen people of God, living out lives of goodness based on the covenant.

That was the dream he had shared with the boy's father, his youngest brother Kenaz, but the dream had ended abruptly for Kenaz last year with the bite of a serpent. He blinked his eyes to clear the dimming wetness and prevent it from spilling over onto his cheeks.

Yes, he would enter the longed for Land of Promise along with these youngsters, but this was not his generation. The joy of the day reached deep into the dark memories of his soul, retrieving the faces of many who had shared his dream as they left Egypt: the faces of his parents, his wives, his brothers, and friends who lay now in graves scattered across the desert. So strange, this blessed day. Part of him could not contain the laughter, while part of him could not hold back tears.

With such thoughts Caleb trudged on without uttering a word to the boy at his side, oblivious to the people they passed. Suddenly, two old friends blocked his path, singing lustily and skittering about like kid goats. With a shout of "Hai, hai," Caleb's melancholy reverie vanished and he leaped into the dance. He chuckled with glee at Othniel's grinning disbelief as he hopped and whirled with his friends, arms linked and white hair flying like banners in the wind, each old man singing at the top of his voice until they doubled over in mirth.

Laughing and gasping for breath, Shammai clapped his friends on the shoulders. "What a blessing to live to see this day!" The old man's tremulous voice was young again with energy and life.

"Indeed," Caleb panted. "Shammai . . . Jekamiah . . . you remember Othniel, do you not, the eldest boy of my brother Kenaz?"

Jekamiah's eyes continued to dance in a sun-browned face lined with the wrinkles of a lifetime of laughs. "Ah, yes, and how he has grown. As handsome as his father he is."

Shammai flashed a toothless grin. "Are you one of the lucky grooms getting married today?"

"I wish that I wanted to be," Othniel mumbled, "but, honestly, I don't."

Caleb winced at the strange answer and the flush rising in the young man's face. It was a natural question, since nearly every clan would celebrate the marriages of sons and daughters today. It should be easy just to say "No," but Othniel obviously felt as uncomfortable at the old man's question as he did around the young women of Judah. Caleb spoke up quickly. "For a wedding, you think this boy would miss today's story-telling?"

Shammai and Jekamiah roared in laughter and clapped Othniel's back approvingly.

Othniel visibly relaxed as he nodded. "My uncle knows me well."

"You particularly like the stories of our war heroes, I recall." Jekamiah studied the young man's face. "Nothing so stirs the blood and tingles through every nerve in your body, eh? May you someday lend your strength to such a noble cause."

Othniel blushed again. He tossed his head, swinging his hair back from his face in a self-conscious gesture.

"What a story we have lived," Caleb mused, purposely diverting attention from Othniel.

Shammai threw his arms about the shoulders of his two old friends and pulled them close. "When I look into your eyes, I can still see Egypt, both its grandeur and its brutality."

Jekamiah's eyes sparkled. "Egypt shmegypt! We have seen many sights, we old ones, but this eclipses them all."

"Ah, yes, my friends, Egypt and the wilderness lie behind us forever." Caleb winked at Shammai. "With our own eyes, we are finally gazing at Abraham's promise."

Jekamiah pointed a gnarled finger to the west, cackling in glee. "Right there across the river!"

Shammai leaned close to Othniel's ear, "The forty-year prophecy hung heavy over us. Yahweh promised to lead you children into this land after we old ones were gone." His watery eyes grew wide in wonder and his voice dropped to a whisper. "But sometimes I doubted that any Israelite would ever really live there."

"I think we all doubted at times," his companion added. "All those days of wandering . . ."

Caleb cut off the thought immediately. "Yahweh is faithful. Always."

Jekamiah laughed aloud and stomped out a snappy rhythm. "Myth has become miracle and a few of us old ones have lingered long enough to see it."

"Perhaps we cannot cross over, but I would be quite content to live out the rest of my life right here," Shammai added solemnly.

"Then let us go prepare for the celebration." Jekamiah beckoned to his friend, and the jovial pair went dancing and hopping back toward the tents of Judah.

Caleb chuckled and ruffled Othniel's hair. "Eleazar did not need to call for a day of thanksgiving. How could we keep from dancing when the substance of every story and song lies under our very feet?"

"No need in our house," Othniel answered, watching the two old men until they disappeared from sight. "The very hour all the men returned from the battle, my mother and grandmother announced that we would offer this fellowship offering in thanks to God. They were more impatient than Seraiah and I for the days of cleansing from death-contamination to end."

"Your first time to offer such a thank offering," Caleb said and then fell silent, reviewing the morning.

Beginning shortly after dawn, he and Othniel, along with his two eldest sons, had joined the long lines gathered at the tabernacle with two rams to be shared among the clan. Caleb showed Othniel how to lean one hand on his perfect yearling ram to signify that he was transferring ownership of his animal to the Lord. As soon as each lamb was slaughtered, Caleb drained the blood into one of the holy bowls, while Othniel, Iru and Elah removed the fatty tails and the fat around the organs. Eleazar, the high priest, ceremoniously dashed a little of the blood against the sides of the altar, pouring the remainder at its base, and then burned the fat on the altar. As each animal was sacrificed, Eleazar took the breast and one thigh as the portion for the Levites, then returned the remainder of one carcass to Caleb's eldest son, Iru, and the other to Othniel for the family fellowship feast.

Caleb watched his son sling the ram over his shoulder and head toward the roasting area with a tingle racing down his spine. This was God's holy food, but it would also be his family's food today, each member of the clan receiving life and strength from the gifts they gave to the Lord.

Such a celebration had not been possible during the desert wanderings. The animals grazing on the thin grasses and scrub brush of the wilderness had borne young only rarely. Those lean beasts would have offered meager flesh for a feast, and the herds would have diminished rapidly under such exorbitant offerings as these. Here in this valley, though, the animals were growing noticeably sleek and fat. The mothers of the lambs, kids, and calves gamboling joyfully in the meadows were now producing more milk than their young could drink and bawled for relief by those who tended them. The Israelites were relearning the arts of milking and of making curds and cheese. At the same time, brave honey-seekers, observing the bees buzzing in droves over the flower-strewn meadows, had followed the insects back to their hives in the rocky bluffs surrounding the valley. With heads and arms wrapped protectively with thick wet cloth, they brandished smoking torches, driving the bees from their homes long enough to gather the dripping, golden combs.

"Aha!" Caleb exclaimed suddenly. "*A land flowing with milk and honey.* At last I see what those words mean."

"Mmm," Othniel grunted.

Caleb returned to his solitary reflections, not certain that his nephew was even listening.

The meadow grasses ended abruptly in a barren border of marled lime-and-clay deposits edging the river basin. The pair stopped there, searching for Caleb's sons and Othniel's younger brother, who had gone ahead to build the roasting frames and start the fires. Crowded across this stony expanse, clusters of men were already at work, turning their sacrifices on spits over the flames. Caleb drew in a deep breath. The heady aroma of roasting flesh added yet another pleasure to the joy of the day.

Moses

High on a rocky promontory overlooking the camp, Moses concentrated intently on the words he was penning onto another parchment scroll. Aristocratically handsome despite deep wrinkles and the wild white mane and beard of old age, there was an aura of strength about him solid as the mountains themselves. His massive fist, curled around the quill, had more the look of a lion's paw than a man's hand, yet the markings flowed easily onto the parchment.

He paused, looking up from the scroll, and laughed aloud at the joy echoing across the green plain spread out below. No bickering, no whining in this valley! Today the Lord was being praised. The life-sustaining daily miracles of the Wanderings: the manna, the water spring flowing from the rock that showed up wherever they camped, the cooling shade of the guiding cloud, clothing and tools that never wore out—these on-going miracles were all too easy to take for granted. But Yahweh had again risen with dramatic power for his people in a miracle that could not be discounted. How spectacularly this land had come into their possession!

As Moses listened to the spontaneous bursts of laughter, singing, and dancing, he broke out in song himself: "I will sing unto the Lord, for He has triumphed gloriously . . ." For a few brief moments, Moses was again on the shore of the Red Sea, surrounded by throngs of newly released slaves, staring in stunned silence and awe at the waters that had just closed over their enemies. " . . . the horse and rider are cast into the sea."

Moses' voice slowed and a wistful sadness clouded his eyes as the song went on. That was how the journey had begun: a miracle crossing of the sea. And this is how it would end: the people crossing the water again. This time it was a river. This time it would be without him. As a babe in a basket, he had been rescued from Pharaoh's death squad for this purpose—to lead this people to this place. It had not been easy, but what a journey! Led every step by the hand of Yahweh himself, he could never have imagined how the past forty years would unfold. It had been worth all the trouble and sorrow along the way.

"We have arrived, my children," he whispered at the end of his song, gazing tenderly at the neatly ordered camp below. It was the same, yet not the same. Efficiently and reverently, the Levites had erected the holy tabernacle in the heart of the encampment once more. The tribal tent villages had sprung up around it as they had for forty years, three tribes on each side forming a perfect square. However, instead of hanging limply in the desert heat, their twelve banners fluttered expectantly in the fresh breezes of a richly-watered valley. A growing sense of detachment tore at Moses' heart, and he groaned aloud, "O my children, how can I bear to leave you?

"No," he roared at himself. "I *will* rejoice today with my people." He shook his head to clear every trace of sorrow and lifted his face toward heaven with a passionate cry that roared out to Ears that always hear.

O Mighty Yahweh.
From the days of our Father Abraham
You have been our God;
We, your children.
You have been our dwelling place
Through the long days of the Wanderings.

The Land of Promise lies before us,
The wilderness training behind.
The waters of the Jordan are low.
The season of crossing is now.
But who will lead my people across?
You swore that I would not enter
For in my anger, I dishonored Your name.
I am ready to lay down my staff,
But who, Lord, will pick it up?

As you have always provided for your children,
Raise up a shepherd with an undivided heart.

Do not let your people enter this land
Like sheep wandering alone,
Only to be devoured by lions and wolves.
Before I lie down in my grave, provide for them
A rod of iron and a staff of strength.

His agony spent, Moses finished his lament and returned to the manuscript, assured that God had a plan. There was little left to write. This scroll began with the numbering of God's warriors throughout the tribes when they left Sinai forty years ago. What might have been a glorious tribute to the power of Yahweh, in actuality unfolded as a dismal failure on the part of Israel. But in this valley, that failure had been reversed. He smiled at the story now flowing from his pen, "The Defeat of Sihon and Og." God's army was on the march again. "All that is needed . . ." he mused aloud, "is a final numbering."

Suddenly in a voice that sounded strange to his own ears, he questioned the silence of heaven. "When do we number them, Lord?"

No command came, no explanation. Only a strong conviction that his work here was not yet finished.

King Zur

On the ridge southeast of Israel's camp, a group of royal travelers stopped to rest. Beginning at dawn, the Five had pressed hard across the desert, and the foul mood brooding and building in each of them finally erupted as their servants attended them and their camels with food and water.

"All right, Zur, this is your game," King Rekem snapped. "Where is that miserable seer?"

"He will be here. This is his game not mine."

"This had best not be another chasing after the wind."

"Aye, one failure is more than enough for me."

Zur puffed through his teeth. The plan seemed foolproof, but he too had misgivings. He was not going to shoulder the blame alone if it failed. "You were the one, Evi, who convinced us to send for him the first time." His voice sounded whiney, even to himself. He needed to exude strength.

"I deal with success, not failure, Zur," King Evi growled. "The prophet conjured up victories for me in the past, but now? After that debacle?"

"Rekem is right. This is your game, Zur. Only reluctantly, because of our long alliance and your persuasive arguments, did I agree to this."

Zur felt a wash of panic. Had the prophet cast a spell over his daughter Cozbi to dupe them again? The prophet had nothing to lose after his failed attempt to curse Israel, but he could pull down the entire alliance of the Five if this new plan failed.

"Listen! I hear hoofbeats."

Reba smirked. "Ah, yes. The little donkey."

"Perhaps we should consult with *her* about the plan before we follow him further." Hearty laughter broke the tension and continued as a tall, red-bearded man clattered up to the shady dale where the kings rested. Their derisive spasms of mirth only increased at the sight of the proud rider, his lanky legs flapping on either side of a rather small beast while a purple cape fluttered behind.

King Zur watched from the corner of his eye as the prophet dismounted, head held high, eyes darting warily from face to face as he forced himself to laugh along with them. He did not know why they laughed, but he must suspect that they were laughing at him. He was flustered, and that was a good thing for the kings.

"Greetings, my lords." The Babylonian inclined his head respectfully as he approached.

Zur waited until the merriment was spent before he met the prophet's lizard-like gaze. "At last you have come," he said condescendingly.

"I am pleased to find you in such jolly humor," the Babylonian crooned. He bowed obsequiously, sweeping the corners of his Babylonian cape wide to hold it above the dusty trail.

An image of a lanky waterfowl performing an awkward mating dance burst into Zur's head. *Ridiculous foreigner. Can he not distinguish desert hawks from heron hens?* Zur snorted anew with contemptuous laughter.

The prophet immediately straightened his shoulders, folded his arms defiantly, and struck a wide power stance.

Zur smirked. *If not a true seer, at least he is intuitive.*

"I trust that you have not been waiting long," the prophet prompted when no one responded. An oily smile slid over his face.

"Waiting does not sit well with kings," Evi snapped, his small dark eyes glittering with annoyance.

"I have been attending to the last-minute details of the plan. Asanath's troops will meet us at the top of the Arnon Gorge. They know *exactly* what to do."

Though the outsider winked at the Five as he made his last comment, the desert kings only glowered at him with eyes as hard and dark as obsidian. King Zur scrambled to his feet as his companions rose, turning their backs on the seer one by one as they dusted off their robes. He could not have planned a better power play. Zur waited just long enough for the effect to simmer, then spun around, stretching his short, stocky frame as high as possible.

"Only because of my daughter do I give you this chance to prove yourself, miserable seer," he spat through bared teeth. "She has exceptional skill in reading men's hearts, but if it turns out that you have charmed her for some dubious purpose of your own . . ." He reached out with the toe of his sandal to crush a beetle scuttling along the stony road and then fixed the prophet's eyes with a chilling stare. "We squash useless insects."

Acsah

The camp and the surrounding acacia groves hummed like a beehive in spring. Children were gathering flowers, decking trees at the ceremony site, and shaping mounds of garlands. Newly constructed clay ovens, tended by old women, poured out the rich fragrance of baking bread. Old men were still in the process of assembling long serving tables in the meadow as young women bustled about, loading them with steaming side dishes for the celebration. A few of these dishes, prepared by the cautious ones, were manna-based, overly familiar foods, but many more had not been savored among the children of Israel since the bondage days of Egypt.

Earlier that morning, Caleb's only daughter, Acsah, had joined her Aunt Sarah and Sarah's mother, Hannah, chopping and grinding, mixing and stirring. It wasn't long before the large iron cauldron was bubbling with fragrances more wonderful than anything she had ever smelled before.

Hannah grinned at her, a joyously beautiful smile in a face corrugated with age. "Oh, how good to smell onions and herbs stewing. It is like my mother's warm embrace when I was a girl in Egypt." She wrapped her arms in a hug around herself, grasping her thin upper arms with gnarled hands.

Acsah smiled back. "It is a happy smell to me as well, even though this is the first time it has entered my nose."

Hannah wagged a bony finger in front of Acsah's face. "Just think. You can make the fragrance of this lentil-barley pilaf a comforting memory to *your* children someday."

Acsah laughed, "That will not be anytime soon."

"Don't presume to know God's timing, child." She picked up the spoon again and gave the pot another stir. "We need to finish and get this out to the table soon or there will be no room for it, at least according to Sarah's report."

"If there is no room, the pilaf isn't needed," Sarah stated flatly. "When I retrieved our bread from the oven and put it out, I could see that *it* certainly will not be needed. I have never seen so much food. We could feed an army of strangers with our leftovers."

Acsah tried to catch Sarah's eyes as she replied. "This abundance is a blessing from Yahweh, for certain. A miracle."

But Aunt Sarah had returned to her work, mumbling at the Almighty under her breath. "Why couldn't you have spared Kenaz to see this . . ."

Sarah had been a widow nearly a year now. Acsah missed her jovial uncle, and she knew that her father grieved for him too. Kenaz was Caleb's youngest brother and the two had been close friends as well. Following their father's death, the two sons, Othniel and Seraiah, went about quiet and steady as ever, their pain hidden from view; but Aunt Sarah was inconsolable. Since the loss, she had withdrawn almost completely from the people around her into a dark world of whispered complaints to Yahweh: *"Why did you have to take him now? How can I settle in a new home in a new land alone? You told Moses to put up the bronze serpent so people could look and live. Why did you wait until Kenaz was dead?"*

"Don't you agree, Aunt Sarah . . . a miracle?" Acsah repeated, but Aunt Sarah had withdrawn again. Although she was not muttering aloud, Acsah could read complaint on her face and could not connect with her. She turned to Auntie Hannah and took the woman's ancient hands in hers. "The hands that are showing us how to prepare these foods are a miracle as well."

Hannah chuckled. "A miracle, indeed, that we can still do so much work."

Acsah nodded. The past few weeks had been as busy as any she could remember. Even as the warriors purged the battle sites with fire, obliterating the gruesome remnants of war and destroying every vestige of the abominable Baal worship that had taken place in this valley—even as that grim work was being completed—a more joyful work had begun. The gray-haired grandfathers and grandmothers of Israel gathered the women and children together and led them to the empty houses. Together they collected the stores of grain, legumes, olive oil, and wine and hauled them back to the camp. Next they harvested garlic, onions, greens and herbs from the well-tended gardens. They had gathered in food fit for a pharaoh's feast, and the older folk could not keep from smiling as they explained what the various foods were.

As Hannah inhaled deeply over the steaming pot, her dull brown eyes darkened and she stared off into the distance.

"Are you feeling all right, Auntie?"

"Dark days . . ." Hannah closed her eyes and whispered, "The dark days of slavery. How can such wonderful smells stir up such chilling memories?"

Sarah muttered almost inaudibly, "We might as well have died under the slave master's whip. What joy is there in crossing over into Canaan when all those we know and love are gone?"

Acsah had no answer. She looked down at the Egyptian-crafted anklet that gleamed silver and blue above her sandal. Egypt, source of beauty; source of pain. All she knew of it were the stories her father told. Surely its sorrow had left permanent scars on that whole generation.

"Do you need to rest, Auntie?"

Hannah shuddered and blinked. "Memories to be repressed." She laughed as she flicked her fingertips in the air. "Return to your dungeon, O dark thoughts. I banish you!"

Aunt Sarah roused herself and stared at Hannah for a moment. "Acsah is right, Mother. You should rest."

"No! I am quite all right." The light had returned to the old woman's eyes, and she lovingly nudged her niece away from the cook fire. "Acsah should go. You and I can finish up here, Sarah."

"Yes. Let the young enjoy the day. Celebration is for those who still have hope. I wait only to join Kenaz in the grave."

As pleasant as it had been learning to cook new foods with Auntie Hannah, Acsah left the miserable muttering of Aunt Sarah with relief. The freedom of the open sky instantly worked its magic, and soon she was leaping and skipping as she ran across the meadow. Within minutes, the tent village of Judah was far behind and she reached the stony flat where bewildering numbers of men were turning spits to roast the family fellowship offerings, the juices dripping, sizzling onto the flaming coals—another wonderful smell.

The clans of Judah were located at the southern end of this open space, and there she spotted the snowy-white head of her father, squatting by a fire with Iru and Elah, her two eldest brothers. Her three other brothers were cleaning sheepskins along with her cousins, Othniel and Seraiah, and tending to the roasting of another ram. Her cousins were Sarah's sons in every way, reserved and very quiet, but Acsah laughed within herself at the thought of either of them muttering and whispering like their mother. That she could not imagine.

The younger men seemed not to notice her approach, but Iru and Elah rolled their eyes and exchanged critical glances as she threaded her way through the Carmi clan. She ignored them and stopped to greet dear old Shammai, one of her father's closest friends. But before her shadow reached her brothers' workspace, the ridicule began.

"Has our little Acsah rushed out here to finish up our work?" Elah's words were not unkind, but his eyes expressed bitter scorn.

"Nay, brother," Iru answered. "You know that she only comes to be sure we are doing everything right."

Acsah flashed her best sisterly smile at Iru and Elah. Pleasantry always marked their mockery, but Caleb knew the sound as well. He said nothing, but when his bushy white brows pulled low over those glowering gray eyes and he gave them *the look*, her brothers fell silent.

Acsah sighed. The tight bond she shared with her father was always stretched when the entire clan gathered. The tugs were uncomfortable, but unavoidable. There had been three wives and many sons, older brothers who were now all married, with families of their own. Her father loved each member of his large family, and for his sake she tried to as well.

Othniel sat quietly watching, obviously bemused by the family interactions. His family was small and reserved, hers a rowdy crowd. Acsah caught him watching for her reaction, but when she met his eyes, he turned his face toward the sky. With a shake of his head, he flung his hair back over his shoulders, an oh-so-familiar ploy he had used ever since they were children when she tried to catch his eyes. The sun flashed red-gold through his thick curls. *Beautiful hair. Strange habit.*

She gave no more thought to her cousin and ignored her brothers completely. "Father, the cooking is nearly finished. I would like to join the garland-making." She fairly wiggled with anticipation.

Caleb nodded. "Good. Just what I expected. Off with you. Only be sure to look for me and for your brothers when it is time to eat. Don't keep us waiting. This roasted lamb will go fast."

Acsah nearly toppled him with a spirited hug. "Thank you, Abba."

"Whoa," he laughed as he steadied himself. "Take care or you will have a roasted father."

Caleb

As the children spilled out of camp early that morning and began racing about the meadow with fistfuls of flowers, Caleb had encouraged Acsah to finish the food preparations quickly so she could join them. He watched her now, running back toward the meadow, her hair a waterfall of silky obsidian rippling behind. He shook his head in amazement. "So like her mother, my child bride," he murmured. "Where have the years gone?"

He caught Othniel watching him and quickly added, "Perhaps I should have taken another wife. As a toddler, Acsah was already helping me with the women's work. When was she ever really a child?"

"And who took over most of your chores so you could care for a baby girl?" Elah interjected.

Seraiah snickered, but Othniel listened in thoughtful silence, continuing to scrape the sharp flint across the sheep hide.

Caleb chuckled. "You are right. You boys had to grow up quickly as well when you lost your own mother."

"Me too, Abba."

"You too, Naam. I will always be grateful for the way you stepped in to help when Jedidah died. Iru and Elah, you were both newly married, yet your young brides so admirably helped mother my two youngest sons. Seth and Jezliah were so young. A heavy burden as you were starting your own new families."

"Seth and Jezliah still look up to us almost as much as to you, Father, but Acsah deigns to look *down* on us."

Caleb gave Iru an absent-minded nod and retreated from an overly familiar conversation.

Elah would not let the conversation drop. "My wife suckled that mewling infant girl along with our little Irad, and what respect do we get for saving her life?"

"She was lording it over us by the time she could talk. When will *she* be grateful for what we did for her?"

The questions hung unanswered as Caleb slipped into a memory-induced trance of an intense three-year old shaking her pointer finger at men old enough to be her father. "Hah!" A half laugh exploded from him at the memory of that bold toddler, unafraid to correct grown men when they broke any of the household rules. *Why could they not just laugh and stand corrected instead of taking offense?*

His boys had taken to quiet grumbling among themselves instead of bombarding him with more disparaging questions. "Let this smoke alone sully the air on such a day as this, my sons," he said, shaking his head.

Suddenly he remembered the roasting lamb. He had no idea how long it had been since he last rotated it. He gave it a turn, then rose and stretched out his back. "Take over this task for me, Iru. Your doddering father left it overlong before the last rotation." He rumpled his eldest son's hair and winked at Elah. "This is a fellowship offering, not a burnt offering. Perhaps you two will be better at maintaining the difference." Before they could answer, he wandered over to check on his friend Shammai and compare the progress of their roasting lambs.

Joshua

As the sun rose higher in the sky, Joshua made his way up the mountain toward Moses' isolated peak. He bounded up the steep slope like a lean wolf, keen eyes focused on the rugged path before him. He knew just where to find Moses. In the weeks since the battles with the Amorites, while the Children of Israel settled into life on the eastern plains of the Jordan, his master had retired to the same spot overlooking the camp, spending the lengthening days of early spring writing a new scroll. Joshua approached wordlessly, only the shadow falling across Moses' work announcing his arrival.

Moses immediately acknowledged him with a nod, but continued writing. As Joshua watched the effortless flow of words—so different from what he could produce with his own poor skill—he was filled with the same awe and admiration that he had experienced daily as Moses' aide for the past forty years. During the wanderings in the desert, one of the camp tasks that

Moses had insisted on for every Israelite was training in reading and writing: a daily focus on bits of their story, bits of the law, and bits of praise songs.

Joshua understood why. Here in Sihon's valley and again in the highlands of Bashan, God had shown his people the ultimate reality. Their strength lay in him alone. No doubt about it, training in faith was far more important than training in warfare. The children of Israel must remember the covenant. Remember and obey. That was why Moses was writing the scrolls, carefully recording all the stories of God's guidance in the past and all His instructions on how to live in the future.

After a few moments, Moses put down the quill, looked up, and shook out his hand. "I have finished the story of our desert wanderings. We have much to celebrate."

"That is why I am here. It is time."

Moses checked the height of the sun and nodded. He packed his writing materials into his leather shoulder bag. As he rose to his feet, smiling fondly at the valley and camp below, his eyes glittered with the excitement and adventure of youth, bright eyes looking out from beneath wild white brows of age. "May Sihon and Og ever be remembered as defeated by the mighty arm of Yahweh!"

"Your parchments will keep our stories echoing to a thousand generations," Joshua said lightheartedly.

Moses did not respond. Joshua watched as a light breeze ruffled Moses' thick white beard and hair. The wise amber eyes probed the recent battlefield, now transformed into this sunlit valley of celebration, and Joshua wondered what he was thinking. The day of the battle with King Sihon had begun right here, on this same ridge. Did Moses have any idea how terrifying that day had been for him—even before they actually faced the enemy?

Following Moses' orders, Joshua had sent Rabez as messenger to King Sihon with a request for peaceful passage through Amorite territory. The message assured the Amorites that the Israelites only desired to cross the king's valley, to follow the road to Canaan. As

Joshua watched the young man descending the road to Heshbon, he was wracked with doubt.

Why would an Amorite king like Sihon show them favor when Balak, the king of Moab, had not? The Moabites were the descendants of Abraham's nephew Lot, as the Edomites were the descendants of Jacob's brother Esau. Both of those cousin nations had an understanding of Yahweh and an appreciation for the Abrahamic covenant, yet they had refused similar requests for passage through their land. Trekking around Edom to Moab and then around Moab to this plateau had added weeks to the Israelites' journey. From here there could be no more going around. From here to the mountains of the north, the entire eastern side of the Jordan was held in the firm grip of the predatory and brutal Amorites under the rule of two kings, Sihon and Og. The children of Israel were at their mercy for they controlled all remaining roads to Canaan.

As soon as Rabez dropped out of view, Joshua wheeled and strode back to the bustle of camp. Moses seemed to be waiting for his return. But now that he was back, rather than provide reassurance, the old man fixed him with a commanding look. "Organize the army. You will lead our people to the valley below. Use the trail down the creek canyon rather than the main road past Heshbon."

Joshua stared at his master. *Would they not wait for an answer at the hand of their messenger? What exactly did Moses expect? Did he want archers and slingers sent first in case of attack, or just an impressive show of swordsmen or spearmen?* Before Joshua could frame a question, Moses whirled about and vanished into the ranks of Levi without issuing any supporting commands. *Should he follow Moses and clarify?*

Just then Eleazar approached. The ark of the covenant, shrouded with its blue covering, lumbered out of the milling crowds of Levi behind him, borne on the shoulders of four young Levites. "Moses sent us. We will lead with the ark; the army will follow," he said, laying his hand on Joshua's shoulder.

The high priest's warm brown eyes exuded encouragement, strengthening Joshua better than a thousand words of reassurance could have done. *So like his father Aaron. If only the rest of the leaders and captains had offered such support.* When Joshua called for Darda of Judah to lead the way with his company of one hundred swordsmen, he was attacked with a barrage of angry voices.

"No!"

"We refuse to follow them."

"Why should Judah always get the glory of going first?"

"Darda's weaklings need *our* protection."

Joshua fought to remain calm. "Moses assigned command to me. Darda's men are the most agile and quick at moving on rough terrain, as well as being our best swordsmen. They will lead the rest of you." This was not an argument a commander should be having with his men.

Zoar of Naphtali shouted out over the rest, "My archers should go first. Their accurate and deadly darts would be the best protection for all other advance companies."

"Think this through, Joshua," Shaul of Simeon growled. "My Simeonites are the horns of the ox. There is no other tribe as fierce in defense! Should agile 'girls' be asked to defend our people as we descend into unknown peril in this valley?"

Reham of Reuben scowled at Shaul, "My company of spearmen are stronger. Their tight ranks will appear to an enemy as the teeth of a crocodile, and when necessary, we can cast our spears as far as an arrow can fly."

Shaul spit on the ground and answered Reham with a sneer, "If they do not attack us, Simeon is more capable than any other tribe of launching a deadly attack on them."

A high-pitched voice called out in alarm, "Does Moses expect a fight?"

The question pierced Joshua's steely facade. That was exactly what he wanted to ask Moses. Joshua knew the men sensed his uncertainty.

Another growling voice from the ranks of Simeon ripped through his silence, "Why not wait until nightfall and launch a surprise attack on Heshbon?" A barrage of agreement and dissent followed the question, and only Eleazar's calming words dispelled the squabbling.

As ranks of old men, women, and children clustered behind in travel lines, the warrior chiefs reluctantly followed Joshua and the ark down the steep slope beside a gushing brook. They led their tribal divisions according to the orders given, but as Joshua picked his way down the rocky trail, avoiding rocks made slippery by spray from the chain of waterfalls, a flood of agitated voices seethed behind him. The mutinous threats fumed and frothed all the way to the valley floor like the waters cascading from rock to rock beside them. Although the water came to rest in a wider bed on the flatlands and flowed peacefully westward from there into the Jordan, the men behind him did not settle into a placid, unified body once they reached the plains. Only the imminent threat of annihilation provided the unification the army needed.

Just as the last division spilled out onto the valley floor with the ranks of Israel clogging the gorge behind them, a cry rang out, "Look!" Other voices took up the call, but there was no need. Everyone was watching a lone horseman thundering down the road from Heshbon to the valley, galloping across the plain directly toward the army of Israel. The movements of the Israelite army were obviously no surprise to the Amorites. While still at a distance, the rider reined in the animal and dumped a large bundle on the ground.

The Israelites stared in stunned silence as the rider spun his horse about and raced back to the city. No one needed a closer look. Rabez, the messenger, had been returned to them. Joshua immediately deployed two men to bring him in and was grateful for their immediate obedience as they raced out and half carried, half dragged the wounded man back to the safety of the group. His clothing was hanging in shreds and his face and limbs were caked with blood, but he was alive. Choking on a cry of grief and rage at the mistreatment of his messenger, Joshua stooped beside the young man and spoke his name.

Rabez moaned and tried to answer. His eyelids fluttered, but only one eye looked up; the other remained hidden in a swollen purple mass. Joshua laid his finger gently on the man's lips. "Rest quietly, my son. Your wounds say all that needs to be said."

Rabez closed his eyes and slipped into unconsciousness just as the shrill blast of a war trumpet split the air.

"Ethan, stay with Rabez," Joshua commanded as he leaped to his feet, his heart beating wildly. A second signal drew his eyes to the city of Heshbon. He squinted through the morning haze at Sihon's city, a citadel of strength, rising from its rocky foundations a third of the way up the mountain beside the King's Highway, perfectly situated to guard the main route into Canaan. He trembled with a cold chill.

"The hornet's nest awakes," Eleazar whispered beside him. Together, they gaped in disbelief at the army pouring from the city gates like a cataract roaring from the mountains at the coming of a great spring thaw. At first the soldiers were so distant and small that they were visible only because their bronze armor reflected the soft gleams of morning light. Frozen with indecision, Joshua watched a bristling forest of spears advance across the cultivated fields while his ragtag army huddled against the limestone bluffs.

"What do you want us to do, Joshua?" someone called out. "We await your command."

Joshua snorted a half laugh. The spectacle of row after perfect row of spears and helmets marching directly toward them, with the glint of even more bronze spear tips waiting in reserve on the city walls, had unified his troops at last. If their situation had not been so deadly serious, it would have been truly laughable. Surely, Sihon was laughing at his opponent: Joshua, son of Nun, seventy-five years old. Previous experience? One battle in his youth nearly forty years ago and another a little over a year past. Both times Yahweh had given victories—albeit strange victories. Now, here he was again, captain of the Lord's army, barely able to control the jealousies and clamoring of the various tribes and clans, and he had no idea what to do.

"What are your orders, Joshua?" the same voice queried again.

How should he answer? There were no reasonable choices. They were positioned in an indefensible location. The bulk of the tribes blocked any possible retreat back up that narrow water-cut draw, but a frontal attack against such an army would surely be disastrous. As the enemy relentlessly swallowed up the open space, the whispered questions became desperate cries behind him.

"Where is Moses when we need him?"

"We can't just stand here."

"What is Joshua doing?"

Sihon's front lines disappeared into a thick stand of acacias, emerging minutes later from the trees, tightening ranks again with only open meadow, less than a furlong in length, separating them from Joshua's men.

A cringing voice behind Joshua cried out desperately. "Should we charge?"

Joshua looked over his shoulder. Darda's platoon had moved far to the right, waiting. Reham and his men stood in the forefront to his left, also waiting for Joshua's signal to rush forward with his spearmen. The men of Benjamin had spilled out onto rocky ledges on either side, behind and above their brothers. They were poised with slings filled and ready for his command. Their captain, Ezbon, watched him carefully. Accurate as the slingers of Benjamin were, their stones would clatter uselessly to the ground at this range. If the Israelite troops moved forward, those fist-sized missiles would rain down on their own troops. Charge or wait? There seemed to be no right decision.

The enemy was not wracked with such indecision. There was a hoarse command, and the first cloud of Amorite arrows whistled through the air, all hitting the ground without reaching their target. The next volley would be deadly, but still Joshua wavered. He glanced at the high priest standing beside him.

Eleazar's eyes echoed the question. *Will you charge or wait here?*

God, give me a sign.

"Shields up," he howled as the Amorite bowmen prepared to release a second storm of arrows. To his great relief, his warriors obeyed and deflected the deadly rain. Then, with the enemy in range, he signaled for Ezbon's slingers to launch their attack, and hundreds of stones hailed down on the enemy, pummeling the frontline warriors to the ground.

A roar of bestial rage rose from Sihon's army as they regrouped. Still Joshua held back his advance troops. When the metallic ring of the war trumpet sounded again, a wave of Amorites with spears and battle-axes rushed forward, thousands of enemy voices shrieking an unearthly battle cry. Joshua responded with a battle cry of his own. "Victory belongs to Yahweh!" If only his faith could match the words.

The next moments blurred like something out of a dream. The Cloud of Yahweh slipped down the slope and settled around the army of Israel, cool and comforting. Instantly clear-minded and energized, Joshua raised his sword with a baying cry, "Charge. Victory belongs to Yahweh. Victory belongs to the Lord." Joshua's troops hurdled out of the mist, every throat echoing the battle cry until "Victory belongs to Yahweh! Victory! Victory!" rang from all the surrounding hills.

At the same time, the swirling vapors engulfed Sihon's army. Blinded, confused, and surrounded on every side by Israelite victory cries, the charging enemy wavered and then ran back. As they reached the acacia grove, a horde of hornets swarmed from the trees, droning over and around the terrified troops, viciously attacking the fleeing vanguard as they tried to find cover in the woods. Joshua's troops ceased chase near the trees, listening in stunned silence to screams of terror and pain as the insect army inflicted their deadly stings. When the survivors of Sihon's vanguard ran desperately from the far side of the woods with the hornets in pursuit, they met the rest of the ordered divisions marching from Heshbon. Dumbfounded, Joshua watched addled bands of Amorites from both groups stumbling in every direction, swords clashing in the confusion, hornets whirring over it all, every man for himself struggling against the might of Yahweh, attacking anyone he encountered. The perfect ranks stretching across the plain were utterly broken.

Joshua would never forget the feeling of putting away a clean sword at the end of the day. The Israelites had achieved total victory as observers. The extent of their military moves had been to drive the enemy back toward Heshbon like so many cattle, repeating the call, "Victory belongs to the Lord." When the chaos subsided, not an Amorite could be found alive in the capital city of Heshbon, in the surrounding towns, and across the open fields of the entire plain. All had been annihilated by the hand of the Lord.

Within a week, the second battle—with King Og of Bashan to the north—produced a similarly strange victory. The commander of the Lord's army claimed no glory for himself. These successes could not be attributed to Israelite valor or skill in battle. All praise went to Yahweh alone, and the people were eager to celebrate.

Joshua glanced sideways at Moses. "Sir," he said confidently. "It is time to join the celebration.

CHAPTER TWO

A TIME TO DANCE

The shadows of the acacias had withdrawn to dark pools of shade under their canopies by the time Moses and Joshua returned to camp. Only then did the deep wail of the priest's trumpets summon all Israelites to the meadow. As the people gathered, hundreds of couples from every tribe, decked in colorful garlands and radiant smiles assembled hand in hand before Eleazar to have the blessings of marriage pronounced on their love. When the ceremony was finished, Moses addressed the crowds. "Covenant people of Israel, chosen by Yahweh, blessed above all peoples on earth, you stand at last on the brink of the Jordan. Soon you will cross over and lay hold of the inheritance that was wrested from God's people so long ago."

Cheers and hallelujahs erupted from the crowd. With a fatherly smile, Moses waited for the commotion to subside.

"We received this valley as an unexpected gift." More cheers arose, but this time Moses' voice thundered over the noise of the crowds, bringing them to silence again. "The evil kings, Sihon and Og, here sought to destroy us, to wipe the people of Yahweh from the face of the earth. Nevertheless, our God gave victory to the weak. He handed the territory of those kings to us along with the cities and fields of their people. Never forget this victory did not come because of your great strength or skill in battle. It did not come because of your righteousness, but purely because of the love and faithfulness of Yahweh. Today we celebrate his love and honor his holy name by partaking in this sacred fellowship feast with our families and with our God."

Moses turned his great, white-maned head toward the feast tables. The sound that rumbled from deep within him was nearly like a groan, not of pain or sorrow, but of intense and profound joy. "Eat, my children, eat. The tables are laden with food such as our people have not enjoyed for a very long time. Eat with thankful hearts."

Acsah

Acsah searched the tide of celebrants surging toward the tables. At last, across the flood of bobbing heads, she saw the familiar sparkling eyes, flushed cheeks, and dimpled smile, glittering like a bead of sunshine on the waves of the jostling sea. "Abihail! Abihail!" She fought her way crosscurrent to the glowing bride, her best friend for as long as she could remember, until the two met midstream and threw their arms around each other's necks.

"I am so happy that I feel my heart will burst," Abihail cried.

"That is evident by one look at your face." Acsah pulled back and scrutinized the radiant bride at arm's length. "You are always lovely to look at, but never more beautiful than today."

Abihail dropped her gaze modestly, tracing the colorful embroidery on her dress with one finger. "It is the gown. It makes me feel like a queen."

"You have been embroidering it for a full year," Acsah laughed. "No queen could hope for a lovelier garment, and no queen could look more glorious."

Abihail was bumped from behind before she could answer and had to grab onto her new husband, Eliab, for stability. The pull of the crowds was making it more and more difficult for Acsah to hold her ground as well and reminded her that she had promised to find her father straight away. "Care for her well, Eliab. There is not one of our childhood friends who is dearer to—whoa!" Acsah fought to remain on her feet.

"You can be sure that I will." Eliab's face was shining. "I cannot believe that this exquisite creature is mine." Acsah eased into the streaming crowds while Eliab was still gushing about his good fortune. "I feel like a rude slave who has just been handed a princess, a crown, and a kingdom."

"This river is telling me to move with its flow or drown." Acsah flashed one last smile at the newlyweds over her shoulder. "You two enjoy yourselves. I must find food and my family in all this confusion."

She tried to stretch tall to catch a glimpse of her father's white hair, balancing her weight momentarily on the tips of her toes, but there was no stopping in this rush toward the tables. She stumbled in the driving current and was still fighting for balance when the crowd directly in front of her split around a thigh-high boulder. With no time to swerve to either side, she leaped up while the streams of people gushed past on both sides of her rocky island.

"What *are* you doing, Acsah?" a cheerful voice boomed from behind.

Salmon. She knew the voice well, but peeked over her shoulder anyway and grinned. Salmon was leading the way as his whole family washed toward her. Those bright eyes, wide and honest and trustworthy, had shared more of the joys of her life than any of her friends beside Abihail. Although a short, curly beard now complemented the froth of loose black curls framing his face, there remained a hint of childish roundness about his cheeks.

She rolled her eyes in mock disdain. "What does it look like, silly boy? I'm standing on this rock,"

"I suppose for you it is easier to take the shorter path over the rock, rather than go around." His mouth pulled into the lopsided grin that had not changed since they were toddlers, and she knew what he was thinking.

"Don't even think of sharing my island."

As Salmon dodged to one side of the boulder, his little sister Ada cackled. A mischievous twinkle lit her eyes. "Acsah wants to play Master of the Mountain," she shrieked. Her little hands flicked out, brushing Acsah's hem just as Salmon pulled her back.

"Oh, no, you don't, Ada," Nashon's deep voice objected from the other side of the rock. "You must be kind to Salmon's friends if you want him to be kind to yours."

"I was just playing," Ada pouted.

"Another day we'll play that game," Acsah reassured her. "Shalom, Prince Nashon." She tipped her head in a respectful bow at Salmon's silver-haired father, taking care to maintain her balance. "What a day of blessings."

"Blessed be the One who has brought us to this place of joy." Nashon glanced up. A warm smile, identical to that of his son, pulled at one side of his mouth. "Enjoy your perch, Acsah."

"There is a purpose in my stance here," she answered self-consciously. It was incredibly awkward to look down on the prince of her tribe.

"I'm sure there is," he said with a laugh. He took his wife by the hand as they reconnected in front of Acsah's rock.

"I am trying to locate my father," she said to the back of his head. "Have you seen him?"

"Not five minutes ago. In the trees over there."

Salmon and Acsah had grown up together among the other children of Judah during the Wanderings. When the protecting cloud lifted, Moses would call out: "Rise up, O Lord. May your enemies be scattered. May your foes flee before you," and the camp would be on the move again. Often the children begged their parents to let them walk with one or two of their friends during the dusty, dreary marching days. Acsah's first choice was always to walk with Salmon. The family of Nashon, the chief prince of Judah, was always first to start out, following directly behind Moses. Then when the guiding cloud stopped drifting forward, Moses would call out: "Return, O Lord. Rest with the countless thousands of Israel."

Such joy for the children as they ran back and forth helping one another's families set up their campsites. In the settled days, between family chores and daily practice reading and writing portions of the Law, the children played at life skills more than games. The boys taught the girls what they had learned of marching in military units and proficiency with sword, bow, and sling. The tasks the girls were learning of grindstones, cook pots, spindles, and looms did not seem nearly as exciting. In the quiet of the morning and evening sacrifices, Acsah loved to stand with her friends and feel the solemn thrill of inner cleansing, trying to understand how the blood of the lamb transferred the guilt of their childish misbehavior to the interior of the tabernacle, but never doubting that it did.

Acsah's favorite part of that twice-daily ritual was when the priest carried the censer into the tabernacle for the burning of the incense. She had often clutched the hands of Salmon and Abihail apprehensively until Aaron returned. The entire congregation understood how dangerous it was for sinful mortals to come into the presence of a perfect God. They waited in profound silence, straining to hear the tinkling of the golden bells on his hem as he ministered before the Lord on their behalf. When a puff of wind blew the spicy-sweet fragrance of the incense offering to her, Acsah pulled it deep into her lungs like the very breath of Yahweh and breathed it out again as a prayer of love and praise. She felt a holy connection with the great God of the covenant, and it was the purest, highest joy of her childhood. Surely this would be the continual essence of life in the Promised Land.

"Head that way and you will surely find him," Nashon was saying with one last backward glance of his remarkable smiling eyes before he and his family were swept away by the flowing river of people.

Acsah searched for her family in the direction Nashon had pointed, and there in the dappled sunlight and shadow of the acacias, Caleb's hair glowed white as a swan, drifting and turning in the swirl of people to the north of the long rows of tables. He was probably pacing, not drifting, she thought to herself as she leaped down from the rock and plunged into the crowd again, bobbing and joggling, swimming in his general direction.

"I trust I did not keep you waiting long," Acsah said apologetically as soon as she reached him.

Caleb silently handed her an empty platter. His stomach growled noisily.

"Your body speaks for you," Acsah said, planting a soft kiss on his leathery cheek. "I had to find Abihail and congratulate her, and then I was trapped by the crowds." She searched his eyes for a hint of a smile.

"Let's get our food." The looked-for crinkles appeared at the corners of his eyes as he shook his head in mock frustration. "The others will be nearly finished with their feast by the time we join them." When their platters were heaped with steaming delights, Caleb led his daughter to a secluded glen.

"At last, our starving Abba has found her." Iru's caustic barb was the first of a barrage of comments from her brothers and their families.

"Grandpa, Grandpa! Auntie Acsah, where *were* you?"

"As you can see, we did not wait."

"Did you two get some of my stew?" Helah asked. "The children say it is the best."

"I did. It smells delicious." Acsah flashed a smile at her sister-in-law.

"It is *really* good," little Rachel chirped, "but Auntie Hannah's pilaf is my favorite. Have you tried it yet?"

Acsah caught Auntie Hannah's eyes. "Not yet, but it's on my plate. I spent half the morning helping her make it, and the smell was tantalizing. I can hardly wait."

"So why did you?" her brother Elah quipped. He always managed to splash bitter on everything sweet.

Acsah chose to ignore him, smiling at six-year-old Mushi's announcement that came complete with a flourishing two-armed gesture toward one of the platters of roasted ram. "I guarded a large share of the sacrifice for you and Grandpa, the best, most delicious part of all the feast. I would not let anyone take a second portion until you got yours." He glanced at his father who merely scowled. Mushi must have finished before she arrived, for now he had nothing better to do than stand there watching his grandfather and favorite auntie eat.

Caleb

Caleb waited quietly for the banter to die down and then blessed each member of the family. When he finished the individual blessings, he raised a round of barley bread. "All praise to the Eternal One who brings forth food from the earth."

Next he held up a shank bone dripping with oily juice. "As the holy flesh of these sacrifices strengthens our mortal bodies, strengthen, O strengthen, our hearts and keep us holy to you."

He scanned the faces gathered together in celebration. "May the blessings of Yahweh follow this clan for a thousand generations in the Land of Promise." Blessings finished, he lapsed into silence as he ate.

The two eldest of his sons had been but young boys when the family left Egypt. The others had been born in the desert. There in the forty years along the wilderness way, they had grown to manhood and married. There along the wilderness way, they had produced his eight grandchildren. And there along the wilderness way, he had sorrowfully buried one wife after another. His first wife, Shimrith died in the fifth year of the wanderings. His second wife, Peninnah, died in the eleventh year. Through the clouds of his grief, Caleb came to the horrible realization that both wives were among those beyond the age of twenty at the time of the exodus and were subject to the curse of wandering in the wilderness until they lay in their graves. As a silver-haired man in his sixties, he married the third time, carefully choosing the lovely young Jedidah who had been but eight years old at the Exodus—in fact, but two years older than his eldest son. That bright, happy girl helped him emerge from the deep, black cave of his grief once more. For thirteen years he walked in joyful certainty that Jedidah would be at his side when Israel settled into their inheritance. Then, at the birth of his only daughter, he was bereaved for the third time. Only the tasks of caring for the new little one gave him strength to go on living, and he could not bear to take another wife.

His heart lurched at the smothering image that pushed aside all other thought: his lovely, laughing bride so altered in one day, his precious Jedidah lying frail and pallid in their bed, cradling their newborn daughter in her arms. He could see again the pearls of perspiration jeweling a forehead drained of color. Every color paled except black—the black of the gleaming rivers of her hair spilling over the pillow—the black of a future without her. Even now, seventeen years later, the leaden ache twisted and tore at his heart with nearly the pain of that day. Again he saw her raising her head in a final burst of strength, her breath quickening as she drew an Egyptian anklet of silver and lapis lazuli from a bag close to her pallet, her mother's anklet during the days of Egyptian slavery. Jedidah had worn it every day since her mother died as Acsah wore it now.

Jedidah's first attempt to fasten the anklet around the infant's neck failed, and she closed her eyes to rest. Caleb gently reached for it, understanding her desire to pass it on to her own daughter.

"No," she breathed, the blaze of determination in her eyes and voice instantly staying his hand. "I must at least do this for my daughter." Snuggling the infant's head against her cheek, she struggled to anchor the tiny silver hook, failing three more times before the connection was complete. At last, she drew an exhausted breath and pressed her lips against the baby's velvet skin.

Caleb threw his arms around the two of them, burying his face on the pillow. He desperately wanted to tell his wife how much he loved her, how much he needed her. Especially now. How could he raise a daughter without her?

Jedidah stroked his hair. "My dear Caleb. Don't grieve for me. I am ready to rest."

Caleb sat up. How strange that she could speak when he could not, that she could strengthen him while he was bound, mute in his grief. A torrent of love and longing rushed through him. He wanted to beg her to hang on to life, for their children, for him, for this little one, but the look of peace and resolve in her eyes stopped him. He must be strong. For her.

"I have produced two sons for you, my husband, but this babe shall be the crowning jewel of our love. Her name will be Acsah . . . "Little Anklet" . . . Tell her of my mother's courage . . . even under the lashes of Egypt's taskmasters. Wearing this anklet . . . may Acsah always remember . . ."

Caleb laced his fingers through his wife's. "I love you. I . . ." He choked on his tears, embarrassed by his inability to say more.

A faint smile played around her lips. "It is you who taught me courage in the Lord." Caleb had to bend his head close to her lips to hear her next words. "How blessed I have been to know your love."

Caleb felt the soft puffs of her breath grow weaker. "I have been the blessed one," he whispered.

"I love you, my Caleb. Take care of our little Acsah for me."

Before he could reply, Jedidah closed her eyes and slipped into the long sleep of death.

Caleb shook his head, forcing himself to return to the celebration of the moment. Acsah was studying his face.

"You were thinking about Mother weren't you?"

"Is it so obvious?"

"Not obvious to them," she laughed, glancing at her brothers and sisters-in-law who were all busily engaged with their exuberant youngsters.

"Well, it is a day to celebrate, not to grieve. And so I give thanks to God for you."

Acsah reached over and patted his leg affectionately. "I wish I could have known her."

A clattering and the chattering of little voices interrupted. "Auntie Acsah, will you come with us to join the dancing?" The children looked at her with large, begging eyes, not daring to smile until they had her answer.

As if deliberating a weighty decision, Acsah studied their faces one by one. Her lips quivered in the struggle to maintain a serious expression. At last, a stream of giggling mirth burst the dam of pretense and she sprang lightly to her feet, "Yes, yes, yes to each of you. Let's go dance."

"Hooray," they cried. The older two grabbed her hands while the littlest one clung to her dress.

Caleb watched as the children pulled Acsah away from the leafy bower. The eyes of the little ones glittered with adoration.

"Oh Auntie. You look beautiful today with flowers in your hair."

"So do you, Rachel."

"She's always beautiful, Rachel. More than you."

"Auntie, why didn't you get married today?"

"Me? I'm not ready for that."

Caleb smiled at the sweet conversation that was rapidly fading into the distance, chuckling at one last comment from little Mushi.

"Wait for me to grow up, Acsah. I'll marry you."

Othniel

Othniel arose, following Acsah and the children to the center of the festivities. He watched the dancing for a few moments, and then wandered to a spot on the edge of the meadow where a boisterous knot of young men had gathered.

"Othniel." The voice of Jonathan, the grandson of Moses, greeted him from somewhere in the group. "Come try your hand at our contest. It is great sport and—are you surprised to hear?—your own friend, Jonathan, has cast the longest throw so far."

Othniel could not see him, but he caught glimpses of Igal through the tangle of bodies. The oversized young man, grunting like a bear, was lifting a rock the size of a large water bag. He whirled himself around for momentum and heaved the massive stone far across the grassy meadow, taking a deep breath as it sank in a bed of scarlet poppies.

The crowd convulsed in a roar of laughs and cheers as Igal doubled over gasping.

"Astonishing strength!"

"Igal has passed Jonathan's mark."

Jonathan laughed and covered his face in mock shame. "Surpassed by more than three cubits—a mighty man no more."

"When I am assigned to a battle company, I request to be with Igal," Ethan announced with conviction.

"My request as well," added Asriel.

"I also."

"And I," several others echoed at once.

Othniel noticed Phinehas' jaw tense and his mouth tighten as the commotion continued. "We rely on the Lord of Hosts, not the strength of man," he said quietly. Phinehas would succeed his father Eleazar as high priest someday. Othniel studied the tall, overly-serious young priest. It seemed the young priest's future role rested so heavily on his shoulders it had pressed down any capacity for pleasure in boyish banter.

Othniel nodded to acknowledge the young priest's words, but the rest of the group neither looked at Phinehas nor seemed to hear his comment.

"Let's hear it for the Champion of the Rock."

"Hear, hear!"

Jonathan gave Igal's solid shoulder a congratulatory slap. "Well done!"

Igal winced in mock pain, "Gentle, please. It will take days for my body to recover from that bruising weight."

The group roared in laughter again.

"Now, who is next?" Igal asked, panting still. One by one, he surveyed those who had not yet taken up the challenge.

"No point in any of the rest of us trying."

Jonathan snared Othniel with his laughing eyes. "You, my friend, must give this a try. I challenge you. At least aim to reach my mark. Prove us equals, yes?" He moved a step away, pointing into the grass. "See here. This is Ethan's mark."

Ethan rolled his eyes. "Thank you, Jonathan, for pointing out my feeble attempt."

Jonathan ignored him. "Yonder is that of Salmon, then Zebulon, and Asriel. Mine is a man's length short of where the rock lies now." He laughed as he tossed a small rock to Ethan who was standing closest to where the large, water-rounded rock lay oddly cradled in a bright floral bed. "Stop moping, Ethan, and mark the spot reached by Igal."

Othniel turned to leave. "I should see if my mother and grandmother . . ."

"Oh, come. This is a day of celebration. They can dance and talk with the old folks."

"No excuses," Asriel added impatiently as he brushed past Ethan. "Just throw it like the rest of us." He bent over to retrieve the huge rock, grunting as he lifted it, and staggered back to the throw line with the rock on his shoulder.

Othniel was bombarded with cries and cajoling, banter and baiting, all his friends intent on pressing him into the challenge. He shrugged off the attention and silently removed his outer cloak. After handing it to Jonathan, he methodically girded up the loose-flowing hem of his tunic to free his legs for the necessary movement.

"Just hurry," Asriel gasped.

When Othniel's deliberate preparations were complete, he took the rock from Asriel. It was cold, smooth, and much heavier than he had guessed. "Uhh," he huffed as its weight pulled his hands earthward, nearly throwing him off balance.

The group erupted in laughter yet again. "I hope you have new respect for even the shortest throws of your friends," Ethan chortled.

"I should get credit for how long I held the thing," Asriel retorted in good-natured complaint, arching his back and shoulders to stretch the muscles back into place.

Othniel assessed the stone-created hollow in the scarlet poppy puddle ahead of him. Then, looking beyond it, beyond the edge of the meadow grasses, to a gnarled and decaying tree stump protruding from the stony rim of the river basin, he took several deep breaths, shifting his weight as he whirled. A wrenching strain ripped through his arms as he leaped into the forward thrust and pushed the stony missile into the air. It flew past the poppy bed, smashed into the stump, rolled to the left, and fell, tumbling and crashing, down the stone embankment. The rocky clattering ended in a distant splash as the final bounce took the stone into the river.

Othniel looked around at the slack jaws. Even Jonathan, for once, had nothing to say. He quietly retrieved his cloak from his stunned friend and left, grinning as Ethan broke the silence behind him.

"Well . . . now that we have lost the stone, our contest is over."

Caleb

Caleb watched his daughter and grandchildren weaving in and out of the circle of dancers. His toes were tapping and his heart was light. The children called to him, "Come, Grandfather. Come join us."

Rachel dropped out and scampered to his side, taking his old hand in her two small ones, tugging him toward the dance. But just as he took the first step toward the circle, Joshua slipped up beside him.

Caleb quickly gave Rachel a light push toward the dance as Acsah whirled toward them. "Back in with you," he called, "I'll join the next dance." His daughter held out her hand just in time to pull the little one back into the circle and off they twirled with the other children.

"Promise, Grandfather?" Rachel's little voice chirped from behind a curtain of skipping, twirling dancers.

"Promise," Caleb called.

Joshua watched the interaction with amusement. "Don't let me stop you."

"One dance—later—will be enough for me."

"This *is* a day for dancing."

"True, true, my friend, but watching the children far exceeds any pleasure I get from frolicking about at my age."

Joshua's eyes embraced the joyous dancers, and he smiled approvingly. "All the excitement of the day we left Egypt without any of the fear."

Caleb simply nodded. There was no need to chatter.

When the music ended, Acsah rushed over with the children trailing behind her. "What a day, Uncle Joshua," she cried. In an unusual display of emotion, she threw her arms around the old captain's neck. The little ones seized his arms and legs until Joshua all but disappeared in a jumble of boisterous children. This was not an occasion for reserve, even for a man as highly esteemed as Moses' aide and the commander of the Lord's army.

"Here you two are again on the borders of Canaan." Acsah's eyes flashed with adoration. "Heroes to their battle stations!"

There was never a time when Joshua was not a part of Acsah's life. He was a favorite "uncle" who joined their family campfire frequently as she was growing up, telling and retelling the story of spying out Canaan. Joshua seemed to believe that Acsah and her brothers must hear the details over and over until the story came to define who she was—daughter of the heroic Caleb of Judah who stood up for Yahweh against the hosts of Israel with only Joshua by his side.

Acsah had no concept of the terror of that day. Only by the miraculous intervention of Yahweh had they survived it at all. Could Joshua not see that the girl had developed an unhealthy reverence, almost a worshipful awe for a level of courage beyond human? But they *were* human, and humans fail more often than not.

Long ago, Caleb began urging Joshua to cease telling the story, and began an intentional effort to demythologize the two of them in her eyes. "Never forget that you are a child of God, the Holy One of Israel. He is the only true hero." Obviously, looking at her face just now, his campaign had not deflated her exalted opinion much.

Joshua laughed and disentangled himself from the enthusiastic embrace. "Yes, here on the border again. This time with a new generation of Israelites." He tousled Mushi's hair, and grinned at Rebecca and little Shema. "Caleb, my friend, how blessed you are with all these children and grandchildren."

He suddenly widened his eyes and put one hand to his ear. "Ah! The reed pipes and tambourines signal a new dance."

"Grandfather is going to dance with us. Will you come too, Uncle Joshua?"

"Why don't you little ones dance just one more for us, please," Caleb requested with a little bow toward his persistent grand-daughter. "Show these two old men how fast the quick-stepping feet of youngsters can be . . ."

His smile faded along with further comment. Another melody punctuated by the staccato of hand-held drums drifted over the valley. Even the Israelite musicians fell silent just as Caleb had. Every celebrant stopped to listen as skillfully interwoven strains of flute, harp, and tinkling cymbals floated hauntingly, sensuously over the valley, filling the senses in a way no music ever had before. *Our own music seems like the simple, halting attempts of children in contrast.*

"Listen to that!" little Shema piped. "I like it!"

I listen, but I don't like it, Caleb thought.

Everyone stared in the direction of the superior sound and saw a tall, stately man leading a long parade across the meadow. His beard was thick and red, twisted into well-oiled and groomed braids, all cut sharply to one length like a long square chin. His garments of scarlet and purple hung heavy and regal as he strode toward them. The two men who flanked him were garbed in the flapping, black robes of desert-dwelling Midianites. Three more swarthy Midianites with ink-black eyes followed close behind. The flowing head coverings of these five were bound with gold bands, each distinctively decorated with colorful gems. The lead man with the red beard had the bearing and garments of a king. His five companions had to announce their royalty through the flashing colors of jeweled crowns. Behind the group of six men, a large contingent of musicians and pert, young dancing girls followed in a long train stretching back toward the trailhead of the Arnon gorge.

Caleb watched them invading the valley with their music—a colorful, cavorting army, hips quivering as joyously as the brass cymbals on their fingers. He liked the look of them even less than the sound.

"This warrants investigation," Joshua whispered and loped off in the direction of the strange parade.

Caleb too splintered off the stump-still crowd. The ax that crashed against the root of their celebration propelled him toward the intruders with a certainty that it was important to stop them before they reached his family, his people.

A few at a time, other princes and elders converged on their path until nearly three dozen of Israel's leaders rushed to close the space between the two groups. Only when the word was passed to make way for Moses did the pace falter. Spontaneously, the elders paused and split in half, forming an open corridor for Moses and Eleazar to pass through. By the time the elders reformed their solid block again behind Moses, the two groups were face to face. The red-bearded stranger bowed and the performers stopped, the final cadence hanging in the air as a fermata of respect.

Moses bowed deeply before the six dignitaries. "Shalom, friends. Blessed be He who has brought you to us on this day of festivity." His voice boomed over the valley so that all could hear. "We are celebrating the blessings of Yahweh, God above all gods, who has led this people, the Children of Israel, out of Egypt to the place where we are today. I am Moses, his humble servant. This is our high priest, Eleazar, son of my deceased brother Aaron." He turned with a sweeping gesture toward the entire group behind him. "These men are the princes and clan chiefs of our tribes. We welcome you." But the welcoming smile did not reach Moses's eyes.

The tall man stepped a little in front of his companions, holding out the corners of his cape as he bowed again. "I am Balaam of Babylonia, a seer, the prophetic voice of many gods." His pale, yellow-brown eyes were intelligent and watchful, carefully scrutinizing the faces of the men before him as he spoke. Caleb did not trust him, but he did not need to warn Moses. The instincts developed over many years herding sheep in Midian would inform the shepherd of Israel that a predator was studying his sheep.

"The fame of your God and of your people has reached across the desert to the land between the rivers," the man continued pompously. "That fame has drawn me hither along with my companions from the desert: King Evi, King Rekem, King Zur, King Hur, and King Reba of Midian."

A ripple of approving nods and comments moved through the princes and chiefs around him, but Caleb watched in stony silence. A quick sideways glance at Joshua informed him that his friend was also on high alert. The remainder of the elders reminded him of insects trapped in honey, kicking and flailing helplessly until they died.

King Evi bowed a second time. "We kings of Midian greet you as brothers. Abraham is our father as well as yours, and we treasure the knowledge of Yahweh just as you do. We are highly pleased to greet you as our new neighbors."

Moses held up his hands in a gesture of blessing, but his eyes blazed over the visitors with searching fire. "May Yahweh bless you in accordance with your faithfulness."

Balaam's cold, reptilian eyes stared back like an unblinking lizard while Moses continued with traditional hospitality. "Today is a day of celebration for us. We are honored to receive you as our guests."

Balaam again bowed low. "It is we who are honored to be here. Our people knew the name of Yahweh before your father Abraham was called out of Ur. We knew of Him long before the descendants of Abraham, Isaac, and Jacob established the nation known today as the Children of Israel. Our chronicles recount the stories of your bondage and exodus from Egypt, and of Yahweh's interventions on your behalf."

Caleb's gut twisted. The prophet seemed pleased, too pleased, at the positive effect of his words on the majority of the elders as he continued. "Just now, a new story has reached our ears, the story of your marvelous victory over the Amorite nations of King Sihon and King Og."

Moses interrupted Balaam at the suggestion that the victory belonged to his people. "We merely asked for passage through this land, to keep on the road and disturb nothing. But first King Sihon, and then King Og, launched their unprovoked attacks against us. We would have been obliterated by their superior armies, but Yahweh our God delivered us from their hands and has given us possession of their territory." His eyes gleamed at the memory. He looked past the group to the green meadows and the cultivated fields of grain beyond, obviously remembering the battle, remembering the fear and uncertainty, remembering the undeniably miraculous victory. Then, as if suddenly remembering the men standing before him, he locked eyes with Balaam once more.

"My friends, we speak too long standing here. Come, find a comfortable place to sit in the shade of this acacia grove, and we will serve you. After you have refreshed yourselves with food and drink, we will talk some more."

He turned to the elders behind him and began issuing orders. "Joshua, find enough women from the tribe of Ephraim to bring water so our friends can wash."

"Caleb and Nashon, see what meat you can find for our friends. We cannot share the holy sacrifices, but some of our men hunted deer and prepared savory venison. Nathaniel and Abidan, your tribes will be responsible for seeing that our friends have wine to drink. Gamaliel, scavenge for leftover baskets of bread. The rest of you gather up what you can find of other tasty dishes. Serve Balaam and the five kings first, and then your women can serve the musicians."

Joshua

Gawking ceased as the guests were seated. Happy chatter picked up where it had left off. The musicians took up their songs again, and the children of Israel resumed their dance. The simple praise tunes mingled joyfully with songs of birds and the gurgling melody of the river while the visitors feasted. But Joshua was troubled. The arrival of Balaam and his companions threw an unsettling shadow across this setting of light and health and goodness.

When they finished eating, the Midianite musicians gathered in clusters on the periphery of the festivities, subtly adding vibrant cadences to the celebration. Over the next hour, Joshua watched dancers trickle away from the Midianite centers and mingle with the festivities, joining Israelite dance circles with laughter and bold new style. He had to admit that the youthful gaiety of the girls was appealing. He had to admit that they were highly skilled in their dance, but their moves evoked something more than expressions of joy and thankfulness. He suppressed the stirrings of his body and fell into dark brooding, dwelling so intently on this injection of foreign flavor that he did not notice Moses until the familiar voice rumbled just behind him.

"Come. The council of elders will meet with Balaam and the Midianite kings." As Joshua turned, Moses dropped the demeanor of authority and added confidentially, "Perhaps together we can discern the motivations of our honored visitors."

"We are obligated to honor these visitors, I suppose, but they are not honorable. A dark shadow trails their steps." Joshua experienced a rush of relief as he revealed his distaste. "The sooner they return to the desert, the sooner peace will return to this valley."

Moses' authoritative air returned with one sharp look. "Hospitality is our duty, loving kindness our mission. Judgment belongs to God." He tossed the next command gently over his shoulder as he walked away. "Help me notify the remainder of the elders. You go to the right, and I will go to the left."

It did not take long for the seventy elders to gather. When the circle was complete, Moses turned his piercing eyes on the visitors. Joshua hoped to hear a stern warning, but Moses simply greeted them warmly one more time. "You have shown great kindness in coming so far to welcome us. Our people thank you for that. We share our bread with you as friends, and we are eager to know more about you and the people you represent. But, first perhaps, you would like to know more about us."

Evi's eyes brightened at the suggestion. He immediately tipped his head respectfully toward Moses in reply. "We are most eager to hear the details of your recent battles with the two Amorite kings."

"My captain should tell of that as I only observed from afar."

Joshua launched into the story, backtracked, and filled in detail after detail in response to heavy questioning. Long shadows were already stretching across the meadow by the time Joshua finished relating the story, yet the five Midianite kings were not satisfied.

"Joshua, you seem sincere in telling us that the cloud came unexpectedly to your aid," King Rekem said. Then he turned to Eleazar. "You are high priest of Yahweh. You have spoken little about your role in that battle, but you stood at Joshua's side when the attack began. Was it you who summoned the magical cloud?"

Why is it so hard to understand? I have been trying to tell you for more than an hour. Joshua wanted to shout at them, but his frustration was so great that he could not coax a word from his lips.

"It is not 'magical,'" Caleb huffed, clearly as irritated as he was. The Midianites would not give up the search to unearth dark mysteries rather than accept that Israel trusted in the faithfulness of Yahweh.

Eleazar sighed. "We cannot control the Cloud any more than we can control the wind. Yahweh gave it as a blessed shade from the desert sun, as light and warmth at night, and as a symbol that He is with us. Then, in our hour of desperation, he used it to defend us."

Zur eyed them suspiciously and tried another tack. "The old stories of your defeat of the Egyptian army declare that a cloud aided you at the crossing of the Red Sea. Who called on Yahweh to send *that* cloud?"

Moses raised his eyebrows in surprise. "Who told you about that cloud?"

"You have forgotten that Jethro, your own father-in-law, was a Midianite priest?" Zur's voice was raspy with exasperation. "It *was* the same cloud that held back your enemies at the Red Sea, was it not? We simply want to know how you conjure it up when you need it."

Moses sighed and then patiently attempted one more time to make the point clear. "My brother Aaron and I were leading the people that day, but we were helpless as Pharaoh pursued us. The Cloud at the Red Sea, just as the Cloud in this recent battle, was God's idea and His alone."

The five Midianites continued probing. They inquired about the hornets. They questioned the purpose of the tabernacle and the ark of the covenant. They were interested in the minutest details of its construction and showed special interest in the *shekinah* light that hovered over the ark in the most holy place. In a dozen different ways, they asked how the Israelites came to receive it. The more the Midianite kings questioned the council, the less content they seemed with the answers they received. The more they modulated their voices with sweetness, the more Joshua detected suspicion and annoyance under the surface.

All during the strained dialogue, Balaam gazed about almost disinterestedly, an observer cloaked in silence. At last, when civility had all but evaporated, the prophet spoke, artfully dissolving the tension between the two groups. "Enough of your battles. We have learned more than enough to see that the power of Yahweh is great and that you are a blessed people."

He looked around at each of the council members with a smile so broad it revealed all his teeth. "I must relate to you the strangest tale of my life for it regards you and the shield Yahweh your God holds over you even when you are unaware of danger."

As Balaam narrated his tale with pompous expressions and gestures, Joshua gazed beyond the council to a group of Midianite dancers gently coaxing the hesitant Israelites into the spell of their music. Their laughter rippled like silver across the meadow. The charm of these young women was too studied, too perfect. His blood ran cold with a sense of certain danger.

All at once, a hearty laugh, totally discordant with his fears, erupted beside him. Prince Nashon of Judah was nearly doubled over with mirth while tears ran down his cheeks. He caught Joshua staring at him and gasped through his mirth, "God spoke to him through a donkey. Have you ever heard anything so funny?"

Concealed by the blanket of laughter covering the circle, Joshua leaned close and whispered in the prince's ear. "Are you not alarmed by this Midianite invasion?"

Nashon stopped laughing and blinked. He cocked his head to one side, answering question with question in a loud whisper. "What's that you're saying? . . . an invasion?"

Balaam paused in his narrative with an unnerving glare at Joshua. When the prophet finally released his eyes and resumed his story, Nashon flashed a boyish grin at him and winked. With that, the prince of Judah turned back to the storyteller, enthralled.

Acsah

Acsah was catching her breath beside Abihail, when one of the Midianite dancers slipped between them, a synthetic smile plastered on her painted face. "My name is Cozbi. Would you teach me your dance?"

Acsah stared at her in silence for a moment. The face was surprisingly young. Younger than she was, of that Acsah was certain, but like the rest of the dancers, this girl's body was voluptuously curved in contrast to the straight, slim bodies of the young women of Israel. Crisscrossed loops of gold chain snugly bound the girl's shimmering robe of red silk. The large breasts and full round hips could not possibly be emphasized more.

As Cozbi repeated her request, Acsah stared into eyes as cold as deep, black water wells. The lips that framed the words were the color of blood. "We have come to offer friendship to our new neighbors," the girl was saying. "I would be pleased to join your dance. Will you teach me?"

Acsah averted her eyes to disguise the revulsion she felt toward this alien woman. "Actually, our movements are simple, not like yours. Just join the circle and follow." At just that moment, Acsah's friend, Bithia, whirled by holding out her hand. Acsah seized it and the opportunity to escape into the dance. With a hop and a twirl, she was gone, kicking back with her heels at Cozbi's hiss of frustration.

Eliab

Eliab grinned. *Acsah has managed to infuriate at least one guest.*

As quickly as Cozbi's eyes had narrowed in fury, they opened again in sugary enthusiasm. "How joyous your dance," she said to Abihail.

"We are dancing what we feel," Abihail replied. Her smile was adorably childlike.

Eliab disguised his amusement at the differences between these three women. *My little wife is nothing but sweetness and innocence. Acsah, the warrior on guard. And this woman, this Midianite—something else.*

Cozbi leaned out past Abihail and winked at Eliab. "It is our good fortune to have come from Midian on such a day to offer our friendship."

"We are glad you have come," the young groom responded hospitably. He dipped his head politely, then realized his eyes were lingering on her curves. He averted his vision with a flush of shame. "My name is Eliab."

Cozbi smiled coyly.

Her body is stunning, and she knows it. She wants me to look at her that way. Eliab's embarrassment and guilt turned to anger. He placed his arm around his bride. "This sweet girl is my wife, Abihail."

"My name is Cozbi," the Midianite responded, and then forced a slight pout. "I wish I knew your dance."

Eliab nudged Abihail.

She flashed her dimpled smile at Cozbi. "We would be honored to teach you."

"Oh, I would be most grateful. It would be so awkward to just jump in."

"Don't be offended by our friend," Eliab said, nodding toward the circle as Acsah swished by. "She is as cautious as a hawk, but once you have won her friendship, she will defend you with beak and talon."

Cozbi giggled with delight. "Her nose does have the curve of a hawk's beak."

55

Eliab didn't know how to respond, but Abihail would not let the stranger's rudeness go unchallenged. "Acsah is my best friend, and I think she is beautiful."

Cozbi smiled at her patronizingly and then turned to Eliab. "Help me understand the structure of your people. You have many tribes, correct?"

"Yes, there are twelve tribes all descended from the twelve sons of our ancestor Israel—sometimes called Jacob. When the tribe of Levi became the priestly tribe, it was no longer counted with the twelve. At that time the tribe of Joseph was divided into two, named for his sons, Ephraim and Manasseh. So in a sense there are thirteen tribes."

"From which tribe will your next king come?"

"King?"

"King, chief, whatever you call that old man, Moses. Who will replace him when he dies?"

Abihail hopped into the conversation confidently. "Our king is our God. Moses calls himself the servant of Yahweh."

Cozbi rolled her eyes. "We all have gods, but they are not our kings. So which of the tribes is the most powerful?'

"It is hard to say. Reuben was Israel's firstborn, but he lost his . . . position of . . . leadership." He faltered over the embarrassing rush of heat rushing up from his loins. This was not a story for such company.

"Tell on," Cozbi murmured with a slight lift of her brows, seeming to relish his discomfort.

"It's a lusty story," he mumbled.

"Those are the best ones." Her lips parted sensuously and she moistened them with her tongue.

A tingling mixture of thrill and dread spread through Eliab as the eager black eyes gripped his, urging him to relate the details . . . but sweet Abihail rescued him with a quick summary. "Reuben surrendered to his desire for the youngest of his father's concubines, the mother of two younger brothers."

"Is that all?" Cozbi laughed. "A common occurrence. A young man comes of age and notices the succulent breasts that nurse the younger children." She tossed her head back brazenly and cupped her own breasts as if offering them to Eliab. "His lust burns until the day his father is away from home, and he takes her. Jacob should have honored his son's burgeoning manhood."

Abihail looked at her with horror. "Such a thing is not done in Israel."

Eliab coughed. "Abihail is correct. Jacob caught them lying together, and Reuben's status as firstborn was lost." He straightened his shoulders, proud that high standards of morality were built into his heritage. "Jacob turned to the next two sons, Simeon and Levi, until they also dishonored him by their cruelty in attacking the town of Shechem."

"Ah, that tale is known throughout this land. So who? The fourth son?"

"My tribe, Judah, descends from the fourth son of Jacob's first wife, Leah. It is the largest tribe, but Joseph was the firstborn son of the favorite wife. As I mentioned, his descendants were divided into two tribes, Manasseh and Ephraim, the younger more numerous than the elder."

"So which is the most powerful?"

"We don't think of the tribes in terms of power."

"Our strength is our God," Abihail interjected. "He has all the power we need."

"Well, from which tribe will the next 'servant of Yahweh' be chosen?" An irritated, demanding tone replaced the playfulness in Cozbi's voice.

Eliab shrugged, "No one knows."

"But we do know how to celebrate the loving-kindness of Yahweh. Come." Abihail took Cozbi's hand. As the little bride pulled the Midianite girl toward the circle, she nodded to Eliab to take the stranger's other hand. "Dance between us, Cozbi. Acsah was right. This isn't difficult."

CHAPTER THREE

BALAAM'S TALE

The trumpet signal, four short, shrill blasts falling to a long, deep-throated wail, ended the dancing and games as it summoned the people to gather. The hills beyond the river had already begun spreading a blanket of shadows over the meadow as the people gathered expectantly to learn from Moses the story of their impressive visitors, but it was the red-bearded stranger who summited the rocky ledge and began speaking.

"People of Israel, my name is Balaam. I have requested permission to address you because I bear good news about the continued protection of your God."

The people looked quizzically at Moses. *Why was this stranger addressing them?*

"You must hear my story from beginning to end."

The whispered questions ceased, but the people stood in stone-faced silence.

"I am a seer from Babylonia, the land that was once the home of your father Abraham. I have been blessed with gifts of seeing, of prophesying, and of gaining the favor of the gods. I communicate with many gods, and have long known of the power of Yahweh.

What did this foreigner have to do with them?

"The Babylonian *Chronicles of the Nations* contain the story of your defeat of Egypt and your years of survival in the inhospitable deserts. A new story was recently added: the annihilation of King Sihon and the people of this valley. But the story did not end there. When all the surrounding nations trembled in fear of what you might do next, the brash and foolish King Og led his vicious army out of the highlands of Bashan against you. Even that giant and his fearsome warriors were no match for the Lord your God. You are celebrating the victory Yahweh granted you over those two Amorite kings, but I am here to tell you how he has protected you since that time."

Balaam's voice rippled over the crowds, rising and falling, floating sweetly, soothingly on their ears like a haunting lullaby. The longer he spoke, the more the crowds relaxed.

"Yahweh has forbidden you to engage in war against Moab . . . or harass their people . . . or covet their land. Moses has revealed this to me, but King Balak of Moab was not aware of the Lord's decree. Desperation pushed him into alliances with neighboring kingdoms. He sent emissaries to the kings of Midian who are with us today and also to King Nahari of Jericho across the river in Canaan. As the kings conferred together, King Evi suggested that they come to me. He well knew the power I wield, for I came to his aid two times in the past, helping him defeat his enemies each time.

"These kings lost no time. They sent a delegation immediately to my homeland requesting me to invoke a spell against you, to render you powerless. They offered me double my normal divination fee for they had a double-pronged plan. They sought power from the gods to defend themselves against any attack from you and also power to defeat you, annihilate you, and divide this valley among themselves.

"I assured them I could only work in cooperation with the gods, and Yahweh is not part of the *shaddayim*, the council of the gods, that normally communes with me. I spent the night seeking a word from him. I pleaded the desperation of Moab and Midian. I begged him to grant me the power to lay enfeebling curses upon you. I pleaded with him for some shred of help for Moab and Midian, but I received only one message from your God: *Whoever blesses*

Israel will be blessed, and whoever curses Israel will be cursed. The love of Yahweh toward you is strong, and His promise to Abraham will endure forever."

The crowds broke into a long cheer, leaving Balaam tapping the toe of one fine leather sandal while he waited for their ignorant enthusiasm to subside.

"It was humiliating to be powerless," he continued modestly dipping his head, "but I had no choice. In the morning, I had my servants dismiss the envoys for I could not bear to face them myself and reveal my impotency in the face of your Yahweh. I later learned that King Balak believed I was holding out for a greater price. So, soon thereafter, an even larger delegation arrived at my door. These were the highest princes of these kingdoms with full authority to assure me that Moab, Midian, and Jericho would hold back nothing if I would only come to their aid.

"How I wanted to go with them, go without delay, but my ears still rang with Yahweh's implacable words. In anger and frustration, I answered the envoys, 'Even if Balak would give me his palace filled with silver and gold, I cannot do anything great or small to go beyond the command of Yahweh.[1]

"One of the princes flung open the largest of the cedar wood chests. 'Do you really wish to refuse this?' he asked incredulously. Oh the gleaming contents that dazzled my eyes! More gold and jewels than I had ever seen. 'And this is only the first installment of your reward,' the prince affirmed.

"What could I do? My desire to help this coalition of kings exceeded their desire to obtain my help. But even as my resolve softened, deep in my heart I knew there was little hope of giving them what they asked for. I invited the delegation to dine with me and spend the night. I assured them that I would go to Yahweh again to see what further word he would give me.

"While they remained with me through the night, I used every incantation in my arsenal to gain permission from Yahweh to go on this mission in their behalf. I argued that the Israelites, the Moabites, and the Midianites were all related peoples. How could he favor one above the other?

"My pleas fell on ears of stone.

"Finally, long after midnight, Yahweh spoke to me. *You may go with the men if they repeat their request to you in the morning, but be sure of this when you go: you will only be allowed to speak the words I give you.* After that, I fell into an exhausted sleep, expecting to speak with the delegation first thing in the morning."

As he spoke, Balaam's pale eyes moved from face to face, peering intently into each set of eyes before moving on. One by one, the people who experienced this shuddered with the eerie notion that he could read their thoughts, but they could no more tear away from his eyes than they could cease listening to this fascinating tale. Relief came only when Balaam's eyes released theirs and moved on.

"Shortly after dawn, a commotion in the courtyard shattered my exhausted slumber. I flew to the window, instantly awake, and was astonished to see the entire troop heading out of the gate. Returning to their own land with their mission unfulfilled, without even breaking fast with me.

"I roused two loyal servants to accompany me. One gathered food and supplies for the trip. The other ran to the stable to get donkeys, saddling their backs with thick cushions for the long ride. I hastily threw on my traveling cloak and packed a bundle of powders and amulets that might be useful in executing my enchantments. We were not more than half an hour behind the delegation by the time we were ready to go, so I pushed my sturdy, little donkey forward as rapidly as possible.

"Just as we rushed through the city gates and onto the open road, my donkey turned sharply into the field on our right. Already irritated by the entire situation and detecting no reason for this behavior, I whipped the annoying animal severely until she returned to the road.

"A little later, as we passed between two walled vineyards on either side of the road, my donkey jerked sharply to the left, crushing my foot against the wall. The stubborn animal froze there, refusing to move forward in spite of my bruising kicks against her flanks. My servants had great respect for my powers with the gods.

What would they think? What would they tell others if I could not control a miserable little donkey? I leaped off and beat her so hard I thought she would never be inclined to defy me again.

"But, not more than a mile farther along, we came to a point where two rocky outcroppings pinched the road narrowly, allowing only one traveler at a time to pass through. As I led the way, the stubborn animal was again determined to turn aside, but as there was no room to do so, she came to an abrupt halt. She stopped so suddenly that my servants could not avoid plowing into me from behind. I kicked the donkey's flanks, shrieking at her to move, but she only dropped to her knees. In a flying rage, I raised my whip, beating her even harder than before. I undoubtedly would have killed her, but she stopped me with a question.

"'What have I done to you that you have beaten me these three times?' Her brown eyes blinked slowly."

Balaam paused at the sharp intake of breath and astonished "Oohs" from every part of the rapt multitude. He smiled knowingly at their reaction. "Without even thinking how odd it was to be having this conversation with a beast, I shouted at her, 'You have made a fool of me! If only my sword were in my hand, I would sever your smirking head from your body right now.'

"My donkey was as reasonable as I was out of control. I can still see the wise look in her eyes, though at the time it only enraged me more. 'Am I not your own donkey, which you have ridden day after day? Have I been in the habit of doing this to you?'

"'No!' I shouted at her, 'but why now?'

"Suddenly, a dazzling being with drawn sword appeared in front of me. I fell on my face before him, shielding my eyes from the blinding light. His stern, hard voice thundered over me, 'Why have you beaten your donkey these three times? I have come here to oppose you because your path is a reckless one before me.'

"My donkey brayed a soft little response and nuzzled my head with her nose, but I could not look up. The brilliant flashes emanating from this being crackled in the air around me, visible even though my eyes were clamped tightly shut. The voice thundered again like the rumbling crashes that follow lightning. 'This little animal saw me and turned away these three times. If she had not, I would certainly have killed you.' He paused a moment to let the fearful words sink in, then added softly, 'I would have spared her. It is your life she has saved.'

"If this was not Yahweh himself, it must have been his angel. With my face still on the ground, I answered in sheer terror, 'I have sinned! I did not realize you were standing in the road to oppose me.' Fearing that his blazing sword would come down on me at any time, I begged for mercy, pleading my ignorance. 'Now if you are displeased, I will go back,' I added respectfully.

"He was silent for such a long time that I finally looked up, hoping that he was gone, but his fiery eyes bored into mine. 'Go with the men, but speak only what I tell you.'[1] His eyes blazed with even greater intensity, and then he completely disappeared."

Balaam was pleased as he scanned the faces in the crowd before him. They were transfixed by his story. He must be careful to reveal only that which would increase their trust in him.

"I continued on my way, still shaken by this encounter, until I came upon the delegation of princes resting beside the road. They were surprised to see me, but well pleased I had changed my mind for they had not been eager to face the wrath of their kings. Immediately, they dispatched a messenger who hurried on ahead, informing King Balak we were on our way. Greater than their relief that I had come, however, was the dark foreboding that fell over me. The outcome of this venture was not likely to be what the kings hoped for."

Balaam squeezed his eyes closed. The details burned like fire in his head. Carefully sifting each part of the story, he culled out the parts he wanted to share, storing the rest for another day, another audience. As he continued speaking, another power took control of his lips. A carefully crafted version of the narrative flowed effortlessly from him as he relived every detail in stark clarity.

The Tale Behind the Tale

The low-slung sun was burning fiery red on the rim of the western hills by the time the prophet and his royal escort clattered up the slope leading to Kiriath-Huzoth. Not far from this city, he had been told, the rocky shoulders of the plateau dropped sharply into the valley where the Israelites camped. Apprehension twisted his stomach at the memory of the bright being who defended them. He was close enough now to read the stony solidarity on the faces of a score of kings and noblemen waiting with King Balak at the city gates. A lone woman stood next to the king, clad in scarlet and black. Her intense scrutiny of him was unsettling, but it was Balak's fierce countenance that devoured every remaining scrap of his confidence.

There was no welcome, no display of courtesy. As soon as Balaam was within speaking distance, King Balak snapped at him as one would speak to a lazy servant. "Did I not send you an urgent summons? Why didn't you come to me? Am I really not able to reward you?"

"Well, I have come to you now," the prophet answered. The pitch of his voice jumped mid-sentence like an adolescent boy. He slid off his donkey and bowed deeply, scrambling for words to explain the limitations that bound him. "But I can't say whatever I please. I must speak only what God puts in my mouth."

Balak's anger suddenly splintered into a wildness, a panic. "Have you no confidence in this assemblage? Here are the five kings of Midian, King Nahari of Jericho, and every important dignitary of the land of Moab. We will reward you well." He seized Balaam by the shoulders, his voice hoarse with desperation as he begged, "Only deliver us from this horde."

King Reba smiled obsequiously and twiddled his fingers in the air, "That swarm of insects pesters all the surrounding kingdoms."

"Pesters?" Balak interrupted. "You fool. They lick up the nations as an ox licks up the grass of the field."

While Nahari of Jericho maintained an aloof detachment and the Midianite kings postured, scrapping for positions of power, Balak babbled about imminent invasion. Balaam was astonished.

What was Balak doing? Kings never revealed such fear. Pity coursed through Balaam's bloodstream. His personal distress vanished, displaced by a sincere desire to be of help—and to be rewarded for his success by honor and riches. But how could he do it? He could not shake the feeling that this endeavor was futile. Or worse, that it would end in total disaster.

Then, in a rustle of crimson silk, everything changed. "I am Asanath, high priestess of Huzoth," the woman announced, swishing close for a face-to-face confrontation. The corners of her painted red lips tightened in a self-assured smile and she drilled Balaam with cold, black eyes. "I know who *you* are and why you are here. King Balak asked me to prepare a Baal feast to refresh and strengthen you. There will be no excuse for failure." She tilted her head in a barely perceptible nod as if soliciting an answer. In that moment, the weight of the entire disastrous day fell on his shoulders. The universe was waiting for the reply of the great seer, but Balaam knew he was only a man like any of them, a frightened man who sincerely wished he had chosen to stay in bed that morning.

The priestess gave one sharp clap of her hands and suddenly servants swarmed over the gear and animals, gathering up everything and rushing off in one direction with donkeys, camels, and even Balaam's personal servants in tow, while the kings and other dignitaries vanished in another. Balaam was suddenly alone with Asanath.

"Neither the servant's tunnel, nor the king's gate is suitable for a foreign guest to the temple of Baal-Huzoth," she said. "Follow me."

This woman commanded with a chilling authority quite different from any Babylonian hospitality Balaam had ever experienced. He was apprehensive about following her, but even more fearful of not obeying. "Let there be no more delay," he replied, attempting to appear eager by rubbing his palms together, but the sticky moisture of his sweaty hands spoiled the intended effect. It didn't matter. Asanath had already turned from him, striding through the broad gates onto the main artery of the city.

He trailed her red cape through the marketplace and up a broad street lined on both sides with solid blocks of red-clay buildings.

All at once the street ended abruptly at a perpendicular street. As Balaam followed her to the left, it struck him as odd that this street was bordered in both directions by blocks of houses and shops quite similar to the last street. When it ended at a new junction, they turned to the right onto a matching street that again ended with the choice of turning left or right. It wasn't long before Balaam lost track of the turns, disoriented by nearly identical buildings constructed of the same red clay, one bewildering street after another, row after row of houses and shops, row after row of doors, always the same no matter which street they took. *How on earth did the inhabitants of this place recognize their own homes, let alone find their way anywhere?*

"Are you coming, prophet?"

Balaam looked up, startled. Asanath waited at yet another corner, arms folded across her torso, impatiently tapping the fingers of one hand against her upper arm. He was surprised at how far he had lagged behind.

"Follow closely. Kiriath-Huzoth is, quite literally, a maze," she informed him curtly. "You could wander for days should you become lost."

"I noticed," he mumbled.

He was short of breath, puffing as he matched her long strides through the labyrinth of streets, each turn sloping steadily upward until at last they reached the steps of a sunbaked temple at the highest point in the city. There the king and his cronies waited in a cluster at the base of a broad, polished stairway. Asanath immediately mounted the lowest step as two young boys in white loincloths scurried down to meet her, falling at her feet like cowering puppies. As she held up one foot at a time, they removed her jeweled sandals, not risking so much as a peek at her face. He could well imagine what would happen to them should they displease her.

Balaam slid into the crowd beside King Balak.

"Leave your outer cloaks and shoes here," Asanath commanded with a sweeping gesture that took in all the kings and dignitaries.

As quickly as the men shed sandals and coats, their belongings were scooped up by another troop of servant boys. Balaam watched the priestess glide up the well-worn stairs on bare feet, her scarlet cape trailing behind her, then billowing wide as she wheeled on the uppermost step and peered down like a ravening hawk. He froze, suppressing the urge to scurry for cover. Asanath caught his eyes and held them, toying with his apprehension. Her crimson lips curled at the corners as if to say, *Too late, little mouse, you can't get away from me now.*

Balaam definitely did not wish to experience whatever she had planned for him in her lair, but escape back through this maze on his own was impossible—and his servants, his donkey, now even his cloak and shoes were gone. An involuntary shiver passed through him, but he deliberately straightened his shoulders. He was no mouse. He was a far-seeing eagle of Babylon, summoned here by the king himself. He soared high in counsel with the gods. An eagle does not fear a hawk.

Asanath laughed. He had the distinct impression that she was able to read his thoughts. "Come to the feast prepared in your honor, prophet," she announced. Then her features softened, and her invitation floated, gentle as a feather, to the men below. "Enter the presence of Baal, my royal guests. Enjoy his gifts."

King Balak had regained his regal composure. "Come, my friend." He grasped the prophet by the elbow in a brotherly gesture while the royal entourage swept the two of them up to the temple, bare feet greedily slapping up the steps. A quaver of excitement shivered through Balak's words as they ascended the steep stairway. "Baal's food. Baal's power. Just what we need for tomorrow's task."

At the top of the stairs, they entered an enchanted world, glowing with hundreds of votive lamps, a fairyland of flickering flames lighting an expansive portico. Between a pair of stout central pillars, a low table groaned with large platters of sliced red meat, pots of gravy, baskets of breads and other baked delicacies, trays of toasted almonds, and bowls overflowing with grapes, figs, pomegranates, and apples. Beyond the table, a troop of female musicians with glossy black hair cascading over bare arms and shoulders, lounged on scarlet cushions. A cloud of spicy incense billowed from six braziers around a large bronze statue of Baal.

The fumes enveloped the royal visitors, and Balaam's head swam with the heavy sweetness of it as the players took up harps and lyres, flutes and pipes, cymbals and drums. His body seemed to float on the vapors and join the ethereal strains flowing from the instruments. He stabilized himself against a pillar.

As he watched deft little fingers plucking strings and rosebud lips blowing across reed flutes, the earthy allure of feminine flesh anchored him to earth again. He recognized dimly that these girls were all very young. Not more than ten or twelve summers, judging from the softness of their facial features, but none retained the slim, straight body of a child. Thin drapings of fine white linen, fastened with a silver clasp on one shoulder, barely concealed breasts as round and promising as sweet, ripe figs. The prophet licked his dry lips, staring like a fool. What diabolical mind had crafted this invasion of body and soul?

King Balak was grinning for the first time that day as he squeezed Balaam's upper arm. "You find our temple girls pleasing? Come, sit beside me." He led the prophet to the elevated cushions at the head of the table while the other kings and the retinue of courtiers jostled for lesser seats. Balaam burned with agitation as he settled beside King Balak. It was not honor he craved at the moment. Even the vapors billowing from the food could not distract from those exquisite musicians even though hours had passed since his midday meal.

"You crave satisfaction for more than the belly, eh?" The king tossed him a knowing look and then gave a nearly imperceptible nod to the priestess who had taken a position across the courtyard in the shadows of an arched doorway. At her signal, two young girls emerged from the dark interior, prancing toward Balaam with shy smiles. The prophet sucked in his breath as his eyes dropped from their sweet faces to the physical charms tantalizingly revealed beneath that same gauzy linen.

Balak snickered and nudged him with an elbow. "Baal's newest brides, groomed to serve you."

"These . . . serve?" Balaam stammered. "But the food is already on the table."

"The rest of us washed long ago," the king chuckled. "You have endured a long journey over desert sands and are obviously in need of cleansing." He playfully brushed imaginary dust from Balaam's beard.

"So these are servant girls? But you said 'Baal's newest brides?'"

"This will be their first encounter, their marriage to Baal. It is the culmination of six months of training. Enough questions. You need a washing and they are waiting." He flicked his eyes up toward the girls who had now crossed the expansive pavement and hovered behind Balaam.

The prophet was overcome with a sudden bashfulness at the proximity of the sweet young things. Well aware that an entire table of men watched with amusement, he dropped his gaze, studying the grime between his toes.

King Evi beamed. "I think you will find this Midianite practice delightful. We are quite proud of our newly-flowered desert blossoms."

"Go, go, my friend. You stink of sweat," the king of Jericho urged. He scrunched one eye in a mocking wink. "Besides, you are far too tense to enjoy the meal King Balak has provided."

A burst of laughter circled the table. Balaam blushed. He *was* tense, and their jibes didn't help. He had to move while he still had a modicum of dignity. Forcing himself to his feet, uncomfortably aware of the eyes fixed on him from every side of the table, he inclined his head toward the young maidens in an attempt at civilized deportment. "Thank you, my dears. What a lovely custom. In my country only the meanest of slaves wash dusty feet." With girlish, giggling glances at each other, the novitiates took Balaam's hands and led him to the inner part of the temple accompanied by hooting and foot-stomping approval from behind.

When Balaam returned to the table a short time later in a clean white temple robe, Balak studied him with an unsettling grin. "Our washing rituals are quite effective, are they not? You look much more relaxed. Now perhaps you will have an appetite for our food." He forked several thick, red slices of beef onto Balaam's plate and poured a puddle of creamy gravy over the top. "Eat plenty, my friend; you will need strength for the task ahead."

Balaam groaned with delight at the first taste. *Such juicy, succulent beef!* He leaned toward the king, shouting over the noisy clatter and conversations of royally ravenous men. "This is the best I have ever tasted."

Balak flashed a broad, confident smile. "The taste of fertility. We steep each calf, Canaanite style, in a mixture of its own blood and the cream of its mother's milk before we roast it on the altar fires before Baal. Six months of this food, along with the blessings of Baal and Asherah, transforms our female children into these temple nymphs."

The king gestured toward the Five. "The local Midianite clans have become avid devotees of the Canaanite religion, and their daughters are my personal favorites."

Balaam feasted and laughed, enjoying the camaraderie of these foreigners, draining his cup as often as Balak refilled it. Engulfed by the warmth of the wine, filled and contented by the rich food, he finally leaned back from the table and belched loudly. "I will sleep well tonight."

"Better than you imagine," the king said with a sly wink. He pointed toward the inner temple doorway where two figures, swathed in long shimmering veils of scarlet and purple silk, waited in the shadows. Balak grinned. "That is the same Midianite pair who attended you earlier. They have shed their servant garments for the bridal dance. Now your marriage to our cult begins in earnest."

"My marriage?"

"Your fusion with the power of Baal."

The glint in the king's eye stirred a fleeting hint of danger, but Balaam quickly dismissed it when he heard the next words. "They are yours for the night." His skin tingled at the thought of those soft, sensuous hands on his body once more.

The music stopped. The room grew silent in anticipation. As demure as any brides, the girls had pulled the folds of their veils across their faces so that Balaam could see only two sets of doe-like eyes turned toward no other man in the room but him. He read shades of fear in those lovely, glowing eyes. Surely Asanath's expectations for this dance were high and one would not want to displease that high priestess. Feeling almost fatherly, Balaam nodded and smiled reassuringly.

Then the music began again, a lush new melody, slow and seductive, encircling Balaam's senses like the tendrils of a growing vine, binding him to the delicate little flowers that swayed to its rhythm. Filmy drapings of scarlet and purple silk fluttered over bare flesh as they twirled and circled each other, easing ever closer to the image of Baal even as their soft, white arms reached out for him. Stronger and stronger, the rush of virility surged through his body as the pace increased, and Balaam gave up all control of his mind to the beauty and sensuality of the dance. Circling the statue, moving in and out in turn, simulating a marriage encounter with the powerful bronze figure, the little brides led their man, a willing captive, to Baal. It was clear that he, not these little dancers, was the "innocent child" here in Moab.

The rowdy clapping and stomping increased with the tempo of the dance, the men around the table urging the bride-dancers on in a wilder and wilder dance. Through the fogging, triple intoxication of heady incense, fine wine, and sensual dance, Balaam assessed the hard, unfeeling face of the image. That cold bronze could not accept the love offering of these two delightful virgins, but he could. He would accept it and receive the infusion of strength that flowed from their worship of this Canaanite god. Tonight, he would be Lord Baal. The prophet's heart soared with newfound hope. Perhaps the power of this god *could* overcome that of Yahweh.

Balaam's legs twitched with the impulse to leap from his place and claim his brides. When he moaned at the exquisite pain of holding back, Balak leaned close with a confidential whisper, "I believe I will have a powerful prophet tomorrow." The king pointed a jeweled finger toward the temple doorway where Asanath waited in the shadows, beckoning to Balaam. The prophet grinned at her. Her training of the two initiates was impeccable. He raised his hand in a salute of admiration and lunged to his feet, ready for the unforgettable worship experience of his life.

When he awoke the next morning, the prophet's head ached. An odd mix of primal fear and bright hope swirled through him, and he strained to recall what had stirred these emotions. *Was he simply suffering from a foul dream born of indigestion? Or had he received a vision from the shaddayim, the council of the gods? If so, what was their message?* He stared into the dim light, trying to cut through the fog in his mind. The richly carved beams of this ceiling were unfamiliar. His fingers brushed the soft sheets beneath him, a finer bed than he could ever recall enjoying. As he struggled to remember where he was and what had happened to bring him here, a sleepy sigh interrupted his thoughts. When he jerked upright, whipping his neck to the right and then the left, a searing pain drove through his skull. He grabbed his head with both hands, squeezing his temples until the pain subsided, but he knew exactly where he was.

He remembered the panic of the early morning ride, his donkey's infuriating behavior, the encounter with that brilliant, white figure, and the trepidation of finally meeting King Balak. He remembered the entire unsettling adventure that culminated in a night of fertility worship with two newly-flowered Midianite dancers. As he watched them sleeping in the pale, gray light, their little chests rising and falling with each rhythmic breath, he was filled with remorse, actually more horror than remorse. The kohl eyeliner was smeared and streaked, the ruby color smeared across swollen lips, tender virgin throats and breasts were bruised with the marks of an animal appetite.

Now that he wasn't drunk on Balak's wine, or floating on the clouds of intoxicating temple incense, or beguiled by Asanath's pert little musicians and ensnared by their music—reality hit. The flawless little brides who danced for him could have been his daughters. They had been well trained to stir up the drunken passion that trashed their perfection. It was obvious they were not the innocents they appeared to be when they began their dance, but they didn't choose this. What kind of gods were these Baals of Canaan? He would not join forces with some bear-god whose followers slurped honey as they mauled and destroyed innocence. He must find Balak and tell him he would return home immediately.

The idea filled him with sudden panic. Perhaps it would be best if he could exit this place secretly, leaving only a message to face the certain outbreak of Balak's rage. But how would he find his clothing, his donkey, his servants? Even if he did, surely Balak's soldiers would find him wandering about the streets before he could find his way back through the maze. He staggered to his feet, shivering as the frosty air hit his naked body. *Or was it a shudder of fear? Had he already gone too far to escape this agreement with darkness?*

The bedside table held a basin of cold water and a steaming cup of pungent herb tea. He grabbed the cup, gulped down the bitter brew, and found it calmed his nerves and eased the pounding in his head. As he splashed his face, then his whole head with water, he smiled at the irony. The very ones who had planned last night's fogging experience were also aware that he needed mental clarity this morning. Nothing had been left to chance.

When Balaam finished dressing, he glanced up. Asanath was watching him through the open doorway. He had no idea how long she had been standing there, but as soon as their eyes met, she motioned for him to follow, her bare footsteps falling as silent as flower petals on the polished sandstone floor as she turned and walked toward streams of light pouring from a doorway at the end of the dim corridor.

Balaam's mind was spinning with questions to ask in order to be on his way, but he could not seem to voice any of them. Wordlessly, he followed her to the portico, the scene of his seduction the night before. It was empty now and bathed in the blush of dawn, the wholesome chorus of birds the only music. The sound refreshed him and strengthened his resolve to leave this base country im-mediately. He was about to ask Asanath how he could locate his servants and his donkey when Balak leaped up from a seat at the entrance. Balaam's stomach turned at the sight of the king who initiated that barbaric ritual.

"I trust you got at least a little sleep last night." A broad smile bared all the king's teeth. "Don't look so dour. You must forgive me for having Asanath call you so early, but we have a bit of a trek ahead of us."

Balaam did not even remember what had awakened him. He stole a glance at the priestess and met unblinking black eyes. The image of a fly buzzing in a spider's web hovered in the back of his mind. When Balak dismissed her with a wave of his hand, Balaam watched her retreat across the open courtyard with a sense of liberation. Although her body was as shapely as those of the temple nymphs, Asanath stirred up dread and disgust in him rather than desire. The entire temple complex disgusted him, at least this morning in the full light of day.

"It is Asanath who trains the girls of this region and brings them to first blood," Balak said without emotion as she disappeared through the dim doorway. "They serve here until they have produced an infant sacrifice for Baal. Then they are allowed to return home to marry and have families of their own." He winked at Balaam. "As you have seen, Asanath is good." Balaam could not force himself to raise his eyes and look directly at the king.

Balak laid a brotherly hand on Balaam's shoulder. "Last night was only the beginning of a mutually beneficial relationship between us." Balaam shivered in the cold of the early morning.

At the king's command, Balaam's two personal attendants appeared. "I am certain that no ordinary military attacks can defeat Israel. You are the sole hope of Moab," Balak continued as the servants wrapped a warm cloak around the prophet's shoulders. These two had served him faithfully for years. Now with smirking smiles barely concealed, they would not meet his eyes. Balaam was annoyed.

The king's fawning prattle persisted. "My future lies entirely in your hands. *Your* future, however, is yours to control. Assist us in the hour of our need, and you will live out the rest of your days with more wealth than most kings—supplied endlessly by the treasuries of the grateful people of Moab, Ammon, Midian, and Jericho." He smiled confidently, once more showing that full set of teeth in a strong jaw. "No luxury will be withheld from you. If you choose to remain among us, I will build you a home near my own palace, or you may dwell in Jericho, or in the desert towns of the Five Kings of Midian. Whatever you choose, wherever your heart leads you, you will ever be held in highest honor." He gazed up at the sky and his voice resonated with awe. "Balaam the prophet will be immortalized in the songs and legends of our people. Your star will dazzle forever in the night sky."

Balak's tone shifted again as he flicked his gaze to the expansive stone pavement of the portico, and with a look that spoke volumes, beyond it to the temple itself. "If you were pleased with the offerings of this place, a continual supply of both the food and the women will be brought to you. Nothing you desire will be withheld from you. Only use your power to defeat this desert horde."

Balaam again was torn by inner conflict. As much as he craved the prestige and promised treasure, he could not shake the haunting conviction that this venture would be his undoing. He looked straight into Balak's eyes. "Balak, my friend, I open my heart to you. I will not deceive you. Nothing would please me more than to fulfill your urgent request, but I am only a poor seer, a prophet . . . not a god."

"Your modesty belies the reports I have heard of your efficacy."

"The reports do not lie. I have been gifted from childhood with special power to determine when the gods are angry and how to regain their favor. Often during the night, I am swept up into their council and instructed by them. When kings and captains come to me, I already know what the gods require to placate their anger. This case is different."

He outlined a circle on the smooth pavement with his great toe and sighed, "Yahweh is not part of the council of *shaddayim*. I have known of him, but until you called for me, he had never spoken to me. When I was still in my own land, Yahweh informed me that he alone controls the words that I say here. I fear that his words will not be pleasing to you."

"But you must try. King Evi has spoken of the great potency of your words."

"Know this: I will do all in my power to cause those words to line up with your needs."

Balak clapped a hand on Balaam's shoulder once more. "That is what I wished to hear. Let us waste no more time. My confidence in you is complete. We will go to Bamoth-Baal. From that point, you will have a clear view of that accursed camp. The priests there believe that this will only increase the strength of your curses." His broad smile faded into a grim hard line. "What will you need to conjure up your curses? Asanath suggested that we might sacrifice the two virgins who slept with you last night."

Balaam looked at him in horror. "Good heavens! No. Yahweh would not be pleased by the sacrifice of those children."

Balak looked at him blankly. "Then what?"

"Seven is a strong number to Yahweh. Build me seven altars at Bamoth-Baal," he said quickly. "Bring seven bulls and seven rams. We will offer them together, you and I, the king and his prophet. Surely that will please Yahweh."

No sooner had the supplies Balaam requested been assembled, than King Balak marched the troop north out of Kiriath-Huzoth. The king and Balaam rode their donkeys side by side at the head of the procession with the Five and the delegation of princes forming a long line behind them. A small group of stone workers with a wagonload of supplies and two animal caretakers driving the fourteen animals followed.

Within the hour, they reached the base of a steep trail leading up to the highest peak in the region. As they rounded the first bend, the dark outline of the sanctuary of Baal appeared above them silhouetted against the pale morning sky. It was well situated with a sense of sacred strength about it, as if drawn from roots in the massive rock ridge. With the sun on his back and such an inspirational view above him, Balaam fully relaxed for the first time that morning. Balak had given him complete control over the proceedings. The promised rewards were as good as in his hand. He reached out and patted his little donkey's neck. "Behold, how far you have brought me, old girl."

The trees close to the city had given way to small shrubs and clumps of grass sparsely scattered in the clefts of a chalky rock wall that rose steeply on the right-hand side of the pathway. As they climbed, these rocks alternately obliterated the view of the top then opened up again to reveal the sanctuary looming larger with every turn of the path. A greater degree of power and strength filled the prophet with each new glimpse. By the time they reached the summit, the golden warmth of full morning had swallowed the early chill. In the sunlit haze of the valley below them, the tents of the Children of Israel stretched out in blissful ignorance of the plot against them. It looked like a toy camp constructed by a child, and the sight filled Balaam with hope.

As soon as the masons had constructed the simple stone altars, the animals were slain and their entrails removed. Then in ceremonial dignity, Balaam and the king moved down the row of seven altars, Balaam solemnly repeating his incantations over each ram and bull while the king, carrying a torch lit from the eternal flame of Bamoth-Baal, touched the bundles of sticks beneath the sacrifices with sacred fire. The princes of Moab and the five kings of Midian formed a half circle behind the seven altars, chanting, "Cursed be Jacob; blot them out. Cursed be Jacob; blot them out."

When the altar fires were all blazing and crackling, Balak grinned, "Surely Yahweh will be pleased with us. What next?"

"Wait here. I must complete my divination alone." Balaam turned sharply to the servants who held pottery jars filled with the sacrificial entrails. "Follow me." He led the way to a rocky promontory protruding from the ridge a short distance from the temple and motioned for the servants to set the containers at his feet.

Gazing down on the Israelite camp in the valley, he clenched his fists, praying loudly, earnestly over the bloody viscera. "O great Yahweh, your ways are only vaguely known to this servant of the *shaddayim* and to Balak the king, but we implore you sincerely. We have spared no effort to please you. We have offered both bulls and rams for your pleasure. We have multiplied our sacrifices by seven to gain your ear. We vow to honor you above all other gods if only you grant our request. Shatter the strength of the people spread out below us in this valley. Empower our coalition of kings that they may prevail over Israel in battle. Affirm the curses I proclaim against Jacob according to the truths revealed in these sacrificial organs."

Balaam stooped down to study the kidneys and heart of the first slain ram, searching for portents of Israel's future. There were only signs of long life and peace. He cast the bloody organs aside and studied the next set. More of the same. His hands were covered with greasy clots of blood and fat by the time he reached the bottom of the second bowl, but he had not found a single sign of famine, war, death, disease, dismemberment, or even bad luck. As he wiped his hands, the anxiety that had been creeping up from his bowels suddenly erupted in full panic. He had never needed to lie before about the results of his divinations, but how could he do otherwise today? He must give Balak what he wanted. What he needed.

Suddenly the same shining being he had encountered on the trek from Babylonia appeared before him. He spoke no words, but the blazing eyes drilled into his, seeming to read his every thought. Balaam's head pounded with pressure, nearly exploding with words that were not his own. He staggered back to the temple, all the while praying frantically to Baal, to Asherah, to the gods of Babylonia. One by one, he silently addressed every god of the *shaddayim*. Eloquent words abandoned, his prayers devolved to a simple plea, desperate and bare, for the power to curse Israel.

The princes still surrounded the altars chanting, "Cursed be Jacob; blot them out. Cursed be Jacob; blot them out," but Balak paced impatiently in front of the temple. The moment he saw Balaam, the king ran to him, searching his face. "Well?"

As Balaam scanned the distant view of the Israelite camp, he fell into a trance. His lips were frozen while the words churned in his head with mounting pressure.

"Balaam! What of the curses? I dislike your silence."

Suddenly, Yahweh's message shot out of his mouth. He could no more stop the utterance than he could stop a sneeze.

Balak brought me from Aram,
  the king of Moab from the eastern mountains.

His first words staunched the incessant chant. The princes leaned toward him, smiling with anticipation.

"Come," he said, "curse Jacob for me;
  come, denounce Israel."
How can I curse
  those whom God has not cursed?
How can I denounce
  those whom the LORD has not denounced?
From the rocky peaks I see them,
  from the heights, I view them.
I see a people who live apart
  and do not consider themselves one of the nations.
Who can count the dust of Jacob
  or number even a fourth of Israel?
[If only I could] die the death of [these right-living people],
  and [my posterity continue as blessed and happy as they!"][2]

King Balak's face blanched whiter with every line of Balaam's message. "What are you doing? I summoned you to curse these invaders not bless them."

The controlling force released Balaam's tongue, and he bellowed angrily, not at Yahweh, but at the king. "I told you. I can only speak the words of Yahweh ."

Balaam steeled his heart to flee this escapade, defeated, hands empty of all promised rewards. "I take my leave of you and your land," he declared with a respectful dip of his head. "Yahweh will not allow what you desire. His will is set in stone as hard and fixed as the mountain we stand on." Eager to get away while there was enough daylight to begin the homeward journey, he summoned his servants, instructing them on what gear to gather and how to pack it, while Balak stormed into the temple to consult with the priests of Baal.

Balaam mounted his donkey and was already starting down the steep roadway when Balak called to him. "Wait! We aren't finished."

Balaam stopped. There was nothing more he could do. After such a crushing failure, no amount of riches or honor could induce him to try to curse Israel a second time, but even as the thought that Balak might seize him and have him killed played in the dark shadows of his mind, he reigned in his little donkey and turned her around. This doomed undertaking could only go from bad to worse, yet he waited, watching the king race down the temple steps toward him.

"The priests proposed a solution to our dilemma," Balak puffed. He paused to catch his breath, but when he tried to smile, his face contorted in a sneer. "I had heard that you were a powerful seer, but apparently you are overwhelmed by the vastness of this people. You must come with me to another peak where you can see only a small part of them. Later we will lead you to several places from which you can view the remaining parts of this horde—to curse them bit by bit."

"You insult me. Yahweh tried to dissuade me from coming. He told me I could only speak his words here. I will never set foot in Moab again."

The king spat on the ground and shot the next words at Balaam in the form of a challenge. "If you leave, you prove yourself to be a coward worthy of scorn—or an imposter worthy of death. If you are a prophet of any god, you should be able to curse these foreigners in part."

Balaam's resolve wavered. He had risked his reputation trying to gain the king's rich rewards despite the unnerving dealings with Yahweh. Balak had just made his actual situation clear. If word of this failure got out, his days as a prophet were over. His very life was in danger if Balak and the five kings decided he had deceived them. Perhaps these priests were not so ignorant. Perhaps their suggestion would work.

"All right," he answered feebly.

Balak quickly issued orders to all the servants. "Hurry now to Zophim plateau on the peak of Mount Piscah and repeat the preparations just as before."

Balaam shot an accusing glance at the king. "Have them prepare better than before. Instruct the stockmen to find the best of the rams and bulls this time. Be certain that they do."

Balak grunted, resenting the implication that some fault on the part of the Moabites had brought about this failure. "Know that it is in your best interest, Balaam, to finish this task with a reputation shining as brightly as when you arrived." He pushed past Balaam on the trailhead. "You heard him," he said to the stockmen. "Seize the cattle and sheep we need in the town below. No inferior animals." Then he disappeared around the first bend with the train of princes, servants, stoneworkers, and stockmen trailing behind.

At the top of Piscah, there was no temple, only a stone wall, built nearly shoulder high to conceal Moabite scouts as they spied out the valley below during the Amorite wars. Close to this wall, at a point overlooking part of the Israelite camp, seven new altars were quickly constructed and the animals prepared for the sacrifice just as before. When the king and prophet had again ceremoniously sacrificed a bull and a ram on each altar, Balaam said caustically, "This time, remain standing in the midst of the row of altars as I asked before. You must do your part to achieve success. I will go apart to see which of the gods will come to our aid. Yahweh will not curse His people."

With servants following him again bearing the jars of entrails, Balaam withdrew from the group to a rocky point with a good view of the eastern block of tents. He raised his hands to the heavens and began calling on the names of the most powerful of the Babylonian gods as well as the gods of Canaan. "O Marduk, you have never failed me in the past. O Ishtar, do not hide yourself from your servant. O Tammuz, arise in strength. O Baal of Bamoth, Baal of Peor, all Baals of Canaan, show your strength against Israel and Israel's god. O Asherah, goddess of . . ."

The words caught in Balaam's throat as the blazing-eyed form of Yahweh's messenger appeared again. "Go to Balak with my message."

Balaam did not need to ask what that message was. His head throbbed with it, and it was even stronger than the previous curse turned blessing.

Before Balaam reached the group surrounding the king, Balak called out to him, "What did Yahweh say?" His voice trembled. "I saw his light."

Once more, unbidden words gushed from Balaam's mouth.

Arise, Balak, and listen;
hear me, son of Zippor.
God is not human, that he should lie,
not a human being, that he should change his mind.
Does he speak and then not act?
Does he promise and not fulfill?
I have received a command to bless;
He has blessed, and I cannot change it.

No misfortune is seen in Jacob,
no misery observed in Israel.
The LORD their God is with them;
the shout of the King is among them.
God brought them out of Egypt;
They have the strength of a wild ox.
There is no divination against Jacob,
no evil omens against Israel.

It will now be said of Jacob
and of Israel, "See what God has done!"
The people rise like a lioness;
they rouse themselves like a lion,
that does not rest till it devours its prey
and drinks the blood of his victims.[3]

Balak's frozen rage shattered into a shriek of fury. "Miserable prophet, must I rip your tongue from your mouth? If you cannot curse them, remain silent, but do not bless them!"

Balaam bellowed back, "Did I not tell you from the beginning that I must repeat whatever Yahweh puts in my mouth?"

The king calmed himself with obvious effort. "Let us not quarrel. We need each other." He took Balaam's arm firmly. "Come, we will go to one more mountain top. It is the most powerful place of the Canaanite Baals. Perhaps Yahweh cannot prevent a curse on Israel from there."

The exhausting day had nearly ended by the time the group scrambled to the top of Mount Peor. A magnificent temple crowned this peak. Priests bustled in and out of the portico while scores of temple nymphs lounged on the steps wearing only beguiling masks painted in kohl and crimson and the alluring temple tunics of fine linen, the promise of another unforgettable night of wild worship under the stars. He was gripped with the distinct assurance that success awaited him on this powerful peak. *Here on Mount Peor, I will celebrate victory at last.*

He turned from the temple and trudged toward the precipice. As before, the king's servants prepared the altars and sacrifices close to the rim of the plateau. "Do not bother collecting the entrails," Balaam said glumly, "Yahweh cannot be controlled by divination or sorcery as can the other gods."

The prophet went apart one last time, carefully keeping his back to the camp in the valley below, looking eastward toward the rising stars. These gods of the night, appearing one by one in the darkening sky over the desert, had proved to be feeble help in his dealings with this most obstinate One. He would not anger the Israelite god by further appeals to any of them.

Yahweh did not have a place in the Babylonian star system, and Balaam addressed him now as Lord over all the star gods. "O Yahweh, I will not resort to sorcery before you. Incantation and divination are an insult to your majesty. I appeal to your justice and mercy. Your dealings with the descendants of Abraham have shown you to be superior to all gods in those virtues. I appeal to your goodness. King Balak has offered me rewards greater than any I have seen in my life. My reputation as a seer is on the line. If I . . ."

The prophet hesitated at the crunch of gravel. King Balak was creeping close to hear. "If I fail here, I may as well end my life; then I would be absolutely no use to you. Give me the words to curse these people, and I will be your prophet." Balaam closed his eyes and waited. Surely, he had stated his case in a respectful and appealing way.

Nothing happened. He opened his eyes just enough to see what the king was doing. Balak was holding his breath, watching him closely, and waiting as anxiously as he was. After several more minutes of oppressive silence, Balaam wheeled around to face the encampment in the valley. "Where are you, blazing messenger? Show yourself!"

Suddenly, he was overcome by the view of row upon row of tents, cook fires glowing like constellations around the tabernacle with its blazing cloud. He fell into a trance as the Spirit of Yahweh possessed him and a third blessing thundered into the night.

> *The prophecy of Balaam son of Beor,*
> *The prophecy of one whose eye sees clearly,*
> *The prophecy of one who hears the words of God,*
> *who sees a vision from the Almighty,*
> *Who falls prostrate, and whose eyes are opened.*[4]

Balaam's mind exploded with a startling new message. The true star story, gleaming clearly from the constellations rising up from the east: the Water Bearer, the Virgin with her sheaf of wheat, the High King on his throne, the Bull, and the Lion. His eyes were opened. These were not miscellaneous tales of various gods, but one story of one God with one mission who had chosen one people to accomplish his purposes.

> *How beautiful are your tents, Jacob,*
> *Your dwelling places, Israel!*
> *Like valleys they spread out,*
> *like gardens beside a river,*
> *like aloes planted by the LORD,*
> *like cedars beside the waters.*
> *Water will flow from their buckets;*
> *Their seed will have abundant water.*
> *Their king will be greater than Agag;*
> *their kingdom will be exalted.*[5]

"Nooo . . .!" King Balak sprang at Balaam, seizing his throat with a strangling grip. Balaam knew enough of Canaanite history to recognize the humiliation couched in the reference to Agag, ruler of the Amalakites who had savagely attacked Israel shortly after they marched out of Egypt, but like the rest of the blessing, these words did not originate in his head or heart.

Priests, who had witnessed the event from the temple steps, ran to the pair and pried the king's hands from the gasping prophet's neck. "This may be a battle of the gods," one of them warned. "Never interfere in such a case."

Balak thrashed against the restraining hands of the priests, and when he could not act, he shrieked at the failed prophet. "Out of my sight or you are a dead man!"

Balaam could not stop the words of Yahweh. He looked the Moabite king in the eye, drew in a deep breath, and finished the prophecy.

> God brought them out of Egypt;
>   they have the strength of a wild ox.
> They devour hostile nations
>   and break their bones in pieces;
>   with their arrows they pierce them.
> Like a lion they crouch and lie down,
>   like a lioness—who dares to rouse them?
> May those who bless you be blessed;
>   and those who curse you, be cursed![6]

"I brought you here to curse these people," Balak croaked, "instead, you have blessed them not once or twice, but three times. I would have made you rich, but this Yahweh has put a spell on you."

Balaam rolled his eyes. "I told the messengers you sent me, 'Even if Balak offered me his palace filled with treasure, I have no power to say anything, good or bad, beyond the words Yahweh puts in my mouth,' but still you urged me to come." He felt the force of Yahweh's holy words building within him again and fought to suppress it. More of these disturbing prophecies could only make the situation worse, but he had no power to control the gush of words coming from his mouth:

Now I am going back to my people, but come, let me warn you of what this people will do to your people in days to come.[7]

Balaam thrust out his hand, pointing with his long, white index finger at the thousands of points of light glowing in the valley below. The priests signaled the servants to bring Balak's donkey and take him away before Balaam cursed the king himself. The prophet's eyes rolled back into his head and he fell to the ground once more, overcome by the vision and the message that would not be silenced:

The prophecy of Balaam son of Beor,
　　the prophecy of one whose eye sees clearly,
The prophecy of one who hears the words of God,
　　who has knowledge from the Most High,
who sees a vision from the Almighty,
　　who falls prostrate, and whose eyes are opened:

I see him, but not now;
　　I behold him but not near.
A star will come out of Jacob;
　　a scepter will rise out of Israel.
He will crush the foreheads of Moab,
　　the skulls of all the people of Sheth.[8]

Balak leaped on his donkey and bolted toward the trail, covering his ears with his hands. "No more! No more!" he shouted. He cringed at every word and kicked the flanks of his little beast to go faster until it tottered on the steep path. With the white-faced princes of Moab and Midian at his heels and the entire retinue of servants scrambling to catch up, the king fled. And Balaam's words continued flowing, resolute and clear, over the starlit landscape.

Edom will be conquered;
    Seir, his enemy, will be conquered,
but Israel will grow strong.
    A ruler will come out of Jacob
and destroy the survivors of the city.[9]

Balaam writhed on the ground, struggling to seal his lips against the prophecy—the future of Israel under the ruler who was to come. For a moment he lay, spent and quiet, then invisible hands lifted him. He felt like a temperamental child grasped by his father's hands and pulled unwillingly upright until he landed stiffly on his feet. Although he flailed and jerked to resist, his arm raised prophetically once more, his bony index finger pointing to the lands of the Canaanite nations one by one in a sweeping arc:

Amalek was first among the nations,
    but their end will be utter destruction.

Then Balaam turned toward the craggy mountains of southern Canaan:

Your dwelling place is secure
    your nest is set in a rock;
yet you Kennites will be destroyed
    when Ashur takes you captive.
Alas! Who can live when God does this?
    Ships will come from the shores of Cyprus;
they will subdue Ashur and Eber,
    but they too will come to ruin.[10]

Balaam was shaking when the Spirit released him at last, but he was finally able to move and speak on his own. "Those were not my words," he sputtered as he staggered to the top of the trail. Balak was nowhere in sight. The prophet shouted into the blackness, "Those were not my words!"

A loud roaring erupted all around Balaam. Blurred images rushed to clarity as if he had been swimming beneath the waters of the Euphrates, and suddenly breaking the surface, could see clearly again. He gulped. Looking out at the crowds massed in the meadow below him, he remembered the plan bestowed by Lord Baal on the night of his dismal failure. He remembered that he had been addressing Israel. The words had been flowing from him so effortlessly as he relived his experience that he had no idea what he had revealed or what he had concealed. But he knew with certainty that the power controlling his voice this time was not Yahweh.

His eyes swept over the people. The daughters of Midian were interspersed throughout Israel, cheering his tale. The crowds were laughing and praising Yahweh.

"The Lord showed Balak a thing or two."

"What a God! Using your own donkey as a prophet to you!"

"Yahweh surely has a sense of humor."

"Praise God for the blessing and curse of Abraham."

The prophet smiled. Exactly the response he had hoped for. When he glanced at the Midianite kings beside him, Evi winked. Everything was going according to plan.

CHAPTER FOUR

OUTBREAK

Eliab

Eliab pushed through the door flap of his parent's tent. "What is so important, Father? We should be present for the morning sac—" He stopped abruptly. Three young women smiled and nodded at him despite his rude entrance. Eliab's face reddened. He recognized them as members of the troop of Midianite dancers and singers that came with the prophet. Shimmering folds of bright-colored fabric lay in the center of the floor beside a small chest glinting with gold jewelry. Eliab's mother, Mara, was serving the sticky-sweet honey cakes she had recently learned to make while his older brother Jamin sat directly opposite the door nibbling one of these delicacies from the fingers of a beautiful Midianite woman. Jamin's eyes flashed irritation when Eliab entered, his mouth twitching in the effort to hold back one of his usual caustic comments.

"Come in, come in, Eliab, my son." Achor was flushed and overly animated as he stood up to greet him. "I would like for you to meet our guests. Jamin and I have had an unbelievable education over the past week."

Cackling with glee, Mara held the platter out to her younger son. "You will love these wonderful girls, Eliab. Such helpful neighbors." She threw back her head and laughed loudly. "Can you picture them, dressed in such fine gowns, leading your father and Jamin around the hills gathering honey for two entire days? Rumpled and soiled, they all were when they returned at the end of each day, but no one complained. Least of all me when I have gained six pots of wonderful honey." She waved the platter in front of his face. "What are you waiting for, son? Go on. Take one."

"No, thank you. I just finished my manna porridge."

She laughed again. "You don't know what you are missing. Father cannot stop praising my honey cakes."

Achor nodded and sighed with remembered pleasure, "The tastiest morsels of my life." Then, with an idiotic grin nearly splitting his face in two, he added, "You must join us in this learning venture, son. Two full days of honey gathering . . . then, yesterday, they showed us a secret place where only a few chosen men may go to gather rare mushrooms."

Jamin shifted in his seat, licking the last sticky crumbs from the girl's fingers. He addressed Eliab without breaking his intimate eye lock with the Midianite. "You've missed out on a wealth of learning, Little Brother."

Eliab wondered briefly if Jamin's wife, Hattil, was as enamored with this foreign beauty as his brother was.

"Father thinks we need to include you. If you are man enough, that is." Jamin glanced up at him, one eyebrow raised arrogantly.

Mara set down the platter. "Oh, Son, Abihail would love those mushrooms. I put them in some lentil stew last night—and oh, the flavor."

She waved one hand before her husband's face. "Achor, don't you dare tell the other men where to get them. My stew will be the talk of all Judah, and I don't want just anyone knowing my secret." She threw him a coquettish smile. "And don't think I haven't noticed your increased virility. Mahalath says it comes of nibbling at raw ones."

The young woman closest to the tent entrance giggled, rose to her knees, and gently pulled Eliab's hand, "I don't think there is any doubt that you are 'man enough' to enjoy the secrets of wild mushroom hunting, or go honey gathering, or learn anything we Midianite women have come to teach." She laced her fingers through his. "There is so much I can teach you. You are definitely 'man enough' for me."

Eliab cringed. Abihail was certainly woman enough to object to this girl teaching him much of anything.

The Midianite stranger slid to one side of the large cushion, tugging him gently toward the other half. "Come. Sit. Don't you remember me, Eliab?"

"Remember?" he said hesitantly, freeing his hand from her grasp. She definitely was Midianite, but with similar clothing, face paint, and hair styling, they all looked alike.

"Don't stand there gawking. Sit down," his father said jovially, giving Eliab a gentle shove.

As Eliab tumbled onto the cushion beside the girl, he fell into her open arms and found himself slumped against the exquisite softness of very full breasts. "We have all day to get better acquainted." She laughed and gave him a light embrace as he scrambled to right himself. "My name is Dinah."

"My name is Eliab," he responded, pulling away stiffly. "I am the younger son of Achor and Mara here, and husband to the beautiful Abihail. I don't remember you at all."

"Obviously, you made more of an impression on me than I did on you." She leaned close to his face and hummed a bit of a Midianite dance tune. "Still don't remember?"

She was trying to reel him in, but he was no fish and had no intention of taking her bait. "You are obviously a Midianite dancer, but I am quite certain that I never met you before," he said, fighting to keep his eyes on her face.

"Well, you are one Israelite man I haven't forgotten. After you taught Princess Cozbi the rudiments of your Israelite dance at the celebration last week, she handed you off to me. We danced the last two dances of the day while the princess went off in search of her perfect partner."

"Oh . . . I do remember," he mumbled. "Yes . . . Just before the prophet Balaam told his story. *Princess* Cozbi, you say?" He had not heard that title when he met her.

"Perhaps you would have hung on tighter had you known that you danced with the daughter of King Zur?" Dinah's voice turned up leaving the playful question hanging in the air.

He stared at her blankly. *I don't know who that is either.*

"Stop feigning such ignorance. Everyone knows that King Zur is one of *the Five*, and you can be certain that his precious daughter holds more power than any girl in Israel. If Cozbi wants something . . . she gets it." She leaned uncomfortably close, the sweet, minty fragrance of her breath as nauseating as her flattering words. "I was surprised that Cozbi left such a handsome man for me to dance with. She rarely leaves any of us girls someone we would want."

Eliab took a deep breath. Surely, he had slipped into a wild dream instead of his father's tent. He tried to clear his head. "You danced with both my wife and I," he stammered. He willed himself to rise and leave the tent . . . or move to another cushion . . . or . . . but roots seemed to grow from his body anchoring him in place. Why couldn't he force himself to run back to the safety of his own tent, the safety of Abihail?

Dinah touched his hand. "Are you all right?"

"Look, Eliab!" his mother cried, hovering over the chest and holding up an intricate gold necklace set with three rubies. "See the wonderful gifts our new friends brought this morning." She set down the necklace and lifted another piece. "This one is for Abihail, and there is another for Hattil. Would you *look* at this veil?"

As his mother chattered on, Eliab felt a squeeze on his arm and glanced at Dinah. Her eyes smoldered with passion as she lightly traced a finger around the knuckles of his right hand. "I've been looking for you all week," she said softly.

Desire shot through him like fire. He fought against it even as he tingled with the thrill of danger. He looked quickly to see if his father or Jamin were watching him, but they were fully preoccupied with the other two women. What was wrong with everyone? He fought for a foothold of sanity.

Suddenly his mother's voice broke into the ensnaring moment. "Eliab, you are not even looking at the gifts I'm showing you!"

"Women's trinkets, Mara," Achor broke in brusquely. Then, uncharacteristically, he checked himself with a smile, broad to the point of being silly. "We will enjoy seeing those things later. When our guests have gone." He stole a guilty glance at his wife as he patted the knee of the woman who had attached herself to him. The foreigner coughed lightly, adroitly flipping her silken gown back to uncover her knee and catch his father's clumsy pats on her bare skin while Mara hummed, swathing her head and shoulders in purple silk, oblivious and happy. Eliab's stomach turned as he watched Achor's hand slide higher.

"Father," he fairly shouted. "Why did you summon me here? Abihail is expecting me back at our tent."

"Wha—?" His father jerked away from the woman, fighting to untangle his hand from the folds of her garment. "Why . . . what?" he stammered.

Mara looked up in surprise. "Achor, you *do* need an education. The answer should be very obvious." She fingered the ruby-studded chain she had just hung around her neck. "We summoned you to begin learning, my son. To begin learning."

"I told you, didn't I?" Jamin snorted condescendingly. "He isn't man enough to even see the possibilities."

The girl at his brother's side chided him coyly, flashing a jeweled finger just a few inches from his face. "Not even Moses knew he needed a Midianite education until he met the seven daughters of Jethro after fleeing from Pharaoh. Now he is the leader of your people. With Dinah to teach your little brother, who knows what he will become?"

Achor had regained his composure. He cleared his throat. "Mahalath, we must tell Eliab about the invitation."

Achor's flushed face provided ample warning that anything they offered should be refused. "What invitation?" Eliab asked cautiously.

Achor cleared his throat, pausing with a look of affected dignity. "We have been invited to a feast tomorrow night on Mount Peor. The kings and princes of Midian and Moab will be there, and they have asked us to come."

"Their feast is at night?"

The women giggled, and Jamin glared at Eliab. "You are an embarrassment. That is their custom, get it? We have been chosen as ambassadors from Israel."

Mahaloth nodded. "You are right, Jamin. You and your father have accepted the honor of ambassadorship." She smiled sweetly at Eliab from across the room, addressing him as one would a child. "We women have been sent not only to teach you how to live well in this valley, but we are each to bring an Israelite ambassador for the most sacred festival of the year. It is our way of honoring those of our new neighbors who are most open to our ways. Your father has suggested that we include you. And Dinah . . . well, Dinah has yet to find her special guest."

Eliab could feel the provocative pressure of her hand on his, but he didn't look at her. "There will be a sumptuous feast," Dinah added as Mahalath finished. He resisted a response even when she cooed softly in his ear, "Nothing that would satisfy you will be held back." The layers of unspoken meaning terrified him.

"So what do you say, son? Jamin and I definitely will go."

"Please say that you will come." Dinah's voice was petulant. "There is only one man in Israel that I desire to have at my side."

"Only if I can bring Abihail," Eliab mumbled.

Suddenly all eyes were on him, patronizing smiles on each face. "How sweet, Eliab," his mother gurgled.

Mahalath drew a long breath, and then explained, "It is our custom for only male guests to come to this Baal-Peor festival. We are celebrating the seed-sowing so essential to the fertility of our land. There will be other celebrations for the wives."

"I . . ." Eliab hesitated. He looked at Dinah.

She ran her tongue over her lips. "Are you not pleased with me?"

"No. I mean . . ." He struggled to phrase his refusal as politely as possible. "Abihail . . ."

Suddenly the demeanor of the Midianite changed. Her eyes flew wide open with astonishment, and she exclaimed, "Would your wife forbid you to come?"

"No," he retorted. "I can go where I want."

"All right!" She sprang lightly to her feet. "I will go with you to your tent right now. Your wife will be pleased when I explain how you have been singled out for this honor."

Achor chortled with glee. "You bumbling little boy. I was beginning to think you were going to refuse her." He leaned over Mahalath and gave Eliab an awkward hug. "It will be a high point of our lives, the three men of *my* family dining with kings and princes—to say nothing of these enchanting ladies."

Dinah stooped to scoop up gift items from the floor, smiling up at Eliab demurely. "I know Abihail will be very pleased with the gifts we have for her. She is such a sweet little thing. It will be lovely to see her again."

Eliab pushed through the door flap following Dinah into the bright sunlight. He was not so certain that Abihail would be pleased, but he resolved that, if he went, he would sample nothing but food and drink at this celebration.

Balaam

The sunset sky flamed orange as King Zur and the prophet Balaam climbed the stairs to the top of the city wall. They quickly found a vantage point with an unobstructed view of Mount Peor. The rising moon was just clearing the peak, a perfect orb of luminescent gold, large and glorious in contrast to the darkening silhouette of the mountain. They traced a small line of lights crawling up from the base, tiny points flickering like stars, their brightness increasing as the few became many, increasing in number until the single points coalesced into a stream, a glowing river outlining the serpentine trail leading to the temple. They watched until the base was left dark and empty and the mountaintop blazed with torchlight.

"Your daughter has choreographed an excellent dance in a very short time," said Balaam.

"The dance of the cobra." Zur made an undulating, snaking motion into the air with one hand, imitating the fiery trail, then touching his fingertips to his thick lips, he finished with a wet smack. "May it end in the kiss of death!"

"Indeed." The prophet grinned. "The numbers are far greater than we hoped for."

"You can see what benefits come from cooperation with these Canaanite Baals. If all goes as well as Cozbi expects, full rebellion should break out within the next week. Our restive initiates will be most eager to cast off the repression of Moses's rule."

Balaam lifted his eyebrows philosophically. "So, tell me, King Zur, is this a blessing or a curse for the descendants of Abraham?"

"Both, I would say," the king answered without hesitation. "The curse is that Israel will no longer be a rampaging bull 'licking up the nations like grass' as King Balak described it, but he will rest among the heifers, his appetite well satiated. Is that not a blessing?" He gave Balaam a lighthearted nudge with his elbow.

Balaam covered his mouth with his fingers in a polished titter. "To the seer a revelation is given: Yahweh's bull charging out to meet the lowered horns of the Five only to discover that our Midianite heifers have dehorned him. Blessing turned deadly curse."

King Zur roared with laughter, staggering toward the stairs, drunk with merriment over the joke. "Follow me. It is time to celebrate."

Balaam sedately followed him down the stairs and through the dark streets to the North Wall Inn, confident that his star was about to ascend to a fixed place in the heavens.

As the evening dragged on, strong barley beer cast a net of drowsiness over the prophet, yet considering the bitter disappointments of the previous month, this evening was too sweet to cut short. Through half-closed eyes, he watched a young woman seat herself on the dais in the center of the room. He had seen her before, serving in the dining hall, but tonight she appeared to his eyes as a queen. He blinked back the cobwebs blurring his vision as she arranged the sleek, blue folds of her gown and pushed a glossy, black curl off her forehead.

Cozbi was beautiful. But she had proved to be a spoiled child, useful in accomplishing his purposes, but no longer desirable as a partner in love. This woman was a definite possibility. Every feature of her face was lovely—striking in fact. She did not have the voluptuous form of the Midianite women, but nature had endowed her well enough. From her gleaming raven locks to the polished sheen of her leather slippers, everything about her seemed to glow in the flickering lamplight, utterly radiant with regal grace and brilliance.

An uncommon musician for this common inn, he mused as she picked up an elaborately carved harp. Even her instrument was gleaming and elegant. When she wrapped her left arm around the bold figure of a male lion that formed its head, pulling it close to her breast as her right hand drifted lightly over the strings, Balaam envied that harp. He fixed his eyes on the thick fringe of her lashes, hoping to connect with the mind behind the beauty the moment she looked up.

When she did, the luminescent eyes reflected only sorrow and seemed to look past everyone in the room. "I will sing 'The Legend of Dusk and Dawn,'" she announced.

Odd for one so young and fair. Perhaps such a rare jewel senses that she was born for a higher place than a dingy inn in the disreputable city of Jericho. A perfect ending for the seer's strange adventure flashed before him as she released the first lush chord, a vision obliterating everything else. He saw himself rescuing the flawless, sad-eyed singer from her entrapment in Jericho. He saw Balaam the prophet returning to Babylonia like a conquering king, cartloads of Moabite gold trundling in a long train behind while this queen among woman rode by his side.

Then her instrument came to life. The vision vanished. The beauty of the girl and the melody from her harp mingled into a present and potent brew, intoxicating Balaam, and seemingly, everyone else in the room. Idle chatter fell mute as a voice, mellow as honey, followed the path of the lyrical harp. The singer and the song fused into one powerful force, flowing into Balaam like the first heady sip of fine, strong wine. He sat up. Body and soul had never been more alive.

'Twas a world of dark and storm,
At the beginning of time,
Ere sweet spring showers suckled the earth,
Ere first raindrops sparkled in life-giving sun.
No barley, wheat, or spelt,
No olive, almond, or fig,
No sweet wine flowing from twining bower—
All was void and dark
The day El prepared a Banquet of Love,
The day the hand of Father God,
Waved two fresh females into a bleak world
To savor El's Banquet of Love.

"This song speaks of the creation of the Canaanite Baals," King Zur whispered. Balaam had never heard the narrative before, yet it was as familiar as his own skin, the song possessing him as if its strains were birthed within him, entwined in his very life force. The power of Baal swelled anew in his loins.

O, El prepared bread and fruity wine
And almonds and soft dried figs.
He roasted a slaughtered calf with his fire
To please his Daughter-Brides.
He called for Asherah's silver light—
And her full, round moon lit the night—
To illumine El's banquet of Love.

El loved his lovely creations well.
He bid them drink of his wine
And feast on the finest of food with him
To the music of the stars;
And his daughters danced in the moonlight,
Their skin white and fair in the moonlight,
Dancing for El in the moonlight,
Ravished by El's Banquet of Love.

Balaam winked at Zur. "I'm guessing that this auspicious banquet is reenacted on Mount Peor tonight."

"That it is. Every god of fertility sprang from the loins of El beginning with the progeny of those two females, two daughters named Dusk and Dawn who gave birth to seven sons. These grandsons became the seven Baals of Canaan." Zur's hands looped the air then lifted in prayer. "May his offspring possess the worshipers tonight."

"Seven. The lucky number of Israel's God . . ." Balaam mused.

"Perhaps not when he is confronted with the seven-fold power of Baal," Zur whispered back.

To Lady Anath, his Consort,
El gave the newborn seven;
And she suckled and nourished his grandsons
With a heavenly River of Milk,
Life flowed from her bountiful breasts,
Till lusty and strong, they grew—
The seven sons of Dusk and Dawn,
Seven Baals for seven nations,
Born of El's Banquet of Love.

A sudden dissonant chord crashed, and the singer's sweet voice grew harsh. Her face flashed a momentary display of fear, anger, and pain, a vulnerable revelation that touched a tender place deep within Balaam. He too had suffered disappointment and grief. This song was the essence of every passion he had ever known. The singer knew those passions too, and the Baals were lords of them all.

The fiery cadence set the room aflame, and Balaam's body throbbed to the vigor of the changed beat. One man began to clap and another stomped his feet. Balaam looked down at King Zur's lusty clomping with pompous disdain. He tapped his toe in a more refined response, but his blood boiled within him. Surely Lady Asherah and Lord Baal had led him to this place and to this woman as a reward for his faithful implementation of the plan. Empty flagons and mugs thudded against the wooden tables and sword hilts thumped against the stone floor, the sounds uniting with the wild beating of his heart, a single pulse connecting him with every man in the room. And the singer's words soared over the hammering beat like the bewitching call of a sea bird above pounding surf.

O Sons of Dusk and Dawn,
O Baals, inhabit our love.
Throw off the blankets of winter cold,
Rouse unawakened earth with your rain.
Inhabit our Banquet of Love.
Rouse sleeping seed to bud and bloom,
Inhabit our Banquet of Love.
Bid field and herd and wife give birth,
Inhabit our Banquet of Love.
Drive your life-power deep in the earth,
Inhabit our Banquet of Love.
Accept this offering, the seed of man,
O inhabit our Banquet,
Our Banquet of love.

The song slowed. The singer's voice dropped. The clapping and pounding receded as Balaam leaned forward to hear the magical whisper of the final cadences.

Ooooo—
The Baals inhabit Love . . .
O Baal, inhabit our Love.

The dining hall with all its unruly tension dissolved in a haze. For Balaam, there was only this song and the woman who sang it, and the power of it swept him higher than the cloudy skies, higher than the starry heavens, higher than the council of the *shaddayim*. Then from somewhere far off, Balaam heard King Zur chortling. "Imagine this song combined with the allure of Midianite flesh and the magic of moonlight on Mount Peor tonight." He seized Balaam's arm and shook him until the trance was completely broken. "The men of Israel will not be able to resist worshipping Lord Baal."

Balaam smiled shrewdly back at the king. "I told you the plan could not fail."

"You will be a rich man," Zur said. His eyes were bleary with drunken admiration. "A very clever, very rich man . . . my son-in-law and my friend."

Balaam backed away from the gushing enthusiasm.

Zur grinned mischievously and thrust his hand between Balaam's thighs "Perhaps soon you and my little goddess will conceive more than a mere plan."

Balaam was revolted beyond reply.

The beautiful singer was calming the room with an instrumental melody of serenity and rest, but the stream of befouled words issuing from between King Zur's yellow teeth promoted anything but peace. "Don't look so blank. You know that I have no son to inherit my crown. I am offering you my daughter and a share in my throne. I have not missed your admiring glances at her beauty."

Even through the mental fog of tonight's celebration, Balaam knew it would be unseemly, perhaps even dangerous to display the revulsion he felt. He closed his eyes and nodded vaguely in Zur's direction, distracting himself with the rippling sound of the harp and thoughts of the lovely hands plucking the strings. The metallic clunking of brassware and murmured conversations gradually resumed as if nothing had happened, but the seer's vision was permanently altered. This singer, not the vain, petulant princess Cozbi, was the woman he needed to further his career.

"What is the story of this chanteuse?" he asked casually after what he thought was a suitable pause.

"Her name is Rahab, the innkeeper's daughter, a very expensive harlot child a few years ago, but no one can purchase a night with her any longer. Put this singer out of your mind. My little Cozbi is a jealous little thing."

Balaam waved his hand as if dismissing any personal interest. "Not just the singer, but the song itself. I've never heard anything like it."

"Aha, the songs of Canaan. You of Babylonia are but babes in pleasing your gods. Unfailing rivers water your land. Here everything depends on the satisfaction of Baal. If he sends no rain, the land withers. If he sends too much, floods wash away wealth and hope." Zur demonstrated the cycle with a sweep of his hand, then leaned in confidentially. "Since we five kings of Midian depend on Canaan for food, we have learned to join in her worship. Israel must also if she is to survive." The king playfully swatted the behind of the serving girl refilling his cup.

"I thought Israel's destruction, not her survival was your goal."

"We will see. My daughter is quite persuasive, and she has a plan of her own." Zur winked as if they shared a secret pact. "I will be a happy man when I see you sitting beside her as king of Israel."

"I believe Cozbi's plans now include that Israelite boy she has taken up with."

"No, no, my friend. Do not entertain such thoughts. Jealousy will consume your bones. The boy is dispensable. Undesirable, in fact, once he has helped our little goddess reach her goals."

"Shh! A new song. Let me listen." Balaam closed his eyes, slouching back against a pillar. *My new plan is to find a way to this singer's heart. Perhaps I will remain in Jericho until—*

The king snorted. "Listen to her songs, my friend, but don't plan on even one night with her."

Zimri

The sun blazed clear and strong into the valley on the morning following the festival at Baal-Peor and drove any late sleepers from the close heat of unopened tents. Although those who had spent most of the night on the mountain were sluggish and irritable, the camp of Israel hummed with the usual business of the day. No one particularly noticed a young couple skirting the margin of the camp and slipping secretively down the road that approached the fords of the Jordan.

The warm days of spring had raised the water level of the shallows to the knees, and the young woman hesitated at the river's edge. The young man shook his head incredulously. *Had she never relished the pleasure of splashing through flowing water? We both grew up as children of the desert, but perhaps all she has experienced was a dependable well and a bathing pool in her father's royal house. How fortunate I am for all the days spent frolicking with childhood friends in refreshing, ever-flowing waters. It really was astonishing how the cloud that led Moses to each new campsite always brought them to the same rock, the miracle rock, gushing with streams in the desert.* Then his Midianite princess flashed her engaging smile at him, and childhood memories evaporated like a mirage.

His stomach flipped and his knees grew weak yet again. This had nothing to do with getting her feet wet. This was another invitation for him to take her into his arms. He tucked the flowing hem of his robe into his belt, then gallantly swept his personal goddess high above the water, sloshing into the current, her arms eager and tight about his neck, her body warm and soft against his chest while her giggles of delight mingled with the song of the waters. He had never dreamed of such a woman.

When they reached the far shore, he lowered her to the ground and pulled her close for a lingering kiss. She ran her hands boldly down his bare thighs, tempting him to take her again. If they did not have to hurry on to Jericho to meet with her father, he would have found a discreet bed of grasses and ferns hidden among the fragrant oleanders right here beside the river.

She sensed his indecision. "I would not hesitate to keep my father waiting just a little while . . ."

"Later, Cozbi my love," he whispered hoarsely as he pushed her hands away and freed his robe.

She stepped back, observing him with a smirk as the robe fell swishing about his ankles again. "You are so dutiful, Zimri."

He did not feel dutiful as he took her hand in his and led her up the long road to the city gates. He felt as if he were Adam, walking through the perfection of Eden with the flawlessly beautiful Eve. He could not imagine any paradise exceeding this.

The reality of Jericho, however, was a harsh contrast. Although the gates were open, a grim line of spearmen effectively barred the inner portal while their grizzled captain scrutinized the two of them warily. It quickly dawned on Zimri that the old lecher had given him but one quick glance and the scrutiny of those debauched eyes was exploring Cozbi from head to toe. Before Zimri could think how to respond, the princess threw back her hood and took control. "I am Cozbi, daughter of King Zur of Midian."

The captain grinned, frothy spittle collecting at the corners of his mouth and oozing onto his grizzled beard. "Mmm," he mumbled, with a suggestive lift of his brows. "Just so. Your beauty was obvious even when cloaked."

Zimri suspected the vile man had been imagining Cozbi's beauty entirely uncloaked. He glared at him and placed an arm protectively around his woman.

"I suspected you were no ordinary traveler, my princess," the captain said with a sweeping bow. He stretched himself back to full height. "Do let me know if there is anything at all that I can do for you. We have been instructed by King Nahari himself to help you in any way we can."

Zimri scowled as formidably as possible as the captain's eyes continued wandering over Cozbi's body, lingering where they should not.

As if he had suddenly caught the scent of Zimri's displeasure, the captain turned with a snarl. "You are not Midianite, nor Canaanite. I could easily be convinced that you are a skulking Israelite spy. Do not let me see you around the city without *her*." The captain jerked his head towards his platoon, signaling that the detainment was over. "Let 'em pass."

As soon as the line of guards split, Zimri pulled at Cozbi's arm and marched her through the opening. *Soon I will enter this city as King Zimri of Israel. You will lick the dust from my feet and feel my gratitude with a kick in your teeth.* He snorted out a disdainful laugh. "Insolent dog," he muttered.

Cozbi shot a reproving look his way. "I would not be quick to laugh if I were you. That dog would crush you like a flea, but for me."

"Lucky for me I wouldn't be caught dead in this city without you."

As they launched into the crowds streaming toward the bustle of the city plaza, the young couple was bombarded on all sides by vendors, and the impudent guard was forgotten.

"My lady, I have the softest linen from Egypt."

"Sweet-smelling ointments from the east. A gift for your woman, young man. How she will thank you tonight!"

"Honey, fig cakes, dates! Special price just for young lovers."

Zimri was dazzled by the abundance on display everywhere he looked, but Cozbi pulled him relentlessly through the marketing frenzy without a glance to the right or left.

Suddenly, the words of a leather worker cut through the babble. "Young man, I can see that your sandals are worn. I will make a pair for you today. Yes?"

Zimri faltered mid-stride, pulling from Cozbi's grip. *Worn sandals?* He had not noticed before, but it was true. One lace hung together by the thinnest filament of cowhide. He stared at his feet in astonishment as the princess forged ahead without him. He had outgrown many pairs of sandals in the desert wanderings, but he always passed them on to younger boys even as he received larger ones from older boys. Never had he seen such scuffed leather or such frayed straps in his entire life. A phrase from the teachings of Moses echoed uncomfortably in the back of his mind, something about Yahweh's tender kindness even to the point of not allowing a shoelace of one of his children to wear out during the Wanderings.

"Look here, my lord, I have the finest leather."

Zimri fled from the cobbler's stall, shouldering his way through the shoppers to where he belonged—at Cozbi's side. Desert days were behind him. Yahweh might keep old garments and shoes from wearing out, but Baal blessed his worshippers with life and wealth and pleasure he had never dreamed of.

Just as he reached Cozbi and took her hand, he heard the vendor's cry over the chaos of the marketplace. "You cannot run far or fast in those old sandals. Let me make a new pair for you today."

Cozbi was looking at his feet now too. "I thought you stopped for the services of that cobbler. You must before we return to camp. I will not be accompanied by a frayed commoner."

What was it about this relationship with his princess? One moment he was soaring high above the earth. The next, he was groveling in its dirt. Please let these sandals see me through this important meeting.

Cozbi dislodged his troubled thoughts with a sharp nudge and favored him with another of her intoxicating smiles. "Look, my love." The swirl of shoppers and vendors and noise had given way to the comparative hush of a narrow street lined with houses stretching all the way to its end. There a large oak door had been built right into the city wall. A sign hanging above it read: North Wall Inn. She pointed toward the sign. "Behind that door, a king and a prophet await us."

Renewed vigor surged through him. He straightened his head and shoulders. No matter how ragged his footwear, he *was* a prince and he had a princess. The thought made him smile from ear to ear. *O, do I have a princess! She makes me feel like a bumbling oaf more often than not, but only because I grew up in Israel's insulated camp. Cozbi chose me, and I will prove myself worthy of that choice.*

With his princess by his side, Zimri marched up the stone steps and grasped the brass handle boldly. He gallantly pulled the heavy door wide, offering Cozbi entrance ahead of him as a cloud of warmth and fragrance greeted them—along with two hulking forms that completely filled the doorway. The two husky men, clad in the green garb of Jericho's royal guard, elbowed their way down the steps, shoving Cozbi back into his arms. As Zimri and his princess tumbled down the steps onto the pavement, the door closed with a dead thud.

"Watch your step," one guard snickered.

"How dare you push *me*," Cozbi shrieked, but the guards merely laughed louder as they ambled down the street.

"King's business trumps yours, sweetheart."

"I'll see you dead for this," Cozbi muttered under her breath.

"Fools," Zimri growled. He glanced at his beautiful companion sprawled indignantly on the street beside him and shouted at the backs of the guards. "You will not be so amused when you learn who it is that you have insulted."

He sucked in a deep breath, listening until the noisy footsteps tramped off into the hum of the city. The sharp edge of the stone steps had caught him across the lower back, and the site of impact stung fiercely. "I hope I broke your fall, my sweet, because the fall nearly broke me." He managed a weak smile. "Let me rest a moment before I help you up."

Cozbi was too angry to respond. As the pair lay sprawled in the street nursing their injuries, the heavy oak door creaked open and a sweet voice asked. "Are you hurt?"

Zimri scrambled to his feet, ignoring the bright, compassionate eyes peering at them through a narrow opening in the door. He must show himself powerful, not pitiful, in this city. "We *will* right this wrong, Cozbi my love," he said, stretching out his hand to help his princess up.

The door flew open wide. "Oh. Are you Princess Cozbi? Your father is here in the dining hall. We have been watching for you. I can't believe that the king's guards toppled *you* on our very doorstep." She skittered down the steps to offer her help. "Our king seems to have a penchant for surrounding himself with ignorant louts, but there is little ordinary citizens can do about it. Come inside, and you will receive the treatment you deserve."

Cozbi scowled and dodged the helping hands. Scrambling to her feet and dusting off her robe, she effectively brushed off help from either of them. "I want the names of those guards," she said.

"Forgive their incivility, my friends. The whole city has been edgy since the invasion of the valley across the river. King Nahari put out the word that you are involved in a plan to stop Israel. His guards obviously didn't guess your identity or they never would have treated you so poorly." She smiled graciously and reached toward Cozbi. "Please come inside and accept some refreshments as a gift to you and your companion."

"Don't presume to touch me."

The serving girl did not blink as she stepped back and gestured toward the open door. "This is my father's inn. It is our privilege to honor you."

Zimri was impressed. "We appreciate your kind—"

"There is no honor your family could offer us under any circumstances," Cozbi snapped. "My father honors this . . . this dark hole in the wall by his very presence. You, servant girl, are keeping his royal highness waiting by delaying me." She flipped her cloak arrogantly and marched up the steps, muttering through clenched teeth, "Only the dead bodies of those guards will honor me now." When Cozbi was abreast of the girl, she lashed out with a snarl and a shove. "I don't need your pity."

As the innkeeper's daughter adroitly hopped down a step to regain her balance, avoiding her own tumble into the street, Zimri caught her arm and their eyes met. The girl had been startled by Cozbi's actions, a little embarrassed perhaps, but she wasn't angry. She laughed lightly. "This is not a good day for lingering on these steps."

Zimri hoped that his eyes expressed the appreciation he dared not voice, but Cozbi looked back just in time to catch the interaction and gave him a withering look. "Consorting with a common Jericho harlot, my prince? I thought that you were better than that."

Fear coiled in Zimri's stomach. He had no idea why this amazing woman had chosen him as her consort and lover, and he had no idea what it would take for her to reject him. On this morning of mornings, he must strike a pose of power—with Cozbi as well as with King Zur. "This time, I will lead the way into this churlish establishment," he said boldly and pulled the heavy door open again.

Baal had entrusted Cozbi with the plan, and last night's festival had solidified his place in it. He would not let this momentary doorstep offense ruin everything. He knew what he must do. He had gone to Moses and the council of elders numerous times on behalf of a grievance in his tribe. How different could the process be in this city? As soon as they located Cozbi's father, he would leave her to give their report while he obtained the names of those guards. The innkeeper's daughter made it clear that the king of Jericho supported their cause. Surely as Cozbi's advocate, he could tap into that royal authority and urge that the guards be whipped and dragged back to the inn. He would see that they groveled with appropriate remorse, begging mercy and forgiveness.

Zimri smiled at the thought as he waved the women into the warmth of the inn and stepped over the threshold. Cozbi would learn how well he could protect and care for her, even as he demonstrated his leadership ability to her father. The door creaked heavily on its hinges behind him, cutting off the bright morning light with an emphatic clunk.

While the innkeeper's daughter hurried into the bright dining hall, Zimri held Cozbi back in the semi-darkness of the antechamber. "I will never let such a thing happen to you again," he murmured. He ignored the stiffening of her body, and her resistance to his arms as she reached up to fold back her hood. He took her left hand gently, slid it down to the dagger sheathed in his belt, and held it there.

"I swear to you. My friend here will penetrate the belly of any other lout who would disrespect my princess."

Cozbi relaxed into his embrace at last, fondling the smooth bone handle. "I've always found men's weapons arousing. But they must be ready when needed." The angry tones had disappeared.

"Duly chided. I won't be caught unaware like that again." He released her and valiantly stepped into the brightness of the dining hall, striking his most warrior-like posture as he scanned the room for Cozbi's father.

There were only a few customers in the large pillared room, and he was certain which one was King Zur even before his eyes had fully adjusted to the interior lighting. The man's back was toward the door as he leaned forward, talking rapidly, circular hand motions sweeping the air—a characteristic he had noticed in all the Midianite kings. Jewels twinkling on the band around the midnight black headscarf, confirmed his identity. The red-bearded man relaxing languidly on a cushion across from the king could be none other than Balaam the prophet. Unfortunately, the king did not turn around, and the prophet was mesmerized by the contents of the heavy bronze goblet in his hands. Neither man noticed his bold stance.

Zimri leaned closer to Cozbi as she shrugged out of her cloak. He gently turned her shoulders toward her father's table. "Over there, near the stairs. Take my arm for a grand entrance, befitting the couple who will soon rule Israel togeth—"

"There's that serving wench." Cozbi pulled away and rushed across the room, leaving Zimri standing at the portal feeling awkward yet again. Before he could think what to do next, her shrill demand pierced the muted conversations of the dining hall. "Give my father the names of the two guards who knocked me down at the door."

Unruffled, the innkeeper's daughter continued filling King Zur's goblet. When Zimri reached them, she was wiping a dribble of wine from the tabletop with a small towel. She glanced up at him through her eyelashes. "Please pardon the jitteriness of our city, my lord," she said to the king. "The princess has just cause for her anger. Two of the king's guards behaved quite rudely on our doorstep."

"The names—" Cozbi spat the repeated command through her teeth.

The answer was barely audible. "Uzal and Hadoram."

Balaam looked up with a smirk. "What do you want, princess? Their heads in a basket?"

"Impaled on their own spears outside this inn would be more appropriate. They *shoved* me. Uzal and Hadoram, I will not forget."

Zimri flinched at the black fire in Cozbi's eyes. His stomach turned with the same sick dread that he had known all his life when the stories of Yahweh's wrath were told. One must avoid getting on the wrong side of all gods, even a lovely little goddess-in-the-flesh such as this one.

King Zur held up his arms toward his daughter. "Greet your father properly, my child. Uzal and Hadoram. I will deal with this matter in due time." As Cozbi leaned down to kiss his plump cheek, he spoke gently, "Calm yourself, my ruby-lipped darling. I will be meeting with the king in a little while."

"All this rancor makes me thirsty," the prophet announced. He had taken advantage of the distracting exchange to ogle the striking face and form of the innkeeper's daughter as she lingered across the table from him. He bared his teeth in an engaging smile, holding his cup high. "If you don't mind, Rahab my dear."

"At once, sir." She fixed her eyes on the cup as she poured, then immediately bent her head and shoulders in a courteous bow toward the king. "More for you, your highness?"

It amused Zimri to see the prophet rebuffed so subtly by the innkeeper's daughter. *Well done, Rahab. The man is as slippery as a snake.*

"You just filled my father's cup," Cozbi snapped.

The girl courteously turned her attention to the princess. "We offer you anything you would like from our kitchen at no cost. Would you like hot tea this morning or some spicy mulled wine? We have bread, hot from the oven, and barley porridge sweetened with dates. There are dried figs, raisin cakes, and some succulent, sweet melons. If you have a taste for flesh foods, we have roasted lamb, suckling pig, or fresh fish broiled with almonds and leek sauce. Only tell me what would please you and I shall have it here right away."

"Nothing from your hand," Cozbi snapped. She turned her back on the girl and whispered loudly to Zimri. "I heard that this Rahab was a popular harlot in Jericho once, but she is used up now. She is just a common serving wench."

"Hardly common," Balaam shot back with obvious irritation. He tried connecting with the girl again, that oily smile sliding onto his face. "No one who has heard her sing would call her common," he gushed.

The word *slippery* definitely summed up this man. *Don't trust him, Rahab.* Zimri tried to project the thought directly to the girl without speech.

Cozbi grinned and tossed her head contemptuously. "Aha . . . methinks the great prophet of Babylonia hopes to seduce his 'uncommon' singing servant girl."

Zimri winced.

Cozbi turned to the girl again. "Well, sing then. Use your uncommon skills to lure him to your bed, wench. I certainly have no interest in him."

Rahab bit her lower lip and left them without another word.

"Stop this childish petulance at once, Cozbi," Zur commanded. "A thousand pardons, Balaam, my friend. My feisty little daughter does have her moods."

Cozbi stroked her father's cheek endearingly. "I'm sorry, sweet Baba. You could alter my mood immediately if you would only go to King Nahari at once. All the joy of this wonderful morning has been sucked out of me by this boorish place."

The king winked and touched the cushion beside him. "Let's give Nahari plenty of time for a morning romp with the girl you selected for him. I'll talk to him after she has sweetened his mood."

"Good thinking, Father. Atarah will put him in the mood to give you anything you ask for. Just don't forget their names, Uzal and Hadoram."

"You are quite the charmer, young woman," Balaam muttered.

Zur patted his daughter's well-rounded behind as she snuggled into his embrace. "The future of all the nations in the region is tied up in what you are doing, Cozbi. My friend Nahari will be sure to agree that only honor is due you. There will be justice." He turned to the prophet. "Uzal and Hadoram. Help me remember the names."

Zimri watched the transformation of his volatile princess with amazement. Exhilaration flashed from her eyes, totally eclipsing the former ire. Cozbi brushed her father's beard lightly. "Have we permission to give our report, O exalted king, my father?'

"Ah, the sunlight of my life shines again," the king chortled. "Balaam, my friend, can you see what a treasure I have? We must not be kept waiting any longer. The news she brings this morning with those dazzling eyes will be well worth hearing."

"So then, do we have your royal permission to speak?" Cozbi turned her eyes down coyly.

Balaam leaned forward, annoyed by the game. "Speak, girl. You know that is why we are waiting here."

Cozbi shot a disdainful glance his way and continued the playful encounter. "Father, you remember Zimri, do you not? I introduced you to him on the day of that tiresome Israelite celebration."

She looked up. "Sit, Zimri."

Zimri did not have time to blink before she resumed her lighthearted banter with the king. "He was the only interesting man I found. Remember, Baba? I said he had promise . . ."

Zur watched with a vacant stare as Zimri seated himself beside Cozbi. Obviously, he did not remember him. *Look royal not ridiculous,* Zimri warned himself

Cozbi wagged a finger close to her father's face and went on in a chastising tone, "My lord, a little respect is surely due him. His father, Salu, is the prince of the tribe of Simeon. This young man was born to rule."

Zimri raised his chin proudly under the glow of her approval.

While Zur took a second look at Zimri, Cozbi lifted her father's cup to her lips and drained its contents. The king mumbled aloud, "Strong square chin, full sensuous mouth, thin straight nose, broad, noble forehead, and a hint of cruelty about the eyes. He does have a royal look despite being an Israelite." He nodded to Cozbi as if they were discussing the purchase of a mule. "Quite so, a royal look."

Cozbi laughed, "The best part is that he *is* an Israelite prince. Just what my plan requires."

"Perhaps," Zur said slowly, meeting Zimri's eyes. "Perhaps you can be useful to our, uh, project." It seemed to Zimri that on this third glance, Cozbi's father finally saw a person.

Balaam scoffed. "Israelite inheritance is in birth order as in most other nations. Simeon was but the second son of Israel. The second son may as well be the tenth unless the two of you plan to murder the competition. That would be the whole tribe of Reuben, I believe."

"You do not know our history, sir," Zimri spoke up defensively. "Isaac was the second son of Abraham. Jacob was the second son of Isaac."

"Zimri *is* the eldest son of Salu, Father. Soon his name will be on the lips of every descendant of Jacob. My own Israelite prince," she cooed, brushing the side lock of his beard. "No one seems to know what will happen when that ancient leader of theirs dies, so . . . why not my vision?

"Father. Prophet Balaam. Let me introduce you to the future King Zimri of Israel."

"My vision, young lady, is that you are naive and premature. Your father's vision is that there be no Israel to need a king. Now give us the report."

Cozbi stared icily at Balaam. "Zimri was my companion last night at the festival. He should be the one to tell of our success."

Balaam slammed his fist down on the table with a fierceness that shocked Zimri and drew a startled cry from Cozbi. "I don't care who speaks. Give us the report!"

"Yes . . . uh . . . success," Zimri stammered. "Success. Everything you hoped for on Mount Peor, my lords. The majority of the princes and elders of all the tribes attended the festival . . . and engaged in the . . . uh . . ."

Cozbi burst into gleeful laughter. "Even the stuffiest old codgers. Good food, good wine, enticing music, a little intoxicating incense, and to a man they fell . . . copulating with amazing vigor under the spell of Asherah and her union with Baal."

King Zur joined in the laughter, but Balaam's jaw went slack. "You're saying they all actually *worshipped*?"

"Well, a few tried to back out . . . of the actual worship." Cozbi's words bubbled up in frothy phrases floating on ripples of laughter. "But they weren't willing to give up what their companions of the night offered." Balaam joined their uncontrolled mirth and then clapped his hands in sheer joy when she regained her composure enough to finish, "Yes, yes! They *all* eventually worshiped Asherah and Baal."

Cozbi's silver laughter cast its spell over Zimri. Her cheeks were flushed and her eyes aglow with wine. *If only we were alone right now.* He gave her a look he hoped expressed the ardent longings of his heart as he squeezed her knee.

Cozbi sensed the electric current tingling from her body to his at the touch and lowered her voice seductively. "We Midianite women know how to delight a man's heart." She took his hand and slid it up her inner thigh with a little moan.

Zimri could feel his face flush as he pushed her away, gently but firmly, making every effort to address the two older men with dignity. "Balaam, sir, you have given a true blessing to the people of Israel. Yahweh was a helpful god while we dwelt in the wilderness, but our laws would never allow us to please Baal and Asherah and reap the bounty of this fertile land as the Amorites and Canaanites do."

He turned enthusiastically to her father. "In one night our people have learned more than in our entire lives before. The nourishing breasts and fertile hips of Asherah have won our devotion and have showed us how to control the great storm god Baal."

Cozbi broke out in ripples of laughter once more. "Get us a room, Father. Asherah's devotee needs to express his devotion."

"Enough, Cozbi," the king growled.

Zimri was taken aback. *That must have been a potent cup of wine.* He struggled to his feet pulling Cozbi up with him. "Later," he whispered in her ear. "I want to speak to your father about us."

He bowed deeply and respectfully to King Zur. "Thank you, sir, for allowing me to spend these past few weeks with your amazing daughter." He paused hesitantly. "This is hard for me . . . Israelite fathers are not so free with their daughters, but I am totally captivated. I assure you that I will never abandon her. When this is over, I pray that you will discuss terms of marriage with my father. He is more than willing to pay whatever dowry you require and—" Zimri gazed into his beloved's bewitching eyes. "I never dreamed love could be like this." Tightening his arm confidently around Cozbi's shoulders, he turned his eyes back to the king. "We have dedicated ourselves as a couple, our entire lives, to the transformation of my nation."

Zimri had been looking down or at Cozbi throughout his rehearsed speech. Now that he dared look at the king, he found him scowling darkly. "You may do that, but it is time for my daughter to return home to her own people. Her year in the service of Asherah is nearly over, and considering what you have told me, she has more than fulfilled what was required of her."

Zimri felt the blood drain from his face. His arm fell limply from Cozbi's shoulder. "But I thought . . ."

Cozbi touched his lower lip with her finger. Suddenly, her demeanor was wholly sober. "Shush, my love. Let me handle this."

She took up her former playful expression and tone with the king. "You wouldn't deny me, would you, Baba? I entered into this for you—for Midian." She knit her creamy brow and pursed her lips in a frown. "You can see that I haven't tired of Zimri in the least. Perhaps I never shall. And we still have *work* to do in that dull camp."

"Don't push this, child."

When she did not get the response she wanted, she turned to the prophet, "Seer Balaam, surely you can see that our mission is not yet complete."

"The curse on Israel most probably is complete, but I can see that your thirst for power is not satiated."

Zur leaped to his feet and clutched his daughter's arm. "Cozbi, do not defy me. Your safety concerns me. War is imminent. It will be dangerous for you to stay in the Israelite camp any longer. And I say when and to whom you will be wed."

A chill ran down Zimri's spine, but Cozbi began weeping pitifully. "I would willingly risk my life to be with Zimri. Is that not how you felt about Mother?"

The king softened his tone and released his grip. "Come home, Little Dove. Let things settle down for a month or so. Let's consider all your matrimonial options. Then if you want to find your Simeonite prince again . . . we'll see. It *is* time for you to marry."

"No." Cozbi's eyes flashed. "Zimri will be king someday. He needs me at his side to make the conversion from Yahweh to Baal complete. I will not leave Israel for a single day. Not until all are worshippers of Baal." She paused and giggled with self-assured delight. "I will stay until one of us girls has snagged the old man himself."

Balaam rose slowly, "Don't rouse the sleeping beast, Princess. I have looked into the Lion's eyes, and this I know with certainty. Even you, most enchanting lady, could not tempt that man."

Abihail

"Good morning, Abihail!" The voice broke through the fog of fever. "How is your handsome husband faring this morning?"

Abihail lay abed beside Eliab, chilled and faint, staring at the dark goat-hide ceiling above her. The hour for gathering manna had come and gone. Although the sound of her friend's voice was most welcome, she could not summon the strength to raise her head.

It was the third morning after the full moon. Her groom of one and a half months had taken ill the previous day, and she had been all aflutter with worry. She could not have endured watching his pinched white face, but for her friend Acsah. When the two of them met to gather manna just past dawn yesterday, Acsah immediately detected her fears and took charge, sending her home with instructions to give Eliab water and to apply cool compresses to reduce his fever. Acsah brought meals throughout the day and tended to the needs of their cow and two sheep as well. More than anything, her composure soothed Abihail's anxiety.

Eliab was worse today, much worse, and Abihail had been so woozy when she got up for manna gathering that she nearly collapsed while trying to dress. Like a bolt of lightning, the realization struck her: she was ill too, and it was a judgment from the Almighty. Acsah had helped her through every grief-pierced moment of her life, and there had been plenty in her short seventeen years, but how could she explain this to her best friend? She winced at the flood of bright sunlight when the tent flap lifted and Acsah stooped to enter. Shrinking back into the warmth of her coverlet in shame, she closed her eyes against the light.

"I couldn't get up," she whispered weakly.

"When you weren't out in the meadow this morning, I guessed that Eliab was no better or perhaps even worse. I gathered enough for all of us." Acsah rustled quickly to her side, placing her hand on Abihail's forehead. "You have the fever now too. And look at those dark, sunken eyes." She poured water into two cups, encouraging each of them to drink.

"Whoa, don't drop that Eliab," she said taking the cup back from him. She dished up some manna porridge. "What is going on?" she mused aloud and handed Abihail a bowl.

Abihail took one small bite, but her stomach roiled against it. She watched wordlessly as Acsah turned her attention to Eliab. He did not lift a hand to take the proffered dish. He did not even open his eyes. After that small sip of water, he closed his eyes and didn't move.

"Is he . . . breathing?"

"Yes, my dear, he is still breathing, and the good news is that he is no longer burning hot like yesterday morning." Acsah removed the strips of wet woolen cloth they had used to reduce his fever the previous evening. "This is so strange. A number of families have come down with a similar sickness."

Abihail's insides churned. She took a second bite of the porridge, mushing it around her mouth, but her throat closed against it. Acsah's piercing eyes seemed to penetrate her guilt-laden sham, and she fought for the courage to confess. "Curse . . . from God," she mumbled through the obstructing bite of porridge. She swallowed hard, fearing that her voice was too weak to be heard. *Please don't ask me to repeat the awful words.*

Acsah frowned. "How could that be? Yahweh protects and blesses his covenant people. There has been no rebellion, no complaining against him here in this valley."

"Baal." The word cut like a dagger on Abihail's tongue, but Acsah could not have looked more horrified if Abihail had plunged a knife into *her*.

"Baal? What do you mean?" she whispered.

"Baal-Peor. A temple on the mountain." She paused to summon strength for the telling. "Eliab went with his father and Jamin . . . the night of the full moon. It was supposed to be a feast of welcome to Israel." The words poured out, and then Abihail lay still, out of breath from the effort of speaking.

Acsah shrank back as if her best friend had been transformed into a viper.

Abihail was compelled to continue. "Three of the Midianite women invited Achor and his sons to go as ambassadors, their special guests. They brought gifts to Mara, Hattil, and me. Thousands of Israelite men went to the festival. Then . . . when they were merry with food and wine . . ." she swallowed and tried another bite of porridge. "I don't know how to tell you . . ."

Acsah placed Eliab's untouched bowl of porridge beside Abihail's. She reached over to touch his forehead again. "He is in a serious state, Abihail. Cold and clammy. Almost the feel of death. If he went to a temple of Baal, he is getting what he deserves. I don't know how I can help a man suffering under the curse of Yahweh."

Abihail felt silent tears spill onto her cheeks. "Pray for us. Please."

Acsah's face softened a little. "I will leave the water skin here by the bed. You must encourage Eliab to keep drinking and eat a little too, if he can."

Abihail drew a long, tremulous breath. "Achor came down with the plague just before Eliab. I want you to understand what happened. Eliab didn't go to worship, just to be a good neighbor. The heads of many of the important families of each tribe were there—along with some of the younger men like Eliab. I don't think many of them suspected what the Midianites had planned." Exhausted by the effort of speaking, Abihail closed her eyes and took several quick, shallow breaths. "By the time the feast was ended, all of them had been enticed to please the gods of the land. The festival was deviously designed to lead them all to worship."

"Worship? You mean coupling in those disgusting rites we saw depicted on the murals and statuary in this valley?"

"But that is how the people here control the rain."

"How could men of Israel believe such lies? Did they convince you too?"

"I wasn't even there. Acsah, don't look at me like that. You are my best friend."

"They did convince you." Disgust contorted Acsah's face.

"No," Abihail protested. "I know that these idols are not gods . . . but the women brought the loveliest jewelry for my mother-in-law and for Hattil and me. They were so friendly." She paused and added, "They acknowledge that our God conquered theirs. They say they are willing to learn how to worship Yahweh."

Acsah's expression had not changed, but Abihail kept talking. "See this veil." She reached over to retrieve the shimmering cloud of purple and held it up in her trembling hands. "Have you ever seen anything so lovely? It comes from far away across the desert, far beyond mountains and rivers in a land we never dreamed existed."

"Beautiful, yes, but I would not touch anything contaminated by this evil."

"Acsah, *I* didn't worship Baal. You don't think we wives were taking part in Baal worship just by receiving their gifts, do you?"

"You took the gifts *and* you let your husbands go with them to a heathen temple."

"But they came as friends . . . our new neighbors. We never dreamed our husbands would worship Baal. It sounds foolish to me now too when I look at you, but they convinced Mara, Hattil, and me to let our husbands go up to Mount Peor as . . . as ambassadors of Yahweh."

"What kind of ambassadors are they if they ignore the commands of the God who gave them victory over the Amorites? They may not have dreamed of Baal worship, but they didn't run from it."

When Acsah was angry, the angular beauty of her high cheekbones, finely chiseled nose, and strong chin gave her a frighteningly fierce look—more like a warrior than a daughter of Israel. Abihail had seen that blazing look directed at dishonesty or bullying in their childhood, but it had never been directed at her before. She closed her eyes to hide from it now and lay quietly, mulling over all that had happened and all she had learned in the past week. Without opening her eyes, she spoke again. "Acsah, did you know that this valley used to belong to Moab? The Amorites drove them out years ago, and now Moab welcomes us as better neighbors."

"And you accept the gifts of a new neighbor who seduces husbands and fathers as part of welcoming them to the neighborhood?" The horror in Acsah's voice was as hard to bear as the look of her face.

"But to these people, Baal worship is the path to prosperity. They only meant to share their blessings with us."

"You foolish, foolish girl. You were blinded by greed for those gifts. You still are."

Abihail reopened her eyes in time to see Acsah gathering her things and moving toward the doorway. "Acsah, please . . . don't leave so soon."

"How could you welcome Eliab back to your bed after participation in their degrading worship? We know enough from what we have seen across this valley to be thoroughly disgusted with these practices. That is why you are suffering now."

Abihail remembered how wild Eliab had been in his lovemaking when he came home from his experience on the mountain. A hot flush of shame spread over her face, and she turned away. "Acsah, I can't bear your anger, but I could never turn away from Eliab. I love him more than life."

"That love may well cost you your life."

"Please try to understand. We have all been friends as long as we can remember. You know that both Eliab and I are devoted to Yahweh and the covenant."

"I'm not sure what I know of you anymore, either of you."

"It's just that . . . Eliab's friend, Dinah, told us that the Midianites know and respect our God, as do the people of Moab." Abihail lifted her hand weakly, reaching for her friend. "The Moabites are related to us, you know."

"Yes, children of Lot's incestuous elder daughter," Acsah spat her last words over her shoulder as she pushed against the door flap. "How much of the truth of Yahweh and his commands do you think *that* mother passed on to her son and her grandchildren?"

Abihail looked at Eliab lying white and still on his bed. Acsah was right. They had been ensnared by something more diabolical than either of them could have imagined. If only they could go back and make those choices again.

"I need you, Acsah. Don't —" The flapping of the tent door was the only response to her plea.

Yahweh, I need your mercy. We have broken covenant, but we want to return to you. We will each bring one of our sheep as a sin offering if you will save us. Both sheep and our cow, if we must. Only forgive our foolishness. Do not count this as a high-handed sin against you.

She sobbed over the lost connection with Acsah. She sobbed over her blind stupidity. Eliab would not have gone if she had begged him to stay. She sobbed bitterly over the pain of betrayal. She had been devastated when she learned of Eliab's worship. Now she saw how she had betrayed the Lord. Death from this plague would be justice, but O how she needed mercy instead.

O Holy One of Israel, enthroned between the cherubim on the seat of mercy, restore us to the covenant. Restore Eliab to health. Restore me. And please, restore my friendship with Acsah.

CHAPTER FIVE

PLAGUE

Joshua

Joshua loped up the familiar trail to Moses' retreat, but this was not a routine run up the mountain. Anguish etched deep lines in his face. He glanced at the moon hanging pale and misshapen in the soft blue above the western hills, one edge shriveled down like a piece of rotten fruit. First Day next, the moon would be new again. If only the camp could be. If only they could return to the happy innocence of the victory celebration of the last new moon.

Sometime in the middle of the night, Joshua had awakened in a cold sweat, the images of his dream too real, too frightening to allow him to fall back to sleep. Those images still cycled in his head as he scaled the mountain, oddly starker and more frightening now that he was awake.

The dream began with a scene precisely like the thanksgiving feast—the Midianite Five and Balaam joining the celebration just as on that day. The Midianite girls danced exuberantly through his dream, and he watched with the same ill-defined unease. Then King Zur's daughter turned and faced him with her arms raised above her head—exactly like the terraphim. Even in the dream, the resemblance hit him with seismic shock: the full, rounded body, the coy smile, the arms raised—a perfect replica of the little fertility images his army had gathered up and burned when they took possession of this valley. The dancing princess in his dream grew. As she stretched toward the clouds, her body began to glow like metal in a fire, and the heat of her body ignited the tents of Israel. Joshua raced from tent to tent trying to beat out the flames, all the time calling for someone to help him.

That was when he awoke. His heart was racing. He tossed restlessly for a time, the drums of his dream still taunting him. There was no hope of sleep, and since he could no longer stay abed, he arose to walk the camp although it was still dark. The beating of the drums was louder now outside the tent, and the sound of revelry drew him to the high place outside the camp of Simeon. There, the dream was reality. Constructed of crimson fabric, luridly aglow from within, a Baal tent crowned the ancient high place they had demolished less than a month previously.

It was nearly dawn by the time he reached Moses' tent. The old man was already gone, but a huddle of elders milled about in confusion. He listened to several reports of similar activity throughout the camp and of an odious festival at Baal-Peor on the night of the full moon. Within thirty minutes he had heard enough. He brushed away a new crowd of elders lining up to speak with him, and headed up the mountain trail, berating himself as he climbed.

Why had he relaxed his vigilance? How had he missed such treachery? Like a days-old carcass in the desert—intact above, rotten underneath—the decay had progressed undetected. Now the stench was overpowering, the camp was running amok, and he did not know how to turn it around. But Moses . . . Moses would know.

The summit was just above him when the sun broke over the eastern ridge. He normally loved to watch the first golden light reach into the shadowed valley, gilding the features of the rugged rocks as it pulled them out of the shadows, but this was not a morning for inspirational strolls. He quickened his pace, though he was already panting from the exertion of the climb. Bounding up the last few rocks, he scrambled onto the crest and located Israel's leader some twenty paces away.

"Moses," he huffed, more out of breath than he realized.

The old man acknowledged him, as he always did, with a wave and a nod, barely interrupting his writing.

Joshua tried to repeat the name again as he approached, but the sickening horror writhing inside him crawled up from his belly and strangled the attempt.

Moses looked up sharply at the choked sound, the fatherly smile kinder than Joshua deserved. "What, my son? What brought you up from camp with this grave and despairing look?"

Joshua could not bear to look into those wise and compassionate eyes. "The camp . . ." He took a deep breath, focusing on a hawk circling the morning blue. "The camp. That is . . . reports began coming to me early this morning." He raked his beard nervously, praying for the words. "It started with the prophet Balaam."

"Balaam? It has been weeks since Balaam returned to Babylonia."

"So we all thought." His tongue felt thick. His throat was dry. "I have been so absorbed in managing the affairs of camp, taking inventory of the towns we conquered, and mapping the river as you asked." He paused and watched as the hawk wheeled and screamed, then plummeted to earth in a dive that meant death for some small creature. "I . . . uh . . . sensed danger. All those Midianite women coming into camp day after day . . . teaching our people local 'living skills.'"

Restraint modulated Moses' voice. "I, too, accepted them as friends, cousins, in fact, despite my qualms."

The master's unrelenting gaze trapped his eyes for just a moment, trying to read him. Joshua wanted to tell Moses. He *had* to tell Moses, and yet, in his disgrace, he could not face those burning eyes. He looked at the ground.

Moses's words continued flowing, like a stream in the desert following rain. "Common courtesy demanded such acceptance . . . unless we had evidence to the contrary." His rising inflection implied a question.

"I tried to follow up," Joshua said quietly. "Whenever I checked up on their activities, I couldn't detect anything." When he finally risked another glance at the leader he had failed so miserably, Moses was no longer looking at him, but at the tents stretched out in the valley below. *He does not yet guess the enormity of the problem or my guilt.*

"The Midianite women did corroborate Balaam's story," Moses said after a long pause. "I overheard many of them telling our people that it was impossible to curse our camp . . . and they seemed genuinely . . ."

At that, Joshua's repressed emotions exploded into words. "They came with the motives of darkness."

"How so?"

Joshua paced back and forth mumbling almost incoherently, "Our men . . . on the night of the full moon . . . I only just learned this . . . they worshipped . . ." He stopped mid-stride. Taking a deep breath and squeezing his eyes shut he forced the words out. "They worshipped in the fertility rites at the temple of Baal on Mount Peor." He turned and resumed his pacing, but with a calmer more measured stride now that the truth was out.

"They have continued in this. Then last night, under the cover of darkness on the knoll beyond Simeon, our own Israelite men erected a tent of Baal harlotry, red as blood. I woke up not long before dawn to see it, Israelite men coming and going like ants on their hill—a nest of fire ants. On the very spot where we tore down that repulsive Asherah pole just weeks ago."

He collapsed onto a large rock and caught his head in his hands. "I don't know what to do. The men of Simeon and Reuben—even some from Judah—were guarding that vermin's nest. My own Israelite brothers threatened my life when I demanded that it be torn down."

Moses scooped up his writing materials and packed them away as he spoke. "I too was uneasy . . . but more with Balaam and the kings than the women." He stopped and looked up at Joshua.

This time Joshua met his eyes unhesitatingly. "It was Balaam who instigated all this."

"Balaam?"

"Apparently, after his failure to curse us, he hatched this plan with the five Midianite kings to separate us from 'Yahweh, our jealous God.' The express purpose of the *friendly* woman infiltrating our camp was to carry out this plot for him."

"I've been negligent. I was too eager to record Balaam's story. When he returned home, I thought the danger had passed."

"Balaam didn't return to Babylonia. He has been right across the river in Jericho since the festival."

"I wondered what kind of tree this prophet was. Now the fruit appears." Moses calmly pushed himself to his feet and threw the leather bag over his shoulder. "How widespread is this?"

"More than half of the princes . . . mainly the older ones, those who should know the consequences. The majority of the clans follow."

Moses sighed as he headed toward the trail. Before they began the descent, he gripped Joshua's shoulders with his massive hands as a father reassuring a young son. "Do not blame yourself. If anyone should have been more vigilant, it is I."

The morning light gleamed across a sheen of tears in the old man's eyes as he turned to begin the descent. "I am so glad Jethro and my darling Zipporah did not live to see this Midianite evil. Those women hardly seem the same race as the Midianite tribe I lived with for forty years out in the Sinai desert."

"They are not! Not at all like Jethro's family. Your Zipporah was a virtuous woman of God."

"I should have been more vigilant. I questioned their statements of allegiance to Yahweh—allegiance simply because Midian was also a son of Abraham—but there was nothing I could pinpoint as evil."

The two men did not speak again as they picked their way down the rocky trail. Joshua could not stop the wrenching memories of another trip down a mountain with Moses—that descent of Mount Sinai just over forty years past, catapulting them into the confrontation with Aaron to stop the worship of the golden calf.

How many died that day? Would this be any less ghastly?

Acsah

Acsah fled the oppression of Abihail and Eliab's tent, dashing through the door into unrelenting light. The brightness was blinding after the dimness of the tent, and tears of frustration blurred her vision. *My best friend? Oh Abihail, you disgust me. Eliab's unfaithfulness terrifies me. You defile the holy covenant and make excuses. Abba, Abba, if ever I needed your wisdom, it is now.*

The back route home was the thing. She would not display her distress in front of meddling neighbors. Only half seeing, she stumbled between the rows. Not far now. Three more tents and she would be home.

"Nooooo . . ." The cry was like that of an injured beast.

She froze. It was her father's voice, she was quite certain. Curious and wary as a cat, she slipped closer. She tilted her head to listen.

Scratching, scrabbling sounds came from the far side, the entrance side where her father often sat. But this was not the sound of Caleb sharpening or using a tool. It was not the rustle of wind in leaves. There were no trees close to her tent. She heard other male voices now, but she couldn't determine what they were saying.

A cold blade of fear pierced through her. The open space between tents suddenly seemed too open. In a panic, she darted to the shadow shield of her father's tent, and when she did, the crunching gravel under her feet whispered the solution to the mystery. The source of those strange scrabbling sounds was the scuffle of sandals, the scraping and scratching of more than one pair of sandals. *But who? More significantly, how many?* She hugged the protective shadows like a spy and listened.

"You cannot stop us, old man," someone growled.

She could not quite understand her father's response. Moving quietly as a spider, she crept forward along the side of the tent, finding a scanty hiding place between a stack of newly shorn fleeces and the tarp-covered collection of household tools. Pressing into her cover, hardly daring to breathe, she crouched to listen.

"I cannot understand this—not from any of you." Her father's voice was high and strained, almost unrecognizable.

"You will understand only when you begin worshipping Baal and Asherah—as we all must."

"But your covenant with Yahweh!"

"Yahweh, hah! Baal is the god of this valley. *He* is the key to a good and prosperous life here."

Acsah recognized the two voices confronting her father: Shaul and Eran, both clan leaders of Judah, often the most vociferous elders at tribal councils. Her heart twisted. *What had possessed them to speak so?*

"It was not Baal who defeated the armies of the Amorites. It was not Baal who turned the curses of Balaam back on him. Do you think our people could survive a month without Yahweh's blessing?"

Her father's distress was answered by a sneering laugh.

"My good men, you share with me the leadership of our tribe. Come to your senses."

"We've come to 'r senses." This voice belonged to another clan leader of Judah, gray-bearded Haggi. Now that was an elder who had outlived his wisdom, in her opinion. This morning his words were not only foolish, but slurred. "Yahweh 'az a tent. Why not Baal?"

He is drunk, and it is not yet noon.

"Haggi has the right of it. The high place is so . . . exposed." Shaul snickered. "Do you not wish to shield the eyes of our children?"

"Shaul . . . Eran . . . Haggi!" Her father's voice crackled with desperation as he called out each of their names. "How can you laugh? I am warning you as a friend. This evil is no joke. It *will* be purged from camp and you with it, if you choose to cling to it."

"Are you threatening us?" Eran growled.

Yes. Unleash your celebrated warrior skills on these reprobates. Acsah tightened the grip on her basket. She could feel the pulse throbbing in her neck. She stooped down and picked up a fist-sized rock, coiling herself to spring out and . . .

But her father fought only with words. "All covenant-keeping people will join in judgment on such behavior. Is that thought not threat enough?"

Acsah discarded her rock as not sufficient for aiding or defending her father and snatched up a broken length of tent pole.

"Surely, Nashon does not condone this."

"Our *prince*? That laughing fool couldn't stop us if he wanted to."

"The tent stays, old man. Stand aside."

"Better yet, join us." Shaul snorted with a mocking laugh. "I'd guess you haven't been between a woman's legs since Jedidah died, true?"

Caleb cut him off with a loud, hoarse cry. "Tear down that abomination. Tear it down, or I will get the Levites to help me do it."

Shaul's reply was cold, menacing, "Try that, and your daughter will be servicing the next one."

"You will not touch—" Caleb croaked, and a storm of sandals crunched in the sand again.

"Let go of me, you withered lizard."

The scuffling ended in a heavy thud that shook every supporting pole of the tent. Acsah stiffened in shock and horror. There were no more sounds from her father.

"Is 'e alive?" Haggi asked hesitantly.

"Who cares? Stupid old man."

"Shaul's idea was good. You know, get Acsah. We'll teach her a few tricks those Midianite girls know and deliver her to Zimri and Cozbi."

"Ag-zah?" Haggi sounded confused. "Sheeze an Israelite girl."

"I heard Zimri saying that the little Midianite fillies have to return to their temples. They need to train Israelite girls for the ride."

"I'm just the trainer to break in Caleb's feisty colt."

"Thiz mornin'?"

"No better time. No better way to show Princess Cozbi that the elders of Judah are serious supporters."

Shaul snickered. "We don't want to let Simeon supplant us as the preeminent tribe, now do we?"

"Bud Ag-zah'd never . . ."

Eran's laugh was sinister. "Haggi, you old fool. That will be the fun part."

Acsah edged under the tarp. In her rage, she had thought to avenge her father. That thought dissolved into horror. The jagged shaft in her hand was not sufficient defense against three lust-crazed men.

"Af-er *me*," Haggi mumbled gleefully. "Fur the tribe zinche I'm th' eldest. Buh ... thiz-iz-er-tent. Where-iz-she?"

Acsah inched back between the small loom and a large pottery jar of barley corn until there was enough free tarp to tuck under her feet. She held her breath, but her pulse pounded in her ears.

"I saw her heading toward the Carmi clan about an hour ago."

"Her friend . . . Achor's pretty little daughter-in-law . . . The one with the dimples?" Eran whinnied, and the others broke out in crazed laughter.

"Firs-come, firs-gets . . ." Haggi's befuddled speech faded along with the scuffle of their sandals.

Whoever heard of anything like this? Never in the Israelite camp I grew up in. Acsah remained in the stifling stillness for what seemed hours, daring to take only the shallowest of breaths. She strained to hear the normal bustle of life in the surrounding tents. *Why is it so quiet? Why did no one come to defend Caleb? If I cried out, would anyone come to my aid?*

Her imagination began spinning out pictures of neighbors either celebrating at that foul high place or crouching fearfully in their tents. Then those images dissolved into a terrifying one—the blood-spattered image of her father lying crumpled and broken before their tent.

"Where are you, neighbors?" she cried aloud. "You cowards." She no longer cared who heard her. She cast the tarp aside, keeping a firm grip on the jagged section of tent pole. "May all of you come down with the plague!"

Looking both ways, she crept into the path fronting their tent row. The evil trio was nowhere to be seen, but at the tent door, a swath of white hair, a bared arm, and a leg protruded at divergent angles from the tangled heap of her father's pale wool robe. In spite of her previous imaginings, the sight jarred her to the core. Caleb of Judah, her father, her fortress. She had never seen him anything but strong. Now, she wasn't certain he was even alive. She held her breath, immobilized momentarily by the terror of that possibility.

Then the jumbled tangle stirred. Caleb straightened his legs and grunted. He lifted his head, touching the back of one hand to his forehead and groaned, "They will bear the responsibility . . ."

Acsah rushed to him, her head churning with a clashing mix of relief and anger.

"The guilt . . ." Her father continued to mumble as he rolled onto his back. "For themselves and for all who follow them."

"I know who did this," she sobbed.

"Acsah? You are *here*?" Caleb gasped. "We must get you somewhere safe." He pulled himself to sitting and tried to get up.

"They're gone. Off on an evil quest . . . for now." Her eyes scanned for blood, but found only bruises. "We'll worry about you right now, my Abba. Where are your injuries?"

"The damage is more to my heart than my body," he mumbled. As he struggled to his feet, she hooked her arms under his to stabilize him.

"I'll be fine. Really." He gently brushed her away and stood breathing heavily.

"What is wrong with those men, Father?" Now that her concerns for his safety were removed, her anger bubbled up full force. "How could they treat you like this?"

Caleb explored a knot on his head with his fingers.

"Come, Father. Lie down in the tent."

"And leave the likes of those three running amok?" Caleb's tone was uncommonly brusque. His bushy brows pulled together as he brushed off his robe with short, quick strokes. "I don't need to lie down. I just need to catch my breath."

"Foolish men. Drunk and it's not yet noon."

Caleb dropped heavily onto his favorite cushion by the tent entrance. "More than foolish. Reckless. More than drunk. Besotted. Their breath tells me they are controlled by brewed mandrakes."

"The same plant that Rachel bargained with Leah for?"

"Precisely. It has been known since ancient times to excite the passions. Rachel traded a night with Jacob for Leah's mandrakes thinking that increased passion would help her conceive. Even the Canaanites call its fruit the "Devil's Apple" for all the trouble it causes."

"Like Eve's apple?"

Caleb gazed at some distant point.

"At least Rachel and Leah used the mandrakes to excite their husband."

"This is diabolical," Caleb mumbled, continuing to stare at the horizon. "We are God's covenant people on the threshold of our inheritance, but we could lose our Eden forever, like Adam."

"Abba, please get some proper rest inside on your bed."

"Rest? When those rebels could return any moment and find you? This high-handed sin against God must be stopped."

"Would you like some water?"

"Just let me rest here a moment."

"Listen then while you rest. Let me tell you about my morning."

"At Eliab's tent?"

Acsah stiffened. *I will no longer call him by the name Eliab, "God is my Father." He is no true son of God.*

"You did go to Eliab and Abihails's tent this morning, did you not?

"O Abba, the very sound of the names . . ."

Caleb's head whipped up and then he winced again at the sudden movement. "Here, my warrior daughter," he said with a grin, patting the cushion next to him. "Sit beside me where I can see you without breaking my neck."

"Warrior?"

Caleb's eyes crinkled with fatherly love. "Don't think after seventeen years of watching you I can't read those flashing eyes. And then there is this." He reached out and retrieved the broken section of tent pole she had dropped in order to help him. He studied it for a moment and shook his head in wonder. "You were going to help me fight off three men, weren't you?"

Acsah melted in a puddle next to her father. What a comfort it was to be understood without explaining.

"Now, what happened when you went to help your friends? Tell your tale."

A shudder of silent rage drove through Acsah again. She wrapped her hands around her knees to steady herself. "I do not know the woman I tended this morning, Father. I no longer have a friend by the name of Abihail."

Caleb raised an eyebrow "My guess is that this is the very time she needs a friend."

"Her husband joined himself to the enemy. She still sleeps beside him."

Caleb's voice was gentle, his eyes, sad and distant. "Before this is over, you may need your friend as well. What enemy of yours have they conspired with?"

After a few moments, Acsah haltingly began to relate what she had learned. While she found release in the telling, Caleb's face grew more and more grave. At the end, he leaped to his feet. "Go to Nashon's tent."

"Father, you haven't told *me* what happened to *you*."

"You know enough." There was a commanding urgency in his voice. "Go to Nashon's tent. Tell him to meet me in front of the Tent of Meeting. I have no idea what he knows, but I cannot believe that he has been entangled in this. And Acsah, please . . . hide yourself there with Salmon and his mother until this craziness is past."

Acsah rose slowly to her feet. She vaguely heard his last muttering words. "Will these young Israelites never learn the lessons of their fathers?" Then he was gone.

Acsah numbly obeyed, her head spinning as she made her way through the tents of Judah. Not a month had passed since the children of Israel celebrated victory over Sihon and Og. In one day, the aura of that golden joy was transmuted to dark, leaden horror. She dodged a woman meandering toward her only to have a heavy fist strike her in the back. She balled her fists and wheeled around to defend herself.

"I'm so sorry, Acsah. I didn't expect you to step out in front of me."

"Hamul, you lumbering bear. You belong in the woods, not on the paths of human traffic."

"Sorry," he repeated. "I . . ." His eyes were hauntingly sorrowful and he seemed to have no more words. He pressed past her; then broke into a halting run, cutting around and through the increasing knots of people filling the pathway.

Acsah felt a stab of guilt. "Forgive me, Hamul," she called. "I was the one who wasn't watching."

He pushed on without a backward glance, and Acsah looked around her, really looked for the first time since she left her tent. *Why were so many people milling about this time of day?*

She spotted Othniel coming toward her down the tent row. Her cousin, the notable "watcher," wasn't watching at all. He was staring at the ground before his feet, his mouth tight, his normally solid steps dragging. He did not see her even when she was just in front of him.

"Othniel? What has happened?"

He looked up, startled, and then acknowledged her with a half nod that flowed into that familiar, self-conscious toss of his head. He carried a water bag and a parcel that smelled of fresh manna cakes.

Acsah waited while he shook his long, thick hair back from his face. "Where are you going?"

"Uncle Jacob's tent."

She made an effort to stir up a laugh. "You need to take provisions? Planning a long stay?"

He shrugged one shoulder to adjust the tightly stretched goatskin hanging from his shoulder and lifted the food parcel as if he needed to show her. "From my mother."

"For Uncle Jacob? Is he ill?"

"And for Grandmother Hannah. He has been ill for the past two days, and she was caring for him. Now they have both succumbed to this . . . this fever."

"Is Auntie Hannah in her tent? I will go to her."

"No. Stay away. She is at Uncle Jacob's too. She began feeling weak and feverish last evening, and insisted on staying with her brother so none of us would contract the illness. She made us promise to leave provisions at the tent door and not enter at all."

Acsah pushed back the surging rush toward panic. "Eliab and Abihail have fallen ill as well. Abihail tells me that it started with her father-in-law."

"Achor too? It *is* a plague, and it's spreading throughout the camp rapidly." Othniel looked up and locked eyes with her for a fleeting moment.

The sun caught the amber glint of a startlingly unusual pair of eyes. It was an unexpected connection. Oddly, she could not remember looking directly into his eyes before, and she was fascinated by the mind revealed there—sad, wise, mysteriously impenetrable.

With a start, she realized that Othniel was still talking. ". . . I fear it was not a wise or safe choice."

He was staring at the food parcel, waiting for her to respond. She guessed that an appropriate response would have been difficult even if she *knew* exactly what he'd been saying. "Auntie Hannah is at Uncle Jacob's tent, you say?"

"Stay away." Othniel tossed one last dark look at her as he sidestepped past.

Acsah had always thought of her cousin as a rock—not stony and cold—simply strong and unemotional, but the wrenching sorrow chiseled onto his face just now disclosed a depth of grief she had seldom seen on anyone. She watched him trudge slowly away.

"I love Auntie Hannah too," she called.

He didn't answer.

Acsah watched until her cousin disappeared around a corner. *It's them. All of them: Achor, Eliab, Uncle Jacob, and who knows who else? Filthy, selfish men who have unleashed disaster on the whole camp.* Anger and frustration boiled through every fiber of her body, and Acsah ran the rest of the way to Nashon's tent.

Father had urged her to go there for safety. But it was not safety she craved. She desperately needed to talk. Harbored anger was like rot in the bones. Her father had taught her that. But how could she not be angry? She needed a kindred spirit to ground her sanity, and, having lost Abihail, she could think of no better confidant than Salmon. He was more like a brother than a friend—more of a brother than her father's many sons. They were older men who had long been married and had families of their own and who seemed to resent her no matter what she did.

Ada popped out to greet her even before she reached the tent. "Here to see Salmon?" A cheeky grin spread from ear to ear.

"Actually, I have a message for your father."

"He went off a little while ago. Salmon can tell you about it." She gave Acsah a coy look. "You can find my brother behind the tent."

Acsah followed the steely sound of stone on bronze and found Salmon sharpening a sword. He raised his head at the sound of her footsteps, and his brows arched in greeting as soon as he saw her. A half smile pulled at one side of his perfectly sculpted lips. "Acsah. A beam of sunlight on a dark day."

Looking into his round, bright eyes, she had no idea how to begin relating her frustration. "My father requests that your father meet him at the tabernacle."

The smile vanished "Father . . . isn't here," he answered slowly. A dark shadow of fear eclipsed the sparkle in his eyes.

He understood. He read her fear and frustration, and it stirred up apprehensions of his own. "Where is your father?" she asked.

"He left early this morning. The camp of Simeon, he said." Salmon inspected the weapon in his hands. "Shortly after dawn, Heldai brought an appalling report of Baal worship there. Father bade me sharpen the swords and wait here for him to return. When other elders came, Mother had to direct them on to Joshua." He laid the sword on the ground beside a second one and stood.

"He must expect a battle. I . . ." Looking past Acsah, he stopped mid-thought.

From the corner of her eye, Acsah caught sight of Ada flitting toward them from the side of the tent, holding out a cup.

"I brought you some water," she chirped, her eyes darting back and forth between the two of them.

Ada, Ada, how do you always seem to know when I need to have a private talk with Salmon?

Acsah took the cup, and masked her annoyance with a smile. She drank deeply. It was so cool and revitalizing that she could honestly express her gratitude. "Thank you, Ada. I didn't realize how thirsty I was."

"I'll get more if you like."

"No, thank you. That was refreshing, but sufficient."

Ada lingered, watching.

"Thank you, Ada." Salmon said, with a look that clearly meant *go away.*

"I could get a drink for you, too."

"No, Ada. I need to talk to Acsah. Alone."

Ada turned slowly, exaggerating her disappointment with slumped shoulders and drooping head.

"Don't even think of listening."

Ada stopped mid-step, turned, and wrinkled her nose at her brother.

Salmon bent closer to Acsah. "I need to go find my father and give him Caleb's message, but quick, tell me what is going on." He laughed lightly. "Something serious has stirred the flames of your ire."

"I think we may be—," Acsah started.

Salmon held up one hand with an exaggerated wince. "Whisper please." He lifted his eyebrows playfully. "Little ears may be spying in spite of my threats."

Acsah hesitated a moment. *His manner is far too playful. He has no inkling of what is happening in camp. Where do I start?*

"Perhaps you have noticed some unusual activities in camp," she finally said, beginning at the beginning as if she were explaining things to Ada. "I rather think they are all related." She tilted her head and studied his large expressive eyes. "Have you talked to Eliab recently?"

"No . . . now that I think of it. I haven't seen him around for the past week." Salmon's irrepressible grin reappeared. "All consumed with pleasing his new bride, I would guess. What do you know?"

"Let me tell you, but it is not a pretty story." In Salmon's easy company, all the bitterness, anger, sorrow, and fear gushed out like a spring flood. Acsah briefly outlined the events of the morning from the time she entered the tent of Abihail and Eliab, to the attack on her father, even to her encounter with Othniel.

In the few minutes that it took her to tell the story, a small crease appeared between Salmon's eyes, deepening to a vertical furrow of grim determination. "I thought it was strange that so many men have missed morning and evening sacrifices this past week." He reached down with trembling hands, fumbling as he retrieved both swords. "Father could be in danger. Tell my mother that I have gone to help him."

Acsah could not think of a more unlikely-looking warrior as he tramped off, carrying the two weapons as if he were presenting them as a gift.

Salmon, Salmon. Do you not have a sheath?

Joshua

Joshua followed the wild, white mane and broad back of his master down the steep path. The sun was halfway to its zenith already, the colors of the valley washed pale by its light. Not a word had been uttered during the long descent to help still the churning of his mind. Mid-morning. Nearly to the end of the trail, and the day before him unknown . . . unsettling. Normally, he would be thick into whatever projects needed to be done, finding satisfaction in his work. But the tasks of this day? The only thing he knew for certain was they would be anything but normal or satisfying.

"To the tabernacle." Moses said the words without so much as a backwards glance and then erupted from the base of the trail, heading toward camp with long, swift strides.

Joshua paused, as he often did, and glanced back up the stony face of the mountain. It never ceased to make him feel small, but today he felt doubly so, small and inadequate. When the murmur of distant voices pulled his attention back to his mission, Moses had already passed through the acacia grove and had encountered someone in the meadow beyond. He couldn't catch the words and he could no longer see him, but his voice was unmistakable. He broke into a trot, his sandals crunching out a reprimanding rhythm

141

in the sandy trail as he closed the gap. *"Keep up with the Moses, Joshua. Keep up."*

Through a break in the trees, he caught sight of Moses conversing with two burly young men more than halfway to the border of the tents of Judah. *How does he do that?* Joshua wondered briefly. *I can barely catch him, yet he never appears rushed.*

By the time Joshua was within fifty paces, the conversation had apparently finished for the young men stepped to the side to let Moses pass. That was when Joshua saw the litter. Moses bowed his head in a majestic gesture of sorrow, his hand raised in blessing. Then with one unhurried glance over his shoulder, he resumed his swift, dignified pace toward the tents of Judah.

Joshua was near enough now to read the tear-streaked grief on the faces of the young men. They must have heard him at the same moment, for both looked up and nodded respectfully in perfect synchronization. Their bear-like size identified them as sons of the Shelahite clan of Judah.

"Of which family are you?" Joshua asked.

"I am Igal, son of Alvan. This is my brother, Hamul."

"Today we are the sons of sorrow," Hamul cried out. "We bear our father's father to his grave, and our father himself is close to death."

Igal lifted the face cloth to reveal the identity of the dead man. "Do you know him?"

Joshua took one look, and inky black spots danced across the sun-drenched meadow. He did indeed know the man lying white and still on the pallet. It was his friend, Shammai, one of the few remaining old ones, a jolly, now toothless comrade from the days of Egyptian slavery, a companion of many an evening of campfire tales through the long years of the wanderings.

"My dear young men," Joshua groaned when he finally found his voice. "I am overwhelmed. I have known Shammai all my life." He glanced at the retreating form of Moses and knew he dare not pause longer. "God comfort you, my sons, and give you strength."

Joshua raced to the tent rows of Judah, and on through them toward the tabernacle, catching up with Moses just as he reached the field between the tents of Levi and the courtyard. Eleazar had already intercepted Moses with his own fears, but he would not be waylaid.

"Eleazar, sound the trumpet to summon the elders," he ordered sharply. "Then help Joshua."

"Joshua, gather the priests and Levites while I inquire of Yahweh."

Eleazar tightened his lips and blinked rapidly.

Joshua could not drive the bloody images of another day from his head, the time when the Levites had taken up swords against their brothers to stop the worship of the golden calf. He suspected that Eleazar was thinking of that time also.

Moses stopped and turned toward them from just inside the curtained door of the tabernacle. He answered their fears bluntly. "Instruct the Levites to bring their swords." His face softened, and he regarded his nephew with a brief, pained look. "I do not know what Yahweh will demand of us, but we must be prepared. Gather your brethren. Wait for me here."

As Moses disappeared into the Holy Place, a deafening thunderclap, punctuated by flashes of lightning, broke from the Cloud and it sank like a black shroud over the tabernacle. The heavy atmosphere pressed down on Joshua as he and Eleazar raced through the tent villages of Levi. Today more than ever, the people needed this protective encampment between themselves and the holy dwelling place of their God. But the Levites were more than a passive barrier; they were sworn to defend the tabernacle with their lives.

"Levites arise. Moses calls for you," Joshua repeated over and over. "Wait for him inside the courtyard. Bring your swords. Alert your fellow Levites to do the same."

Over the next half hour, silent as shadows, the men of Levi gathered on the eastern side of the sanctuary courtyard. Their faces mirrored inner horror and dread as they surrounded the bronze laver and the altar of sacrifice. Caleb and a handful of other elders and princes collected at the courtyard gate. A few of the elders discussed the rumors and events of the day in low worried voices, but the Levites huddled together in silent dread. They knew their history. It was at such a time as this that they as a tribe had first been dedicated to the service of Yahweh.

Too soon, Moses emerged from the tabernacle. His eyes, dark and brooding, swept over the men who had gathered there. In spite of a deep sigh and a noisy clearing of his throat, his voice broke with his first words. "Yahweh . . . has spoken. The leaders of each tribe who will not turn from this rebellion must die. Their bodies are to be exposed here in front of the tabernacle until sundown.

"Caleb, take charge of constructing cross beams for that purpose. Recruit all elders who are on the Lord's side to help you.

"My Levite brothers, our task is yet more grim. We will tear down all sites of false worship. Do not flinch from slaying anyone—brother, father, or son, who chooses evil by attacking or resisting our work. Those who choose Yahweh must come here and cast themselves down before the mercy seat. We must destroy all the Midianite women. They are an army of the enemy, though they do not bear swords.

"Ithamar, Phinehas, sound the short blast of war on both silver trumpets. You will come with me to lead the Kohathite Levites to battle against this rebellion. Eleazar, prepare to receive sin offerings. Pray that many will choose life and turn from this evil. Those who choose death, will find it today."

Acsah

Acsah left Nashon's tent in a daze. There was evil in the camp, but surely those who were faithful to the covenant would be protected from its consequences. She had stayed to reassure Salmon's mother that all would be well. No matter what she said, Abijah only wailed again and again, "This is a day of sorrow and death. I dreamed it. I dreamed it."

In the end, Acsah found herself talking in circles. Her head whirled, and the firm edges of her faith crumbled under the battering of the woman's repeated cries. Now, as she stood in the walkway just outside the tent, she felt weak. She could still hear Abijah's keening and Ada's voice piping like a little bird, "Don't cry, Mama. Don't cry. Father and Salmon will be all right. Acsah said so."

What if everything wasn't all right? She glanced toward the tabernacle. The war cry of the trumpets had been followed by the summons for all the people to gather there. That's where her father would go. That's where she should go, but the sanctuary did not appear as a place of comfort and safety at this moment.

The high, white cloud had vanished. In its place, churning black billows hid the dark tabernacle coverings, which were normally just visible above the tents from anywhere in camp. Flashes of lightning cracked and sizzled from that darkness. The blare of the priestly trumpets sounded again, dual blasts, urgently repeating the call to war, the summons ringing as a metallic echo to Salmon's last words, "Father could be in danger . . . in danger . . . in danger." Eerie wails of grief over the dead and dying bombarded her from every direction, chasing the pitiful cries of Abijah down the halls of memory, while the thunder from the tabernacle rumbled through the echoes of Shaul and Eran's chilling threats. A storm of judgment raged all around, and she was suddenly a child alone in that storm.

Crowds clogged the walkway ahead of her now, some rooted like plants with faces turned toward the Cloud of Judgment, others milling aimlessly like trails of ants disturbed. A few pushed purposefully toward the tabernacle, and still others headed out of camp bearing the shrouded corpses of loved ones. As Acsah stood, uncertain of which way to turn, a blur of widow's black slammed hard against her and then dodged back into the crowd.

Acsah staggered to maintain her balance. "Watch your path, woman. A crowd does not give you license for rudeness."

The woman looked back with dark, empty eyes. "Death in camp. Death everywhere."

Before Acsah could respond, the woman was gone. *A crowd is no license to speak irritable words either. Just go to the tent and find something profitable to do until Abba . . . no . . . not safe. Better find Auntie Hannah. Perhaps Othniel will be there. Maybe he could help her find her father.*

All at once, Acsah came upon Igal's mother, rocking and wailing shrilly in front of her tent oblivious to the confusion streaming past her. She stooped beside the grieving woman. "What is it? Can I help?"

The woman lifted reddened eyes. "Too late. He is gone."

"Who?"

"Father Shammai."

"Gone? Dead? Oh God! No . . ." Acsah felt faint. "When?"

"Just this last hour."

Acsah closed her eyes and she could see Shammai's face. She loved to listen when he came by to chat with Caleb about the old days. No matter how dismal the tale, his mouth would always stretch into that toothless grin of his, and he would say, "But you have a whole lifetime ahead of you in Canaan, Acsah. Fortunate, fortunate girl!"

"Igal and Hamul have already taken the body. My husband, Alvan, will be next . . ." the woman broke into a choking sob. "Then what will become of me?"

"Alvan is not dead yet. Do not borrow sadness. Pray. And remember that your sons are good men. They will care for you should the worst actually happen."

"My sons . . . they are good men. They are faithful men in Israel, but God's judgment has fallen upon us all. I begged Alvan not to go to Mount Peor."

Acsah's heart stopped. *Achor . . . Eliab . . . now Alvan? Othniel called the sickness a plague. Surely it was retribution for Mount Peor. Just retribution.* The rage she had first felt in Eliab's tent returned full force, hot and blinding. She croaked out the question burning inside her. "Surely, Shammai did not go?"

"No, only Alvan. Only my husband went. See what he has unleashed on our family."

A wave of disgust washed over Acsah along with the certainty that Uncle Jacob had also been among those who worshiped at Peor. *Foolish, selfish old men.* She fought to calm herself. Laying an encouraging hand on the woman's shoulder, she intoned a blessing she did not feel. "May God strengthen you and give you peace."

She began to stumble away, then with a pang of guilt at leaving the woman alone in her sorrow, she called over her shoulder. "I must hurry to check on someone." Her only thought was to get to Auntie Hannah's bed lest she die, but progress was slow and the chorus of grief around her grew louder as she passed more and more families bearing loved ones out of the camp. *So many? How could it be? Yesterday there were only a few rumors of illness.*

Joshua

Joshua had to lengthen his stride in order to stay abreast of Moses as the pair led the way from the tabernacle to the far boundary of Simeon. Phinehas and Ithamar, carrying the trumpets of the Lord, followed wordlessly behind them, leading the band of armed Kohathites. They plunged into the grove of acacias and all too quickly passed through the shadows to the sunlight on the far side. There, the woods gave way to an open, grassy slope rising to the high place. Joshua squinted into the brightness. The hill was lovely and green with a band of worshippers dancing around the tent at the summit. A wave of nausea swept over him at the contrast with the somber silence behind him. *What would happen when the Baal-worshippers noticed the Levite army moving through the shadows of the trees?*

Suddenly, a roar of fury fractured the air. Moses sprang forward in a blurred rush. *What? Was this a signal to charge?* Then, as Moses dropped to his knees, Joshua saw it—a body twisted, tossed against the rough trunk of an acacia like rubbish. Moses groaned as he bent his ear to listen for breath. "The fruit of this wickedness . . ."

Joshua knelt beside Moses. Hoping against hope that life remained in the man, he gently turned the shoulders. "Friend, we are here."

The head rolled loosely to the side, a familiar face with dark, round eyes staring lifelessly at the sky. A small trickle of blood stained the corners of pale lips. There was no breath. The crooked half-smile he knew so well would never grace those lips again. "Nashon," he whispered.

Moses wept. "Such a good man. Such a good man."

Joshua tenderly closed the dead man's eyes with his fingers. He removed his own outer cloak and covered the body. *Why? O why, Lord God of Israel? Shammai. Now Nashon . . . Yahweh God, these are my brothers. Those men at the top of the hill are also my brothers. What do you want?* He instinctively turned to Moses.

His master's eyes flashed. "Go. Tell the Kohathites to take up their positions and wait for my command."

By the time Joshua returned to Moses' side, the worshipers had formed a line at the brow of the hill and the half-clad dancers stood behind them still as statues, all glaring down in defiant silence while distant thundering rumbled in the heart of camp. Moses' words roared like the voice of God at Sinai. "Yahweh has spoken. Turn from this wickedness. Cast yourselves down before the Lord, for He is merciful. I beg you, do not choose death."

A few men jeered. Fewer still silently slipped down the hill, heading for the tabernacle, fear and confusion written in dark strokes across their faces. Most remained where they were. At Moses' nod, the trumpets blasted the command for the army of God to advance. With a hoarse, grief-filled cry, Moses called out, "Tear down that site of evil. Use your swords against any who try to stop you."

The sound of the priest's silver trumpets ripped over the scene again, battering their ears, echoing from the surrounding hills. A naked man leaped from the Baal tent in wild panic. "The trump of Yahweh," he howled. "The Levites attack." A storm of shrieks and curses rose from the women as they clawed and fought each other to pack into the scarlet tent. "We are going to be slaughtered," one cried.

A red-faced ox of a man scooped up a large stone and hurled it toward the advancing Levites. "We have the high ground," he bellowed at his companions. "We can stop them." His bravado helped organize the resistance. Those without weapons began scrambling for rocky missiles, taking up positions beside the big man while those who had swords formed a defense line behind him.

As the Levites rushed past him up the hill, Joshua felt as if he were floating over a surreal world. The very fabric of the covenant was rent and ruined, all that Israel had woven with her God through the trials and tests of the past forty years. Massive bloodshed could not be avoided, but to what end? *O God, give this horror some meaning.*

"Joshua." The sharp tone of command cut through the dreadful thoughts.

"Sir?"

"That young Levite. The one with the long curly hair. Bring him to me."

"That wiry one?" Life seeped back into his dead bones with the orders. Any action was better than simply watching. He was already sprinting by the time Moses' voice rang out behind him.

"My grandson."

Joshua barely recognized the pale, frightened youth he pulled out of the uphill charge. "Moses calls for you, Jonathan."

"Abandon . . . the charge?" the young man asked in confusion.

Joshua nodded curtly and Jonathan followed meekly and quietly against the current of the charge until they reached Moses. There he caught sight of the bloodied body at his grandfather's feet.

"No!" he cried out in horror. "I know him." He clapped his hand against his chest in disbelief. "Surely, he wasn't one of the rebels?"

Moses shook his head. "No. A victim of their rebellion."

"His son, Salmon, is my friend." A barely perceptible quiver shook his chin.

"That is why I called you," Moses answered. "Take the body to a place of honor outside the camp where the family can pay tribute and lay him to rest. Notify the family, especially Salmon. Remind him that he is now the new prince of Judah."

Moses turned to the young priest standing at his right hand. "Phinehas, go with Jonathan. When you are finished, report to your father."

"Ithamar, take both silver trumpets and return to the tabernacle. Blow them long to summon the entire congregation to the sanctuary of the Lord again. Don't stop until all have gathered. Reassure

149

Eleazar that he may accept the sin offerings of all repentant malefactors, even these. He will need the assistance of every priest."

Acsah

Acsah pressed her way through a camp that seemed more and more like a macabre nightmare. At Aunt Sarah's tent, she found Othniel kneeling beside his mother, comforting her in gentle, soothing tones. He looked up sharply even before Acsah spoke, his cheeks flushed, his chest heaving. He had obviously just arrived in a rush.

"Auntie Hannah?" Acsah asked hesitantly.

Her cousin turned his reddened eyes away while his mother stared into the dark void of her imagination. There would be no answer from her. Othniel's breath shuddered and he managed one choked word. "Gone."

Acsah did not know what to say.

Othniel focused on the disorderly stream of people flooding the walkway behind her. "Not ten minutes ago," he added impassively. "Uncle Jacob just before her." His mouth opened again as if he would say more, but he did not.

One moment Acsah was watching Aunt Sarah's hollow stare and Othniel awkwardly patting her back, the next she was wandering again. She did not remember anything more until she heard her father's voice in her head. *This may be the very time she needs a friend.* Auntie Hannah was gone. Acsah did not know where her father was, but she knew where her best friend lay, weak and fevered, sick with sin. She would return to Abihail's tent and help her get to the tabernacle for cleansing and forgiveness. Eliab too if he was still alive.

The Cloud still loomed over the tabernacle, thundering and black. But now yellow-gray billows of smoke rose into the western sky beyond it, slowly drifting toward her, choking out the blue. It was the smoke of death. Funeral pyres consuming the diseased remains of untold numbers of Israelites were already burning on the barren limestone flat where her father and countless others had roasted thanksgiving offerings only a few short weeks earlier. Acsah coughed and pressed her fingers against her temples.

Clouds of smoke blurred her vision; clouds of confusion obscured logic. When death tolls rose with the serpent infestation last year, God gave Moses the antidote: a defeated serpent, cast in bronze, held high on a victory pole. One look, believing in God's salvation, cured the dying. *Could there be an antidote to this? If this plague was indeed a judgment to punish the guilty, why would God allow the innocent to die?* No matter how much she wanted the ways of God to make sense, today they did not.

The way to Abihail's tent was congested. As she slogged through the crowded lane, she noticed Ethan and his sister, Bithia stumbling toward her like wraiths out of the billows of smoke, vacant eyes staring but not seeing. "Have you seen my father?" she asked, purposely blocking their path.

Bithia blinked, her eyes startled wide.

"Is Caleb among the sick and dying?" Ethan whispered.

"No . . . no . . . he is well. I just don't know where he is." Her voice sounded high-pitched and shrill even to herself. She concentrated on sounding calm. "He went to consult with Moses and Eleazar this morning."

"We have not seen him," Ethan replied.

"So many deaths." Bithia's voice broke as she seized her friend's hand.

Acsah studied her face. "Have you lost anyone in your family?"

"No," Ethan answered for his sister. "Well, God willing, no. All our neighbors have lost loved ones. We actually don't know where our parents are. They were not ill this morning, but . . ."

Bithia's eyes welled with tears as he spoke. "More and more people are dying, Acsah. I'm so afraid. Who will be next? What is happening?"

"It is a plague," Acsah answered in a matter-of–fact tone. Suddenly, something broke within her. She found herself shouting and could not stop. "What is wrong with our people? We are people of the covenant. How can Yahweh protect us when we choose these abominations?" She sucked in a deep breath to continue, but her lungs filled with acrid, murky air, and she succumbed to a fit of coughing.

Still she could not stop. Between coughs, she continued adding the blast of her words to the noxious fumes. "Shammai . . . is . . . dead. Auntie Hannah is dead." She coughed again. "Why? Because of men like Alvan and Jacob . . . because of families like Achor and his sons . . . because of clan chiefs like Shaul, Eran, and Haggi. The evil ones . . . live . . . and the good ones die. It is not right. It is not just." She felt hot, and her whole body was shaking with her coughing.

Bithia began stroking Acsah's trembling hands gently. "You are not well. I will help you get to the tabernacle. Ethan will look for your father while he seeks our own parents."

Suddenly Acsah's head cleared. "I . . . I'm sorry. I am not ill, but I am distraught by these things. I need to check on Abihail. Come with me. I could use a friend."

Ethan was watching her as anxiously as was his sister. "You should lie down."

"Truly, Ethan, I am well, but there are others who need help. Othniel lost his grandmother and great uncle in just the past hour. I did not see his brother, Seraiah. Perhaps he could use your help. If not, Igal's family lost their grandfather this morning, and when I passed their tent, Alvan lay dying."

Her voice was raspy and weak when she finished, but Ethan seemed to gain energy as she spoke. In a quick, wordless, chin-up salute, he acknowledged her suggestion and headed back in the direction of Othniel's tent.

"Come Bithia . . ." Acsah's sentence ended in another paroxysm of coughing. She forced an encouraging smile in response to the look of alarm and wheezed out words of assurance. "It is . . . just this smoke."

Bithia studied her uncertainly. "You should go to your tent. You need rest."

"God is good. It is not I who suffer from the plague, but Abihail and Eliab." Acsah turned rapidly, took a few steps, and suddenly felt faint. Everything slowed and grew dark. Then as she leaned on

Bithia's shoulder to support herself, a long screaming blast from both tabernacle trumpets juddered through her skull.

"Acsah . . . Acsah!" Bithia's face came into focus, and Acsah realized she was slumped in her friend's arms. As she pulled herself up to balance, stabilizing her weight on her own feet, she noticed a curious flurry of movement in the clots of people ahead of her.

"I don't know what is happening," Bithia cried out in alarm.

Acsah looked with watery eyes. Nothing made sense. The disturbance in the mass of people reminded her of the frothing water that fish made when she tossed a bit of food into a sheltered pool.

All at once, Phinehas and Jonathan emerged from the rabble, dodging and twisting, slicing a path straight toward her. "Salmon," the young priest called out. "Have you seen Salmon?"

"He went to find his father," she answered.

"Can you tell us what is happening?" Bithia asked.

"No time to explain. Which way?" The words were clipped, almost desperate. Phinehas bobbed impatiently while waiting for her reply as if she were holding him back from beginning a race. Jonathan hovered behind him, mute and ashen.

"He went toward the camp of Simeon."

"How long ago?"

"A half hour at most."

"His mother?"

Acsah shrugged. "In the family tent a short time ago." She looked at Jonathan and restated Bithia's question, "What is happening?"

"Acsah . . ." Jonathan's eyes pleaded for comfort, but his cousin cut him off, barking orders as fierce as his countenance.

"Jonathan, go to Abijah. Lead her to the place where we put the body. I will loop back to find Salmon. Acsah, Bithia, obey the trumpet summons. Go to the tabernacle." He gave them one last urgent look. "And pray."

Acsah stared as Phinehas and Jonathan vanished in different directions. *Why was the dignified grandson of Aaron racing madly through camp shouting orders? Why was his fun-loving cousin, Jonathan, running in his wake, eyes rolling in terror, like a frightened calf?* She had the strange sensation that she did not know anyone anymore—not them, not Othniel, not Abihail, and certainly not Shaul and his companions.

"War in camp," someone shouted. "It's the Levites. Run for your lives."

Acsah tightened her grip on Bithia's arm as a cloud of confusion swept toward them. Suddenly Shaul and Eran stormed past, elbowing roughly through the clogging mass. Bithia screamed and jerked her to the side of the walkway as the evil pair dodged between the knots of people in the tangle of traffic. Now they could see the older, more feeble Haggi, trailing behind while a man in a Levite turban ran in hard pursuit brandishing a sword. People scattered like quail before them, diving into tents or the spaces between them.

Suddenly, Haggi broke to the left and crouched between two adjacent tents as the Levite continued the chase. "No!" Acsah cried. "Haggi must not escape." She stepped into the lane, pointing toward his hiding place, and was nearly trampled by a second Levite, following close on the heels of the first.

"There," she shouted, but he was already raising his sword and lunging left. The impact sent Haggi's sword flying into the roadway, Blood sprayed high, spattering the surrounding tents, and the severed head tumbled to a stop at the girls' feet. The two-handed swipe of the Levite sword was well-aimed. It was obvious that he had already seen Haggi split from his companions, that he did not need her direction. A scarlet rivulet pulsed from the headless body, trickling into the sand, and Acsah squeezed her eyes shut against the image.

"The Levites have gone mad!" someone shrieked. *Yes, this is madness, but it isn't the Levites who have gone berserk.*

When she opened her eyes again, the Levite had positioned Haggi's bloody head on his chest and was wrapping him with his cloak. Then pandemonium exploded through the crowd a third time. A band of three more Levites, brandishing swords, rushed around the corner following the same path as Shaul and Eran, shouting, "Make way. Make way."

There was no need to shout. The path was clear. Two of the Levites ran by in a blur, but the third came to a halt at the sight of his blood-spattered brother struggling to lift and carry the body by himself. He seized Haggai's feet and the two Levites began bearing the corpse toward the tabernacle while the stunned spectators peered silently from their hiding places.

The trumpet sounded, long and urgent again, and the call of one of the Levites echoed back to the crowds. "If you are on the Lord's side, obey the summons. To the tabernacle without delay."

"To your tents, brothers," someone snarled. "Do not let them herd us to the tabernacle for destruction. Arm yourselves with sword and spear before the Levites slay us all as they did our fathers at Mount Sinai."

A second menacing voice sneered, "I will go to pray that God strike every Levite butcher dead."

Acsah was incredulous. "Which side are you on?"

"The side of life," a man with grizzled gray hair growled.

The urgency of the trumpets interrupted the chaos again, the authority of Yahweh drowning all speech in unrelenting repetition.

"Yahweh is angry," Bithia whispered.

"Not at us," Acsah answered. "The faithful can always go safely to his sheltering protection." Even as she was speaking, she wondered where the words came from. That confidence did not reflect the state of her heart.

"All the same, the thunder and lightening in the Cloud terrifies me."

Acsah nodded. "Honestly, it terrifies me as well, but we must obey the call. God is merciful. Surely, we will find our parents there."

The trumpets at last pulled the confused eddies of people into orderly streams flowing toward the thundering heart of camp, and the two girls slipped into the current. Acsah took one last look over her shoulder. "Later, Abihail," she whispered. "I pray I will not be too late."

CHAPTER SIX

BLOOD MOON

Zimri

Zimri's eyes blinked open as he hit the floor. Brilliant sunlight already streamed through the high window and Cozbi was laughing as she drew her foot back under the covers and leaned over to peer down at him.

"Wake up, my darling," she cooed. "It is full morning already, glorious and beautiful."

"Gloriously beautiful," Zimri mumbled sleepily, squinting up at her. "You. Not the morning." He relaxed against the stone floor, drinking in every intoxicating feature of the face hovering above him. "I love every inch of you—even the little foot that just kicked me out of bed. But you, you seem only to love abusing your most ardent admirer."

"I am not being abusive, my ardent admirer. We need to be up and going."

Zimri yawned and stretched. "What's the hurry? We did not get back here to sleep until the night was nearly over."

Cozbi's eyes twinkled teasingly, as she slid farther over the side of the bed, caught his face between her hands, and pressed her velvety lips against his forehead. "I am inclined to invite you back

157

to bed and remain here all day, but I must learn what transpired after we left the tent of Baal-Simeon."

"Oh!" Zimri's sleep-deprived stupor instantly vanished. "How could I have forgotten? I could not believe the lines of men waiting their turn to worship." He seized Cozbi's hands, pulling her off the bed into his embrace and smothering her shrieks with kisses until she relaxed in his arms. Then, savoring the soft pressure of her body stretched over his, he nuzzled his face into the fragrance of her silky hair and murmured, "I can't think of one of my brothers who would refuse to switch allegiance once they taste the benefits of Baal worship. I believe I can tell you exactly what transpired. Our numbers surpass those of the covenant." His fingers lightly traced the long smooth curve of her spine. "How deliciously power falls into our hands."

A short time later, the pair descended the stairs, entering a room buzzing with words like plague, tumult, and smoke. As Zimri lingered a moment on the bottom step, a lead-like mass formed in his stomach. "Listen. I have a bad feeling about all this."

"Nonsense," Cozbi replied dismissively. She walked her fingers up his chest and slipped her hands around his neck. "Regardless of what is going on here in the city, our success in the camp is assured."

Zimri disentangled himself. "I wouldn't be so certain."

A barrel-shaped man sat alone nearby, toying with an empty mug. Zimri plopped down on a cushion across from him. "What is happening?" he asked, searching the man's eyes, but finding them empty. "War, smoke, plague? What is everyone talking about?"

The man listlessly pushed his cup around in a circle. "A plague has broken out here in the city," he finally said. His breath smelled of strong drink. "And, I don't know . . . across the river? The invaders seem to be stirring again."

"Yes!" Cozbi exclaimed, her face glowing with excitement as she nudged Zimri with her knee. "Our revolution! Hurry—to the camp!"

Zimri was still struggling to his feet by the time she was halfway across the dining hall. Before he could catch up with her, she had pushed the heavy door open—and was swallowed by swarms of flies and the smell of rotting flesh. "Oh! Foul! Foul!" She ducked her head and turned her back to escape the overpowering stench and the buzzing cloud of insects.

"I can't believe *that* is good for business," Zimri chuckled as he reached out and drew Cozbi back inside. He couldn't help laughing. She had been so delighted when the heads of the two offending guards finally appeared on either side of the doorway, skewered on the ends of their spears like tasty morsels of meat at a banquet.

"Today vengeance is not so sweet, eh, my love?" He bowed to each head in turn. "Uzal, Hadoram, watch your odor. My lady finds even greater offense in you today."

Cozbi threw him a blistering look and slammed the door closed against the stench. "Don't *ever* make fun of me," she hissed. "See that the innkeeper moves those heads now. To the top of the wall, for all I care, but don't allow them to be taken down. I want them to hang until the birds peck every bit of stinking flesh from their skulls—but not where I have to walk and breathe."

"Move the fly bait. Orders understood," Zimri muttered. "Meanwhile, I'll get a straight story on what is transpiring this morning."

"Just get the heads moved." Cozbi located an empty table and sank down on one of the cushions. "I'll wait here, but we must hurry."

He looked down at her with as authoritative a look as he could muster. "Something is going on in Israel, and I want to know what before we get in the middle of it."

"*I* can tell you without hearing more," Cozbi snapped. "Salu and our followers are beginning to take over the camp."

Zimri had a heavy, sick feeling that she was wrong. "I don't think my father has the numbers to strike yet. I want to learn more. We must go back prepared."

"We must go back, period, but I will not walk out that door until those putrid heads have been moved. Find the innkeeper," she commanded as if he were her slave rather than her lover."

Zimri glanced around the room and spotted the innkeeper's daughter. He motioned to her and then watched approvingly as she maneuvered toward them supporting a large pitcher on her shoulder with one hand. There was artistry in the way she moved, almost a flowing dance as she smiled and nodded to the patrons she passed. She had a beauty of a calmer, gentler kind than the woman by his side. He recalled the day Uzal and Hadoram shoved Cozbi aside. This simple tavern wench demonstrated a regal diplomacy, attempting to soothe the bruised dignity of an irate princess with amazing skill. Someday, when this time of transition for Israel was over, and he and Cozbi were living in tranquil happiness together, he would gently reform the ways of his fiery woman. *How could the passion that was so exciting to him coexist in the same body with serenity and discretion?* He shrugged and smiled to himself. *He would have to wait to find out.*

Cozbi looked up just then and misread the meaning of his smile. "I don't like the way that tavern kitten is playing you. She should have learned that I have claws of my own. Very sharp claws."

The raw jealousy in Cozbi's eyes alarmed Zimri. "My kitten does not need claws to hold me." He reached out playfully to pat her head.

Cozbi dodged his hand. "I am *not* your pet kitten."

Zimri gave up. He took a solid step forward into the girl's path, carefully keeping his expression and tone impassive. "What is the news this morning, *servant*?"

"Servant?" The girl lifted her eyebrows.

"What is the news?" Zimri repeated coldly.

The girl warily glanced from him to Cozbi. "This past night brought change across the river, but we do not know what it entails. We do know that a plague is running rampant through Jericho. They say even King Nahari and his Midianite consort have been stricken."

"Bad luck for me," Cozbi interjected. "It has just occurred to me that another head is needed outside this door as a warning to anyone who thinks to cross this princess."

"Another head?" The innkeeper's daughter replied lightly. "Have you been outside? We have two too many now."

Cozbi glared deadly daggers at her.

Rahab tilted her head quizzically, searching Cozbi's eyes for some clue to the cause of her wrath this time. "Who . . . has offended you today?"

"A tavern cat who supported the ruffians from the king's guard when they insulted me. A cat who seeks to toy with my lover's affections."

"Do you mean one of our patrons—here in this room now?"

"You are the daughter of the innkeeper, correct?"

"Yes."

"*And* one of the harlots who service your father's guests?

Zimri flinched at the look of pain in the girl's eyes. "Cozbi, this isn't necessary."

"Who has offended you, princess?" Rahab asked, her brows pulled together in genuine concern. "Be plain, and we will try to make it right."

"What is your name?"

"Rahab."

"Speaking plainly, that is the name of the one who offends me."

"The lady jests," Zimri broke in with a feeble voice. "Cozbi, you already dislike the reality of your demands. Would you fill all of Jericho with flies?"

Cozbi ignored him, studying her fingernails with a detached look. "If the king were not ill, this harlot would know my power this very day."

"Cozbi, forget this nonsense. I need to get information." Zimri stepped between Cozbi and the girl. "We hear of strange occurrences. A commotion across the river. What can you tell us, Rahab?"

"Strange occurrences . . ." Her voice wavered. She stepped sideways to look directly into Cozbi's face instead of his. "A storm settled over the valley east of the Jordan several hours ago. Thunder and lightning in dark clouds right over the heart of the Israelite camp even though the sky is perfectly clear and blue elsewhere." She did not risk a glance at Zimri as she relayed the reports. "Some say it is the cloud of Israel's God showing anger. Others say it is the storm god Baal reclaiming his territory. Rumors run wild that many of the Israelites are turning to Baal . . . led by you Midianite girls." She paused. The response in Cozbi's face was unreadable. She risked a quick glance at Zimri. "I can't imagine that to be true."

"And why not?" Intimidation crackled through Cozbi's words.

Rahab met the challenge with conviction. "All my life I have heard stories of the wondrous powers of Israel's God. If even half is true, I would not expect his people to abandon him readily."

Zimri frowned. "You might be quite surprised. Things are not always as they appear from the outside."

"Are *you* an Israelite?"

Cozbi forestalled Rahab's question. "Your treasonous ideas would make one would think *you* were an Israelite."

"Would that I were," Rahab answered under her breath.

"I would that you were too. My understanding is that they stone harlots."

"Cozbi." Zimri sighed. His princess had a way of constantly derailing conversation. "This girl can help us. She hears every rumor that rumbles through Jericho." He addressed Rahab with urgency, careful to keep his tone businesslike. "The princess is under considerable pressure, and she got little sleep last night. Can we begin this conversation anew? What causes all these people to speak of war? What evidence?"

Rahab nodded her head. "Several hours ago, people began hearing shouts of conflict and trumpet blasts across the river. Those who have gone up on the wall say they hear the sounds of war, but they cannot see a battle. Multiple reports testify that the miasma over the valley is not all storm. Black smoke pours into the sky as well. The cause cannot be determined from here."

"You call that evidence?" Cozbi tossed her head.

"Those are the reports. No one here has actually been across the river, of course, so all talk of war is merely speculation."

Zimri could feel the blood drain from his face. "War alone could be a good thing, but I have a very bad feeling about the so-called *storm*. The Cloud has been known to perform in strange ways on behalf of Israel. I suggest we wait here this morning, Cozbi, until we learn what all this means for us." He slumped down on the second cushion at Cozbi's table. His hands were shaking.

"You were supposed to be working out what to do about the stinking heads that prevent me from returning to camp," Cozbi hissed with exasperation. She stood and thrust her face inches from Rahab's. The loathing and rage twisting her lovely face choked all music from her voice. "Tell your father I want those heads repositioned. I want them placed where I can see them, but not smell them. And I do not want a swarm of flies following me down this street when I leave. Do you understand? If this does not happen within the hour, King Nahari will hear of it and serve up a rather pretty head for me on the end of another spear."

Rahab chewed on her lip as she listened and then fled to the back of the room. Her sense of urgency, as she interrupted her father's banter with his guests, was evident even from this distance. *The poor girl had done nothing to deserve such cruel treatment.* But the warm flood of Zimri's compassion froze instantly under the icy blast of Cozbi's next words.

"I find no pleasure in a man whose knees weaken at the first sign of danger." She wore the expression of one who has just discovered maggots on her plate. "Show yourself to be a man if my love means anything to you."

"But Cozbi, my concern is for you. Remember your father's words about your safety."

"And do I tremble in fear? We have made much headway in the Israelite camp since the night at Baal-Peor. I have an army of faithful devotees over there. Would you throw that all away at rumors of a storm cloud and rumbling thunder?" Cozbi dropped down to her seat again. "Summon her back," she demanded, flicking her hand toward the innkeeper's daughter who was now working her way through the room, serving guests. "I need a drink."

Zimri rose stiffly, motioned for the girl and sighed as he seated himself again on the cushion close to his princess.

"Bring us two cups," Cozbi ordered as soon as Rahab was within speaking distance. "And a flagon of your strongest brew. My lover needs something that will stiffen up his courage." She laughed coarsely, slipping her arms around his neck and pressing her body against his.

Zimri did not respond.

Cozbi pulled back from him and leaned against a pillar regarding him silently.

She views me as weak. And she hates to admit how much her plans depend on me. Zimri dropped his head, not looking up even when Rahab returned, setting cups at their places. She filled them and left without a word. Still Zimri did not move. He was certain that his stomach would revolt if he tasted even one drop.

"Zimri, we have no other recourse," Cozbi said in an uncharacteristically reasoned tone.

When he finally looked up, she was taking a slow, thoughtful sip and smiling at him sweetly. *She has figured out that her bold advances are repulsive while I am anxious and distraught. She's shifting tactics, playing me for a fool. Her head-over-heels-in-love fool. Steel yourself, man. Don't let her coerce you into doing something foolish. Yahweh God . . . Lord Baal . . . Someone help me. If I let her have her way, she will surely get us both killed.*

"This revolt is necessary," Cozbi said as serenely as if she argued for an outdoor picnic lunch. "It is what we planned together."

"We need not abandon the plan. Let's just lay low until we learn what is going on."

"We dare not hold back or delay a single day. If the flame of Asherah is crushed out, it could take months to fan it back to life. If there is a rebellion and we don't support our new devotees, all will be undone. And if there is not a war going on over there, we have to begin training Israelite girls in the ways of Asherah or how can our worship continue? Asanath has already begun pulling the girls back to their temples."

Zimri tipped up his cup and let the first burning gulp slide down his throat. *She had a point. Maybe I was unreasonably fearful. But then, Yahweh had a way of undoing plots against his people.* He smacked his lips together. The strong drink was exactly what he needed, settling his stomach, tingling and warming his entire body, infusing him with strength, enough strength to deal with the wild, defiant woman beside him. *Oh Cozbi, Cozbi. More than anything, I could not bear losing you.* He searched carefully for the right words.

"Never have I even dreamed of someone like you, Cozbi. I just want to protect you."

"I do not want or need your protection," she replied flatly. "I was born to rule. If we lose the foothold we have gained among the tribes of Israel, there is nothing for our love to stand on."

The bottom dropped out of Zimri's core. His heart and his stomach—and all his vital organs seemed to slip into some unseen abyss. "Do not even suggest that our love stands on shaky ground. There could be no other love for me in the entire world. Cozbi, my darling, I could not live without you, so how can I risk endangering your life?"

"How sweet." Cozbi took his hand, her voice oozing with honey. "But the gods have decreed a higher destiny for us, my love, than just enjoying each other."

For the next hour she pleaded, coaxed, and teased Zimri as she plied him with cup after cup of the potent liquor until all his anxiety dissipated and his only resolve was to follow his indomitable partner—if necessary, into the very jaws of death.

Acsah

The tabernacle was all but hidden by a seething, roiling black mass looming above the heads of the crowds pressing into the heart of camp. Acsah winced at the pain of another rumbling peal of thunder as she scanned for white among the sea of dark heads. Bithia had found her parents, but Caleb was nowhere to be seen. Acsah coughed. Her lungs burned, laboring against the leaden weight of the air. Her head pounded, spinning with fear and anxiety. It was not only the smoke. The wrath of Yahweh hung over his covenant people like a weight with measurable, ever-increasing heft.

Those who had reached the tabernacle before her began falling to their knees as they approached the courtyard curtain, so at last she was able to see the entire expanse east of the tabernacle. It was a simple matter now to locate that unmistakable white mop, her father lying prostrate directly in line with the entrance to the

165

courtyard. His hair spilled over his shoulders and onto the earth, his arms outstretched toward the Holy Place of God, but between him and the courtyard was a hideous forest of crude, acacia-branch crossbeams. Scores were empty, but too many were not. A mere body's length from her father, Haggi hung from one of those crosses, his severed head tied beside the blood-soaked corpse. Acsah's knees weakened as she comprehended the need for the hundreds of crosses remaining. She stabilized herself with a wider stance.

Beyond the death zone in front of her father, the curtains of purple, scarlet, and blue were tied back, a brilliant gateway in the white linen walls of the courtyard. Within the yard, Eleazar and his sons bustled back and forth between the blazing bronze altar, the laver of water, and the penitent with their guilt offerings. Farther back, a second set of richly colored curtains remained closed, shielding the entrance to the dwelling of God. Moses stood, hands upraised to Yahweh, at the outer gate, outrageously framed by its glorious colors, as if he stood interceding at the very door of heaven. His huge frame sagged as he alternately begged the people to repent, then pled with God to cleanse the camp and end the deadly plague. Joshua stood beside him, limp arms hanging at his sides, head bowed in sorrow.

Acsah made her way to Caleb, carefully stepping over and around prostrate worshipers. She followed a hunched, weeping man as he led a ram in a meandering path toward the courtyard. On the edges of her vision, she could see anguished tribal princes plodding one after another to the crosses with bloodied swords and crimson-stained robes. Pairs of young Levites followed, bearing limp, lifeless bodies to be tied high on the crossbeams, adding to the shield of judgment between the grieving people of Israel and the thundering cloud of their God. Actually viewing the kind of revenge she had wished for earlier turned her stomach. She swallowed back the bitter taste of bile.

Staring numbly through the constructed forest of crosses past the interceding Moses, Acsah forced herself to focus on Eleazar tending the flaming sacrifices. His garments gleamed with blue, white and gold authority as he spattered deep crimson blood against the sizzling sides of the bronze altar and then poured the remainder on the ground. In contrast to this fiery judgment against sin, the face of the high priest told a story of heavenly love and compassion for the worshippers, and the flashing colors of the twelve stones on his breastplate seemed to glow with unearthly light.

The burnt offerings were so numerous that both of the sons of Eleazar as well as Ithamar and all three of his sons were needed in constant assistance. The bloody rites had never seemed so precious. One way or another blood would be shed. Who would not choose that it be the blood of a lamb? Who would not choose the rituals of mercy provided by a holy God rather than judgment and death?

Acsah numbly found her way to her father and sank to her knees in the slim space beside him. Caleb did not acknowledge her or even seem to notice as she stretched out beside him, closed her eyes, and simply listened to his prayer.

"We dare not claim to be more compassionate than you, our God and our guide . . . or more wise . . . or more just. If our unholy hearts are crushed . . . our feeble minds overwhelmed with this carnage . . . how much more your heart above all hearts must be breaking now.

"Almighty Yahweh, God of our fathers, do not abandon us to the consequences of our sin. Remember your promises to Abraham, to Isaac, and to Jacob. We are their children. We are *your* children. We do not deserve to be, but you have chosen us above all peoples of the earth. You led us out of slavery and lovingly shepherded us these forty years. You have shown the nations that you are not like their gods. You are a God, not only of incomparable power, but of holiness, justice, and tender mercy.

"O Most High and Holy One . . . You who directed the path of our father Jacob and transformed him from Jacob the Deceiver to Israel the Overcomer, do not abandon us. Transform *us* as you transformed him, O Lord. Do not let the tragedy of this day be empty. You can do all things. You *can* purify Judah. You *can* purify every tribe. You *can* make of us a holy nation. This alone would restore the honor of the name of Yahweh in all the earth."

As Acsah listened to her father's words, her disgust, anger, and frustration dissolved into shame. His thoughts were so much nobler than hers. She had been irritated at the stupidity of people like Abihail and Eliab who brought down trouble on herself and her people. She was revolted by the lecherous insanity of Shaul, Eran, and Haggi. She was appalled at the specter of death in the camp. This prayer provided her with a momentary glimpse into the mind of God. *Holy Lord God, purge my heart and my tongue. I am no more righteous in your sight than the unfaithful of Israel. Oh, but I long to be . . . I long to be holy. I long to be worthy of our covenant with you.*

She had no idea how long she lay there, embraced by her father's words. Was it only minutes? Hours? She gradually became aware of the growing volume of the prayers around her, thousands of voices blending in a single hoarse roar of sorrow.

"Yahweh, have mercy. Forgive your people."

"We have broken covenant with you, the Holy One of Israel. Restore us again."

"Cleanse us and heal us."

She raised her head to look around, dully watching two Levites with grave faces and hollow eyes as they fastened another corpse on a cross. There were almost no empty crosses left. *Was it nearly over then?* The head flopped to one side as the Levites trudged away. She gasped. *Shaul.*

At the sound, Caleb lifted his head and shoulders, supporting himself with his forearms. He acknowledged her with a quick lift of his shaggy white brows. "Dreadful. Dreadful day. No words for it." He looked down at the rough, gnarled fingers pressing against the earth. "My own hands helped construct those crosses . . . because he commanded it. It is God's judgment, not man's revenge. "

Acsah looked at him. She was beyond words, beyond tears.

He returned the look. He understood her horror. He felt it too. "What else could God do? Trust him, Acsah. He is not cruel."

"But . . . this?" Her voice broke.

"The rebellious took the stance of war. They were willing to kill us or die trying. Still he was merciful. Only the unrepentant hang there. O Acsah, if our hearts are sick with sorrow, think how much more so the heart of God. I was so afraid that he would abandon all of our people. Or force us to turn back into the wilderness again."

Acsah reached over and stroked the back of his hand. It was not hard to comprehend what that would mean at Caleb's age. He had been prevented from entering his youthful dream forty years ago because of the rebellion of others. He had spent half his life wandering in the wilderness, waiting for another chance to enter his dream. Another delay would be the end for him.

"How long are they to be 'exposed'?" she asked flatly.

"Until the end of the day."

Acsah stared blankly at the crosses, silent for a long time. Gradually, she became aware of Shaul's family, huddling close to his cross, weeping. "I can't bear watching," she whispered. "The guilty have earned their fate, but the families are *exposed* too."

"Selfish choices have exposed those families to shame. If the lies of Asherah and Baal are exposed here as well, perhaps some good will come of it." Caleb's mouth formed a thin, tight line, and he inhaled deeply through his nose. "I pray that the truth has shocked our tribes and brought them to their senses. Those gods cannot protect from disease. Those gods do not promote clear and rational thinking. Those gods do not promote peace or love. May this sound of sorrow be the sound of healing, not mere complaint."

Phinehas

Phinehas took a deep breath as he tramped to the laver for wash water one more time. There were no more guilt offerings waiting. As far as he could tell, the last of the Levites had returned from the bloody battle. Even the roaring sea of repentance was settling into waves of quiet weeping. Surely the story of this grisly day was nearly finished.

He tightened his lips in a grim smile. *The enemy thought to undo us, but with the help of Yahweh, we clawed our way out of his tangled net. Soon Uncle Moses can add this tale of terror to his manuscript. The Book of the Wanderings will be finished and the Children of Israel will cross over into the Promised Land.* He lingered over the refreshing coolness of the water, soothing currents of cleansing passing over and around his fingers as he swirled them in the basin.

What was that? Laughter? Here? Yes, a woman's laughter. Flippant. Mocking. Discordant. He tensed at the sound of it, distant but distinct and disturbing, drifting toward the tabernacle over the drone of the grieving crowds. He dried his hands hurriedly and returned to his place at the altar, searching all the time for the source of the sound.

Then a man's voice called out, "Moses? Where is Moses?"

Grief and groaning had already ceased as necks craned throughout the crowd. Now it seemed that even the rumbling Cloud paused to listen. Phinehas could see them now: Zimri of Simeon, tall, handsome, and utterly irreverent, wading through the sea of penitent, prostate people with a Midianite woman clinging to his arm. The woman was none other than Cozbi, the daughter of King Zur, her beauty arresting, her garb alluring, and her bearing absolutely arrogant. Zimri was drunk.

One after another, individuals on the edges of the crowd rose to their knees to gawk while those in Zimri's path scrambled to clear the way as the couple made their way toward the tabernacle entrance. There was no mistaking the moment that Cozbi saw the hideous judgment scene. As her black eyes appraised the crosses, her laughter shriveled and died. *Where is the grief, woman? Your hands crafted this along with those of the prophet Balaam. Where is your grief, Zimri? Are you too drunk to see your own father hanging here?*

Zimri led the princess directly toward Moses. In the midst of the forest of death, he stopped and turned, regarding the sea of trembling people with obvious contempt, then swept back around, stretching an accusing index finger toward the humble leader. "That man is responsible for all this carnage and for the removal of Baal's tent of worship. Open your eyes, people of Israel. Behold the clear choice—will you have gods of wealth, pleasure, and prosperity, or Yahweh, the jealous God of blood and death?" The pointing finger shook and the words were slurred.

Phinehas averted his eyes from this affront to the Almighty. He could see Caleb and his daughter, Acsah, crouched just past Zimri, the shock and revulsion on their faces reflecting his own feelings perfectly. Like himself, they seemed to cringe in expectation of a blast of fire from the presence of the Lord, consuming this irreverence as it had his father's two older brothers, Nadab and Abihu. Indeed, all Israel seemed to hold their breath with that expectation. But no fire came, and the drunken challenge continued.

"Choose now. Will you crown me as King Zimri of Israel? Will you follow me and Princess Cozbi into an inheritance of milk and honey—right here, right now? Or will you continue to follow the stern shepherd who led our people in circles in the desert until most of our fathers fell in that wasteland, their corpses rotting there to this day?"

Yahweh, where is your thunder? Moses, where is your rod?

Cozbi waved Zimri to silence. "Who would choose a drunken sot as king?" she hissed and then broke from Zimri's side.

"Is that really you, Moses?"

"It is," he growled. He took a step into the shadowy forest of crosses to confront her.

Princess Cozbi began to circle Moses like a prowling lioness. "You are a bloody ruler. Is this how you maintain power?" When she completed the circuit, she stopped in front of Moses, studying his face. "You once knew the joy of a Midianite woman. I have heard that she is long dead and that the lion sleeps alone."

Phinehas wanted more than anything to lunge out and throttle the seductive tone, to terminate the inappropriate glances this foreigner tossed at the revered leader, but he could not make himself move.

"Think what an alliance between our peoples would mean," Cozbi continued. "Together, we would roar from this valley, Israel and Midian, lion and lioness, conquering and devouring, our power unstoppable."

Phinehas remained frozen in his place, but Zimri shook off his drunken stupor and lunged forward, seizing Cozbi's shoulders. "No!" he cried.

Cozbi shook him off, leaving her Simeonite lover reeling, as much from her betrayal as from his cups.

"Yahweh is the Lion of Israel, not me," Moses roared.

"Humility does not become a ruler any more than cowardice," Cozbi sneered. "If you do not crave power for yourself, crave it for your people. The splendor of our united kingdoms would surpass the glory of Egypt or Babylonia. What is this lion banner flying high behind me if it is not you, the one who led Israel out of Egypt and brought them victorious into this valley? This is no time to curl up in the sun like a toothless lion."

Phinehas detected a sea of swords unsheathed in hundreds of accusing eyes in the crowds. They wanted this insanity to stop, but no one lifted a finger to defend the Lord. He wanted it to stop too, but he was a priest. He quickly scanned the lines of Levite regiments. It was their assigned duty to protect the tabernacle, to defend the name of Yahweh. *O Lord Almighty, awaken your warriors to their obligation.*

He stepped forward and bent all his energy into issuing a silent challenge with his eyes. *Stop her.*

"I am only a shepherd," Moses thundered. "But I wield a rod of iron in defense of the people of Yahweh. You will not leave the Lord's camp alive today, either of you."

Cozbi matched his fire. "You think Yahweh will arise for you here as in Egypt? You do not know the power of the gods who rule this valley. They have held this land since the days of Nimrod, the mighty hunter against Yahweh. The deep dragon power of this land drove the descendants of Shem from it then. It will do so again through Lord Baal. Every king of Canaan, as well as Moab and Midian, bends the knee to his rule."

"We do not fear the kings or the gods of this place."

Cozbi smirked and tossed her head seductively. "Those kings may not frighten you, but know that even jackals will join in packs to devour an old lion that sleeps alone. Only with a strong young lioness at your side, will you and your people survive."

Phinehas crept alongside the warrior at the end of the Levite formation south of the gate. He exchanged glances with the man, flicking his eyes to the sturdy bronze javelin in his hands. *Stop her*, his mind demanded, but no words came forth. The Levite handed him the javelin.

"What are you *saying*?" Zimri croaked in a hoarse whisper, scrabbling for Cozbi's shoulders again.

Cozbi lowered her voice to speak privately with Zimri, but Phinehas had no trouble hearing her hysterical, venomous whispers. He had little doubt that Moses and many of the Levites could hear her as well. "I have beseeched the gods for this moment. Trust me, Zimri. As his widow, I will bestow legitimacy on you as his successor."

Zimri swayed unsteadily, looking utterly confused when she pushed him away and addressed the crowds. "Hear me, people of Israel. I am Cozbi, daughter of King Zur, sent by Lord Baal to stop the foolish changes Yahweh seeks to bring to this land. The goddess Asherah intends good for her devotees, but know that her fire will either inflame the hearts of men to worship or reduce them to ashes. She will do to the tabernacle of Yahweh as you did to the sacred obelisks that you demolished and burned in this valley. The death and confusion you see around you is a direct result of rejecting her and Lord Baal.

"Let all the people hear and judge what I have to offer. The armies of Midian and Moab gather as we speak. They intend to wipe you from the face of the earth, but my father will cut a covenant between our peoples at a word from me and you will not be destroyed. Join me and live. This will be your only warning." She opened her arms in a graceful sweeping gesture. "Asherah sent me as her ambassador to teach Israel how to reap the riches of this land through the power of its gods. You have seen the wealth of Sihon's cities and villages. How foolish to cling to the ways of a desert god and reject the prosperity of the gods of this region. I would be honored to reign as your queen." She looked around as if she expected applause.

"Stop, in the name of Yahweh, God of Israel," Moses thundered. "Israel will worship him alone."

Zimri roused himself. The look on his face said, *Why should I fear an old man of one hundred twenty years? This is my moment.* He pulled Cozbi close to his side and bellowed out his own challenge. "There is no stopping the worship of Baal, Moses. Not after we have tasted its delights. Even the fires of Sodom could not destroy our zeal." His eyes flamed with drunken rage, and he shook a warning finger at Moses. "Know this, old man, Cozbi is mine."

Acsah

Acsah was astounded. *Zimri, what has happened to you? How could you be deceived by a woman like her? Do you see your dead comrades? Do you see your own father hanging there?* She wanted to scream at him to look. She wanted to stop him. She wanted to remove that woman from the face of the earth forever. She reeled with shock and silent rage, praying for the fire of Yahweh to flash out and consume such rebellion. But the fire did not come.

All around her, people gaped open-mouthed, but no one moved. Not even her father. She looked at Eleazar. She could see his lips moving in silent prayer, but he did not act. Not one of all the priests and Levites moved. A look of horror and astonishment was frozen on Jonathan's face. And Phinehas? Nearly in his third decade of life, he was always more serious than any of Acsah's other friends. He had left his place among the priests and stood like a commander beside the ranks of the blood-spattered Levite army. His high forehead was deeply furrowed and his eyebrows drawn together. At the moment, he looked terrifyingly fierce. Still, he did not act.

Zimri

Zimri stood straighter, emboldened by the silence. Even Moses did not make a move against him. "What do you think you have accomplished, Moses? The era of your repressive rule has ended." The surrounding hills magnified his words, and he felt like a god.

He pulled Cozbi against himself with one arm and held the other out in invitation to the crowds.

"Hear me, O Israel, the worship at Yahweh's tabernacle is not only dreary, but impotent. Lord Baal rules this land. Come. Follow Baal. Crown me as your king and Cozbi as my queen."

Zimri did not flinch even when he heard Moses cry out. "Who will defend the honor of our God?" Not one man responded. He had never felt so powerful.

"Moses is a weak old man," Zimri murmured in Cozbi's ear. "You belong to the real lion in this camp, ruling as *my* lioness. We will devour the flesh and crunch the bones of all who oppose us."

Cozbi gave Zimri the very look he wanted to see. The fire of Asherah was running hot through her body, and he trembled with longing for her.

He turned his back on Moses and the tabernacle, proudly leading his goddess through the crowds to his father's imposing tent. It seemed to him that the people regarded them as deity. Basking in the awed hush, Zimri paused at the tent entrance for a final bold announcement. "Until we have another, I dedicate this place, the tent of Salu, prince of Simeon, whom Moses murdered, as our temporary altar to Baal."

A collective gasp rose from the crowds.

"Do not fear that old man. Join us. Even you Levite butchers will be pardoned if you alter your allegiance today. Cozbi and I will introduce you to a powerful way of life that has been denied you for too long." His voice was coarse and thick with lust. He liked the sound—the very sound of strength. He threw open the tent flap with urgency, feeling the swelling of his passion as Cozbi loosened her belt, dropping her gown just as she slipped through the portal.

She was brilliant! That quick flash of her naked beauty spoke more eloquently of the benefits of Baal worship than a thousand, thousand words. Zimri lunged after her, pouncing on his princess with the roar of a lion as the door flap closed.

Acsah

Holy Yahweh, stop this blasphemy. Acsah looked around. Her father's forehead was pressed to the earth and he was groaning. Moses and Joshua had turned toward the door of Holy Place. Everyone else seemed frozen with incredulity. Acsah desperately scanned the cowering tribal princes yet again. *Would not one of those blood-smeared, grim-faced men rise up in defense of the Lord?* They were tough enough to confront their own clans, but against this high-handed foreign fist, raised in defiance of Yahweh, not one moved.

Cozbi's cry issued indecently from the tent of Salu. "I am Asherah. You are Ba-a-a-aal."

Acsah fought back the urge to leap up and grab a sword herself. Suddenly, a blurred rush shot past her. She knew the tall, thin back racing toward Zimri's tent. It was Phinehas, a Levite javelin held high above his shoulder like a hunter giving chase. His priestly white robe flapped around lanky legs, long strides flying toward the tent where Cozbi's shrieks of ecstasy were rising ever higher.

Just as Phinehas burst through the tent door, she cried, "We are gods!"

There was a startled squeal. A grunt. Then, eyes closed, breathing heavily, Phinehas emerged without the javelin. He stood in front of the tent, tall and strong for one long moment. Then, as if he were a figure formed of sand, a child's sculpture on the beach suddenly assaulted by a wave, he crumpled to his knees, his face pressed to the ground, his shoulders shaking with sobs.

A voice near Acsah whispered, "Phinehas is a dead man."

Acsah looked toward the speaker in shock. *Phinehas is a hero, a hero today among a throng of cowards.*

The woman on her other side narrowed her eyes. "Zimri's family is known for revenge." She drew a flat hand across her throat in a quick slice.

Obviously, Acsah's assessment was not the majority opinion, and the murmuring multiplied apace.

"If not the Simeonites, surely King Zur will avenge his daughter."

"Indeed," a deep voice boomed. "One way or another, Eleazar's eldest son will not live to succeed his father." This last voice sounded almost smug.

Are they deaf and blind? Phinehas was defending the covenant. Acsah looked to her father, but he neither looked at her nor at the worried whisperers around. He simply raised one finger toward a stirring in the tabernacle courtyard. The blazing altar stood unattended while Eleazar and four young Levites huddled briefly around Moses. Then as Eleazar returned to the altar, the four tramped heavily through the courtyard gate and on through the forest of death toward Phinehas. Moses followed close behind.

"Behold, the bloody Levites go to claim another victim."

"Why did Phinehas not wait for instruction from Moses?"

The Levites trudged ominously through the murky muttering.

"Woe. Woe to the family of Aaron."

"Woe to *us*. The Midianites will avenge the death of their princess."

"The Five are already gathering against us. Did you not hear Cozbi say so?"

"Woe. Woe to us."

When the Levites bypassed the young priest and disappeared into Salu's tent, the grumblers lapsed into silence. Moses planted himself not five feet from the young priest as the first pair of Levites backed out with the limp body of Zimri sagging between them. As the second pair of Levites emerged with the body of Cozbi, the crowds whipped themselves into a greater frenzy.

"Will the Levites not bind Phinehas and hand him over to the Midianites?"

"If they won't, we must."

"Deliver him dead or alive. It is the only way to avert war."

Crumpled and silent, Phinehas remained where he was. He did not look up even when his gory work was carried past him. He did not react to the increasing threats, even when the flood of fear and fury threatened to overwhelm every remaining island of reason. Moses seemed like a mountain of strength in a raging ocean to Acsah, but how long until even his life was in danger?

Unless . . . Acsah looked over her shoulder at the Levite army. *Would they rise up to protect the Lord's anointed? Were their swords enough to stop this horde?*

"So much like the day the camp turned on Joshua and me," her father whispered. The anguish in his eyes sent a shiver down Acsah's spine. She knew the story like the back of her hand. Today for the first time, she felt the terror of it.

Suddenly, there was a rush near Phinehas.

"O Lord, not again—" her father groaned, but his words were cut off by a blazing light.

The mob fell like grain mown by a sickle, shrieks and screams sounding from every direction as lightning split the air, followed by a resounding boom. Acsah squeezed her eyes closed against the brightness. The earth beneath her trembled and shook as one bolt after another crackled from the Cloud of the Lord, flaring red through her closed eyelids. The deafening peals of thunder purged every remaining complaint. When the lightning flashes and thundering began to subside at last, Acsah looked up. The bodies of Zimri and Cozbi hung in disgrace among their followers, their crosses flanking the entrance to the tabernacle courtyard. The crowds on every side lay flat on their faces before the Lord, all but Moses, who stood with his face upturned toward the Cloud, listening attentively to the awesome rumblings of Yahweh.

Gradually, Acsah became aware of a soft, shuffling noise . . . somewhere vague and distant. It was difficult to distinguish the sound at first from the low rumblings of Yahweh's thunder, but it gradually increased in volume, surrounding the entire camp with dreadful whispers. *The sound of rustling robes . . . the shuffling of thousands of feet, but it cannot be our people. They are all here. Could it be the creeping of the Midianite army already? But we did we not see them descending into the valley. And why was there no war cry?*

She squinted into the horizon, beyond the crowds, beyond the surrounding tent cities, but she could see nothing . . . until a small movement caught her eye at the doorway of one of the tents of Judah and a pale, feeble couple emerged. *Who?*

Then a single form appeared between the tents of Simeon, followed quickly by numerous small groups, masses of pale, gaunt figures, hobbling and tottering out of tents on every side, limping, staggering, dragging themselves toward the heart of camp. The fleeting thought that these were the specters of the slain men on the crosses flashed through Acsah's head. A nonhuman army bent on hateful revenge did not seem impossible on this day of horrors. But then the thundering ceased. The Cloud billowed up, towering and white, to its usual place over the tabernacle.

"Here is what the Lord says," Moses announced. "Phinehas, son of Eleazar, the son of Aaron, you have turned my anger away from these rebellious people."

No one moved. The people remained where they were when the glory light first struck them, scattered in heaps like the rubble of broken statues. In the hush, the shuffling and rustling sounded a dreadful accompaniment to the words, "rebellious people."

Moses laughed aloud in reaction to the dead silence. "Do you not understand? The plague is over."

Understand? Over? The words rang through the fog of her confusion as Acsah watched the haggard horde move closer. Then she spotted Abihail and Eliab leaning on one another. Achor and Mara followed with Eliab's brother, Jamin, and his wife. And there was Igal's father, Alvin. These were not those who had died. These were those who *survived* the plague.

All around, the people flung the shroud of judgment aside like an unwanted blanket in summer, releasing ten thousand sighs of relief. "Bless the Lord," Acsah whispered. Whatever would transpire with the Midianites did not matter. Israel was safely in the hands of her God again. Even those stricken by their own guilt had been given the strength to obey the summons and come to the altar.

"Therefore, Phinehas . . ." Moses continued. He gave the grandson of his beloved brother Aaron a look of great love and compassion, but Phinehas didn't look up. "Fear not, my son. Hear the words of the Lord: 'I, the God of Israel, am making a covenant of peace with you. Because you were zealous for my honor and made atonement for all Israel, I am bestowing a lasting priesthood on you and your descendants after you.'"

Acsah's heart leaped with the rightness of this blessing. Phineas had risked his life and reputation for Yahweh—and his God had answered. Still Phinehas remained, flat on his face by Zimri's tent. *He didn't hear. Moses, tell him again.*

Then, as if he had heard her, Joshua ran from the tabernacle courtyard. "Rejoice. The plague is over. Young Phinehas has stayed the hand of death." While he was speaking, Moses lifted his nephew to his feet and everyone leaped up with a mighty cheer. "Phinehas! Phinehas stayed the hand of death!"

Eleazar began a hymn of praise while Moses led his son back to the altar, and as he sang, the faces of the plague victims seemed to brighten. Many joined in singing Eleazar's song as they merged with their brothers and sisters around the tabernacle, a wave of straighter backs, stronger steps, and the flush of health began visibly moving over those who had come so close to death. Acsah joined in the singing, but could hardly hear herself in the rush and roar swelling all around like the revelry of a waterfall, the sound of life gushing forth, full and rich in praise to God. The rebellion was over. The plague had ended.

With his head tilted to one side and tears streaming down his face, Eleazar held out his arms like a loving father embracing all Israel.

Joshua

The sun set darkly that evening. The dead had been relegated to the purifying flames. The crosses also pulled down and burned. But now the night came, grief-filled and ominous under a starless, smoke-shrouded sky. The clans gathered, clinging to each other for comfort, but an unearthly stillness displaced the usual singing and storytelling. What story could override the horrors of the day? How could they sing when thousands of places around those evening campfires were forever empty? And the smoldering remains of the day obscured all messages of hope from heavenly star patterns. A stiff evening breeze tried desperately to claw ragged openings in the smoke shroud, even allowing a brief appearance of the belt and sword of the Warrior. The moon when it rose was the color of blood, and by its light the people found their way to bed much earlier than usual.

In the Levite camp, however, the families of Moses and Eleazar remained huddled in their campfire circle as the blood moon climbed the sky. Joshua had joined them, as he often did since he had no family of his own. He listened as Eleazar read the story of the Exodus from Moses' second book, watching numbly as the great leader nodded his approval over the tale as set down on parchment for generations to come. He felt a heaviness bordering on despair, as he joined in singing "The Dwelling Place."

We are consumed by your anger,
And terrified by your indignation.[11]

The words, composed by Moses after the horrors of the golden calf incident, tingled down Joshua's spine with cold reality. Once in a lifetime would have been too many times to experience that anger and indignation. Now, the story was finished, the song ended, but Joshua was in no hurry to leave. Tired as he was, sleep would not come easily tonight.

"The Serpent orchestrated this rebellion."

Joshua welcomed the rumbling voice of authority and settled deeper into his place to listen.

"It was not the prophet Balaam. Not the Midianite kings . . . nor any other man." The hint of a sardonic smile touched Moses' lips. "Nor any woman for that matter."

Moses paused and drew in a long, deep breath. Joshua knew the look well—intense amber eyes peering into the past, sorting through more than a century of memories to make sense of the day. When he spoke again, they would hear wisdom and they would hear love.

"Our Enemy is more powerful, more cunning, and more treacherous than we mortals can comprehend. He wants our worship—but he is no god. Yahweh demonstrated that in Pharaoh's court the first time Aaron and I stood before him. We came as emissaries of a deity Pharaoh would not acknowledge. We came with the preposterous request that the greatest monarch of the world give his slaves freedom to worship a different god. Yahweh wanted Pharaoh's worship as well so he arranged a battle of serpents, using the Egyptian's own myths and beliefs to convict him.

"How well I remember the teaching I received in my youth, how the power of the serpent Mehen coiled around Egypt's Pharaoh god to protect him from Apep, the serpent god of chaos. When Aaron threw down my staff, it became a serpent signifying disaster, a symbol of Apep. The magic of the priests produced serpents as well, but the power of Mehen could not protect their Pharaoh. Their staves had only the appearance of life. My staff proved the lie when it swallowed up theirs. The Serpent has power, but only Yahweh can create life. He *is* life. God spoke Pharaoh's language that day, but he wouldn't hear it. He chose death."

Moses squeezed his eyes closed. He shook back his shaggy white mane and roared into the night of the blood moon, "O my people, choose life. Forever and always, choose life."

Joshua wondered how many in camp heard. Of those who heard, how many understood the words? Moses held his face uplifted, contorted with agony and bathed in the strange, red light. Joshua knew he was interceding for the future of his people.

"Life . . ." Moses whispered as his features relaxed and he lowered his face. "Life and love. Indescribable, powerful love." He scanned the circle of faces, but the piercing amber eyes lingered longest on his. "The full force of that love and life surged through me for the first time on Mount Sinai. You saw him, Joshua, from a distance; you and Aaron and the seventy. Remember that pavement of blue sapphire. So strange to see such a thing on that mountain. It was as if the touch of God's feet melted the rock and reformed it as blue glass. Then he called me to him. The moment I stepped onto that sapphire sea, the life of Yahweh boiled through my body, a searing flame of exquisite pleasure that left me both strengthened and filled with profound peace.

"The Serpent cannot imitate it, so he usurps the blessing God bestowed on the union of man and wife. The wild sex and intoxicating incense of idol worship combine in a poor imitation of the true presence of life. But through those pleasures, the Serpent seduces mankind again and again. We reject the life-giver and bow in worship that leads to death."

Joshua watched the firelight reflecting along Moses' broad, sun-browned forehead, highlighting his strongly-shadowed cheekbones, and piercing amber eyes. The thick white mane and beard fairly glowed in the dark. Joshua mused on Moses' reply earlier to Cozbi—that *Yahweh* was the Lion of Israel. But no one was surprised when she referred to their leader as a powerful, old lion. The older the humble shepherd of Israel became, the stronger the lion-like qualities of his face.

Moses met Joshua's eyes momentarily and then looked around at his sons, his grandsons, his nephews, and their wives and children, studying their faces one by one. His eyes, crested with thick white brows, were always lit with wisdom and kindness. Tonight, they held a deep sadness as well. "Thank you all for your support today, my dear, dear family," he said, breaking the long silence. "I love you more than you could know.

"Phinehas, you acted with incredible courage. Taking the life of another will change you forever. You may long be haunted by the pain of your deed. Never question the fact that you did it, not in passion or revenge, but to defend the honor of God and to protect His people. That is the task of the entire tribe of Levi, even the priests when necessary." He fixed his eyes on the young man with a look as unforgettable as his words. "When these memories disturb you, find an act of love that you can pour your heart into—and do it.

"Eleazar, you have the same gift of love and compassion for the people that Aaron had. I sense that the people already love and respect you as they did him."

Eleazar silently nodded his acknowledgment of the approving words.

"At times like this, I truly do miss my brother." The voice of sorrow, deep and grave, dropped to an almost inaudible level as

Moses shook his great head slightly. "Perhaps I have lingered too long."

Joshua felt a stab of nameless, cold fear. The chill shuddered through the entire group, and they hardly dared to breathe until at last Moses resumed his comforting commentary on the day's events.

"Thousands died in this plague and purge, but Yahweh has restored the remnant to the covenant. The smoke obscures the stars tonight, but they are there, real as ever, and so is their story. We look at the figures and love to recount the tales: the Enemy appearing in the forms of the Serpent, the Dragon, or the Scorpion. Yahweh opposing him in the forms of the Lion, the Bull, the Arrow, and the Warrior. But God has also placed the Ram in the sky, not as a powerful male, charging with horns down like the Bull, but as a Lamb of sacrifice.

"The Lion will defend his people. He is awesome in his judgments. We dare not cling to any form of evil because he will eventually shatter every perverted, hurtful thing. But his love for us is as fierce as his wrath. As I think about all the blood that flowed in this judgment today, and all the rams offered to restore us to the covenant, the symbol of the Ram in the sky gives me more hope than any other. The stars are telling us that our awesome, magnificent Yahweh would sacrifice anything to save us . . . even to laying down his life if a god could do such a thing. When you bring your sacrifices . . . when you see the Ram in the sky . . . remember the sacrificing love that cleanses the Lord's erring people and draws them back to the covenant."

Another long period of silence ensued. No one moved. Finally, Moses looked at his family with a trace of a smile crinkling the corners of his eyes. "It has been a long day. A tiring day. Go now. Take your rest. I am well past ready for bed myself, but first I must speak with Joshua. Alone."

Joshua glimpsed a fleeting shadow cross Jonathan's face. He could tell that Moses had seen it too, but Jonathan avoided meeting his grandfather's eyes as he rose and left the firelight with his father, Gershom. Moses watched the young man sorrowfully, not speaking until all the family members had left.

"Joshua, why did you come to me with the crisis this morning and not inquire of the Lord yourself?" His gaze bored into Joshua's heart.

Joshua stammered. "You are our leader, Moses. And I . . . well, I . . . I so often am wrong." He looked down at his hands. "Remember when I wanted to silence the men who were prophesying from their tents? I thought I was protecting you and the Lord's chosen ones." He winced at the memory. "I felt so stupid when you silenced *me*."

"I will not always be here with you," Moses said gently.

"But you are now, and we need you." Joshua gazed sadly into the crimson glow of the embers. He had disappointed Moses yet again. "God speaks so clearly to you. I try to do the right thing, but I'm so afraid it will be the wrong thing. Too often it seems to be. Your wisdom gives us a sense of security, a sense of comfort. I cannot give the people that."

He felt Moses' eyes on him, but when he looked up, he discovered a bemused smile rather than a look of condemnation.

"It is not a leader's role to make people feel secure and comfortable, Joshua." Moses reached over and patted Joshua's knee. "More often he must lead people from a comfortable place to an uncomfortable one."

Joshua pondered that statement. He was not sure he fully grasped its meaning.

"Joshua, you have been like a son to me for more than forty years now. You are a good man, and you will be a great leader in Israel. You must learn to go to God yourself. He may not speak to you face to face, but don't be surprised if he does. He will, if you need it. But you have something I did not have: the books of the law which God instructed me to write." Moses looked down at his rough, leathery hands. He slowly curled then uncurled his fingers. "I have prayed that I will leave out nothing that the people need and that He will not take me until the scrolls are complete."

"Don't speak of God taking you, Moses. Not here on the very brink—"

"Enough," Moses roared, holding up one hand in a gesture that brooked no argument. "I have settled this with the Lord. You must not attempt to dissuade me from my acceptance of his will. I am finally at peace with the fact that I will never set foot in the Land of Promise."

"Wrong again," Joshua mumbled.

Moses shook his head slightly and his lips pulled into a tight smile. "I do not have many more days with you, and God has revealed to me the final things I must do. First, Eleazar will organize a census of the men twenty years and older, just as we did after we left Egypt. God's holy army is on the march at last and they must be numbered. Next, God has commanded that we avenge the deceit and treachery of Midian."

"I will begin organizing and drilling the troops tomorrow."

"Not this time, Joshua. God has called young Phinehas to lead the army."

"Phinehas? But he is a priest! He is so young . . . he has no training or experience."

As Joshua stuttered and stammered in surprise, he caught a look of disapproval in Moses' eyes. "Did you hear me, Joshua? *God* commanded that Phinehas lead."

Joshua could sense only love in Moses' steady gaze in spite of the reprimand.

"How much experience did *you* have the first time you led the army, eh?" Moses chuckled. "God doesn't need experience. You know that. *He* has the experience. What he needs is a responsive heart. Phinehas demonstrated that today, and I believe that God wants to honor him and prepare the people to accept him as high priest in a difficult era."

"Well, then, sir, do you want me to help Phinehas?"

"Yes. I plan to climb the mountain again before dawn. I have been impressed to add the story of Balaam's treachery to the history of our people. I just completed the story of the blessings turned curses. Balaam wrote out the words the Lord placed in his mouth. He gave them to me when he told me the story. He seemed so sincere . . ." The lion's mane shook from side to side as Moses wagged his head sadly. "I would never have guessed that he had already gone to the Midianites with this viper's plot. But he was right, absolutely right. Seducing Israel from their covenant vows is the only way to curse them."

Moses rose to his feet. "I will need a full day of solitude to record that story. Perhaps more, depending on what God leads me to record. I know you can handle anything that comes up in camp." He stepped back from the fire. "Eleazar may need your help in organizing the elders for the census in the morning. That will be the first priority. When the numbers are announced, I want you to make God's plan regarding Midian known to Israel."

Joshua looked up at Moses sharply. He remembered the sullen expression on young Jonathan's face. The boy's grandmother was Moses' Midianite wife, Zipporah. "Considering their Midianite heritage, wouldn't it be best if one of your sons . . . or grandsons?"

Moses closed his eyes and tightened his lips.

Joshua checked himself. "I will talk to Phinehas in the morning to see how he would like to proceed against Midian. I will help him organize the divisions if he wants me to. If we form our plans while the census is being carried out, we can make an announcement together by the time it is finished."

"Good." Moses took another step, then paused on the very edge of the circle of light. "When I have finished writing, I wish to address the entire congregation. I want to review the story of our people from beginning to end, rehearse the law in full detail, and renew our covenant with God. Then I will have peace about leaving my flock to another shepherd."

Joshua nodded. He stood, picked up a stout stick, and pushed the burning logs to opposite sides of the fire pit. When he looked up again, the darkness had swallowed the great leader of Israel. A coldness crept into his bones as he finished spreading the dying embers as if the fire within him was dying too.

Who would take Moses' place? His sons, Gershom and Eliezer, had always kept themselves a bit apart from the leadership of the tribe. They were free children of the desert who had never known slavery in Egypt. It was hard to picture either of them replacing Moses. Jonathan was well integrated into the tribe of Levi, but he was young and unstable. Would it be Phinehas? No, he would become high priest after Eleazar. Whoever it was, would the new leader want or need his help?

Full of self-doubt, Joshua looked at the sky. The faint ruby glow of the moon, smoldering forebodingly through a smear of black mist, was misshapen, a damaged, incomplete orb. The lurid gleam knotted his stomach. It was the color of the blood that streamed through camp that day, the blood of brothers shed by brothers. He blocked out the dismal thoughts and retrieved the coal pot. *This day of trouble is over. There is no value in raking through its embers to try to remake it.*

While he knelt by the dying fire, gathering enough coals for the morrow, the moon threw off its smoky shroud, flooding the camp with hideous red light. "Good night, *blood moon*," Joshua said pragmatically. He rose and left the smoldering fire circle with long, loping strides. "I don't wish to see the likes of you ever again."

CHAPTER SEVEN

NUMBERS

Acsah

The first thin, dawn-light diffused red through the smoky remnants of the funeral pyres, the smell heavy over the valley, and the memory of yesterday's horrors heavier still. Gatherers filled their baskets silently, moving through manna-white meadows with no more interaction than a herd of grazing cattle. The customary laughter and chattering had, quite literally, gone up in smoke.

Yesterday, Acsah's senses had been battered numb. Today her head churned with questions. *Why had God brought them into this valley? Why had he allowed such a devious and deadly temptation? Why had so many faithful Israelites died when guilty ones survived? Better to pick these flakes off rocks and dry scrub brush in the wilderness than this place where beauty masked evil and death.*

Every time she closed her eyes, Acsah was sickened by images of Nashon, his bright eyes and endearing smile replaced by an empty death mask. The widow Abijah wept inconsolably yesterday evening as Caleb helped lay the prince of Judah in his grave, but little Ada glared at Acsah. It was as if her assurances that Nashon would be all right somehow made Acsah to blame. She wanted to say that *her* faith was shaken too, but words seemed inept and hollow. The worst part of the burial ordeal was watching Salmon.

His body was there, staring with dark, expressionless eyes, but that miserable frame was no more Salmon than the lifeless corpse they laid in the ground was Nashon.

After campfire, Caleb brought Salmon to the tent and counseled with him in the eerie red moonlight. Acsah left them alone, tried to sleep, but fragments of her father's words and Salmon's broken responses too easily penetrated the goatskin walls of her sleep chamber and echoed through her thoughts even now.

"You can not indulge despair or bitterness. Your mother and sister need your strength, and the tribe needs the new prince of Judah."

"But how? I don't know what is required of the head of a family, let alone a tribe. I can't do it."

"You can and you will." As usual Caleb's compassion was expressed in practical advice. "Do one thing at a time, whatever must be done. In service to your family and your tribe you will find healing."

There was a long poignant pause. Then the tear-choked question, "How can I even get out of bed tomorrow?"

"Sometimes that is our greatest act of faith. Get up. Lace up your sandals and step into the day with the strength God gives you."

Will that work for my pain too, Abba? Lace up my sandals . . . and what? What do you want me to do, God? Surely not just gather manna?

Acsah noticed Abihail working nearby, and felt again the stab of betrayal. Abihail avoided Acsah's eyes as she filled her basket, and Acsah had no wish to communicate with her. It was Abihail and Eliab, along with Eliab's family and others like them, who had brought all this devastation on Salmon and his family, on Auntie Hannah and dear old Shammai. On all Israel. She concentrated on her work. She ignored Abihail.

Suddenly her father's voice sliced the silence, *"My guess is this is the very time she needs a friend."* The words were so startlingly clear that Acsah looked around quickly. Caleb was nowhere in sight, and no one else seemed to have heard.

She felt a flash of rebellion at the unbidden thought. *At least Nashon received a proper burial. Those that died of the plague were tossed onto the funeral pyres like rubbish. There will be no stone cairn marking the resting place of Auntie Hannah, Shammai, and a host of others whom I will personally miss. Salmon needs a friend. I need a friend, a true friend. But the guilty must live with the pain resulting from their actions.*

Her father's words sounded through her head again, *"This is the very time she needs a friend."*

Acsah clenched her teeth. He was right. She knew it, however difficult it was to admit. Her bitter and unforgiving thoughts were consuming everything joyful within her. *The greatest act of faith is to lace up my sandals . . . and what? Love someone I don't feel like loving? God give me strength.*

Acsah forced herself to move closer to Abihail as she scooped up moist fingerfuls of manna. Abihail seemed to sense her closeness and met her eyes with a guilty, anxious look, then instantly dropped her gaze. *She probably reads resentment all over my face.*

Acsah forced herself to say words she did not feel. "Good to see you here. I'm glad you are well . . . and Eliab also."

Abihail nodded. "God is good. We have much to be grateful for."

Acsah went back to gathering the soft white flakes. Grateful. I need to be grateful. *Remind me, O Mighty One of Israel, of your goodness to all of us . . . for our daily manna . . . for deliverance from the plague . . . for not abandoning us even though we deserved it.*

Wooooo-hooooo-hooooo. An insistent blast of a war trumpet suddenly stopped her prayer. All the manna gatherers lifted their heads and listened. This was the particular call that summoned the princes and elders—the military leaders. War again? The whispered question moved through the group like wind. Acsah remembered Cozbi's words that the army of Midian was already gathering against them. Was it true then?

Through the smoky haze, Acsah watched murky outlines, dreamlike shapes of men making their way from every corner of camp to the tabernacle at its center. With a glance at her basket, Acsah checked herself. *Less than half full. When the sun breaks through this haze, it will melt the manna into the grass. Stop gawking and work, Acsah. You will find out what is going on soon enough. There's no point in us going hungry today on account of your curiosity.*

Cycles of hope and fear, courage and dread invaded the remaining task-filled hours of her morning. Acsah milked their herd of five cows and led them, along with their small flock of sheep and goats, to grassy pasture. She built a fire, stirred up a pot of morning porridge, and baked manna cakes for later in the day. Still she waited for her father's return. She picked up her spindle to resume the pleasant task of transforming clouds of fleece wool into yarn. Sunlight had finally pierced the smoky clouds, warming her back and bathing her workspace with wan light, and she tried to recapture the joy of the recent shearing day. But in the same way the haze lingered over the valley, no amount of sunlight could drive away the somber memories of the previous day.

Nothing, that is, until she heard the sheltering, soothing sound of her father's voice and saw him striding down the tent row with his usual confident steps, intensely engaged in conversation with her cousin. Her father always lifted her spirits, and she smiled now to see Othniel talking so earnestly with him. Normally, her cousin watched rather than spoke, and if he spoke, his words were brief. But there was something about Caleb that changed the people around him. He was the most amazing man, the most amazing father.

Bubbles were plopping to the surface of the porridge, and Acsah removed the pot from the fire. "Othniel, won't you eat with us this morning," she invited, "I seemed to have gathered more than we will need. And you and my father obviously have much to talk about."

Othniel's face flushed, and he turned toward Caleb questioningly.

"Yes, yes, I should have thought to ask you the moment I smelled that honey sweetness. We can't keep leftover manna, now can we?" Caleb grinned at Acsah and nodded toward the empty bowls. "Fill them up, my dear."

"Thank you," Othniel mumbled, stealing a quick glance in her direction as Caleb handed him a bowl.

Acsah laughed to herself. *My boldness stirs up discomfort in many young men, and I know it makes some of the elders angry, but Abba treats me with all the respect he gives his sons.* "So tell me, Abba, why were you summoned to the tabernacle? My mind is about to explode with curiosity."

"The summons regarded a census of all the men of fighting age," Caleb explained.

"Midian?" Acsah whispered, but Caleb had withdrawn into himself and Othniel apparently had nothing to say.

The three ate without speaking until halfway through their meal when loud sandal-crunches on the gravel path interrupted the silence. Jonathan suddenly burst around a corner, racing down their tent row with puffs of dust trailing behind. His black curls swung wildly, his cheeks were flushed, and his eyes flashed. *What a contrast to the grief-stricken young man running through camp with Phinehas yesterday!*

"Uncle Eleazar sent me—" he huffed as soon as he drew close. He stopped and bent over, resting his hands on his knees, gasping for air.

Acsah giggled, "Whatever time you saved running so fast is now lost in waiting for your breath to catch up."

Jonathan's eyes sparkled. "You are right . . . but the news is exciting." The group waited while he took several more gulps of air. "Joshua was with Uncle Eleazar so he already knows. The two of them sent me to you, Caleb. The numbering is finished. The total number is 601,730 Israelite men."

"Not so exciting when the census forty years ago was greater—603,550 to be exact," Caleb interrupted.

"But, I haven't finished. Not one of the men counted this morning is the same as the group that was counted when Israel left Egypt—except you and Joshua."

"All . . . gone?" Caleb dropped his head and was silent for a few moments. "This plague and yesterday's slaughter took *all* the rest of them?"

The old man closed his eyes absorbing the meaning of this news. Acsah held her breath knowing that the announcement was more important to her father than the others could guess.

Othniel had been watching Jonathan's display of energetic reporting with the hint of an amused smile. Now he turned attentively to Caleb. His face did not betray his thoughts.

Jonathan shuffled his feet and glanced at Acsah. Like the others, he waited for Caleb to break the silence.

Caleb finally looked up. "You mentioned Eleazar and Joshua. What does Moses say?"

"My grandfather went up the mountain early this morning to continue his writing. When he is finished, he plans to speak to the whole assembly."

"He doesn't know?"

"Uncle Eleazar thinks the Lord told him about the numbers . . . which is why he ordered the census."

"Well, then," Caleb responded slowly, "the time has come. The faithless army of the Lord has been replaced by a new one, trained to faith in the wilderness. Nothing hinders us from crossing over into the Land of Promise."

"Not a thing," Jonathan declared and flashed a huge smile at everyone.

Acsah's hand flew to her breast in horror. "Is that all the numbers mean? Were Nashon and the other good fighting men we lost merely a hindrance? Mere numbers to be eliminated? What about Auntie Hannah and dear old Shammai? Just excess old numbers?"

Caleb's piercing scowl was a wordless command for her to hold her tongue. Acsah leaped to her feet and began vigorously stirring the remainder of the porridge.

Jonathan cleared his throat. "Say, that porridge smells wonderful. Do you have enough to share with a ravenous man?"

"Ravenous men," Acsah snapped, surprised by the irritation of her response. "Which one did you mean?"

Jonathan gave her a sweetly pleading look as he nodded, "The one who stands right here, sorely in need of morning manna."

She scraped out the last of the porridge and handed it to him brusquely.

As he took it from her hand, his fingers brushed hers. His smile was too warm and too sweet for this moment of horror. "It's good that you are here to help finish this," she replied, "or the worms would get it tonight."

Jonathan stared at her for a moment and then began eating hungrily. "We Levites have been so busy taking the census all morning," he mumbled good-naturedly through the first mouthful, "that

I haven't had time to eat yet. At least I didn't take the opportunity earlier, which is all the better now." He fixed his large, luminous eyes on Acsah. "I don't think I've ever tasted better porridge nor had fairer company to eat it with."

"Fair company?" Caleb coughed. "If you think I'm fair now, you should have seen me fifty years ago."

Jonathan's brow crinkled. His neck whipped around to look at the old man's face. Othniel smothered a laugh, and Acsah rolled her eyes, concentrating on chasing her last bite of porridge around the bowl. In a split second, Jonathan recovered his composure, slapping his forehead with his hand to acknowledge the joke. Soon he had everyone, even Acsah, laughing along with him at colorful stories of the morning's counting procedure.

Balaam

It was mid-morning by the time servants unlocked the large exterior doors to King Zur's palace and flung them wide to receive the guests. Balaam entered the courtyard with the express intention of positioning himself favorably for the gathering. He threw himself down on a cushioned bench directly across from the entrance where he would be the first seen by each guest as they arrived. Leaning his head back against the wall and closing his eyes, he savored the sun's warmth as he reviewed his strategy.

"Sir, are you awake?" a voice interrupted hesitantly. "My lord bade me bring you something to eat."

Balaam opened his eyes to see a servant standing before him with a pottery drinking jug and a platter of dark amber dates. He motioned for the platter to be placed beside him on the bench and took the jug. He tipped it up and drank deeply. The cool camel's milk curdled refreshingly on his tongue before it slid down his throat, quenching his hunger as well as his thirst. Life was good.

He laughed aloud over his success in the past few weeks. What a contrast to the bitter disappointment of his disastrous endeavor with Moab's King Balak. He had set out on that journey without fully plotting his course and without the full approval of any of the gods. The mere thought of his foiled attempts to curse Israel soured his stomach, and he reached for one of the soft, plump dates. As it melted, sugary sweet in his mouth, he smiled again, smacked his lips, and picked up another in long, thin fingers. The sunlight gleamed on the deep gold of the wrinkled fruit, beautiful and perfectly delicious, precisely like his day of success, doubly sweet after the bitter taste of defeat.

He had overcome the Abrahamic curse. The promise to Abraham was that those who cursed Israel would be cursed. He hadn't been able to *curse* them, but he had *blessed* them as he had been blessed, blessed them with the joyous freedom of Baal worship and the assurance of prosperity. Therefore, Yahweh must bless him for it was written into the promise: *He who blesses Israel will himself be blessed.* The plan he had received from Baal the night he threw himself down before the image on Mount Peor was a double success. It had given him status among the Midianites and it would gain him Balak's promised gold.

The prophet nibbled the golden flesh. *My current situation is so utterly sweet. Date sweet. Israel no longer has a supernatural advantage. On their own, those pathetic desert wanderers are no match for even the weakest kingdom that might attack. Even a fort city as small as Ai across the river could trounce that ragtag army.*

Balaam retrieved the jug of camel's milk and drained it, planning his strategy for the assembly as the curds washed down his throat. He must impress on the Midianite kings the necessity of striking before any other nation guessed Israel's weakness. The five kingdoms of Midian could undoubtedly defeat that rabble without help, but the coalition would grind Israel to powder. Half of Midian's crack camel riders would swoop down from the high eastern plateau while the other half swung northward, sweeping down through the highlands of Bashan, then push against the Israelite camp from the north end of the valley. Jericho was poised to prevent escape westward across the Jordan and Moab would wall Israel in on the south. By the time the Midianite infantry from the southern tribes followed the divisions of the Five down into the valley, there would be little fighting left to do.

"Hah! The blessing Yahweh forced from my lips described the people of Israel as numerous as the stars. It should have been 'as numerous as dust'—dirt to be trampled underfoot."

"Our enemy is only dirt, eh?" King Zur smirked as he approached the lanky prophet.

Balaam looked up and grinned sheepishly. He didn't realize that he had spoken aloud.

Zur's smile revealed both rows of yellowing teeth. "Good, I see you have received some refreshments. Would you like some pistachios? Some barley bread? Any more to drink? Is that bench satisfactory? Is there anything else I can do to make you comfortable?"

Balaam shook his head, "No. I am beginning to feel a bit sleepy. I will doze here in the warmth of the sun while we wait for the others."

"Good, Good. Your confidence is assuring. The others have been instructed to be here by noon. They are eager to hear the details of your plan of attack. Several of them are hesitant . . . because of Yahweh's past interference, but I believe your arguments will convince them as readily as they convinced me."

Before the king had left the courtyard, a clattering of hooves and a commotion at the gate doused Balaam's drowsiness. He squared his shoulders and lifted his red-bearded chin. But only a common courier approached the king. He slumped back against the wall in disappointment.

"King Balak bid me deliver this message, sire. He will not come, nor will his army leave the borders of Moab to assist you."

As he was speaking, a second messenger galloped up to the gate. This time the messenger was from King Nahari of Jericho, but the message was similar: "We have contributed gold to fund your cause, and we hope to have good diplomatic relations with the new Israelite-Midianite regime ruled by Queen Cozbi and Zimri of Israel, should they be victorious. But we will not station our forces at the fords and become embroiled in their civil war."

The messenger from Moab backed away from King Zur's scowling face. "Would you care to reply, my lord?" he asked hesitantly.

Balaam leaped to his feet. "No reply for cowards! Get out of here while you can. Both of you."

A third courier arrived, this one trotting through the gate on his donkey. He glanced warily at the messengers scuttling away in obvious distress. "The Midianites of the Sinai desert will not join your fight against Israel," he called without dismounting. "Our chiefs warn you to give it up as an ill-fated, ruinous endeavor."

As the messenger wheeled and raced away, Zur broke into a shrieking fury. "What is it with these cursed people?"

Balaam repressed the gnawing fear that the plan might unravel even now. It must not fail. It could not fail. Reason must control his thinking, not fear or anger. "The southern tribes have never allied themselves with the Five," he replied with forced calmness. "Remember, Moses lived among them and took the daughter of their priest as his wife. I never really expected their help. And Jericho sits so securely behind her walls that her support in gold has always been the most we could hope for."

"But Moab? Balak was the one who first felt the threat of Israel."

"We don't need Moab." Balaam locked eyes with the king, his voice iced with chilling conviction. "Balak will regret this insult." Suddenly, he lost control over his rage, prophesying with shrill, rapid bursts of words. "When this is done, we will watch that dog grovel. He will beg to be part of the alliance of the Five and the new Israel, but any connection with us will cost him twice the gold he originally promised. We will wring heavy tribute from him if he agrees to be our vassal. If he refuses, we join King Zimri in annihilating Moab, adding her highlands to Israel's conquests. Balak's stupidity will cost him his crown. It will increase Cozbi's power in the region, and flood our coffers with Moabite wealth."

King Zur laughed and clapped Balaam on the back. "You did well to convince me to leave my little queen-to-be in Israel with her Simeonite prince. You are right. We don't need Moab!" He picked up a date, chomped it vigorously, and spit out the seed. "Except for dessert." His brow crinkled and his eyes darkened with concern.

"But, we must be certain to send a messenger to them before the attack. Not only should we notify Zimri to marshal his forces from within to coordinate with ours, but we must be certain that Cozbi is safely sequestered in Jericho until the fighting is over."

Balaam relaxed, confident and calm once more. He smiled broadly. "Yes, above all we must protect that girl. She has been invaluable. Thousands joined with Baal at Mount Peor, and who knows how many have converted since? With such large numbers rising up to help us from within the camp, our attack against Moses will be a mere toddler's sport."

Acsah

Acsah nearly dropped her porridge bowl as trumpets shattered the quiet for the second time that morning. While she was still drawing in a deep breath to calm the pounding in her chest, Jonathan demonstrated an exaggerated, jumpy, alarm reaction and laughed. "My cousin Phinehas doesn't seem to be able to keep that thing out of his mouth. I think he enjoys startling everyone."

"Dual blast," Othniel said, ignoring Jonathan and staring in the direction of the sound. "Everyone to the tabernacle."

Caleb rose slowly and stretched his back. "Time for the official account."

Jonathan leaped to his feet and bowed to Acsah. "May Othniel and I walk with you?"

Before she could answer, Caleb coughed. "Certainly, you young folk go on ahead."

A priestly threesome surrounded Joshua at the gateway to the tabernacle courtyard. Eleazar and his brother Ithamar flanked the silver-haired commander while her friend Phinehas seemed to hang back in the shadows, more behind than beside his father. Moses was conspicuously absent. Questions and speculations about that absence buzzed all around, but Acsah's attention was immediately drawn to the two sons of Aaron. Both were noticeably older and grayer, but there was a striking change in Eleazar's bearing. His head was tilted a bit to one side, soft brown eyes lit with love as he watched the clans and families packing together in tribal groups—the very image of the high priest she had grown up with. After the savage rebellion that ripped throughout the tribes yesterday and the gaping holes left by so many deaths, this Aaronic resemblance provided a comforting continuity.

She ignored Jonathan's attempts to chat, preferring to watch her high priest and listen to the rushing and roaring created by the combined chatter of all twelve tribes of Israel as they poured into the assembly area. When the streams dwindled to the final few gurgling trickles, Eleazar raised his hands for silence.

"Moses commanded us to take this census here on the plains of Moab. He has already returned to his mountaintop retreat, intent on finishing the Book of the Wanderings. The numbers are an important part of that story, therefore every man, twenty years and older in every tribe, was counted this morning. As we prepare to cross the Jordan and enter the land of our inheritance, the army of the Lord is more than six hundred thousand strong. The exact number is 601,730.

"Not one of these warriors was among those numbered in the desert of Sinai forty years ago—not one save Caleb, son of Jephunneh, and Joshua, son of Nun. They alone trusted that God would bring them safely into possession of the land. The word of the Lord declared that your fathers—the unbelieving Israelites of the last census—would surely die in the desert. Only the children would pass over into the Land of Promise. Now it has come to pass. It is time for this generation to take possession of Canaan."

There were no cheers. Acsah could see heads turning throughout the crowd, looking for the gray of ancient heads. But all were gone. She felt an overwhelming sense of loss.

"This land is God's land and we are the people of his covenant. Canaan is our inheritance, and it will be distributed according to this census taken today. The sections of Canaan will be distributed by lot among the larger and smaller groups—to a larger tribe, clan or family, a larger inheritance, and to smaller ones a smaller inheritance based on the number of those listed today. That will be your inheritance forever.

Reuben, the eldest son of Israel:
the children of Reuben;
Hanoch, of whom cometh the family of the Hanochites:
of Pallu, the family of the Palluites:
of Hezron, the family of the Hezronites:
of Carmi, the family of the Carmites.
These are the families of the Reubenites: and they that were numbered of them were forty and three thousand and seven hundred and thirty.

The sons of Simeon after their families:
of Nemuel, the family of the Nemuelites:
of Jamin, the family of the Jaminites:
of Jachin, the family of the Jachinites:
of Zerah, the family of the Zarhites:
of Shaul, the family of the Shaulites.
These are the families of the Simeonites,
twenty and two thousand and two hundred.

And the sons of Judah after their families . . .
of Shelah, the family of the Shelanites:
of Pharez, the family of the Pharzites:
of Zerah, the family of the Zarhites.
And the sons of Pharez were;
of Hezron, the family of the Hezronites;
of Hamul, the family of the Hamulites.
These are the families of Judah according to those that were numbered of them, threescore and sixteen thousand and five hundred.[12]

The rhythm of Eleazar's voice, as he called out the clans of each of the remaining twelve tribes and the total number of men in each, soothed Acsah with a warm feeling of belonging that eased the sting of loss. *These that remained, these were her people. They had been her family while wandering together, landless, in the wilderness. They would remain her family as they grew roots in Canaan.*

Caleb was standing beside her brothers a few feet away, strong and vigorous despite his white hair. Othniel had lost his father. Salmon and Abihail . . . most of her friends, in fact, lost theirs. She still had her Abba. How could she not be grateful for that?

His gray-green eyes caught hers and crinkled in a fleeting smile before moving on to her cousin and Jonathan, saluting each with a quick lift of his wild white brows. Her losses were insignificant compared to his, yet he listened this report, the replacement of his generation, with serene acceptance. She was a beneficiary of his faithfulness.

When Eleazar finished reciting the numbers of the twelve tribes, he paused to survey the families of his own tribe, the guard posted around the tabernacle. His voice grew even more intimate and affectionate. "This census has been taken to number the warriors ready to serve in the army of the Lord. The descendants of Levi, the third son of Leah, have not been included in the numbered tribes for they are not part of that army. For this reason, we Levites will not receive an inheritance as you will. In fulfillment of the prophecy of our father Jacob, we will be scattered among the tribes. But that fate has been transformed to a blessing by the faithfulness of the Levites at Sinai. Our tribe will not be absorbed and lost, but will serve you as your priests and teachers. The Levites are a gift to all the tribes from the Lord. The number of our males, a month old or more, is 23,000."

Amid the roar of responses, Acsah thought she heard a faint choking rasp beside her. It could have been Jonathan. There was an uncharacteristic tightness to his jaw, but he did not return her glance. It was definitely not Othniel. She shrugged and turned her attention back to the proceedings.

Eleazar raised his hands for silence again. "Moses will address us all when he completes his writing. In the meantime, the Lord will not leave us with idle hands." He smiled grimly. "Joshua."

The silver-haired captain lifted his chin high. He scanned the throng briefly, his eyes keen and intense, his head moving slightly to the left and then to the right, assessing his surroundings like a wolf sniffing the air. When he finally spoke, he barked his announcement in clipped phrases, a strong, urgent tone that contrasted sharply with Eleazar's and quickly stirred the crowd to full attention.

"The vengeance of Yahweh will fall on Midian. God has commanded his army. Twelve thousand men, one thousand from each tribe."

If Moses is the lion, Acsah thought, *Joshua is the wolf. The pack listens when he speaks.*

"Yahweh bids us exact retribution for our dead, for all those who died of plague. Even for the covenant breakers. Even for the rebels who suffered the consequences of their rebellion. All this death resulted from the treachery of that desert people. We deemed the descendants of Midian our brothers and sisters, but their women slipped into our camp with the cunning of vipers. Now their day of judgment has come, and Phinehas will lead the troops."

Joshua stopped abruptly. He faded into the shadows before the crowds realized that he had finished, and Phinehas, aglow in white linen, stepped into the pool of sunlight he vacated.

"Hear, O Israel. You are the army of God," he called out with authority, "chosen to lift up his holy name in the earth."

Acsah clutched at her chest in awe. Phinehas was no longer simply one youth among her group of friends. In one day, he had risen to his place as a leader in Israel. Handsome, almost kingly with his towering height and strong, chiseled features, he fully looked the part of the future high priest in the line of Aaron. The gleaming, gold emblem, attached to his turban and lying on his high forehead, said it all: "Holy to the Lord."

The young priest must have had the same effect on the entire crowd. Someone shouted, "Phinehas, son of Eleazar, holy to the Lord."

"Phinehas, future high priest in the line of Aaron," another called.

"Speak, Phinehas, and we will listen."

The name—Phinehas—*mouth of brass*—that had seemed strange when they were children, was wholly fitting today. Acsah clutched Jonathan's arm and her praise gushed out. "Can you believe that is your cousin? What a blessed gift to Israel."

Jonathan leaned close to her ear. "Didn't you hear Uncle Eleazar? All Levites are God's gift to Israel. So there you have it. I am God's gift to you."

"Jonathan, you are so silly." She giggled, but when she looked into his eyes, they were uncomfortably serious. Othniel's inscrutable gaze followed the exchange closely. She rolled her eyes and swished past her cousin, sidestepping her brothers, and found a place in the ever-comfortable company of her father. She was not about to let two socially inept young men ruin this momentous day.

Caleb grinned and pulled her close. "They are lifting up the name of Phinehas in quite different tones than they did yesterday, eh?"

She smiled and nodded. *Yes.*

"Hear, O Israel," Phinehas repeated. "Those numbered in this census make up an army of God more than 600,000 strong, but God has only called for twelve thousand to go up against Midian. The twelve tribal princes will serve as captains over thousands. Each of the twelve will draw ten lots, men to serve as—"

Someone called out, "Only twelve thousand? Every man here has lost family or friend because of these Midianites. Why not send the largest army we can muster?"

"That is not what God commanded," Phinehas retorted with flashing eyes. "We *will* obey the word of the Lord." He paused. If there was another who questioned God's plan, he dared not express it.

Acsah found her father's eyes. "Even his voice has a new ring of confidence," she whispered.

Caleb just beamed his approval.

"The captains of each division of one hundred will be chosen by lot. Each of those will select their one hundred men by lot. The chosen will receive a summons this afternoon to meet with the captains. The rest of you must help gather adequate arms to outfit your tribe's one thousand men. Tomorrow morning beginning at first light, Joshua will help me drill the divisions in our formations and fine-tune our strategies. We will rest on the Sabbath, setting out at sundown to cross the desert at night. We will strike the first of the Midianite towns with a surprise attack early on First Day morning."

Phinehas stepped closer to the crowds, holding out his hands in a gesture that reminded Acsah of his grandfather, Aaron. "Those who remain behind are still a war camp. Each day that we are gone, Eleazar will guide you through a time of community prayer following the evening and morning sacrifices." His voice was now as gentle as his father's. "This army must be fully committed and faithful to Yahweh, undaunted by danger, strong in the face of evil. We need your prayers."

Grandfather, father, and son, Acsah thought, *links of love and holiness connecting us to our God.*

Preparation Day was a busy one across the entire camp of Israel. As families busied themselves with the normal preparations for Sabbath, twelve thousand men drilled for war. Acsah found herself with twice as many chores as usual. She had gathered the double portion of manna and prepared food for both Preparation Day and Sabbath. She had drawn a double quantity of water from the river and stacked extra wood for the fire. She tended the animals. In the late afternoon, she was bustling busily inside the tent so everything would be in order for the holy day of rest when she heard a noisy throat-clearing just outside.

"Father, is that you?"

"It is only me," a tentative voice answered. "Othniel."

Acsah came to the tent entrance. "Father hasn't returned yet."

"I know. He volunteered to lead Judah in the place of Salmon since that family is in mourning for Prince Nashon. He and the other captains of thousands are having a last meeting with Phinehas."

Acsah studied her cousin with curious amusement. "Well then, this is a rare encounter. What can I do for you?"

"I was wondering . . ." He blushed slightly, tossing his head toward the sky. There was a blaze of tawny gold shot through with sunlight as the long, heavy hair fell back over Othniel's shoulders.

He continued gazing at the clouds as he spoke. "If I could . . . I, uh . . . I want to ask you . . ."

There was a long pause. This would be a serious request. Acsah steeled herself for a challenge.

"Could you . . . would you . . . help my mother while I am gone?" Othniel's voice was so low that she had to lean forward to hear.

Acsah checked the impulse to laugh. "Is that all? Of course."

Othniel looked down and stammered. "I . . . don't want to be a bother. I know . . . Uh, you will have a lot to do . . . since Caleb will be gone too."

"I am happy to do what I can to help." Acsah stretched her neck forward, trying to catch his eyes again, but they were lashed to his feet. "Aunt Sarah is family after all."

"She is worse than ever since Grandmother died. She can't seem to complete the simplest tasks around the tent, let alone care for the animals by herself."

"Othniel, I'm honored that you asked me, and I will do whatever I can."

When he slowly lifted his eyes to return her gaze, the low-slung sun lit them like the dark-rimmed pools of a forest. She was struck with certainty that wisdom resided there and knowledge worth pursuing, but he turned away, closing the window to his thoughts and emotions.

"Thank you," he mumbled as he hurried off.

From sundown to sundown, the Sabbath was a somber one as twelve thousand families prepared to send their men off to the deadly unknown of battle. Anxious thoughts of impending loss were relieved only a little when Moses returned to camp in time for the Sabbath eve sacrifice and addressed the people with a message of hope and assurance. The next morning and throughout the day, each clan clustered around the warriors who had been chosen to go to war. The newly installed elders in each tribe and family were nearly tongue-tied by inexperience as they attempted to remind the younger ones of God's mighty acts in the past on behalf of Israel, halting over stories that had been so familiar when their fathers told them. The faith of every family was stretched.

Acsah clung to her father most of the day, resenting any family members who engaged his attention. Now and then, throughout that long Sabbath, she sensed Othniel lingering nearby, watching her and her father, but he did not speak to either of them. At last the blazing evening sacrifice marked the close of the Sabbath. As Eleazar disappeared into the holy tabernacle with the evening incense offering, Acsah prayed with such urgency that her nails dug into the flesh of her clenched hands. *O Mighty Lord of angel armies, keep our losses small. There have been too many deaths. May our efforts to obey your command be as sweet in your nostrils as this incense is in ours, covering the stench of sin and blood and burning flesh.*

Then, as the sunset colors faded to the deep purple of bruises, the army left camp. Leaving the tabernacle, Acsah trailed behind Salmon, who walked with his arms around his mother and sister, all three of them hunched and desolate. She understood why her father had been chosen to *lead* Judah, but why was Salmon not included at all among the men who would administer God's justice? That would be the quickest road to recovery for her if she were in his place.

From there, her thoughts spiraled ever downward in disapproving analysis. *This is the first time Israel has ever sent out an army to attack. Why did God command that it be so small? He could have sent one hundred times more men and still have warriors aplenty left to protect the camp.* "Stop it," she said aloud as she reached her door. "You know better than to question the ways of Yahweh."

She was not hungry, but she took the two manna cakes remaining from her sixth-day baking. The rest she had given to her father. The fact that manna would not keep overnight except for the Sabbath was a little miracle of God she had known all her life, reminding her week after week of Sabbath sacredness: special food for a special day. Special or not, this evening she had to force herself to eat. She had no desire to throw out a wormy mess tomorrow morning.

A rapidly multiplying set of stars jeweled the sky as the glow of the day faded. Normally, she watched the adorning of the night sky with joy and assurance. The stars told so many stories of deliverance. There above the eastern horizon was the Arrow directed at the heart of the Scorpion. Tonight it seemed more alarming than reassuring. She shivered and closed the tent flap against the chill of the night. She sat in the semidarkness a moment. It was too early for bed, and her head spun with worry. *I will not succumb to this dark mood. I will break out of it,* she told herself as she finished the last bite of her manna cake.

Before this is over, you may need your friend as well.

"But how, Abba?"

A picture of girlhood days with Abihail flashed into her mind, and suddenly she knew. *A walk along that flower-strewn meadow above the river. Tomorrow morning.* She lifted her hands in a gesture of submission and laughed aloud. "All right, Abba, this is for you. I'm lashing up my sandals. Actually, I'm already wearing my sandals, but I'm getting my cloak." Before she could change her mind, she threw the warm covering over her shoulders and set off to find her friend.

Abihail's face broke into dimpled delight as she agreed to meet Acsah following the morning chores. She clasped Acsah's hands. "It will be like the old days when we were children. Time to walk and talk. I have missed you so much."

"Like the old days," Acsah mused aloud. *Was that not just a few short weeks ago? Before the plague, before the wedding, before the day of the victory celebration.* It seemed like years ago now, and this friendship might be just what she needed to recapture that joy. Simply planning such a time together was a warm dose of medicine for the chill in her soul.

"See you in the morning then." She gave Abihail a quick hug, and then as she walked away, she pulled her cloak tight to hold in the warmth of love. Just before she turned the first corner, she took one last look back. Abihail was still watching from her tent doorway looking so happy. *My dear Abba, you always know what is best.*

As soon as she entered the tent, however, the door covering flapped softly closed, blocking out the stars and extinguishing the warm glow in her spirit. The place had never felt so empty. A mournful night bird was calling in the distance as she slipped into bed and lay staring into the darkness.

Even when she drifted off to sleep at last, there was little rest. Vivid images chased each other through her dreams: Phinehas' medallion of holiness gleaming red-gold on his forehead as he led the army to war, one white-haired warrior leaving camp on the back of a donkey, the afterglow of sunset reflecting brightly on his back, twelve thousand foot soldiers following their captains, trudging up the steep hill in formation as dusk deepened to purple. Darker images rose like smoke: the faces of death carried out of camp on litters, crossed acacia branches, flames reaching skyward, and a blood-red moon leering through ragged shreds in the smoke shroud.

Picture the meadows and the sunlight, she told herself each time she awoke. *Picture the walk with Abihail. Feel the joy of her friendship.*

It was hopeless. The visions of plague and war stormed darkly through her dreams whenever she fell asleep, awakening her with stark fear and sweat. Over and over, with cold beads of perspiration drying on her forehead, she prayed for the army of Yahweh, prayed for Caleb, prayed for Phinehas, prayed for each friend by name until she fell into troubled sleep once more.

CHAPTER EIGHT

THE MIDIANITE WAR

Phinehas

The moon-silvered wilderness stretched gradually upward, ending where a long slow swell in an ocean of desert met the horizon. Beyond that, Phinehas could see nothing. Undoubtedly, the land would drop to another seemingly endless stretch of sparse grasslands. He did not expect to reach Midianite settlements for several more hours, but he could not afford to be careless. "Let's ride ahead again and see what's over that rise," he said quietly.

The sound, guarded as it was, seemed to him recklessly loud in the silence of this place, but Jonathan shifted in his saddle with a broad grin, answering in full voice. "Right. We wouldn't want any surprises, would we? What if we encountered a fox or an owl in this desolate land?"

Phineas stiffened at the jaunty self-assurance so out of keeping with the gravity of their mission. He hoped he had not made a mistake by giving in to his cousin's pleas to come along as his aide.

"We need to push our foot soldiers as fast as possible in order to reach the first town before dawn, but a responsible commander . . ." Here, he gave his cousin a pointed look. "Needs to know what lies ahead lest he march his whole army into a hornet's nest."

Jonathan nodded, his white teeth still glinting in the moonlight. Phinehas exhaled audibly. The indomitable smile was beginning to annoy him. He glanced over his shoulder at the swift-moving shadows following behind. They had been giving this march all they had since dusk and still they pressed tirelessly on. Wonder and dread shivered through him. Just a few days previously, he could not have conceived of any of this. The deceit of the prophet Balaam, the wholesale apostasy of the princes and elders of Israel, the treachery of Zimri and Cozbi, and least of all, this assignment given to a high priest in training.

"What are Levites like you and I *doing* here?" he whispered into the night. With no expectation of an answer, he urged his donkey into a gallop with a light kick.

Jonathan didn't miss a beat. "Riding donkeys at the head of Israel's army, I believe," he replied with mock seriousness, his donkey matching his cousin's stride for stride. "And a small, but fine army it is. Twelve thousand foot soldiers plus twelve, noble division commanders, led by the noble *us*."

Phinehas was losing patience with the flippant responses. "I'm serious. This whole mission is . . . We're Levites, you know. I mean, any one of these men behind us is more qualified to do this than either of us. While I was learning the fine points of ministering sacrifices and you were immersed in the book of the law, the rest of the tribes were mastering the craft of warfare."

Jonathan had not stopped grinning. "I can wield a sword as well as most, and you certainly proved your skill with the javelin."

Phinehas winced. He pushed his little beast on ahead to escape the maddening grin and called over his shoulder, "Hardly skill. Just protecting the camp and the tabernacle of Yahweh. That's all our basic weapons training was intended . . . What's this?" Phinehas interrupted himself as he crested the hill. An endless expanse of black tents darkened the plain beyond. He reigned in his donkey and signaled for Jonathan to halt, but his cousin, riding just a pace behind, jerked to a stop so suddenly that the nose of his little beast slammed against Phinehas' thigh. Jonathan stared at the tents, rows and rows of them marching to the horizon. "God save us."

Phinehas surveyed his cousin's suddenly sober face with self-satisfied amusement. "Still glad you begged to come along as my aide?"

"Midian already on the move." Jonathan was whispering now. "It is too late for a surprise attack on the towns."

"Summon the twelve."

Jonathan wheeled his donkey around, galloping frantically back down the slope into the ranks of foot soldiers in search of the twelve tribal commanders.

In no time, Phinehas found himself scanning a circle of fear-darkened eyes. He found a sort of dark humor in the speed with which a subdued Jonathan managed to assemble the twelve men.

"The warriors of Midian have saved us the trouble of finding them." he said sardonically.

"There are more tents here than in all Israel, and we come with only twelve thousand men." It was Palal of Asher. His youthful chin showed only a hint of beard.

"Per . . . haps we should retreat before they see us," lean-faced Jared of Dan stammered. "They will chew us up and spit out our bones."

"The Lord's strength does not depend on numbers," Phinehas replied curtly. "I wonder though . . . If I were commanding that army, I would sweep down into the valley from two sides. Easier to crush the Israelite camp in a pair of deadly jaws."

"We must warn them!" young Ornan of Naphtali cried.

"We must get help. You cannot ask us to face this Midianite horde with less than every fighting man in Israel." This voice sounded more angry than alarmed, but Phinehas could not see which of the captains was speaking.

This time Caleb cut off the speech. "God has given us exactly what we need: twelve thousand under the direction of Phinehas. Trust God in this, my sons."

Phinehas nodded. *Good old Caleb. If his twelve commanders wavered, how would he get the common soldiers to respect and obey him? Lord of the heavenly hosts, give me a plan that will inspire them to follow.* "I was pondering the possibility of this being but half of the fighting force," he mused hesitantly, "but I am reluctant to divide . . ."

Caleb's demeanor was unruffled, almost serene. "May I suggest scouts? Perhaps, my nephew Othniel and one of his companions. The boy has senses like a beast of prey. If there is another army of this size moving against Israel from the northeast, he will easily sniff them out and be back before first light with the report."

"Excellent idea." Phinehas felt the knot in his stomach loosen. He was so grateful for the wisdom and capability of the old war hero. Humble as Caleb was, willing to support and follow a young inexperienced priest, there was no greater warrior in all Israel other than Joshua himself.

He turned to give Jonathan the order and almost laughed at the lines crisscrossing the troubled young brow. *Where was that grin now?* "Courage, cousin. We're the army of the Lord. Find Othniel and Ethan. I need to see them now. Right here."

As Jonathan rushed off to retrieve Othniel and Ethan, another of the captains began to grumble. "Our numbers are too small. If this is not the entire Midianite army . . ."

Phinehas could sense the weight of the gold medallion on his forehead. His duty was to see that this army unerringly carried out the orders of the Lord and somehow, personally, to maintain the perfect holiness of the priesthood. He did not reply but fixed his eyes on the grumbler. His captain did not miss the look and fell silent.

Dropping his voice so low the twelve were forced to press close to hear the words, Phinehas laid out the battle strategy. "We will strike this encampment silently from every side within the hour. God has given us this opportunity to surprise our enemy while they yet slumber." His mouth relaxed into a grim smile. "We will be a bad dream from which many will never awake."

Phinehas proceeded with his orders, brusquely and systematically. "Judah will attack from here in the center. Jared, move your men into position across that knoll over there. Ornan, take your men to that patch of broom beyond them. Palal . . ." The young captains nodded approvingly. His own confidence in this hastily adapted plan increased in response to the support of his men. By the time, he had assigned each captain a position, his assistant had returned.

"Jonathan, light the captains' torches with fire from the holy censer. Captains, shield your flame from view until your entire force is in place. When your tribe is in position and ready, raise the flame of holy light high as a signal. Work quickly. Not till I have counted all twelve lights ringing the dark tents of Midian, will I signal the attack."

Acsah

Morning chores were completed, and Acsah wandered to the river's edge to wait for Abihail. The sun, warm on her face, was quickly drying the dew-wet grass at her feet. The twittering of birds rising from the thickets of the zor mingled with the silver sound of the river. Breathing in the earthy freshness of the morning was like diving into an ocean of peace and joy.

"Sorry I'm late. Mara needed help." Abihail's words were a happy intrusion. Her cheeks, flushed by the exertion of running, were a healthy red again and her eyes gleamed with vibrant life. "I have not only taken on a husband to care for, but now it seems, a mother-in-law as well. I wonder if Mara will *ever* regain her former strength."

Acsah brushed excuses aside and took her friend's hands. Life-long affection diffused warmly through her veins again at the touch. Forgiveness had bestowed healing, surprising and deep. "Thank you for coming. A day with you will be good medicine for a heavy heart." She stepped back and viewed Abihail approvingly. "You are your beautiful self again."

"Oh, it's good for me to be out here. I feel so alive." Abihail stretched out her arms and whirled around. Then she stopped, mid-twirl, her face suddenly solemn. "I hope we never have to endure anything like that plague again."

"The morning is far too glorious to spend dwelling on dark times," Acsah said. "Let's walk along the river this way." Walking, however, was impossible this morning. She skipped off, but within a few hops, stopped short in a knee-high patch of yellow blossoms, stooping to uncurl a coiled stem. "Aren't they wonderful? Tiny shepherd's crooks covered in even tinier golden trumpets."

Abihail nodded as she bent beside her. "Now I don't miss the anemones so much. Gold replaces red. Who would have thought that common grass and rock could produce such splendor?"

Acsah rose to her feet. "I have a lot to learn about this cycle of flowers. When those first red anemones faded, I was literally grieving. It seemed we had left the dead scenes of the desert only to discover that Canaan would not be much different."

"Not you alone. A lot of us reacted similarly to the loss. Those flowers were like crimson jewels nestled around our tents when we set up camp. Symbols of the rich inheritance God was giving us. We expected it to stay that way."

Acsah laughed. "I can't wait for Abba to return so I can tell him what I learned from the flowers."

"That there will always be new blessings?"

"Yes, and more. Looking forward with expectation . . . *and* letting God run things *his* way. Even thanking him for blessings that fade away instead of grumbling about the loss."

"That's deep, Acsah." Abihail giggled with the same carefree laughter Acsah had known since they were toddlers. "Even your father will be impressed."

As the girls proceeded northward following the margin of the zor, the morning shadows shrank. The bird chorus diminished to an occasional tweet as little feathered wings darted to hiding places deeper in the thick foliage of the Jordan jungle. All at once an allegro sonata of *chi-wit, chi-wit, chi-wit* called the girls out onto a hummock of pale marlstone with an open view of the river where a flock of small yellow birds bathed in the spray along the bank. As Abihail crept closer, a pebble dislodged by her toe clattered down into the ravine and the bathing party ended in an explosion of yellow wings.

The birds disappeared into dense foliage, and although the girls waited as silent and unmoving as the riverbank, they did not return. After awhile, Abihail whispered, "Kings of the earth could learn from those little creatures. They are rich with gold and use it to bring joy all around, but their adornment is drab—only gray crowns and black bibs. Kings hide their gold away in vaults except for their crowns and the jangling chains they drape around their necks."

Feeling like children once again, Abihail and Acsah clambered up and down the rocky edge of the ravine, at times scrambling along on a level with the meadow and then scuttling partially down into the zor closer to the muddy Jordan twisting along its serpentine path through luxuriant foliage. The sun was straight above them when Acsah silently pointed to the pale stone walls of a city set luxuriantly in a grove of palms in the hazy distance beyond the river.

"I wonder what those people are thinking about our people," Abihail whispered.

Acsah nodded but said nothing.

"I mean, what will happen when we cross the river?"

"Only God knows," Acsah breathed. She dropped down and wiggled into a slight depression on a water-smoothed outcropping. Relaxing with her back against sun-warmed stone, she gazed thoughtfully at the city.

Abihail plopped down beside her and opened the lunch pouch. "Shall we eat here?" Without waiting for an answer, she handed Acsah a manna cake and a cluster of dried grapes.

Acsah stared at the palm groves around the Canaanite city across the river as she munched the crispy pan-fried cake. "The most luxuriant of the oases we found in the desert could not support so many trees. How many springs do you think they have?"

Abihail shrugged, but her eyes sparkled, "You can count springs if that is what excites you. I want to see what their houses are like. Can't you just imagine the beautiful things they have?"

Acsah pulled a sweet, shriveled grape off the dry stem with her teeth. "Mmmm, so good. For me just living in a land of such bounty is enough. Cities and stone houses do not intrigue me. I would be quite content to live out my life in the airy openness of our tent."

"Not me. I want to live in a real house."

The deep, gulping cry of a bittern sounded a sudden summons. Acsah tightened her lips in a closed smile and looked at Abihail out of the corner of her eye. "Did you hear the invitation to visit *her* home? I think I'd like to take her up on it. The oleanders are glorious, and who knows what mysteries wait to be discovered in that dense green thicket?"

Abihail's eyes opened wide with alarm. "It *is* beautiful, but it's hardly safe. The people of that city might find us, and . . . There may be beasts lurking in the shadows. Eliab says that he has heard lions and hyenas down there at night. No exploring for me. I will just enjoy the beauty from here."

"You are right, but it intrigues me just the same. Besides, don't forget the lesson of Baal-Peor. Our greatest danger comes from the idol-worshiping people of this land and their gods, not the wild beasts."

Abihail tucked the empty lunch bag in her belt. "O Acsah, I am so grateful that Yahweh granted us a fresh start. His blessings astound me: the fruit of this land, our daily manna, and His great mercy even when we fail to keep our half of the covenant."

The girls stretched out on their backs, enjoying the heat of the sun-warmed rock, nearly dozing in the silent serenity of the afternoon until a high-pitched yapping and growling surrounded them. In flashes of red, four fox kits rolled and tumbled past, wrestling their way down the slope. Acsah and Abihail sat up as one, spontaneously motioning each other to keep silent and tightening their lips to stifle any laughter as they watched those furry, fighting bundles.

There was a moment of panic when a quick, deep growl sounded close by. Then the mother fox, carrying a dead rabbit in her mouth, moved protectively between her little ones and the girls. She threatened them with another throaty growl and then barked a command that drove the foursome back to their den. As soon as the little fox family disappeared, the pent up mirth bubbled out and the girls fell back on the rocks laughing. When the merriment was spent, Acsah took a deep breath, gazing contentedly at the sky.

"Remember when we played with the same carefree abandon as those little foxes? It seems like such a long time ago."

"But it wasn't. Not much more than a year ago, we still enjoyed the freedom of children. Then that slithering viper killed my father . . . and my mother gave up and died of her broken heart."

Acsah was quiet for a while. "I feel so blessed to still have my father when so many of you have lost your parents."

"I do feel the loneliness sometimes, but I am blessed to have Eliab—and he loves his orphan girl."

Acsah did not answer. Puffy clouds drifted across the sky like a hundred sheep grazing in a blue meadow. "I never get tired of watching the changing sky here in this valley," she murmured lazily.

"Nor I. The wilderness sky was the same every day, stark blue outside our great sheltering cloud."

"But, praise Yahweh for shielding us in the desert."

"Acsah, I was just thinking about the first real memory I have of you. Do you remember that day when rainstorms caused the desert to bloom almost overnight?"

"Yes. You and I . . . we couldn't have been much more than three or four years old. We were gathering flowers and sticking them in the sand."

"You decided that we were making 'Canaan Land.' Do you remember? We formed houses by heaping up little piles of sand, squaring them off, and surrounding them with flowers."

"Until your brother Jezliah came by with Jamin and Eliab and started stomping them down."

"Eliab was laughing and stomping around like a naughty little boy, but the two older ones frightened me."

"I remember. You ran away and hid."

"While *you* stood up to them. I could hear you lecturing them from my hiding place."

Acsah smiled to herself. "I was so self-righteous. I remember telling them that being cruel and destroying 'Canaan' was breaking the covenant. Yahweh would throw them out of Israel if they didn't stop."

Abihail giggled at the memory. "You were amazing even then."

"Well, I didn't have much effect on the older boys. Before they ran off, they pushed me down on the last of our little sand houses and laughed, 'Oops, there goes the last of Canaan.' I grabbed a big stick and chased them clear to the tents of Levi even though I had no idea what I would do if I caught them."

"Eliab stayed behind to help us rebuild." Abihail was silent for a while. "That was the day I fell in love with him. He came and found me where I was hiding and held out a handful of flowers. It was so sweet, but all I could do was cry."

"And I ran smack into Phinehas and Jonathan." Acsah paused, remembering. "When I explained what had happened, Phinehas said he would come and stand guard. Of course, it sounded like an adventure to Jonathan so he came too." Acsah chuckled. "So you found the love of your life, and I found the priests and Levites."

"Well, at the time, that was important. I wasn't afraid of Jezliah and Jamin when we had our own priest guard."

"I felt pretty smug, too, having a tall, older boy like Phinehas on our side. Who would have dared to attack *him*?"

Abihail's look was distant and dreamy as she retreated into her favorite memory. "While we rebuilt the 'houses,' Eliab kept running back and forth, gathering more and more blossoms off the desert shrubs and bringing them to me."

"And Jamin and Jezliah never did come back to bother us."

Abihail sat up and looked at her friend sharply. "To be perfectly honest, Jamin scares me a little even today."

"Really?" Acsah sat up too and scrambled to her feet. "I don't trust him either. Eliab seems so different from the rest of his family."

"It's true. I avoid Jamin as much as I do Achor. Sometimes I think even Eliab is a little afraid of his family, his mother included."

She got up and brushed the grass from her cloak. "Acsah, do you ever wish we could just go back to the desert—you know, return to the easy way of life we had as children?"

"On the brink of the Promised Land?" Anticipation shimmered through her. "Who would want to go back? An adventure lies ahead of us."

"But the camp has been so safe all our lives . . . until now. We always knew just what to do, and no one tried to entice us away from Yahweh."

"Well, no one could entice *me* away from him. You just have to be strong." Acsah got up and took an arching leap from their stony lunch table to a patch of soft grass. "It's time to head back to camp."

Abihail scrambled to catch up. "Acsah, it has been so good to enjoy a day with you again. It was devastating to feel your anger."

"I wish I didn't get angry so fast. Anyway, I am glad you are out of the clutches of that evil. So what did you do with the Midianite gifts?"

"I packed them away for now. I will use them to make my home beautiful someday. And when I see them, I will remember that we must always be faithful to the covenant."

"If I were you, I would burn them."

"But you won't be mad at me if I don't? I just could not destroy such beauty." Her dimples flashed in a mischievous smile. "It would be like the boys stomping on our beautiful 'Canaan.'"

Acsah gave her a quick hug. "I will always love you, my dear, dear friend, no matter what."

Phinehas

The sun was up. The battle ended. Enemy dead included two of the five kings. Phinehas surveyed the scene with satisfaction. It was still chaos, but a quieter, safer kind. Soldiers were pulling up the last remaining tent stakes, folding the black goat hides, and binding them in bundles with their tent cords. Others were bundling the weapons and usable articles of clothing they had stripped from the dead, packing them onto ox carts already loaded with barley beer, cheese, flat bread, and bushels of parched grain and strips of dried goat meat. The very carts that carried supplies to sustain the Midianite army would carry their plunder. Phinehas snorted at the irony.

Jonathan galloped back to him just then. "Do you find humor in death, destruction, and discomfort? Or does it merely amuse you to think of errand after errand to send your cousin on?"

"What?"

"What next?" Jonathan tilted his head and raised his brows in an impatient prompt.

"Nothing," Phinehas laughed. "No more messages. You can go rest if you would like. Get some sleep if you can, we still have a long day ahead of us."

"Sleeping wouldn't be fair while others still work so hard." He waved his hand in a sweeping arc across their view of the field. "Besides, I'm too riled up to sleep."

"Well, I would rest if I could. I'm exhausted although I can't tell you why."

"Why wouldn't you be? You are the commander."

Phinehas shook his head slowly. "The twelve thousand endured the long march on foot. They charged into the fray as soon as we could organize, brandishing weapons, dodging attacks, responding to my orders, fighting till nearly dawn. They had no chance to rest, and they are cleaning up the field as we speak. Their commander? Here in the saddle, pretty much where I was hours ago before the battle began."

Jonathan rolled his eyes. "Your mind has worked harder than any of us. I know because I carried those thoughts to your captains, riding back and forth, back and forth."

"Ho! Over here." Phinehas abandoned the trivial banter, kicked his donkey's sides lightly, and trotted toward his scouts. He acknowledged them with a nod and simply their names. "Othniel . . . Ethan."

"Just as you suspected, Phinehas," Othniel began without ceremony, "there is an equally large force of Midianites north of us. That way about three hour's ride."

Othniel pointed as if Phinehas did not know which direction was north, his face as impassive as if he were describing the location of a watering hole.

Ethan's furrowed brow hinted at the need for urgency. "They were beginning to stir as we left the area," he added quickly.

"Their plan," Othniel continued with thoughtful consideration, "is, undoubtedly, to set out toward Bashan at first light. If we march hard from here without delay, swinging west as well as north, we can intercept them within two hours."

"Jonathan, summon Ira, Heled, and Abiel. I'll send their divisions on ahead immediately. God willing, we can surprise that Midianite division as we did this one."

Othniel's amber eyes, wide-set above prominent cheekbones, were grave. "I don't believe there will be an element of surprise."

"I suspect you are right," Phinehas said, stroking his chin thoughtfully. "I had hoped to choose the ground for the next battle."

"Perhaps the surprise will be the discovery that their backup force does not have their back," Jonathan added cheerfully, "and that we have cut off retreat back to their towns."

Phinehas did not grace his cousin's happy assessment with even the hint of a smile. "After you have notified the captains of Reuben, Gad, and Manasseh, ignite those piles of corpses with the censer of the Lord. If no element of surprise, perhaps the smoke of funeral pyres will add the element of fear."

Jonathan grinned with a joy ill-suited to the assigned task and lifted his chin in a snappy salute. "At last you give me something to do beyond delivering messages."

"So tell me what you learned, Othniel. Numbers? Camels? Terrain?"

"That division is much like this one. The corral included countless numbers of camels as well as oxen for nearly as many supply wagons as you rounded up here. They are evidently prepared for a long campaign."

Phinehas suddenly realized that Jonathan had remained beside him to listen. "Get going, cousin, or we'll not catch the enemy before they reach our people."

"Phinehas, please. Let me fight this time," Jonathan begged. He patted his weapon. "My sword was itching to leave its scabbard all through this long night."

"Killing is not play," Phinehas replied softly. The image of Cozbi's face flashed up and remained frozen in his mind. *Could he ever forget the look of pure hatred and terror as he drove the javelin through Zimri's lower back into her belly?* "Go," he commanded and waved Jonathan off.

"The terrain becomes more rugged as you move north." Othniel resumed his report to the drumming hoofbeats of Jonathan's donkey. "I could discern but one road down from the highlands that would be suitable for their ox carts. If we are fast enough, we might be able to establish a foothold on high ground to the west of them along that road before they detect us and set up their own welcoming party. If you like, Ethan and I can guide . . ."

"Othniel! Ethan!" Jonathan interrupted from halfway down the slope. The censer of holy fire swung crazily in his outstretched hand after his abrupt stop. "You missed quite the spectacle. A wild stampede. We shooed all the surviving camels back into the desert." The flash of his white teeth was visible even from this distance. "No surprise, you say? Hah! Wait till those droves of hairy beasts arrive home without a single rider. Now that *will* be surprise!" He cackled like an old crone as he turned and galloped away.

Hours later, Ethan guided Phinehas and the main body of troops into a shallow valley where the vanguard had stationed themselves in hastily-formed lines at the base of a mounding hill. The Midianite army stood shoulder to shoulder at the top, and both groups appeared to be waiting for him. *Surprise,* Phinehas mused. *The surprise is that Midian waited for us to arrive. Did they think our initial three thousand were bait for a trap? A miscalculation perhaps that saved them from slaughter.*

Phinehas set up his fielding station on a large rock platform shielded by thorn bushes on three sides. From this downslope vantage point, Phinehas could view the whole of the Midianite line. He sent charge after charge driving straight up the center, then from the left, and then the right. As soon as one battalion was repulsed, he sent another. He dispatched distracting feints. He drove boldly into apparent points of weakness. Jared of Dan nearly reached the top at the extreme left, but again the enemy drove him back with long cruel swords before he could establish a solid toehold. The blessing was that he made it back down at all.

The scene replayed itself over and over no matter which route he chose, the Midianites defending their high ground like a fiendish living wall. Although more and more black-garbed bodies littered the hillside, a seemingly endless supply of fresh warriors continued to fill the gaps.

Phinehas sucked in a deep breath of spicy, sweet incense from the smoldering censer at his feet. *We didn't choose this battle, Lord. You sent us here, yet the Midianites continue to hack their way down the ridge, driving back every charge I send against them. Your day of judgment is about to go down in defeat. I do not have the skills for this.*

Drumming hoofbeats announced that Jonathan was galloping back to the command post again. Each time Jonathan sped off to this tribal prince or that with an adjustment in strategy, Phinehas's own donkey brayed his disapproval at being left behind. Now she nickered her greeting and stretched her nose toward the returning pair. Phinehas reached out and patted the fuzzy heads of both beasts as they nuzzled each other. *You spoke through Balaam's donkey, Lord. Couldn't you send a message through one of these?*

Jonathan remained waiting expectantly in his saddle. When he received no new orders he fairly shouted, "The Midianites are poised to pour down any slope of the hill, at any time."

"I believe that is obvious to everyone on the battlefield," Phinehas muttered. "There is no way to outflank them. There is no way to strike from the rear. I have run out of options." He was not certain whether he addressed himself, the donkeys, Jonathan, or Almighty Yahweh. He could not bring himself to look at his cousin. "I have no more messages for you."

Jonathan scrambled off his donkey, tying it to the thorn bushes beside its companion. The donkeys continued their affectionate nuzzling as Jonathan took up a silent post beside Phinehas. His cousin's support was comforting, but what he desperately needed was guidance. "If only I had the breastplate with the Urim and

Thummim, the glowing stones of *light* and *perfection*, to clearly show the will of Yahweh."

Jonathan picked up the censer and swung it in slow circles. "There is a lot of black cluttering that field. How many do you think they have lost?" he asked.

"More to the point, what is left of our twelve thousand? And how much longer can we sustain repeated frontal assaults?"

Jonathan continued swirling the cloud of incense in front of them. He seemed to be praying silently.

Balaam

Side by side atop the ridge, Balaam and King Zur watched the fighting from the backs of their camels. Zur had planned the military campaign with the prophet's approval. Now he had lost nearly half his division and the remainder were losing their nerve. *Advance, retreat. Advance, retreat. Back and forth, back and forth like the lapping of the tide. Midian pushes down, but Israel comes back —as unceasing as the tide. This should not be happening.* The prophet's camel swayed beneath him, amplifying the nauseating waves of anxiety.

At the center of the battlefield, King Evi sent his crack division of mounted camel cavalry stampeding downslope once more, but Balaam didn't need an oracle from the gods to know that this would be another futile surge. He watched the assault slam against the enemy with a force that should have broken through, but again like an ocean wave against a rock, the formation shattered, camels and riders fleeing the flashing blades of mere foot soldiers. Evi did not disguise his fury. He plunged his camel into the retreat, venting the full force of his frustration with a long arching swing of his scimitar on the commander who failed. A bright plume of blood looped into the air along with the unfortunate commander's head, a clear message to the remainder of the rattled riders.

Suddenly, the same frustration broke out close beside him. King Zur shrieked maniacal curses at his foot soldiers. "Reverse that retreat with the points of your blades," he roared at his captains. His reaction was just as hysterical as Evi's, though less messy.

A few moments later on the far side of the Midianite position, the downward thrust of King Rekem's charge broke. As his division withdrew incoherently back to the ridge, Rekem leaped from his camel, screeching and kicking sand in his front-line commander's face as he fell on his own sword before his king. "I don't want your blood. I want theirs!"

The impasse was wearing the edges off the sanity of the three kings. Their captains were not incompetent. Something else was going on. *Open my eyes, O Baal. This is your war for survival in this land, not the mere grasping for power by ambitious kings. This is your plan.* Then as if a cloud had been swept away from his eyes, Balaam spotted the priest. "I see. I see," he shouted jubilantly. Ignoring Zur's scowl, he sent for the other two kings.

Evi drove his camel recklessly through the masses of reserve troops on the ridge top, black-robed foot soldiers scattering before him like bats from their cavern. Balaam's confidence wavered momentarily in the face of such anger and the screams of outrage and agony rising from the trampled wake of the king's fury. He stabilized his certainty with another glance at the priest. He watched the assistant hand him the smoking censer before mounting his donkey and riding off to deliver another message to a harried Israelite captain. There was no question that he had located the source of their superhuman resistance, but it would require all his diplomatic cunning to regain the trust of these hotheaded kings.

King Evi reigned in his camel nose to nose with Balaam's. "Tell me, sage seer, what *do* you see?"

"Trust that I do see. And very well." Balaam carefully masked his contempt of one with so little self-control. "You are all brilliant commanders. Your troops are feared throughout the region, yet you do not prevail against the weakest of the weak today. I am not a commander, but I can see that we must rethink our strategy. O, trust me. The seer sees."

He lifted himself in his stirrups to hail the approach of the third king. "King Rekem," he called, forcing a broad smile.

"How long can an infestation of mice continue assaulting a bear and not be mauled to oblivion?" Rekem wailed without acknowledging the greeting. He mopped the beads of perspiration from his brow. "If only Hur and Reba were here to attack from the rear. Have you no power to summon them from afar?"

"It is not Hur and Reba that we need," the prophet responded confidently. "We already have the advantage: good ground, greater numbers, superior weapons . . . and yet we do not prevail. I am convinced that all the forces of Reba and Hur, even Moab and Jericho, and all the armies of southern Midian added to our numbers would not make a difference. Yahweh has risen in defense of Israel again.

"My physical eyesight is as keen as my prophetic eye. Look to the eastern horizon. The smoke rising there is a portent of doom for our companions. Did the Israelite army not approach from that direction, precisely the position of Reba and Hur's forces? Even if I could summon your fellow kings, I believe it is too late for them to respond."

The three kings turned toward the east. While Rekem and Zur paled in silence, Evi's glowering look deepened. "So our great seer admits that he is a failure yet again. I thought *the plan* could not fail."

"The plan has not failed," Balaam replied calmly. "I believe Israel attacks with so small an army because this is all that remains who have not bowed the knee to Baal. These few are still bound in covenant to Yahweh. It does not take a seer to see that our blades bounce off their bodies without inflicting damage. Their power emanates from that young priest down there." He paused to let his words sink in.

"I'm not a warrior of renown as you are. I'm a mere seer, but hear the words of my mouth, for this is the vision of Balaam son of Beor:

I see a smoking censer linking Israel's priest to the mind of Yahweh,
I see a youth in white linen racing back and forth from the priest to his captains.

I see the messages thwart our every offensive.
I see that the tide turns when that messenger arrives
    and our advances become retreats.
Through that priest, Yahweh commands this army.

"We are undone," Rekem cried in despair. "The remnant of Israel that survived Cozbi's revolution is stronger than our entire army."

Balaam squared his shoulders authoritatively. "Ordinary tactics will not prevail, but the Israelites have foolishly left their priest with no guards, only that single rider, relaying messages from Yahweh. All we need to do is eliminate him and take charge of his censer."

"But how? We obviously can't charge down the hill to his position. We can't get past their first line."

"O my kings, hear me. Prepare for one grand assault. All the remaining troops on this hill. Rekem will advance with his foot soldiers from the west while I myself lead King Zur's division down from the east. At the same time, Evi will charge straight down the center with his entire mounted division. Hold nothing back."

"How is that different from the surges we've launched all day, other than that it will consume all our reserves?"

"Ah, this. This will be the difference. Zur, as father of Queen Cozbi of Israel, you will have the honored assignment. While our diversion engages these swarming vermin, take one bodyguard and slip down the gulch on the backside of this hill. Circle around as secretively as you can to the priest's rocky table and make it an altar of sacrifice to Baal. After you have slain the priest and his messenger, set the bodies ablaze. Let this rabble army see and despair. Then, bring the censer to me."

"I have little faith in your *seeing* at this point," Evi grumbled. "Look at the bodies littering this slope. Do you see any that are not garbed in black? Would you have us lose our entire army?"

"We have no other option," Rekem wailed. "They do not break or bend. If we must lose every man in our combined army to get that priest and win the day, so be it." His face was a mask of despair, but Balaam had won him over.

King Zur grinned at his good fortune. "I accept the honor of my assignment. Our friend is seeing clearly. I am certain of it."

"O yes. My eyes are unquestionably open." Balaam dismounted his camel stiffly. He much preferred the soft Babylonian cushions with which he saddled his donkey to this hard Midianite seat. He was saddle sore, but faith in the plan tingled through every nerve and sinew like the crackling spidery branches of summer lightning. He grinned up at the three kings. Even Evi's face had softened.

"Once we have that censer, we will be unstoppable."

Phinehas

Phinehas stared blankly at the battlefield, keenly aware of his cousin's silent, supportive stance by his side. No more strategies came to mind. No messages for his troops. No answers to his prayers. A scornful laugh escaped through his nose. "We are not our grandfathers, are we? No plagues to unleash, no miraculous midnight deliverance, no dividing of the sea into an open path."

"We can pray side by side as they did," Jonathan said quietly. He stooped down and rummaged through the supplies in the saddlebags for another package of incense. After he sprinkled the fragrant mixture over the live coals, he broke off a dry twig from the thorn bushes, crumpled it into tiny bits, and stirred the dying censer to life with a bronze fork. The flame flared with new vigor as he rose to his feet and a strength-giving aromatic cloud billowed around them again.

Phinehas did not even know what else to pray. Instead he grumbled. *Twelve thousand hapless Israelites will be slaughtered if you don't intervene, Lord. I have nothing left to offer—nothing to offer you or these twelve thousand. I don't understand why so many warriors remain in the Valley of Acacias, but twelve thousand is the number you sent with me. I only ask that you reveal your plan for deploying them. Arise to save us before it is too late.*

Suddenly, bestial screams rent the air. The ground shook and it seemed as if all the Midianite foot soldiers remaining on the summit were charging down against his men at once. They poured from both sides of the ridge, their long curved blades slicing and hewing like woodcutters gone mad. As Phinehas watched his troops stumble and fall back, courageously parrying off the attack, not breaking, not fleeing, camel riders crested the hill and entered the melee, slashing wildly from high on their saddles. He watched a black-bearded Midianite head fly high in the air, showering a mist of blood over the fighting. Obviously, the riders swung their weapons blindly with no regard to the identification of their prey. He watched a band of men from Asher dodge the hacking swords of black-robed foot soldiers only to turn and run back again, chased by the frothing teeth and trampling feet of the camels. With admiration, Phinehas noted many brave islands of defense forming in the sea of chaos.

Jonathan seized his arm, "Phinehas, please. I beg you! Give me leave to join my sword to that of my brothers. This must be the last charge of these barbarians and our final opportunity to win the victory."

Phinehas hesitated. "You are a Levite, not a warrior."

Jonathan ignored the argument. "Every Israelite is fully engaged in the fury of the battle. You said you no longer have orders for me to deliver to the captains, and who could receive them in this confusion?"

Phinehas nodded reluctantly. *Surely there could not be too many swords. Jonathan was willing, and Jonathan was needed.* "Give me the censer," he said, reaching out and grasping its golden chains even before Jonathan remembered that he held it.

As Jonathan sprinted up the hill, Phinehas waved the censer, surrounding his station with a thick cloud of holy smoke. He prayed he would not have to explain to Moses why his grandson, a Levite no less, had been killed in battle.

No need to worry, he laughed bitterly. *If the Lord does not intervene soon, none of us will return to Moses.*

Too soon, Jonathan was swallowed up in the fray near Othniel. Although Phinehas could no longer see his young cousin, Caleb seemed to appear in every opening between fighters. White hair flying like a breeze-tossed banner, the old warrior brandished his sword with lightning swift strokes. Sparks flew as bronze met bronze, shields cracked and flew from the hands of the enemy, even camels could not block his path. He watched amazed as Caleb drove his sword into the belly of a great beast, jumping back as it crumpled beneath its rider. He watched Caleb spring for the kill, dispatching the rider while he was still reeling from the fall. In spite of the ferocity of the enemy's downward push, the old hero was edging slowly upward toward the top of the ridge. All at once, Phinehas caught sight of Caleb's goal, the lanky form of the instigator of all this evil, Balaam himself.

Balaam, here? O Lord, do not let that man escape, he breathed.

While Caleb was working his way toward the red-bearded, devil prophet, Phinehas could see Balaam's protective ring of bodyguards loosen their circle, dropping back to lay a snare for the old captain. He watched them reform their noose around him. Caleb was fighting his way into a death trap at the heart of the battlefield, and there was not a single warrior of Israel nearby who was not hard pressed with life and death struggles of his own. He fought alone, and Phinehas did not have a messenger, even if a message could be sent into that confusion. He swung the censer on Caleb's behalf. There were no words for his fear.

Without warning, a steely whisper sighed behind him. Wheeling and ducking, he barely escaped the sword swishing across the top of his priestly turban and found himself staring into a pair of hate-filled black eyes. The well-armed Midianite lifted his sword again with a curse. "Baal take you, you filthy priest of shepherds and sheep dung. Less shocking, still an insult! Who sent *you* to war against a real army?"

Phinehas scanned the rocks and shrubs around him, dancing from foot to foot. There was no easy escape route. He had no weapon. And a second assailant was closing in from the other side. He looked again at the second man. He knew that face: those small black eyes, the magnificent black bush of a beard, and the mold of those heavy lips. Even if he hadn't seen the jeweled headband, he knew the man.

"King Zur," he said with feigned nonchalance. "How kind of you to come greet me." He continued to weave and dodge as his eyes darted from one man to the other. "You know your cause is lost."

Both men exploded into action at the same time, lunging at him, snarling like dogs. The king seized Phinehas just as the first man raised his sword in both hands over his head like an executioner. "Stand back, your majesty. I will end his miserable life."

"You stand back. The priest is mine," the king grunted. "I hardly needed a bodyguard when Israel has foolishly left her commander alone and unarmed."

Phinehas felt curiously calm even though Zur whipped a long bronze dagger from his sleeve.

"I want to watch you die *after* you understand that the worship of Yahweh is finished in the Jordan valley." The king flashed the bronze in his face, his thick lips twisted into a self-satisfied grin.

Bright blade. Gleams like a woman's bronze mirror. Was one of Zur's servants assigned the task of constantly polishing it?

King Zur pulled him into a headlock and positioned the blade at his throat.

Phinehas did not flinch. He felt an insane confidence. Head pressed down, voice muffled, he answered the king with the poise befitting his office. "Yahweh finished? To the contrary, his fist has already crushed the power of Baal in the Valley of Acacias, and he will deliver you into our hand."

"Not likely into *your* hand," the bodyguard scoffed. Phinehas watched the feet circle and scuffle as if the man still sought a target for his blade.

"The majority of Israel's princes and clan leaders now follow the Lord Baal of Peor," King Zur announced pompously. "Isn't that why you come against Midian with so small an army? Did the rest refuse to come against us?"

There was a mocking laugh as the knife rasped over the short curly hair under his chin. He could not feel the sting of a cut, but a clump of his beard slid onto his chest. He had no doubt that Zur's blade was not only shiny, but sharp. Still he did not quail. "The name of our God will endure forever," he said.

"Ignorant fool, listen and despair before you die." King Zur's voice was choked with hatred. "Moses and Eleazar no longer rule that sheep station of yours, that cattle camp you call Israel. While your pitiful force has been out seeking us, Prince Salu of Simeon initiated a rebellion and civil war in your camp. Yahweh *is* finished in that vale."

Phinehas listened with increasing incredulity. His response was slow and cool. "I find it very satisfying to inform you that it is Baal worship that is finished there. Your rebellion failed."

Zur lowered the knife and snapped the young priest's head up, glaring into his eyes. "You do not know my daughter. Moses has been toppled. Zimri, son of Prince Salu of Simeon, will be the puppet-king of Israel in an alliance with the Five of Midian. Cozbi will reign as queen at his side, and . . . Baal . . . will . . . be . . . their . . . god." He spat the final five words one by one into the young priestly face.

"Your daughter," Phinehas responded without losing contact with the king's eyes, "and her lover are dead." He slowly raised the censer of holy fire, brushing it against the flowing royal robe.

"He lies!" the bodyguard shrieked, swinging his sword up and back. "Stand aside, your majesty, while I cut out his deceiving tongue."

Phinehas read a glimmer of confusion in the king's eyes as the vise-like grip loosened. King Zur stepped back to better search the priest's eyes for truth. "My daughter? How could she be dead?"

"Believe it," Phinehas said without emotion, standing up straight again and slowly lowering the censer. As he locked eyes with the king, a line of flame crept up one long, black fold of Zur's robe. "Slain by my own hand three days ago."

"If this is true—Aaaaaai!" The king's eyes were narrow with rage and then flew wide in shock and pain as fire suddenly erupted all around him, crackling and billowing into his face. His dagger clattered across the rock.

"Get him," the king cried to his bodyguard. "Avenge Princess Cozbi!" He flung himself onto the ground below, rolling in the dirt to smother the blaze.

As the bodyguard lunged toward him, Phinehas swung his censer at the man's knees and dove for King Zur's cast-off weapon, but before Phinehas could lift the blade against his assailant, flames also enveloped the bodyguard. He too cast himself from the rocky platform, dropping and rolling on the ground a stone's throw from the king. Phinehas leaped onto the groveling monarch with the bronze dagger leading the way, the impact driving the blade into Zur's rotund belly. Phinehas was drawing a ragged breath, trying to regain his equilibrium, when he realized that the bodyguard had struggled to his feet and was staggering toward him, wrapped in a fiery shroud.

All movement seemed to slow: the blazing arm raising the curved sword, Phinehas pulling the dagger free from Zur's belly, then swinging it at the burning man with a desperate upward arc. In a dreamlike daze, he watched the severed hand fly through the air, losing its grip on the sword, dark blood pulsing from the blazing stump. The bodyguard, still sheathed in flames, reeled with the blow and crashed into the thorn bushes.

Phinehas had but one inane thought. *Definitely a sharp blade, a very sharp blade.* He scrambled to untie the donkeys as the barbed branches clawed and tore at the struggles of the flaming figure. By the time the bodyguard ceased writhing and shrieking and submitted to the prickly embrace of his funeral pyre, Phinehas had retrieved the censer and was leading the two terrified donkeys away from the flames. The golden bowl of incense swung from his hand, tracing circles of prayer. *Thank you Lord for holy fire.*

Only then did he notice that the battleground above him had grown eerily quiet—only the distant, dull thudding of a handful of riderless camels fleeing into the desert. Mounds of tan fur dotted the barren hill where the less fortunate beasts had fallen and all around them the slope was carpeted with the crumpled black of Midianite corpses. Here and there soldiers remained standing. None in black. And all were staring at him. Then at the top of the hill, a movement caught his eye. Old Caleb lifted his sword to the sky. In a deep baritone, not quavering with age but rich with experience, the Song of Moses rang out. *I will sing unto the Lord . . .*

A higher tenor answered, *"For he has triumphed gloriously."*

Several voices sang together: *Yahweh is my God, my Strength, my Shield . . .* One weary soldier after another joined in, until thousands of voices united like the roar of the sea, and when they finished, they sang it again.

> *I will sing unto the Lord*
> *For He has triumphed gloriously.*
> *The horse and his rider have been cast into the sea.*
> *Yahweh is my God, my Strength, my Shield!*
> *He has become my Victory.*[13]

Hours later, the hungry flames shrank in exhaustion. Having devoured the hideous debris of battle, the feeding frenzy of the blazing beast fell into slumber. A mound of ashes, like a great cat, curled in smoldering rest with only an occasional flick of a hot red tongue licking at a last hidden morsel. A second caravan of oxcarts, fully loaded with plunder, had been tarped and tied, readied for travel. When the scavenging, the burning, and the packing were done, the exhausted men collapsed on the turf to sleep, their meager cloaks the only comfort against the cold desert night and the hard bare ground.

Phinehas lay on his back staring at the sky. No stars penetrated the black tent of smoke. It was that night of plague and retribution repeated when out of the joy of the promise, a dragon of destruction leaped out to attack the Lord. Phinehas closed his eyes, but images of death continued their taunting—plague victims on litters, lifeless brothers and sisters fed to the hungry flames, rebels hanging limp on crosses before Yahweh's holy altar, and always the fury of the beautiful face, frozen forever at the moment of death, defying his right to ever sleep peacefully again.

O God, I didn't ask for this job. It is my birthright, my duty to defend your name. How long must I live with the horror of that day? How long until this bloody business is over? How long? O Lord, how long?

When he looked up again, he could see, or imagined he could see, the faint glow of a ruddy crescent moon crawling ominously up from the horizon. *The east. The Midianite towns. The end of this battle was not the end of the war. The Dragon was still there, masked by the smoke of the battle, lurking in the towns and settlements of his collaborators. How would he find them all? And if he did not?*

The others might fall into exhausted sleep, but Phinehas's mind churned with plans and preparations for tomorrow.

He coughed at a choking breath of smoke, the foul stench of death and destruction, and that breath brought new visions of terror, visions of what might have been. What if the plague had never fallen? Never brought the people to their knees before the tabernacle? What if Cozbi and Zimri had succeeded in binding so many to Baal there was no turning back? What if it had been the Midianite army that swept down on a sleeping camp instead of the other way around? It would not merely be the seed of Abraham extinguished, but the truth of Yahweh and his righteousness.

There was a soft, rustling in the grasses, the sweet movement of fresh air across his face. A breeze swept the plains, driving off the stagnant smoke and clearing his head. The plague had seemed like a cruel punishment for the rebellion of the people. But it had turned the people away from a headlong rush to self-destruction.

Phinehas pulled in a deep breath, welcoming the clean, crisp aroma of the desert night and listening to its speech. Perhaps the Dragon was terrified of what God's covenant people could do. He pictured the Law in its gilded chest. It was a gift entrusted to Israel to bless the world. It was light in the darkness. Its truth would sweep away the black clouds of the Dragon's breath, and the nations would look. They would see a people living in the very presence of the One and Only True God. They would stream to that light.

As this image filled his mind, the heavy mantle of responsibility lightened, lifted, and followed the fumes of the smoldering fires. He would do his best. That was all he could do. The lullaby of rustling grasses soothed Yahweh's battered and agitated child like the gentle shushing of a heavenly parent. Phinehas at last succumbed to the healing of sleep along with his men.

Jonathan

The Israelite troops slept well, but once the sun blazed up from the horizon the next morning, they organized and headed southeast within the hour, pressing hard to the realm of the Five. Their bodies were fueled by the abundance of Midianite provisions and their spirits by the energy of duel victories, every man fired with a fierce eagerness to finish the job. The enemy, it appeared, was just as eager to stop them.

As they rode into the first town, a young girl's voice lisped the alarm, "The enemy is at the gates." Then all was chaos. Flocks and herds stampeded directly into their path, shrieks and curses issued from the rooftop, and projectiles flew into the street from every direction. Jonathan jerked and joggled, fighting to remain astride his donkey through a jumble of terrified livestock. Phinehas was driven from his side in the confusion. Just as he spotted his cousin on the far side of a flood of wooly black sheep, he saw a chunk of broken pottery the size of a small saddle strike Phinehas mid-back. The priest-commander toppled off his donkey, but instantly scrambled back. All along the flat rooftops lining the street, an army of old men, women, and girls appeared, flinging stones, broken pots, and curses in an increasing storm, the projectiles thudding against heads and shoulders, hammering against the wooden shields of those with the foresight to hold them up, cracking against the trundling plunder-carts as they creaked slowly forward.

"Ira, Heled, and Abiel, send your men house to house. Clean off those rooftops. Capture every one of those women and children."

Startled by a stinging impact on his own forearm, Jonathan looked up into a deadly pair of eyes carefully calculating the lethal distance to his head. He ducked as a melon-sized rock hurtled toward him. He watched it explode into the milling herds. Cattle bawled and stampeded back the way they had come. Sheep twisted and leaped, uncertain of which way to run, then decided to follow a curly-horned ram as he charged madly into the front ranks of the foot soldiers. All at once, boys as young as five and six, armed with knives and sticks, charged fearlessly out of the swirls of dust and churning stampedes of cattle, sheep, goats, and camels into the orderly lines of Israelite foot soldiers.

As Jonathan looked about frantically in search of cover from the hail of stones, a sharp pain shot up his thigh. A dusty little boy, shrieking animal-like screams of rage, was attacking his leg, stabbing wildly with a knife so large that he had to hold it in two hands. As Jonathan leaped from his donkey and seized the boy's hands, the knife fell harmlessly into the dust, but the child exploded into a bundle of frenzied biting and kicking.

"Secure those boys," Phinehas thundered. "Take them all captive. Kill only in self-defense."

Jonathan was fighting the flailing arms and legs, struggling to force the boy face down on the ground. *Secure them all? I can barely restrain one.*

Othniel scooted out of the confusion and picked up the knife the boy had dropped. He tucked it into his belt. "I wouldn't leave this for another of those little foxes to use against us."

"Thanks for that," Jonathan grunted. "A little assistance would also be appreciated here."

"I'm keeping your path clear of stampeding livestock. What more do you want?"

"Maybe some rope?"

Without a word, Othniel turned and shouldered through the chaos to a heavy cart of Midianite plunder stalled nearby. The driver was sheltered, tortoise-like, inside a large iron pot. "Any rope in there?" Othniel asked, addressing the pot as if it were an ordinary sight. The clang of a stone against the metal vessel punctuated his question.

"Take anything you can find." The echoing answer sounded very much like Igal. "I'd help, but I have my hands full."

Under other circumstances, Jonathan would have laughed, but this was not funny. He had no shield and no free hands. He could perish at any moment from a rock bomb or an attack from the companions of this little ruffian. He watched Othniel rummaging methodically through the contents of the cart with one hand, holding his shield up with the other. "I'm so glad that both of you have cover," he called.

By the time Othniel returned, Jonathan had managed to clamp his legs around the boy's legs to stop the kicking, but he was still struggling to maintain a firm grip on the amazingly strong little hands.

Othniel began lashing the boy's feet and hands together, and Jonathan had to admit that it really hadn't been that long. It only seemed to be an eternity while he was struggling. *The oddities of time.* Jonathan was still contemplating this when a large pottery shard smacked his cheek. Others clattered all around. A sudden rain of missiles focused on them now.

"I appreciate your help, but hurry!" he gasped. "I think they see us."

"Finished," Othniel replied calmly.

"Othniel. Jonathan," Igal called, easing the huge cart close beside them. "Under here." Igal replaced the shelter of his iron pot, and Jonathan dove for cover under the overhang at the back of the vehicle. Incredulously, through the tangle of cow legs, sheep, goat, and donkey legs, and the occasional set of camel legs, he watched Othniel drag the restrained, shrieking bundle of curses out of the traffic.

"Wouldn't want the little fellow to get trampled, would we?" he called out.

Othniel ducked in beside him just as an assortment of boy legs began darting among the livestock. Soon there was an army of children, circling, dancing, and jeering around the cart. One little face, twisted in a spiteful smirk, peered into their shelter and pelted them with stones.

Othniel grimaced. "O look! We have more of them to save."

"Where did they all come from?" Jonathan whined.

"They're locals."

Jonathan could not believe how calm Othniel was through this. He adjusted his tone. "I thought Phinehas sent bands of men to clear out the houses ahead of us."

"Apparently, the boys weren't home. Let's go get 'em."

"You jest."

"Commanders' orders. *We* are to secure them."

Jonathan rolled his eyes and groaned. "Wouldn't it be ironic if, after being twice victorious over the warriors of Midian, we were defeated by their children."

"Can't be victorious hiding under here." Othniel sprang out and snagged two of the closest hooligans. Their friends immediately scattered, though from the cover of the milling livestock, they continued lobbing poorly aimed projectiles at the one who dared capture their companions.

Jonathan sighed and left their scant cover. "My turn to scavenge for rope."

"I'll cover you," Igal shouted, thrusting his head out from under the pot again. He reached into his stockpile of unorthodox armaments and lifted a long tent pole high as a platoon of children darted in for a more daring attack. Jonathan seized several lengths of rope and dove to help Othniel while their heavy-footed, bear-like friend labored skillfully above them, keeping the attackers at bay with smacking blows, occasionally flipping a bronze dagger into the air or deflecting a stone missile with his pole.

"Why are we taking these captives?" Caleb's voice roared over the din. "Say the word, Phinehas, and my men will slay the lot of them."

"Thank you, Caleb," Jonathan breathed. *Who ever heard of cleaning out a hornet's nest by capturing and holding the hornets?*

The message his cousin trumpeted back was not what he wanted to hear. "Neither God nor Moses has instructed me to put these little ones and their mothers to death. We will take them back to camp."

Caleb's voice cracked. "Back to camp? You mean we will go through this over and over as we move from town to town, village to village, only accumulating greater and greater numbers of these spiteful captives?"

"That is exactly what we will do," the answer rang back.

Jonathan glanced at Othniel. His friend was listening, but the look in his eyes was totally unreadable. "Give me the straight-forward swords of their fathers any day," he said and was gone.

Remembering the last harrowing half hour in the battle yesterday, Jonathan was not certain he could agree. He spotted Othniel's bent back between two goats and dove in to help him restrain another young assailant. For hours, the three worked as a team, Igal with his pole, Jonathan and Othniel rounding up and roping droves of snapping, snarling boys into groups and securing the livestock as they went. It took the better part of that day for the main body of the army to clear the clogged dirt streets while the vanguard platoons dashed ahead of them from door to door, emptying rooms and rooftops, sweeping the corners of every dwelling until they had captured every one of the screaming, cursing women and their daughters. The few old men of the village fought fiercely at their posts, most finally leaping to their deaths rather than be captured.

More than two weeks elapsed before the last Midianite outpost and town was reduced to smoldering ashes and the army headed west. A long train of captives, wagons of plunder, and great numbers of livestock trailed behind them, slowing the homeward journey, but at last, on the seventeenth day, they pulled up at an overlook on the edge of the high desert plateau. Jonathan's heart leaped at the beauty of the ordered rows of tents nestled in the green valley, each tribe marked with its fluttering banner. Home.

Through his tears, the tabernacle of Yahweh at the very heart of that camp appeared brighter than ever before, the cloud starkly white against the black backdrop of the dark outer covering, the bronze laver gloriously reflecting the sun, and the great bronze altar aglow with the ever burning daily sacrifice—God's dwelling framed with the white of the courtyard wall and surrounded by the tents of Levi. His tribe. Defenders of the tabernacle, guardians of truth. His tent nestled among those on the eastern side with the children and grandchildren of Moses. What an honor. His own beloved grandfather was not only clan chief, but shepherd of the most blessed people on the face of the earth. He glanced at his cousin, the future high priest of Israel. He had never before felt such kinship and admiration. The innocent abandon of their shared childhood had vanished into some distant place and time. Somewhere along the way, as they faced death and danger together, this war had forged an iron bond of brotherhood for the grandsons of Moses and Aaron.

Phinehas grinned at him. "Can you believe that only two Sabbaths have passed since we set out on this campaign?"

"Two and a half weeks that seemed a lifetime," Jonathan replied slowly. "A venture that cured me forever of seeking the adventures of the battlefield. All I wish for now is to live in peace and fulfill my role in Israel."

"My young cousin has become a man." Phinehas lobbed a quick, fond look his way, flicked the reins of his donkey, and headed down the steep descent.

The train of men and wagons had not rumbled and rattled more than a quarter of the way down the steep slope before they heard distant cries echoing up from the valley. "They return. They return. The army returns." Soon trumpets amplified the announcement, and people swarmed out of camp like bees from a hive suddenly disturbed.

Jonathan sighed with a strange blend of longing and belonging. He was proud to ride beside Phinehas and could think of no higher honor than to labor at his side for the rest of his life just as their grandfathers had, no greater joy than to take up his role of leadership in Israel, to marry and begin a family. He strained his eyes, searching the crowds as they poured into the meadow, eager to catch sight of one girl in particular.

Acsah

The last woolly tail waggled down the bank, dropping into a fleecy cumulous cloud mounding around three sides of the

243

dammed-up pond. Just when the flock seemed sedately settled, an impatient ewe or unruly lamb would jump up and scramble over the broad backs of her comrades looking for a better spot to sip the quiet waters. "Why must you push and shove. There is room for all of you," Acsah laughed. "What will I tell Abba if he comes home and finds that half of you drowned in the river?"

She was more than ready for the return of the army. The tally of days since they left for the Midianite war now reached seventeen, each day stretching long and worrisome for those who waited and wondered at home. This daily comedy of jostling sheep did not exactly replace the laughter vacancy her father left behind, but it was a welcome reprieve from the common anxiety pervading camp.

There had been little time for leisurely strolls like the one she had taken with Abihail the first day. With Aunt Sarah's flocks to care for as well as her own, morning hours vanished quicker than manna under the sun. The first few days, when Sarah invited her to share a noon meal, Acsah declined because she had barely finished her morning porridge. Her aunt chided her for letting worry ruin her appetite, but when Acsah tried to convince her that it was because her chores had taken so long, Aunt Sarah withdrew into wounded mumbling.

Acsah was quite surprised on the fifth day to discover Aunt Sarah in the meadow ahead of her, nearly finished collecting manna for both of them. A brighter flicker of life lit her aunt's eyes as she cackled over her joke. After that, the mornings settled into a comfortable routine for both women. Acsah milked the cows, drove the flocks and herds to the stream for water and turned them out into an area with adequate grass under the watchful eye of her nephew, Mushi. Aunt Sarah gathered manna, made porridge, and baked manna cakes. By the time the bright rays of the morning sun poured over the eastern hills, Acsah and her aunt were breaking fast together, and Acsah was more than ready to join Sarah for the rest of the day's meals as well.

As they laughed together over stories of Auntie Hannah's antics, they found healing for the void left behind by mother and substitute grandmother. The life-light in Sarah's eyes grew with the telling of her story: the thrilling and terrifying night her family left Egypt when she was just a child, the struggle to adapt to the changes of wilderness living, the joy of falling in love with Kenaz and bearing his sons, but what she could not bring herself to speak of was the despair of losing him last year. Through those days of shared hopes and fears, Acsah gained a new understanding of and appreciation for this woman, and Aunt Sarah nearly ceased her muttering altogether.

A few days into the war, Acsah dedicated an afternoon to Salmon's sister, Ada. She showed the girl which savory herbs to gather and then taught her how to create the delicious lentil-barley pilaf she had learned to make with Auntie Hannah. That evening, Acsah and Sarah joined the child's family for supper, and afterward they all gathered around the fire. Ada was much herself again, jabbering about her day whenever there was a lull in the stories and songs. Even Abijah, draped in the black of mourning, clapped and sang and occasionally joined the friendly banter. Salmon alone remained brooding and silent. He loomed like a melancholy cloud across the fire from Acsah, smothering every spark of life and energy in his shadow. Soon, it seemed, even the flames wearied of dancing for him and collapsed into tired embers. Acsah made no attempt to add new fuel.

"The fire is nearly extinguished and so am I," she said, forcing a breezy brightness. "Do you want help spreading the coals? No?" She dipped her head courteously to Abijah and rose to leave. "Good night, everyone."

On the other side of the dying embers, Salmon mirrored her movement, pulling himself up slowly. "I will walk with you." He didn't look at her, and his voice was dead. It was not surprising that Ada avoided her usual jibes and giggles as her brother left the firelight with Acsah. Even a child knows you don't poke and tease a corpse.

Salmon walked, silent and glum, the entire way to her father's tent, his hands clasped behind his back. At her door, he looked at her for the first time in the entire evening. His eyes pleaded for help, but still no words. In the uncomfortable silence, Acsah found herself wordless as well. What do you say to a black mountain of grief?

Suddenly in a wild impulse, she reached up and brushed his lower lip. "We need to see Prince Nashon's smile here."

His hand rushed up and pressed her fingers against his lips. One side of his mouth curved up weakly. "For you."

Too "im," she thought. *Improper, impetuous, impulsive, and more.* She took a step back. "The whole tribe needs your smile, Salmon. We all grieve for our prince."

Not a hint of the smile had brightened the rest of his face, and as he dropped her hand, the last feeble trace of it sputtered out. "Ada had a good day," he said. "Thank you." He turned and trudged heavily into the darkness, and Acsah did not see him again during the time of war.

Just as the sheep had finished drinking and Acsah was leading them to pasture, Mushi came running toward her, flapping his hands and shouting. "Look. They're coming. They're coming. Phinehas and his army return."

Acsah squinted into the eastern haze. A cloud of yellow dust smudged the bluffs above the valley and was beginning to drift down the steep slope. She could not yet hear the thunder of their feet, but she had no doubt that it *was* the army. "Yes," she cried and swung Mushi into a swirling, dancing embrace. Before the first of the horde was visible descending the steep slope, Acsah was back at Aunt Sarah's tent, breathlessly shouting the news in case her aunt hadn't noticed the bombardment of joyous calls from every direction. "The army returns! See there! Our men are returning."

The older woman continued stirring the steaming pot. "Isn't that just like a group of men to show up at the whiff of food. The porridge is ready."

Acsah pulled the pot off the fire. "The porridge will wait." Without further discussion, she whisked her aunt off to join the crowds pouring out of camp.

By this time, it was just possible to identify some of the figures emerging from the clouds of dust. "O, will we celebrate tonight," she cried, searching for her father's white hair.

Sarah's response was guarded. "The soldiers who made it back will have to be cleansed before we can welcome them back to our tents."

"But it will be good just to have everyone safely in camp again."

"Everyone?"

Acsah refused to start down that negative road. She looked for familiar forms and faces. There was no question of the identity of the one riding tall and noble at the head of the returning soldiers. "There, I see Phinehas."

All around people began to call out other names: "Haniel! Ethan! Reuben!"

"Othniel," Sarah whispered, and tears began to stream down her face. "I see my boy."

"I see Igal," Acsah cried, "and my father." Was that Zebulon with Asriel? A frenzied waving left no doubt that the man at Phinehas' right hand was Jonathan. As Acsah identified more and more of the soldiers she knew, her spirits soared. Surely there had not been many losses.

"Asher!"

"Plunder!"

"Elihu! Jahath!"

"Midianite captives!"

The other words blasted through the happy list of names like sour notes, but the high-heaped, lumbering wagons interspersed with flocks of sheep and goats, herds of cattle, oxen, donkeys and bands of bound and guarded women and children trailing behind the returning army declared them a true part of the song.

Acsah recoiled at the sight of the foreigners. It dredged up the memory of Balaam and the five kings leading that troop of women into the valley. The Midianites weren't singing and dancing now, but . . . "Why would they bring those abominable women back with them? Or their children? Or even their contaminated belongings?"

Apparently, she had been wondering aloud for a woman behind her responded patronizingly, "I'll take your share of those contaminated belongings if you don't want them."

Acsah recognized the voice even before she turned to respond. It was Mara, Abihail's mother-in-law. Both young wives of her sons were with her, one on each side. "Would you want one of those women as a maidservant after what they did to us?" Acsah asked. She was well aware of the incredulity in her tone and did not expect an answer.

Mara laughed. "I rather like the idea of a Midianite slave. I want the very one who thought to be so alluring to Achor. I want to see her laboring over every demeaning task I can find, and if I catch her attracting the slightest look from my husband, I will quite enjoy beating her bloody."

"And do you like the idea of needing a guard every night to prevent her from murdering you in your sleep?"

The two daughters-in-law listened to the exchange with very different reactions. Abihail shrank from the clash and wouldn't even look up, but Hattil tossed out a sly smile. "We may not welcome those women, but why not be enriched with their wealth? Think of all that our camp suffered because of their treachery."

"We didn't need Midianite stuff when they brought it as part of their plan," Acsah said, with a pointed look at Abihail. "We don't need it now."

Abihail did not acknowledge the statement, but she could not have missed Acsah's meaning.

"My husband risked his life out there," someone called out defensively. "Certainly, he should be compensated for that."

"And I say, why should only twelve thousand be rewarded? My husband would have gone to fight, but he wasn't chosen. Shouldn't we be compensated for our losses too?"

"Do you really want to be compensated with idol-worshipping slaves? Do you even want to touch their goods?" Acsah cried in frustration. "The lot of it should have been burned and no one allowed to live."

"After the plague, we gave our Midianite gifts to the priests," a soft voice declared.

"Good for you." Again Acsah tried to make eye contact with Abihail to no avail.

"Hush," Aunt Sarah interrupted. She held up her hand with fingers spread and then closed them as if catching any more words from the women around them. "Hush. Listen." She spoke with such authority that the women all around hushed at her command.

Acsah listened when the chatter stopped, but there was nothing. Only silence. A growing absence of sound that moved like a wave through the throng along with Moses, Eleazar, Ithamar, and Joshua. The wave absorbed her, absorbed Aunt Sarah, absorbed everyone around and drew them back with tidal force, and the leaders passed through a parting sea of people.

Joshua and the priests came to a halt where the rocky shoulders of the mountain pushed up at right angles to the green belly of the meadow, but Moses continued on, long strides carrying him up the mountain road alone, rapidly closing the gap between himself and the army. "What is the meaning of this?" he roared as soon as he was within speaking distance of Phinehas.

The question reverberated fiercely against the stony slope and passed in a wave of trembling through the multitude. "Are these not the very women who brought this whole trouble on our people? Are these young ones not the spawn of wickedness?"

Exactly, Acsah said to herself.

Phinehas

Phinehas did not flinch. "We completed our mission. You neither told us what to do with the women and children, nor whether or not to save their possessions, so we brought them back to you."

The air suddenly seemed heavy as if a storm was brewing. Moses lifted the thumb and fingers of his right hand to his eyes and rubbed as if hoping to make the unwelcome sight of the captives disappear.

"I have no quarrel with the acquisition of this property, but . . . not these captives, Phinehas. Summon the division commanders. I want to hear the full battle report."

The weight of Phinehas's decisions pressed down on his shoulders as he called for the tribal princes. The crowds below must have felt it too for they waited silent as tree stumps in the meadow below. He dismounted, handing the reins of his donkey to Jonathan as he joined the circle of twelve around Moses. But the old man did not address the group immediately, nor even look at them. His face was lifted to the sky, eyes closed, features deeply troubled.

Phinehas scanned the faces of his commanders—some bewildered, some wary, all somber—and was nearly overcome by an upwelling of love. Seventeen days ago, they had been but fellow tribesmen. Today, they were brothers. They had been loyal, followed his commands, risked death for him. Several of them even questioned the wisdom of bringing these captives back. He was not going to let them bear the blame for any misdeed on his part.

He squared his shoulders. "It was I who made this decision," he said. "I commanded. These good men obeyed."

Moses snapped to life, eyes blazing. "What about you? Did you obey? It is a fearsome thing to deviate from the explicit commands of Yahweh."

Moses was furious, but Phinehas recognized in it a parental, protective anger. He would never forget a look exactly like that on the face of his gentle grandfather when he was just a toddler. The memory was set in first light, just before dawn, when he had managed to slip away from the family tent unnoticed and find his way to the tabernacle. Perhaps he followed Grandfather Aaron. All he really remembered was standing just within the entrance of the holy place, awestruck by the shimmer of gold against a backdrop of wildly magnificent purple, blue, and scarlet. One moment, he was watching his grandfather's meticulous trimming of the lamp wicks, the next, the old man caught his eyes through the seven gleaming branches, and he was terrified by the look—love, holy fear, anger, tender concern, and abject terror all rolled into one. He vaguely recalled his grandfather snatching him up, and taking him home. He had a dim remembrance of an excited conversation between Aaron and his parents, but that look was burned vividly into his mind ever after.

Thus began a growing understanding that the Mighty One who freed his people from slavery and cared for them faithfully in the wilderness was also the One who thundered at them from Mount Sinai. The God who loved his people so much that he gave them instructions to build a dwelling place for him in their camp was at the same time, a blazing fire that could not be tamed. Phinehas wasn't sure if he had ever heard the story of his father's brothers, Nadab and Abihu, before that event. But the thought of them reduced to ashes for bringing strange fire to the altar became frighteningly real to him afterwards, and the terror of it was always associated in his mind with the beauty of holiness and that look on Aaron's face.

As he grew and became a young student of the priesthood, he listened carefully to the teachings of his father, his grandfather, and Uncle Ithamar. Would he remember every detail of the protocols they were teaching him? He trembled at the thought of encountering the loving, deadly, presence of the Lord. And so with trembling he watched and carefully imitated the way his father and grandfather presented perfect offerings on the great, bronze altar. He memorized every word of the law. He could not have tried harder to perfect obedience. Surely Moses knew he would never disregard a single command of the Holy One of Israel.

"I carried out my orders as I understood them, Uncle. The five kings, Evi, Rekem, Zur, Hur, and Reba, were already coming against our camp with every fighting man of their people when we came upon them the first night, and we destroyed them."

"All?"

"Every man."

"The towns?"

"I believe we found them all. Found them, subdued them, plundered what our people could use, and left nothing but ashes behind."

"And brought those vile women and their brood back to us."

Caleb met the blazing eyes and interjected a terse report. "The prophet is also dead."

"Balaam?"

Caleb smiled. "Who else?"

"Balaam was there?"

"He was," Phinehas confirmed. "And Caleb risked his life to ensure that he didn't leave the battlefield alive."

"My oldest warrior. I suspect you will risk your life many more times in the coming years." Moses smiled grimly. "Cause for rejoicing. But, Phinehas, tell me about the women. Did they negotiate a truce with you?"

"No."

He felt sick. He made every effort to bring honor to the emblem of holiness that his father had given him to wear. Rounding up these captives had added days to the campaign and had put his troops at risk.

Moses' eyes bored into his. "Did they convince you that they still had things to teach you?"

"No. Not at all. They were doing everything possible to kill us. We surprised them in a few places, and we encountered some towns immobilized by plague, but in most settlements, they were waiting for us. Rounding them up was not an easy task. I certainly had reservations about bringing them back to our camp, but how was I to decide whether they should live or die? I did not have the Urim and Thummin."

"As high priest someday, Phinehas, you must learn to recognize God's voice. He will speak when you need it; more often, he will bring the word of his law to mind. The Urim and Thummin are more for confirming the Lord's will to the multitudes. How did you know it was God telling you to defend the tabernacle against Cozbi and Zimri? "

At the mention of the names, Cozbi's face, bitter, bold, and blasphemous, intruded into the conversation. Phinehas heard the death gurgle again and felt weak. "It is not easy to slay a woman, much less a child," he said.

"You had the word of the Lord. You knew that these women were responsible for twenty-four thousand who died in the plague. They would slit our throats in broad daylight if they could. But that is not the greatest of their crimes. Their ultimate intention was to defeat Yahweh. They intended to wipe the face of the earth clean of all who worship his name. You are sworn to promote the worship of Yahweh, to defend him and his holy tabernacle, yet you did not think it meet to execute the judgment God commanded?"

Phinehas glanced at his cousin. "But the children . . . have you forgotten who they are? Jonathan's father was born in the tents of Midian."

The idea registered visibly on Jonathan like a slap on the face. Until this moment, Phinehas guessed, his cousin had not connected this enemy with his father's kin. "They are his cousins. They are your wife's people, and they are also the seed of Abraham."

Moses closed his eyes and turned away for a moment. His voice was soft and mournful when he spoke again. "Do not think this is easy for me. Could I forget the kindness and hospitality of Jethro? He took me in, a fugitive from Pharoah's wrath. He gave his beautiful daughter, Zipporah, to be my wife. His Midianite clan protected and nurtured me. He gave me a new life among his people as a shepherd in the deserts of Sinai."

"And you would still wipe them out, even the little ones?"

Moses continued without seeming to notice. "I expected to die and be buried in Midian. Life there was good, but God had bigger plans than my contentment in old age. I was eighty years old the day I encountered his holy fire on the mountain and he made me the shepherd of his people. An old man entrusted with a mission and a third life. For forty years I led the Lord's sheep, and now that I have brought them safely to the border of the Promised Land, I prepared to lay down my staff. Then just when I thought the hard tasks of my life were finished, the Lord gave me one more: to avenge the attack on my birth people by my adoptive people.

"I know who they are, Phinehas, which is why their treachery is so abhorrent. More importantly, I know who we are. I know we have been commissioned to take back the land of Canaan and to bless the whole earth with truth and righteousness. Above all, I know our God. I know what he commanded. We dare not disobey."

Jonathan's eyes were dark with dread. "But, Grandfather, I understand that we cannot bring them into camp. They hate us. But can't we let them go? They can find refuge with the southern clans of Midian who know you and love you. Perhaps they would learn to know the true God of Abraham there."

Moses looked from Phinehas to Jonathan and back with quiet resolution. "Their version of the tale would infect any lingering good will the southern clans have for me. They would stir up all Midian against us. No. These children must not live as a hate-filled generation bent on avenging the deaths of their parents and continuing the fight against our God. We cannot set them free. We cannot take them into our camp. Phinehas, you should have slain them one by one as they attacked you. How much harder now that you have brought them back here. Never forget that the sting of a young scorpion can be as deadly as that of a mature one."

The timid face of a young girl, no more than three years of age, peeked out from behind her mother's skirts. "That child?" Phinehas asked.

Moses' face, weathered and strong as a mountain crag, softened. His eyes swept over the masses of captives, and for a long time, he did not answer.

"Only the very young maidens may be saved," he said at last, "those who have never been contaminated by the training rites of Baal worship. They will follow the purification procedures along with our soldiers, and they must be instructed in the ways of our God."

"Jonathan, I will assign the welfare of those girls to you," Phinehas ordered immediately. "Ornan, work with Jonathan. Organize your division to separate out those little ones and take them to the cleansing area. I will see to the rest myself."

The task was too gruesome to relegate to his battered soldiers, but if Cozbi's face haunted him now, he expected that the ongoing nightmare would soon be multiplied by thousands.

"Joshua," Moses called out. "Choose a few men from each division whom you know are capable of that other work. Help Phinehas organize and carry it out. You will then need to stay with the quarantine for the week."

Moses wheeled and faced the masses of Israel who waited quiet as stones in the meadow below. "The Five and their armies are destroyed. Their cities burned to the ground," he announced. "Balaam, son of Beor, has also fallen by the sword."

At the news of the prophet's death, the entire petrified forest of people came to life with cheers and clapping. At the same time the sheep, goats, cattle, and donkeys confined to the steep roadway smelled the green grasses of the valley and began to paw the earth, tug at their restraints, and bawl for freedom. Moses lifted his voice above the din. "Yahweh commanded, and Phinehas obeyed. He led our army out against a people wholly committed to our destruction. Our soldiers preserved God's holy dwelling place and kept our people from being destroyed. But, in fighting this war, they themselves have become unclean. Those contaminated by death are unfit to dwell in the camp of the Lord of Life."

Moses now turned to the waiting soldiers. "We have been preparing for your return, my war-weary young men." Not a trace of wrath clouded his rough-hewn features now. A striking tenderness, sweet as sunlight following rain, replaced the storm. "Your priests sacrificed a thousand red heifers outside the camp, reducing them to ashes in flames fueled by red cedar wood and wool dyed red. Red, the color of sacrifice, produced these ashes of black so when you wash with this ash water as prescribed you will be clean. Yahweh himself gave us these simple rituals so sinful mortals may live and thrive in fellowship with him. May his love bring healing to your hearts and minds during these days of cleansing."

Moses dipped his head toward the high priest. "Eleazar will review the procedures for purification."

While Eleazar climbed the slope and stood catching his breath, Moses began the explanations. "All the plunder must stay by the river until it is cleansed. Once everything is cleansed, Eleazar and the priests will count the animals and goods we have acquired and divide it among *all* the families of Israel."

He nodded at the audible ripple of surprise. "Yes, you heard correctly, and it is just. The entire camp suffered at the hand of the Midianites and all shall receive of this bounty. Half of the plunder will go to the soldiers and half will be divided among the rest of the people. The soldiers will present one in every five hundred from their share of the maidservants and the animals to Eleazar as a gift for the priests. The rest of the congregation will present one in fifty as a gift to the Levites."

Moses nudged Eleazar to begin.

Eleazar cleared his throat. "Yahweh wants us to be a holy people, free of evil and free of all the diseases afflicting the nations around us."

The tone was confident, but Phinehas could easily read the private anguish in his father's eyes. His mouth was drawn, and he averted his gaze from the captives as if he could already see the rivers of blood. "Everyone who has shed the blood of man or been contaminated by touching the dead must remain outside of the camp for the full seven days or you will be cut off forever from the fellowship of the covenant people. The young maidens and all the captured items must also remain by the river until their cleansing is complete."

Moses interrupted. "Be certain not to allow any exceptions. Phinehas told me that there was a plague found in many of the cities and camps of the Midianites similar to that which struck us. There is disease among the animals as well. Some of them fell sick and died on the return journey. If no more sickness is evident after seven days of cleansing, we can combine them with our own flocks and herds."

Eleazar continued his instructions. "This is the procedure. On the third and seventh days, we will send Levites to cleanse your bodies. The rest is your responsibility. Fill your buckets with living water from the river, adding a handful of ashes from the sacrificial heap. Stir them well with branches of hyssop. Sprinkle this ash water over the items to be cleansed and then wash them thoroughly in the river.

"Purify every garment, as well as everything made of leather, goat hair, wool, or wood. Today, cleanse all the cattle, all the sheep, all the goats, and all the donkeys. Tomorrow, cleanse all the saddles and anything pertaining to the beasts. Also, cleanse the tents and rugs made from hides. The third day, cleanse all clothing and sandals as well as yourselves. The fourth day of your purification is the Sabbath. On it you will rest from the work of cleansing. On the fifth day, cleanse the wagons and anything made of wood. On the sixth day, cleanse all the articles of gold, silver, bronze, iron, tin, or lead. All weapons of war that can withstand flame must be put through the fire. And any articles crafted with images or symbols of the gods of Midian, Moab, or Canaan must be burned or melted down to erase the memory of them forever.

"On the seventh day of your purification, the Levites will again purge you with hyssop and you will wash in the living water of the Jordan. That evening you will be clean and may return to your tents and your families. The cleansed animals may be added to your flocks and herds, the captive maidens can join your households, and all the possessions that you took from the Midianites may be brought into the camp."

Moses turned toward the crowds on the valley floor again. His smile was broad and magnificent. "God has blessed, yes?"

"Yes! Hallelujah. Our God has blessed," the people shouted back enthusiastically.

"Before you return to your tents and our brave warriors set up their camp of purification, let's recite the covenant code together. Although we will remain divided for another week, we are bound together by the love of Yahweh and his law."

I am the Lord who brought you out of Egypt . . .

The familiar words resounded all around Phinehas in the deep, strong voices of the twelve thousand men. They echoed up from ten thousand times ten thousand in the valley below and stirred a deeper response of love and joy than he had ever felt before.

> *Because the great and holy Yahweh loves you and wants to dwell with you . . .*
> *You will have no other gods before Him*
> *You will not make an image to distract from His grandeur*
> *You will honor His Name, keep His Sabbaths, honor your father and mother . . ."*[14]

The old covenant was new today, its words permanently burned into his heart. No other nation had ever been so privileged.

Othniel

Phinehas took charge of the cleansing while Moses dismissed the ranks of Israel. First, he called for the young girls to be separated out of the captives. He designated Ornan's division to set up a quarantine for them in a secluded glen at the northern end of the cleansing area. "Men of Naphtali, be kind to these children," he cautioned. "They have suffered much already and are now losing their mothers. Anyone who harms them in any way will answer to me." He nodded toward his young cousin. "Jonathan will be their special guardian until we have gathered a team of women to care for them."

Othniel watched Jonathan pull a screaming toddler from her mother. No smiles, no easy humor today as he wrapped his arms around the small one, speaking tenderly as he carried her down the trail to the valley floor. Before he handed her off to be gathered into a small flock and shepherded across the meadow, he whispered something to the child to make her laugh. The grin morphed to a grimace as he trudged back up the hill. He had chosen to help the men assigned the harder task of combing the bands of captives seeking young girls they could save. Othniel admired his skill in handling the frightened children. Those were not his skills.

He was greatly relieved when the tribes of Simeon and Judah were assigned the cleansing of the animals. As soon as Caleb asked him to supervise the purification of a thousand sheep, he leaped into the work, directing his brigade to divide up their flock into tens to lead down the hill to the river. As Othniel followed, watching for stragglers, sheep bleated wildly all around him, other flocks in the hands of Caleb's other brigades. The bleating of the sheep muffled the sounds of wagons creaking and rumbling off in the distance and the sound of donkeys braying to the north and cattle bawling to the south. He did not know when the repulsive work of exterminating the women and boys began or who was assigned to do it, but he was glad for the animals that drowned out all other sounds.

At the river, Othniel focused on the assignment. One group of men would wait at the water's edge with ash pots and thick-leaved hyssop branches. Their task was the most important in the purification process. They were to thoroughly blacken each sheep, using hyssop sodden with ash water. Then the attending soldier would lead his sheep down into the water where foreign impurities were swept away along with the ash. When no trace of black could be seen, the animal could be brought back to shore where another group of soldiers soothed them with calming words, watching carefully to keep the cleansed sheep separate from the others.

Othniel encouraged speed and order as he raced up and down the bank, inspecting the application of the ash, then checking the emerging animals. "Bring the animals out over here so the next ten can descend into the water the way you did. Move along. You do not have to wait for everyone to leave the water before you enter. We want to get some rest tonight."

Evening fell and the work continued into the night. A waxing quarter moon touched the river with silver and gave them some light, but before the mooing, braying, bleating, and baaing ceased, it slipped behind the western hills. At last, under the star-studded canopy of a moonless sky, the cleansing of the livestock was finished and silence reigned. There were many in camp who had been kept awake by the beastly symphony. Now they, the weary soldiers, and the frightened animals, all fell into an exhausted sleep.

CHAPTER NINE

CLEANSINGS

For the soldiers returned from the Midianite war, the next few days were a blur of washings, busy days slathering each plundered object with the ash and water mixture, then scrubbing and rinsing in flowing water and laying the cleansed items out in the sun. They sorted like items into piles of ten and groups of one hundred for Eleazar and the priests to count. By sunset on the third day of cleansings, every man was eager for the day of rest.

From their quarantine, twelve thousand soldiers watched the smoke of the evening sacrifice spiral into the sunset blush. Phinehas led the men in a psalm of praise and a prayer of blessing. As the Sabbath began, Joshua addressed the men, reminding them that this bitter incident came about because of Israel's unfaithfulness to the covenant. He reminded them of the grace God had showered on Israel following another episode of unfaithfulness, the worship of the golden calf.

"When we least deserved it, God renewed His covenant with our people. He did not choose us because of *our* goodness, but because of *his* goodness. His great kindness seals his covenant in our hearts. We do not deserve the land across the river, but Yahweh promised it to us in spite of our weakness. This bounty we are cleansing and counting—is there anyone who thinks we deserve it after the faithlessness of Baal-Peor? This bounty is a gift from an exceedingly gracious God."

Joshua regarded the sea of tired faces before him as tenderly as a father looking into the faces of his bleary-eyed little ones. "You have endured two weeks of warfare, rigorous days of travel, and three long days of cleansings. I suspect that no one has the energy for more storytelling and singing around campfires tonight. Before we sleep, repeat with me the encouraging words the Lord spoke after the incident with the golden calf."

Yahweh! he called out, and the twelve-thousand joined in unison.

> *Yahweh! God of compassion and grace,*
> *Overflowing with patience, kindness, and faithfulness,*
> *Lavishing love on a thousand generations,*
> *Forgiving their wickedness, rebellion, and sin—*
> *But by no means clearing the guilty.*
> *The consequences of evil fall on their*
> *Children and grandchildren,*
> *Even to the third and fourth generation.*[15]

The declaration thundered over the valley, stirring hearts throughout camp, for even from afar, everyone recognized the sound of those words. Israel was bound by covenant to the one loving, forgiving, and just God. Like a wave of peace, the words ushered in the Sabbath rest, while high above both camps, the Creator tossed handfuls of stars across the darkening sky in bright patterns of promise to a dark world.

Othniel

Early Sabbath morning, Othniel sat breaking fast with his uncle Caleb and a large, boisterous group of young men from Judah. The fire, which had been lit on the preparation day and carefully laid to take the men through the Sabbath, was now but a heap of smoldering embers, no longer needed for heat or light, and yet it seemed natural to linger around it as they ate. He had finished his food, picked up a long stick from the pile of kindling, and was poking at the movement of crimson light in the coals when Joshua approached.

"*Shabbat shalom*, my friends," the old commander's voice boomed over the hubbub.

The youthful warriors fell silent as Caleb welcomed him. "*Shabbat shalom*, Joshua. Won't you come sit with us? Have you eaten?"

"Yes, I have eaten, and yes, I would be delighted to join you."

The young man sitting at Caleb's right hand arose and gestured respectfully for Joshua to take his place.

"This is indeed a Sabbath blessing, my boys," Caleb said with a grin. "Joshua rarely has time to visit old friends these days."

Joshua held up his hands in a gesture of surrender and smiled sheepishly. "The responsibility of running the camp while Moses finishes his writings . . . But we have this whole day to make up for it."

Iru exchanged knowing glances with a companion. "Please excuse us, Father. We will let the two of you reminisce unhindered by our presence." At Caleb's nod of dismissal, they slipped away along with several others. The two old men watched, slight smiles flicking the corners of their lips as the remaining young men left the circle one by one. It wasn't long before only Othniel remained.

"You don't mind if I stay and listen, do you, Uncle?"

"Absolutely not. I am pleased that you wish to remain."

Sabbath rest wrapped comfortably around the three, each man exploring separate memories as they watched the occasional flash of a flame rise from the ashes. Conversation would be minimal, but who needed the constant bombardment of speech? Othniel was happy enough just to enjoy the company of like minds.

"Three months," Caleb mused aloud after a long period of silence "It has been but three months since we defeated the Amorite kings, Sihon and Og. It seems much longer than that."

Othniel regarded his uncle silently for some time. Three months . . . A lot had happened in those three months, but nothing on a par with the battles that gave them possession of this valley. With his own eyes he watched the smashing fist of Yahweh demolish those brutal kings just as he had flattened Egypt with the plagues. The plagues had been a pivotal event, changing everything for the previous generation. As one plague after another fell, the chains of their bondage were broken. The plagues birthed faith in what God could do and launched the Children of Israel into the world as a new nation. It was all God's doing. His people only watched it happen. The defeat of the kingdoms in this valley was very much like that. This time he had been an eyewitness.

"I expect the battle we just fought with Midian will retreat into the shadows of minor conflicts by the time I am as old as you," he said, "but the battles with Sihon and Og will never be forgotten."

"I'll never forget." Joshua puffed out a half laugh through his nose. "The attack by King Sihon's legions, when we were pinned against the bluff, so unprepared, often haunts my dreams. I had no idea what to do, and I was the commander."

Caleb looked at him sharply. "Never let thoughts of our enemies disturb your sleep. Yahweh, our God, always knows what to do."

"And for that very reason, I am grateful for my bad dreams. That battle taught me that the true Commander of Israel's army is the Lord. I don't want to ever forget that."

Othniel nodded thoughtfully. "Sihon and Og." He poked at the fire with a stick and watched a tiny flame come to life. "Even the names have a chilling sound, a good reminder of how desperately we need the Lord."

"Just names," Caleb grunted.

Othniel shook his head in protest. "Not to me. Seeing King Sihon's forces, pouring out of Heshbon, was unnerving enough, but the sight of King Og's army was beyond terrifying. Any one of those warriors made ours look like toddlers, but King Og and his sons were giants among giants, towering over the rest of his huge men. It was a bad dream in the flesh."

Joshua tightened his lips. "That was the very impression made by the giants we encountered forty years ago."

Othniel stared at Caleb and Joshua. Here was a new connection to an old story. "Og and his sons . . . were the giants you saw in Kiriath-Arba like them?"

"Believe it," Joshua answered slowly. "My first sight of that king immediately swept me back to our days of spying—of being 'grasshoppers.'"

"Grasshoppers . . ." Othniel thought about that description for a moment. "Yes. That *is* how we felt charging up that rocky pass to meet King Og and his army."

"Grasshoppers, smashpoppers," Caleb scoffed. "The plagues of Egypt proved that insects in the hands of God will not be crushed underfoot unless it is his will. Tiny grasshoppers can demolish forests."

A solemn, grieved look crossed Joshua's face. "But only for those who trust him. Fear and rebellion won the day when we spies returned to camp. We saw firsthand a panic of grasshoppers."

There was another long period of silence. Then Caleb sighed. "That was the saddest day of my life bar none." He picked up a twig lying at his feet, snapped it in two, and tossed it onto the coals. It smoldered for a moment and then blazed into a small, bright flame before dying back into the ashes. "I have often wondered what became of that woman, Shua, that we met in southern Canaan. Shua and her daughter."

"I have as well. It seemed that God led us to her, then it was all for naught as we turned back into the wilderness."

Othniel frowned. "Who is this? I don't think I have heard you tell of her before."

"Really?" Caleb raised his shaggy brows in surprise. "Have we never related her story to you?"

Joshua winced. "How could we miss telling you the story? We met her at the very end of our forty days of spying. The twelve of us had traveled under the cover of darkness, arriving close to Kiriath-Arba just before dawn. You will remember that we were carrying the fruit samples from Eshkol."

"And Eshkol was but one small valley in Canaan," Caleb interrupted, his face beaming with sheer joy. "Wait until you see for yourself the goodness God is preparing to hand to us, Othniel. The fields of barley, spelt, and wheat stretch on and on, hill after hill, interspersed with groves of olive trees, almond and fruit trees, and vineyards thickly hung with grapes. More than the human heart could conceive of."

"But this Shua woman?"

"Oh, yes. Shua," Caleb chuckled. "Distracted again by the glory of God's gifts. Shua was a demonstration that in the midst of the most horrific violence God has his faithful ones."

This time Joshua interrupted. "The violence of Canaan is as hard to imagine as its goodness." He stared at the distant ridge west of the river, his face dark and troubled as he spoke. "You could read it on the faces of every inhabitant. Lines of cruelty, fear, or both etched their features. Sometimes their eyes did not even seem human. Like wild beasts. Either predator or prey."

"It was evident even in the very young," Caleb agreed. "Children already shaped by the basest greed and violence. The problem is their Baals. The gods they worship reduce humanity to the level of savage beasts."

"Lower perhaps. Beasts kill to feed their stomachs. The Canaanites rape and steal and butcher to feed their twisted lust for power and pleasure."

"The worst was in Kiriath-Arba," Caleb added quietly. "To see such violence in *that* city of all places."

Othniel nodded. "Abraham's territory."

"You know your history, my son," Caleb grinned at his nephew. "Not only do the bodies of Abraham and Sarah lie near it, in the cave of Machpelah, but Isaac and Rebecca, and Jacob and Leah as well. It is as if the torch of truth our fathers held up to the world was purposely extinguished by a city dedicated to blackness."

Joshua snorted. "It was that city with its giants that caused our ten fellow spies to panic."

Caleb's eyes glittered fiercely. "I have been waiting forty years to go back and clean out that viper's den."

A shiver ran down Othniel's spine—along with a deep soul-urge to help Uncle Caleb rid the land of such evil. He wanted to ask about Shua again, but the two old men had retreated once more into the silent world of memories.

Othniel was still pondering what he knew of the land of Canaan and what he hoped to learn, when Ethan approached the dying fire circle. He extended an invitation to join a group of friends in a walk along the river, but Othniel shook his head. "I don't want to miss any of the stories these old warriors tell."

"Oh."

Ethan sat down beside his friend. He looked hopefully at Caleb and then at Joshua. Neither man looked up or spoke. He waited for a few minutes respectfully and then grinned. "Enjoy the storytelling, Oth. Catch up with us later, if you change your mind."

Othniel watched his friend disappear down the trail. *Ethan was too impatient.*

Joshua's weathered face crinkled in a smile. He winked at Othniel. Seeing no evidence that Caleb was about to launch into a story, Joshua said. "It is time we begin telling the stories of *this* valley. You remember how our army broke into bands when King Og fell, heading every direction in pursuit. I was with the men of Ephraim searching a small settlement of those huge black stone houses, when a band of giants burst from the cover of a willow thicket, racing northward toward the highest parts of Bashan. I signaled a small band to join me in chase, just me and that handful of men on the heels of five desperate ogres."

Caleb continued staring into the smoldering coals. It was hard to tell if he was listening or reliving his own story.

After a brief pause, Joshua continued. "We chased them through cattle pastures and oak forests. Pursued them mile after mile until the grass underfoot gave way to nothing but rocky rubble, a desolate tableland inhabited only by gazelles and conies. There in that forsaken place, half walled in by jagged peaks of weathered blackstone, we spied those giants milling in confusion on the edge of a precipice. Far from our comrades, fully expecting the giants to turn on us, we were nearly crippled by the powerless sensation of being insects easily crushed underfoot. But we shouted our battle cry—"Victory belongs to Yahweh!"—and those giants gave us one final, horrified look and leaped into oblivion." Joshua stared off into the distance. "I have often wondered what they saw."

Caleb arched one bushy white brow. He had been listening after all. "Giant grasshoppers," he replied, "magnified by the fear of the Lord."

"No doubt." Joshua's quick laugh was full of incredulity. "We couldn't breathe easily again until each of us peered over the cliff. Even when we saw their bodies dashed to pieces on the rocks below, we still had the feeling that a surviving giant might suddenly roar out from behind a rock and destroy all of us in his fury." He sounded tired and paused with a far-away look in his eyes.

When he spoke again, his voice had regained its vigor. "It took awhile, but at last, we recovered our senses. We stopped looking down at the blood and gore and lifted our eyes to the gift of God. That barren height overlooked a beautiful blue lake and an unbelievably lush, green plain extending in every direction as far as the eye could see. Beautiful Canaan. It was like our first view of the Valley of Eshkol forty years ago, only more distant and far more vast."

"Ah, Eshkol." Caleb said wistfully. "After weeks of fear traversing Canaan . . . after thirty-eight days of revolting observations, we came upon that valley. I still get goose bumps remembering it. Nothing we had seen compared to that jewel." He grinned at each of them, then fell silent again.

Othniel stood and arched his back into a stretch before settling back into place. "What about Shua?" he prompted. He knew the look on Uncle Caleb's face. His memories were stretching back beyond the recent battle with Og, back to the days of spying forty years before. Othniel knew the story well, but with each retelling, he learned something new. He didn't mind waiting.

He tried to imagine Eshkol. While the entire land was beautiful, the twelve spies found fruit larger and sweeter in that valley than words could describe. Only actual samples would do. Othniel had watched the glowing faces of Caleb and Joshua many times as they described that night to his generation: the heady thrill, the child-like gaiety and hilarity of running through the vineyards and orchards in the moonlight collecting pomegranates, melons, figs, and grapes.

Caleb locked eyes with Othniel and grinned as if he had heard his thoughts. "When we cut that giant cluster of grapes and Elidad and Hanniel headed down the road carrying it on a pole between them, we began joking about being chased. If our identity had been discovered, could those two have run without giving up the grapes? Would Paltiel be able to flee without smashing his bundle of soft, sweet figs, each as big as two fists put together? How would Shammua juggle his melons if he had to bolt for freedom?"

With a lift of his brows and a nod, Othniel encouraged his uncle to continue the familiar tale.

"Soon our laughter morphed into serious discussion. There was no way we could blend with travelers on the road with that fruit. No sane trader would head out toward the desert with such perishable goods. We agreed that it was better to cross the hills off-road, traveling all through the night."

The old man fell silent and closed his eyes for so long that Othniel began to wonder if he had nodded off, but Joshua took over the tale. "I'll never forget the knee-quaking, wet-palmed reality of retracing our steps past Kiriath-Arba with that fruit. The giant reigning as king over that city was not only huge, but had terrifyingly pale skin, white hair and red eyes. I did not want to see him again."

"Nor I!" Caleb added. "But the terror of that city made our arrival back at camp all the more jubilant." Othniel understood why Caleb did not sound jubilant as he said it. He knew exactly what his uncle would say next. "Jubilant . . . until the ten convinced everyone that entering Canaan would be a mistake."

Othniel shook his head. As often as he heard it, the story never made sense. "Why would the other spies carry those samples of fruit back to camp if they had such a negative view of the land?"

Joshua regarded him for a moment before he answered. "They did not carry that disastrous report back to camp with the fruit. It came later."

There was another long pause and then Caleb took over the story. "Cheering crowds followed as we marched straight to Moses, holding the samples high. Crowds packed every inch around the tabernacle as Paltiel waved his figs in the air with bulging eyes and dramatic description. I believe his exact words were: 'The bounty of the land is more wondrous than you could imagine. The trees are literally dripping with fruit like this. Never, even in the lushest gardens of Egypt, have we seen anything so extravagant.'

"Then Shammua of Reuben called out. 'Luxurious living awaits us: large houses with fine furniture and beautifully painted pottery jars for storing more produce than you can eat.'

"Someone else, I think it was Elidad, brought up the Canaanite clothing. 'Fine fabrics, skillfully made. Every color imaginable. Trunk after trunk of garments brought to their cities and towns by caravans from the east, the north, and the south. It is an inheritance beyond our wildest dreams.'"

Joshua broke into Caleb's enthusiastic descriptions just as he had forty years before. "As the other spies added more and more glorious details of the wealth of Canaan, I felt compelled to declare that judgment was on the land. Forty days of spying made it clear that God's indictment was just. 'Canaan indeed flows with milk and honey,' I said, 'but the stench of its corruption is also beyond belief.'"

There were no more long lapses, no more gazing into dead ashes. Internal fire blazed through the narrative as Caleb cut in. "'There will be war,' the ten declared. And they began describing the dark side of Canaan as passionately as they had described its glories. We begged the people to trust in God, but the other ten began arguing against us. The more we urged the need to end the violence and evil we had seen, the more the other spies spewed poison."

Joshua squeezed his eyes shut. "I can still see Gaddi of Manasseh shaking his finger at our trembling audience. I can hear . . ."

"We saw eee-vil you could not imagine . . ." Caleb cut in with the exact words, his eyes and nostrils flaring as he imitated the chilling tone. "We saw the hideous sons of Anak. We saw human blood flowing like water in the gutters on their religious festivals. It will be Israelite blood flowing there if we dare try to dislodge those giants."

Joshua broke into Caleb's dramatic reenactment with a hoarse whisper. "The course of the river reversed just that quickly. Rippling praise one moment—a torrent of despair the next. The ten detailed every horror they had seen. They declared that our untrained and poorly equipped army could never stand against those warrior giants. The more they spoke, the more they and their listeners were undone by mere thoughts of Canaan's power. When Gaddi announced that the land mysteriously devoured its own inhabitants, the others took up the same ridiculous assertion."

Joshua shot a pained look at Othniel. "You would not believe how everyone wailed. Caleb and I moved from group to group trying to reverse the tide. 'Put your faith in God,' we pleaded. 'What are giants to the God who battered Egypt into submission? The God who split the Red Sea so his people could pass through? Who drowned Pharaoh's entire army?'

"Over and over, we insisted, 'We should go up and take possession of the land. We can certainly do it.' But we only made the crowds angrier." Joshua's words hung in the air.

Othniel picked up a stick and poked at the coals again. It did not take long for a flicker of red to lick the blackened twig and then retreat back into the ashes. The old men did not resume the tale. "At least Yahweh had you two to remind the people of his power," he said.

Joshua found his voice first. "Yahweh did not need us. We needed him."

Othniel had heard the story of that terrible night many times, the panic intensifying to full hysteria, until by morning all the tribal princes were organizing a return to Egypt. After more than a year of freedom, they intended to beg Pharaoh to take them back as slaves. Even Judah and Ephraim—Caleb and Joshua's own tribes—were prepared to follow. They declared with an oath that no one must speak of marching into that Canaanite death trap again. Dissenting voices should be stoned."

Caleb wiped the corner of his eye. "That is when the mob bound the two of us and began dragging us out of camp. Women and children jeered and shook their fists while their men followed carrying stones."

"I prepared myself for death." Joshua's voice broke. "Moses tried to stop the riot as soon as he realized what was happening. Aaron pled for restraint, but there was no stopping the mob at that point."

Caleb ran his hand through his hair. "I believe they would have killed Moses and Aaron when they were through with us, but God heard our prayers."

Joshua finished the narrative. "The glory of God flashed from the Cloud. He saved us then just as he saved Phinehas after he slew Cozbi and Zimri. We were saved—but the end of the rebellion became the end of our dream."

Othniel took a deep breath. "Maybe Moses should not have sent the spies at all."

Joshua shook his head to indicate a clear no. "Israel needed the forty years of training, but who could have admitted it? It took those events at the camp of Kadesh-Barnea to reveal the feeble quality of our faith. And it took the travails of the past forty years to strengthen it."

Caleb tightened his lips in a grim smile. "So here we are: old men, the last remnants of Egypt, as we prepare to enter Canaan again."

Joshua cast a sideways glance at Othniel. "But here in this valley, this time, our people fought."

Caleb snorted like an old warhorse. "This time God did not give us a chance to give in to fear. The army of Sihon was upon us before we had time to think, and then the army of King Og marched against us ere we had caught our breath. We could only rely on God's deliverance, and as always, his deliverance was astounding."

Suddenly, Othniel remembered his original question. "But who was Shua?"

Caleb and Joshua exchanged a quick look of disbelief and broke into hearty laughter. "You can see why you have never heard of her, Othniel. The two of us distract each other."

Joshua slapped Caleb's knee. "Let me tell the story, old man. This time with no interruptions." He stared off into the distance for a moment, remembering, and then he began with an uncommonly tender edge to his voice. "As the twelve of us passed close by Kiriath-Arba on our return with all that fruit, we came upon a spring sheltered by a large oak tree. It was about a mile from the city—actually quite close to Abraham's burial cave. Though it was barely dawn, a woman was there, filling her water jar. She tried to ignore twelve strange men descending on her alone in that desolate spot, but I could see her hands shaking as she raised the jug to her head. And I felt impressed to tell her who we were. When I did, her fear visibly dissolved into relief, and she urged us to come to her home. There had been rumors of Israelite spies for weeks and the king had dispatched soldiers to find them. Shua offered to hide us until nightfall, promising water and food as soon as she had tended to her young daughter who was ill with a fever."

"Why would a Canaanite woman want to help you?"

Caleb started to answer, but Joshua held up his hand to silence him and continued the story. "Shua's family was from Jericho where her father ran an inn. Her first husband was a Moabite who taught her a little of Yahweh, but when he was killed, she fled to southern Canaan, eventually marrying an abusive merchant. Fortunately for her as well as us, he was away on a trading expedition. She offered kindness, a place to rest, a place to hide."

"But, Joshua, my friend," Caleb broke in. "She gave us so much more. Othniel, listen to this. Shua helped us understand the conflict that began with the sons of Noah. As the generations increased on the earth, the sons of Shem devoted themselves to peaceful living in harmony with their devotion to Yahweh while the sons of Ham formed great civilizations—Libya, Egypt, Babylon, Damascus. All but the youngest son, Canaan. He coveted this land along the Great Sea, but it was part of Shem's inheritance. He seized it anyway, driving out or killing the families settled there until Shem himself came and established a fortified city on Mount Zion, a refuge for his remaining descendants. Canaan's sons formed little kingdoms all around, warring against Shem, but always warring against each other as well. As Shem was nearing the end of his life, Yahweh sent Abraham to reclaim the land, but his descendants were few—until his grandson Israel. Then, according to the Canaanite story, the god Baal took charge. He withheld the rain, creating a famine that drove Israel and his sons to Egypt."

"Caleb, you are launching another distraction," Joshua protested. "The important thing, Othniel, is that Canaan was prevented from founding one great civilization, though many Canaanite kings down through the centuries dreamed of it, admiring the success, the splendor, and might of Egypt—which had been founded, of course, by one of Canaan's elder brothers. So when they heard the reports of Yahweh God freeing the enslaved descendants of Shem from the hand of Pharaoh, they were horrified. They learned how this God of gods still fought for the descendants of Shem, how his plagues laid Egypt's splendor to waste, and how he drowned Pharaoh's army in the Red Sea. Now the Children of Israel were coming to reclaim their long lost inheritance, and all Canaan was filled with dread."

Othniel had never before connected the ancient history of the nations with the promises of land in Canaan. When he looked at Caleb for confirmation, his uncle's eyes had grown misty. "The Canaanites lived in terror of what Yahweh would do next, yet Shua was the only one who showed interest in knowing him. My heart breaks when I remember how she begged to come with us, to become part of our people—a people led by such a good God."

"She wanted to join Israel right then and there?" Othniel asked.

Caleb nodded sadly. "Her husband would not be back from Syria for weeks. It was the perfect opportunity, but we did not have the authority to bring Canaanites back to camp. We prayed for her daughter, Keziah, and she seemed much improved afterward. We also prayed for them to be kept safe during the battles to come, and warned Shua to stay out of the cities when she heard that we had crossed the border."

"We assured her that we would look for her when our people began to settle Canaan." Joshua added quickly.

Othniel stared at the two old men. "I wonder what she thought of Yahweh when Israel was defeated and driven back into the wilderness."

"I pray her faith survived," Caleb muttered. "I pray that she did not attribute the defeat to the power of Canaan's gods."

"We must believe that God rewards those who seek him."

Othniel jabbed at the cold fire pit with his stick and stirred up only a puff of ash. The hours had passed so quickly that when Othniel noticed the fiery-orange sun nearly touching the rim of the western hills, he was surprised. Another Sabbath had come to a close, a good day filled with stories and long periods of thoughtful silence. "Your stories have been as healing as the purification rituals," he said.

"Indeed," Caleb agreed and gave Joshua a slap on the knee. "Don't become a stranger, old friend. You are the only one left who lived those days with me. This *has* been a blessed Sabbath of remembrance."

"*Has been?*" Joshua took one look at the sky and leaped to his feet. "Sundown already . . . I trust Phinehas has begun gathering the troops for evening prayer." His voice trailed behind him as he hurried away.

Caleb rose stiffly and followed, chortling at Joshua's distress.

The voices of the twelve thousand warriors flooded the Valley of Acacias, deep and rich, powerful as thunder. Othniel remained alone by the cold fire pit listening to Phinehas lead his army in the Red Sea victory song, and the old lyrics sank into the marrow of his bones with startling newness.

In the greatness of your majesty
You threw down those who opposed you.[16]

This song was bigger than the dramatic defeat of Pharaoh's army. It was also the story of Balaam, the story of Midian, and it was his story. He was part of a narrative so huge that the world itself could not contain it, his life a slim thread in the tapestry of Yahweh's story.

He watched the smoke from the bronze altar rise over the tabernacle, mingling with the music in a flaming sunset sky, and felt a strong connection to both groups of worshipers, though not present with either. Strange that something as ephemeral as altar smoke could link him solidly to his mother and brother, his clan, and all the people gathered around the tabernacle, stirring up home-hunger, not simply to be with his family, but to return to the peaceful, orderly ways of camp life, to be back where he belonged. At the same time, the voices of his companions reminded him that the war camp was also his home and would be for a long time.

As the song roared to its conclusion, he sensed the message pounding the dark ridges on both sides of the valley: a dirge over the smoldering ruins of Midian to the east, and a song of judgment to the Canaanite hills skulking away toward the west.

> *You stretch out your right hand,*
>> *and the earth swallows your enemies.*
> *In your unfailing love you will lead*
>> *the people you have redeemed.*
> *In your strength you will guide them*
>> *to your holy dwelling.*[17]

The holy dwelling of Yahweh, the tabernacle with its altar of sacrifice and covenant chest covered by the mercy seat was pitched now between the highlands of Canaan and the highlands of Midian and Moab. It bridged conflicts past and future with an alternative: dwelling with God. This song was sung for the first time on the banks of the Red Sea—before there was a tabernacle—but the dwelling place of God had always been part of the song, part of the eternal story.

You will bring them in and plant them
on the mountain of your inheritance—
the place, LORD, you made for your dwelling,
the sanctuary, Lord, your hands established.[18]

It struck him that the tabernacle could have been built after Israel reached the Promised Land, but the Lord purposely planned it to be portable, planned for them to bring it in and plant it. This was his destiny.

He had sung these words countless times in full view of the tabernacle and never saw the connection before. From where he sat, only the dark coverings of its topmost parts were visible and yet he saw it as never before. *Did anyone else standing in full view of God's sanctuary, anyone else in all the masses around the altar with Eleazar and Moses, see it as he did?*

Moses' rich bass tones blasted the hushed expectancy in awesome answer to Othniel's question. Not an old man's voice this, but like the mighty roar of a lion challenging his foes, he sang out the opening lines of another of his songs.

LORD, you have been our dwelling place
throughout all generations.

Immediately, Phinehas trumpeted back.

Before the mountains were born
or you brought forth the whole world,
from everlasting to everlasting you are God.[19]

Othniel's skin prickled into gooseflesh as voices from both camps joined the duel of praise. He did not like to hear himself sing, but at last, he too opened his mouth. The tune he added to the swelling sound might be off-key, but the message rang true. Yahweh was at work, slowly, inexorably regaining control of a world usurped by the ancient Serpent. Once again, Yahweh was establishing his dwelling in it, a place where he could walk and commune with mankind as he had with Adam.

May the favor of the Lord our God rest on us;
establish the work of our hands for us—
yes, establish the work of our hands.[20]

Othniel lingered long beside the ashes of a glorious Sabbath, fired by the challenge. The sky grew dark and the stars appeared. An evening breeze rose, stiff and chilly. The rowdy camaraderie of his brothers called from the distance. Othniel smiled and pushed himself to his feet. It was high time to get his cloak, find some supper, and join his companions.

King Nahari

The king of Jericho drummed his fingers on the carved cedar arms of his throne. He had put off this royal messenger from Moab all day. As shadows lengthened and he was informed that the man still waited in the outer courts, he relented.

Too soon, however, he regretted granting the audience. His head throbbed dully, and he had no energy for diplomatic palaver. As the man recited flowery praise for the city and its monarch, the king stared at the cedar beams over his head. Finally, he slammed his fist on the arm of his chair and shouted, "The point, man. What is your message? What does Balak want?"

"The point, my lord?" the ambassador sniffed and bowed respectfully.

The man reminded Nahari of a weasel.

"Coming directly to the point, my lord. In view of the most recent events in our region, King Balak extends an invitation for Jericho to renew our alliance and make it stronger yet. Certainly, there must be some anxiety here regarding the vermin infesting the plains of Moab just across the river."

"The *former* plains of Moab," the king sneered. "They were wrested from your hands by the Amorites decades ago, and now these *vermin*, as you say, these Israelites, have conquered the Amorites."

"Precisely, but it is quite unlikely that Israel will remain crammed in that narrow valley. Who knows where they will strike next, your lands or ours? Our kingdoms could maintain a watch from both sides of the river. Neither of us would be taken unawares, and the one not attacked could support the other from the rear."

The king scowled and rubbed his temples. "This is why you have called me from my couch? My head aches. I have barely recovered from illness." Irritation tingled through him and increased the pounding in his head. Trapping the messenger's eyes with a fierce look, he hissed. "I do not need your king. I have allied myself with the Five and the prophet from Babylonia."

The messenger blinked slowly. "Then, my lord, you surely *do* need an alliance with King Balak. You have not heard the news. The Five are destroyed, they and their armies slain by the hand of Israel. All that is left of the Midianite towns is ash and smoke. No one knows what happened to the prophet."

Nahari realized that his jaw had gone slack. He clamped his mouth shut and glared at the messenger. He had no response for him.

"These people spread a curse. Perhaps you have fallen under it also." The Moabite narrowed his eyes and studied the king's face. "A plague broke out among the people of Midian and parts of Moab, as well as among the people of Israel after the full moon festival on Mount Peor. Many of the Midianite temple nymphs who celebrated that night have died—along with the men who worshipped with them." He fixed the king with a leering grin. "Perhaps your illness was born of a Midianite wench through the curse of Israel. Hummm?"

The king's skin crawled with an icy chill, but he artfully donned an attitude of detachment. "The problems of Midian and Moab do not concern me. Has Israel shown any interest in crossing the river? I think not. Surely even they know that they must cross before the spring rains and melting snows of Hermon completely inundate the fords."

"But, sire—"

"I do not need Moab any more than I needed Midian," the king growled. "Jericho's strength is in her walls. I defy Israel and her desert god. Be gone, weasel." The king pulled a long jeweled dagger out of his belt and hurled it toward the ambassador.

As the man scuttled aside, the knife clattered across the stone floor. Scrambling to recover his dignity, the ambassador faced the king and pointed at him prophetically. "You will beg for Balak's help one day, but it will be too late."

As Nahari's bodyguard retrieved the dagger and handed it to the king, he watched the ambassador pull a warm hood over his head and hasten out of the room and into the night before he could throw the blade with keener aim. But King Nahari had lost interest in him. He pushed his dagger back into its scabbard and summoned his steward. "Send to the house of the women and inquire after Atarah. If she has recovered, bring her to my bedchamber. Only she, the Midianite girl, will do this evening."

The king rushed to his quarters and paced the floor as he waited for the girl. He need not have rushed. Nearly an hour passed before the young woman appeared. Although her cheeks were pale from her recent illness, her eyes had been carefully lined with kohl and her lovely full lips tinted red. Thick, black curls, plaited with strands of gold, formed lavish loops crowning her head.

"We know each other well," the king said without emotion. He fondled a coil of glossy black hair hanging seductively against her cheek and then ran his hand down to her neck. "You needn't have made such preparations for me."

"All the more reason to give you my best," Atarah replied.

Shrewd little vixen, this Midianite beauty. The king massaged the little hollow at the base of her throat with his thumb as his fingers tightened on her neck.

Atarah nuzzled his hand with her cheek and then slipped her arms around his neck. "Your steward made it clear that your desire tonight was for me alone," she whispered in his ear.

"He told you that, did he?" Nahari said flatly as he disengaged from her embrace. "Well, it is true." He studied her eyes as he informed her of the message delivered by the ambassador from

Moab. "I have received distressing news. My allies, the entire kingdoms of the Five—your people—have been totally annihilated by the Israelites. Surely, none of my other concubines or wives would do for such a night."

Nahari enjoyed seeing the wash of fear whitening her face. It made him feel even more powerful. If the news were true, and he did not doubt the report, then she had no home but this palace.

The understanding of that registered fleetingly on her face, but she quickly masked her alarm and began kissing the hands that had pushed her away. "You know why you called for me tonight," she murmured.

Beautiful as she was, King Nahari felt nothing.

"Our match is ordained, not by marriage, but by the gods. Our united love will bring the power of Baal to the ruler of Asherah's city."

I am made of stone tonight. She knows it, and since she cannot arouse the lust of my flesh, she thinks to inflame my lust for power. He did not like to be manipulated. He shoved her onto the bed with a growl. "Our united love brought me illness."

"How can you say that, my lord?" She slithered back on the soft linen covers as if this were ordinary pillow talk, all the while trying to lock his eyes in an intimate connection, "It is for love that the gods have saved us from this illness. Come to me. Renew your strength as we drink of love."

"Drink of love . . . ?" the king repeated inanely as he inched closer to the bed. He swallowed hard, his chin quivering like an adolescent as she loosened her robe.

"How charming," Atarah laughed. "You are a nervous boy tonight." She pulled her knees under her and knelt on the edge of the bed before him, letting the silky garment slide deliciously off her body into a puddle on the floor. "Your love is always new to me, my king."

"New . . ." His mouth went dry with unexpected passion, and he gasped at the powerful sensations electrifying his body. He pulled her close. Her little heart was beating just under those magnificent round breasts, quickening in expectation of his love. "New and powerful . . ." he whispered.

Sensing his arousal at last, Atarah's mouth softened with a seductive smile, her eyes inviting him to take her. "Kiss me, my lord. We will drink of love as if it were the first time for either of us."

As Nahari yielded to the intensity of his lust, the room dissolved into fog. He saw the jeweled handle of his knife flash before his eyes. He heard someone shout, "I give you justice to drink, not love." He felt the hard bronze blade plunge into soft flesh and heard a pitiful scream dissolve into a fading gurgle.

The fog cleared. The king's passion was spent. He rushed to the window, panting and retching. Vomit splattered the sill and ran down the outside wall. *My final gift to you, Midianite whore. Justice. Justice for the plague you brought. Your death—for death in my city.* He slumped to the floor, wiped his mouth with the back of his hand, and retched again at the smell of blood. He leaned his head back against the wall to gather strength and then bellowed for his steward.

The door opened cautiously. "So quickly, my king? The *great one* must not be himself tonight . . ." The manservant's snickering prattle entered the room ahead of him. "Perhaps I could send for a livelier girl? I thought this one looked pale . . ." As the door swung wide, the steward stopped agape in the doorway and covered his mouth with his hand. "O, my lord."

"Draw me a bath and see that this mess is cleaned up."

The king pulled himself to his feet, leaning on the windowsill to steady himself. "Send for Ahuzzath. I want Jericho cleansed of every Midianite woman. Exterminate all who remain within these walls.

"Tonight, sire?"

"Immediately."

EPILOGUE

Caleb

The seven days of cleansing were complete, and the elders were organizing the tribes for the distribution of plunder. Livestock lowed, brayed, baaed, and bleated, begging for release from the temporary stockade while the cleansed troops watched the assembly gather. Now and then, soldiers pitched high-spirited calls to sweethearts, mothers, and children over a barricade of wagons interspersed with ordered heaps of weapons, tools, clothing, and jewelry, and all the time the boisterous crowds babbled excitedly, eager to welcome their warriors home.

Caleb drew a deep breath, savoring every aspect of the happy hubbub simmering around him. The sights and sounds and smells frothed and bubbled like the aroma of a favorite stew, the taste of home and all that he loved. His daughter was bouncing with anticipation beside his little flock of excited grandchildren. He loved the way they tossed up a flutter of waves whenever he looked their way. He could almost feel the hugs and tugs and kisses. Their parents—his sons and daughters-in-law—waited with more reserve, gleaming eyes quietly revealing anticipation equal to that of their offspring. Caleb chuckled. He wasn't born yesterday. That glint in their eyes was more likely birthed by the spoils of war than by longing for his company, but who could blame them? The Lord *had* blessed. He found himself bouncing on his toes like the children, eager to get this process underway.

Joy came more often in giving than in getting, and, today, he would experience both. He pressed his toe against the bag at his feet just to hear the metallic clink of the surprise he and the other captains had planned for Moses, Eleazar, and Phinehas, and then realized that his nephew was watching. He felt a bit childish, but Othniel signaled his understanding with a quick lift of his brows and a light toe kick to his own bag.

When at last all the tribes had been arranged into clans and families, Eleazar called out, "The time has come to begin the distribution." The words, given with great priestly authority, were swallowed up in all the commotion. For the first time Caleb realized that the silver trumpets used for announcements were among the cleansed items with Phinehas.

The high priest's eyes crinkled in silent laughter. He tilted his head to one side, embracing the people with warm brown eyes as he waited. He was so much like his father, Aaron. He wouldn't be fighting the clamor. The people would realize soon enough the necessity of quieting down when nothing was happening. Part of Caleb wished he had been blessed with Eleazar's patience, for it was all he could do to keep from shouting out for people to quiet down.

He didn't have to wait long for others to do that for him. "Look. Eleazar is waiting to tell us what to do," one woman exclaimed in surprise.

"Do you want to see your fathers and sons, you chattering magpies?" another growled. "Or do you want to wait another week?"

"Quiet. We are holding up our own welcome party."

When the crowd had self-quieted, Eleazar put on a most solemn look. "You are all rejoicing over the seeming abundance of plunder. The truth is that this is but a part of the livestock. Some of the captured Midianite animals died of disease or the hardship of the march. Some went astray, and some were consumed by our hungry soldiers."

The crowd groaned. Eleazar was certainly building up to an-nounce a limited allotment. The high priest paused with a droll grin. Then, as if he had forgotten to mention a minor detail, he added, "Ah! But this is what remains: of sheep and goats, 675,000; of cattle, 72,000; of donkeys, 61,000; and of young maidens, 32,000."

Long cheers broke out so that he could not continue until the men who considered themselves the regulators of noise hushed the crowds again.

Eleazar laughed. "Yes. The wealth is great. Half has already been counted out to those who fought in battle. The priests will now distribute the other half to the remainder of the families of Israel."

Caleb slung his bundle over his back and nodded his prear-ranged signal to the other eleven captains. They, in turn, signaled their captains of a hundred while Eleazar continued his instruc-tions, "Every tribe must give the required share to the priests and Levites out of . . ." He paused and jerked his head around at the jangling sounds building behind him. "Out of . . . what's this?"

"Ha hah!" Caleb answered. "Praise the Most High God." He led the way toward Eleazar with the eleven other captains and the one hundred and twenty under-captains trailing behind, all bearing bulging bags of their own. While the parade clanked and clattered into formation around Moses and the priests, Caleb shouted so that no one in the crowd would miss his words.

"Good news follows good news. We numbered the men of every tribe who fought under our command. Not one is missing. Not one is seriously wounded. Therefore, we captains return *all* the gold articles each of us acquired to the Lord who blessed us." He opened his bundle and let the glinting gold tumble onto the ground before Eleazar. Then, one by one, the remaining captains of one thousand and the captains of one hundred poured additional beautifully-crafted articles on the pile until a mountain of treasure rose thigh-high between the captains and their priests.

"Did your commander order this?" Moses asked sternly. "Thank offerings cannot be coerced."

Phinehas shrugged his shoulders. "This generosity is a surprise to me as much as to you, but I could not be more pleased at their understanding. Is not the warm blood still circulating in the brave men who followed me worth more than this cold metal? Yahweh, our Banner of Victory, is worthy of any freewill offering we can offer him. He has blessed this endeavor beyond what we deserve."

Eleazar caught his son's eyes briefly with an approving smile, then tipped his head toward the captains to acknowledge the gift. "Whenever we use articles crafted from this metal, we will remember this victory and our courageous army. All glory to the Lord of Hosts for preserving you in this fight.

"Now, enough of ceremony. The representatives of each family are already lined up by clans to receive their fair share of the plunder." The high priest's smile broadened even more as he turned toward the regiments of regular soldiers with a congratulatory salute. "You are purified in accordance with the rituals of the law and your share of plunder has already been allotted to you. Now, you may rejoin your loved ones in the holy camp of Yahweh."

Another long cheer arose, followed by a rushing swirl of hugs, smiles, and tears as the separated groups merged into one, but hours passed before the distribution of livestock, young maidservants, and possessions was complete.

Othniel

That evening, Othniel loped toward the gathering of the Calebite clan in an attempt to make up for lost time. The words of the old war hero always stirred his blood, but tonight—tonight the tale would be his own as well. He hadn't meant to be late, but he insisted on doing all the evening chores himself and did them slowly, savoring the simple joy of being home.

He had waved his mother and brother on before him, but now that he approached the leaping firelight alone and began to make out the faces around it, he realized his mistake. His mother Sarah and Seraiah were sitting in the shadows just behind Caleb—with his always-unsettling cousin sitting close to her father's side with her head resting on his shoulder. Trying to give his uncle a quick nod, enough to show proper respect, while carefully avoiding contact with Acsah's lethally piercing emerald eyes was like planning a battle strategy.

He was still circling the gloom just outside the ring of firelight when his mother called out, "Othniel, we're right here."

Caleb twisted around with a welcoming smile. "Shalom, Othniel."

"Othniel is here. Tell us the story, Grandpa. Othniel is finally here."

Caleb laughed and wiggled his eyebrows at Othniel. "Here we have just returned, eager to slip back into our old routines, but all these . . ." He swept a hand around the circle indicating Acsah and his sons, his daughters-in-law, nephews, nieces, and droves of bright-faced grandchildren. "These think the purpose of our return is to regale them with the adventures of war."

"I want to hear you tell the story as much as anyone," Othniel mumbled as he settled into place beside his brother.

"Even you? Hmph. You were there."

Othniel risked a grin. "You never know what you missed."

Caleb's bushy brows drew together in a frown. "The more of battle you miss, the better." He paused a moment, turning sideways to study the row of children with their wide, gleaming eyes. "War is gory, not glorious, but I am blessed with a family worth fighting for. The light in their eyes warms me far more than this blazing fire."

Acsah sat up straight. "War may be gory, Abba, but how would we learn that God is the true hero of every battle if it were not for your stories?"

Caleb smiled fondly at her. "Don't let me forget that." He joggled his shoulders, returning to his comfortable position with face toward the fire, and Acsah snuggled against his shoulder again.

"It is good to be back in this circle," he began. "I have gained a greater understanding of the One who tenderly shelters and preserves his fledglings under his wings—though weapons are hurled against us or plague runs rampant. This is a new song that flamed into my head in bits and pieces through the anguish of these past weeks of war. Listen and then we will sing it together.

> He that nests in the secret place of the most High
> is sheltered by the shadow of Almighty wings.
> I will say of Yahweh, "He is my refuge and my fortress:
> my God; in him will I trust."[21]

Only when the group had learned the old war hero's new verse and had clapped and sung many other songs, old and new—only when hearts were fired by praise—did Caleb lean forward to begin telling of the Midianite battles. His tone was hushed and filled with awe.

"That first night, we came to the crest of a hill and beheld the innumerable hordes of enemy soldiers who had marched out and camped against us. Black tents filled the plain in every direction. We reminded each other that Yahweh had seen fit to guide us there while the enemy slept. Imagine the fear that shuddered through each man with the realization that we came with only twelve thousand men. Were it not for our God, we would have had no confidence to attack with our meager force."

He detailed Phinehas's military decisiveness, the attack, and defeat of the confused enemy. The family smiled and cheered at the triumphant conclusion to the story of the first battle. Then as Caleb began the tale of the second battle—the fierce resistance, the onslaught of wave after wave of Midianite foot soldiers with their long, curved scimitars, of camels crashing through the melee, their riders lopping off heads to one side and then the other, the frustration of finding his men pushed back time and again—hardly a breath disturbed the air. Hardly a breath, that is, until he mentioned catching a glimpse of Balaam.

Othniel chuckled at the collective intake of breath. He had the same reaction when he saw the prophet on the day of that battle. Along with all Israel, he believed that the instigator of all their trouble had returned home to Babylonia.

"Yes, children, I heard your gasp," Caleb said. "Balaam was there, but mind you don't suck up all the air if you want our fire to thrive."

He wagged a warning finger as one of his grandsons took in another exaggerated breath. "It was no joke, Mushi. I saw that red-bearded devil-prophet standing high on the ridge watching the struggle below. It occurred to me that he was invoking the power of Baal and using his incantations to thwart the prayers of Phinehas. He was surrounded by a net of black-eyed bodyguards, but I fought my way toward him with all remaining energy and resolve. The victory would not be complete if that evil man escaped. Justice demanded his death, and I dedicated myself toward that end.

"I was attacked first on one side and then the other, my progress thwarted on every hand, each assailant bent on ending my life. I felt the resistance against me waxing all the more fierce the closer I came to the summit. Othniel fought in my wake, leading his band into the paths I cleared. I took great comfort in knowing that my boys followed, courageously adding their swords to the charge. If I failed, if my sword could not fell that foul prophet, surely one of theirs would."

Othniel was glad for the shelter of darkness at the mention of his name, but Caleb did not turn around to look at him. The narrative continued without embarrassing interruption.

"At last, I managed to come up behind the seer. But I could not kill him that way. He needed to face his treachery, to understand that his work had been undone, so I called out to him, 'Ho, cursed prophet! The rebellion is quelled. Your evil plot has failed.'

"The seer turned and looked at me with wild, uncomprehending eyes. 'Quelled?' he repeated. 'Failed?'

"'Israel rests secure under the sheltering wings of Yahweh once more,' I replied smugly.

"Whether gripped with despair or anger I know not, but Balaam shrieked like a madman, 'What of Cozbi and her prince?'

"I touched my sword to his chest. He had not bothered to wear a breastplate. 'May this be the final revelation to your twisted mind, O seer of Babylon: Cozbi, daughter of King Zur, and Zimri of Simeon are dead. Slain by the sword of our God—and his blade now desires *your* heart.'

"Balaam looked around frantically. His bodyguards were fully engaged by Othniel's band, but the prophet ripped a javelin from the hand of one even as he fought. As he lunged for me, Othniel thrust his sword through the now-unarmed bodyguard and the man crumpled against the prophet. The impact nearly toppled him and was enough to throw off his deadly aim. With a solid crack of my sword, I parried his attack, snapping the wooden staff of his javelin in two. Looking straight into those odious, reptilian eyes, I cried, 'This is your day of judgment!' and drove him through with my sword. Balaam gurgled in the blood that poured from his mouth. Never again would the lips of that false prophet utter his lies."

Caleb paused, looking around the stunned circle. "The battlefield was just like this at that moment—quiet as the eye of a tornado. Hundreds of eyes were watching me from up and down the slope, God's army witnessing the death of the one who brought this trouble upon us. Balaam was the last man on that field to fall."

Jonathan slipped into the glow of Caleb's family fire while the old hero was finishing the gripping tale of Balaam's demise. Othniel had no question in his mind that the one who attracted his Levite friend to this particular family circle tonight was his cousin. He watched his friend flash smiles across the flames, out of keeping with Caleb's account, baited smiles tossed toward Acsah, and Othniel found it deeply unsettling although he could not have explained why.

What Jonathan couldn't hear from the far side of the fire as Caleb concluded were Acsah's adoring words. "You are my hero, Abba. My life is complete again now that you are safely returned." She tucked her hand into the fold of her father's arm and laid her head on his shoulder. Her words were most likely not ones his Levite friend would like to hear.

Caleb grinned and patted Acsah's hand as the attention of the group turned to Jonathan. He was already capering about the fire, amusing the little company with his own account of that same battle.

"Picture the dreariness of acting as aide to a captain who fought with prayer instead of a sword. I rode my donkey over here. I rode my donkey over there. Over here, over there, until I was sick to death of delivering messages. My brothers were fighting for their lives, but my only wounds were from the pounding my backside received from my donkey's saddle. My fingers itched to lift my sword with my brothers, but my cousin always seemed to have another dispatch. At last, when it seemed that the Midianites were making their final charge, Phinehas gave me leave to join the battle.

"I rushed off to help my comrades, but I had not gone fifty paces from my cousin's side when I came on Ethan locked in mortal combat with two assailants at once. I cracked the skull of one of those Baal-worshippers like this, and then turned to assist him with the other." Jonathan's ruddy face fairly glowed as he re-enacted his exploits, becoming more and more animated as his audience laughed in merriment.

He caught Acsah's eyes in a moment of dramatic pause. It occurred to Othniel that this gleaming flash of white teeth in an extraordinarily handsome face would have been appealing but for a discomforting lack of humility. Rather than listening to the story, he found himself assessing Jonathan's perfectly combed and oiled hair and beard and the way the newly acquired Midianite robe was belted low, falling open just enough to reveal hints of the proud young chest within—an odd garment for a Levite since it lacked the tassels shot with blue threads required by the covenant.

Caleb exhaled audibly as he stood up and reached for a pole to stir the fire. "Prance and prattle," he said under his breath. As he shifted the wood, a shower of sparks swept skyward with the smoke, dazzling for a moment, then gone. "Worthless for heat," he muttered. "We prod the fire, not for that, but to encourage the steady coals."

Listen, my cousin. Your father is wise. Listen to him.

Acsah glanced at her father, momentarily puzzled by his cryptic comment; then her attention was reeled back by the charm of the storyteller.

"The ferocity of the battle was indescribable," Jonathan continued, now addressing Acsah directly. "I spotted Othniel in need of support and was hacking my way toward him when a towering, black-garbed hulk on camelback charged at me, swinging a long curved scimitar." He outlined a shape as high as he could reach and enacted swift and mighty sword thrusts toward a point above his head. "I could not help Othniel or anyone else. I was fighting for my life. Suddenly, a spear flew at the rider from the back—a Midianite spear—and the camel dumped the impaled man at my feet. My sword was already mid-swing when the camel ran off, snorting and squalling, and the stroke of my sword was perfectly lined up to put that Midianite out of his misery. I stood, panting heavily, staring at all the blood, hardly believing what I had done, when I heard Othniel shout, 'Behind you.'

"I turned, and all I could see was an arm with a spear rushing for me, directed right at my heart." Jonathan patted his chest and spun in a brisk war dance, face aglow in response to the gasps of his listeners. "I ducked down and out, like this, but it was Othniel who drove his blade into the man's back as he lunged past me. I would have been dead for certain, but for my friend's sharp eye and sharper sword."

The crowd cooed their approval, heads turning as they searched for Othniel and found him sequestered in the shadows. Acsah turned so abruptly that she captured his eyes momentarily in an admiring glance. He blushed and lifted his face to the night sky, shaking his hair back over his shoulders.

"Don't be so shy, my friend." Jonathan said with a laugh. He pushed past Acsah and Caleb to Othniel's dim refuge and nudged his friend's shoulder with his knee. "This young Israelite is well named: Othniel, lion of God. In truth, he should be telling this story."

"Hear, hear," someone called out. "Let's hear from Othniel, lion of God."

Othniel's neck twitched, but there was no way to cast off all this attention with a mere toss of the head.

"Lions don't recount their exploits merely to entertain the pride," Caleb said.

"Maybe he is no lion at all," someone quipped.

"Or maybe just a very shy lion."

A burst of giggles erupted from a group of young women.

Jonathan flashed a look of compassion Othniel's way and added more words of praise. "Shy perhaps . . . but a brave young lion, an honor to Judah's banner." He grinned as the young women showered Othniel with even more unwanted admiration.

"Behold the lion of God," he continued. "Aware of the hunt. Never distracted—he knows exactly what is going on in the four directions around him at every moment. I wouldn't be here to tell this story, but for being personally rescued by Judah's young lion."

Othniel stood as the group cheered. He was taller and huskier than Jonathan, and he felt almost fatherly as he pulled gently at Jonathan's shoulder. "And you are the cub of Levi—always at play. I say it is time for the cub to return to the lair for sleep."

A new burst of feminine giggles brought the flush of embarrassment to Jonathan's cheeks this time, and Othniel joined in with the howling laughter of the men. When the merriment died down, Caleb took charge. "Enough storytelling for tonight. Othniel has spoken rightly. Lions and lionesses, young and old, need their rest. Off to your lairs, all of you."

The clan dispersed as the old man rose and began spreading the fire. Acsah stooped by his side collecting coals for the next one, and Othniel slipped into the darkness with Jonathan in tow, his heart aglow with the flame of family love. It was unbelievably good to be home.

ENDNOTES

1. Much of the dialogue in this section (Chapter 3, Balaam's Tale) is taken from the biblical narrative in Numbers 22 (NIV), including the conversations between the donkey and Balaam, the words of the angel, and the initial conversation between King Balak and Balaam.
2. Numbers 23:7-10 (NIV), v. 10 author's paraphrase.
3. Numbers 23:18-24 (NIV), includes author's paraphrase.
4. Numbers 24:3-4 (NIV).
5. Numbers 24:5-7 (NIV).
6. Numbers 24:8-9 (NIV).
7. Numbers 24:14 (NIV).
8. Numbers 24:15-17 (NIV).
9. Numbers 24:18-19 (NIV).
10. Numbers 24:20-24 (NIV).
11. Psalms 90:7 (NIV).
12. Numbers 26:5-7, 12-14, 20-22 (KJV).
13. Exodus 15:1-2 (KJV), author's paraphrase.
14. Exodus 20:2-12 (NIV), author's paraphrase.

15. Exodus 34:6-7 (KJV), author's paraphrase.
16. Exodus 15:7 (NIV).
17. Exodus 15:12-13 (NIV).
18. Exodus 15:17 (NIV).
19. Psalms 90:1-2 (NIV).
20. Psalms 90:17 (NIV).
21. Psalms 91:1-2 (NIV), author's paraphrase.

The Family of Nations

descended from

Terah

9th Patriarch in the Line of Shem

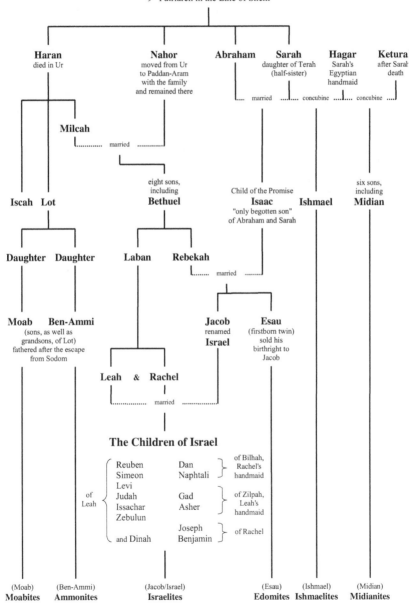

LIST OF CHARACTERS

Bold print identifies the seven main characters. Abihail is the only fictional character of those seven.

Names in italics are fictional characters or unnamed Biblical characters whom I have named.

Names in regular print were actual people included in the Biblical narrative.

ISRAELITES

Abihail (father of strength)	*Acsah's best friend from childhood, daughter-in-law of Achor*
Abijah (My father is Yahweh)	*Salmon's mother, wife of Prince Nashon*
Achor (trouble)	Unfaithful man of Judah, father of Eliab, father-in-law of Abihail
Acsah (anklet)	**Caleb's only daughter**
Ada (beauty)	*Salmon's young sister, daughter of Prince Nashon*
Bithia (daughter of Yahweh)	*Young woman of Judah*
Caleb (capable)	Acsah's father, hero, faithful spy of the tribe of Judah

Eleazar (God has helped) — High priest of Israel, son of Moses' brother Aaron

Eliab(God is my father) — *Younger son of Achor, Abihail's husband*

Eran (watchful) — *Man of Judah ensnared by Baal worship*

Ethan (enduring) — *One of the young men of Judah*

Haggi (festive) — *Unfaithful man of Judah ensnared by Baal worship*

Hannah (grace) — *Othniel's grandmother*

Hattil (doubtful) — *Abihail's sister-in-law, wife of Eliab's brother, Jamin*

Igal (avenger) — *Young man of Judah, noted for his size and strength*

Jamin (right hand) — *Achor's eldest son, Abihail's brother-in-law*

Jonathan (the gift of Yahweh) — **Levite, Moses' grandson**

Joshua (savior or whose help is Yahweh) — Moses' military commander, camp aide, and forty-year disciple.

Mara (bitter) — *Achor's wife, Abihail's mother-in-law*

Moses (drawn from water) — Legendary lawgiver, Israel's leader from the Exodus to the Jordan

Nashon (enchanter) — Salmon's father, Prince of Judah

Othniel (lion of God) — **Acsah's cousin, Caleb's nephew, first of the future judges of Israel**

Phinehas (mouth of brass) — **Future high priest, son of Eleazar, grandson of Aaron**

Salmon (garment) — **Prince of Judah upon his father's death, close friend of Acsah**

Sarah (princess) — *Othniel's mother, sister-in-law to Caleb*

Shammai (desolate) — *Old man who dies of plague east of the Jordan, grandfather of Igal*

Shaul (asked) — *Man of Judah ensnared by Baal worship*

Zimri (musical) — Simeonite Prince, Cozbi's lover, slain by Phinehas

FOREIGNERS

Balaam (foreigner)	Babylonian prophet who plots to destroy Israel

Canaanite

Asherah (straight)	Goddess of fertility and war
Baal (lord)	God of storm and fertility
Nahari (snorter)	*King of Jericho*
Rahab (wide)	**Innkeeper's daughter, singer at North Wall Inn, Jericho**
Shua (prosperity)	*Woman who befriended Caleb and Joshua forty years earlier*

Midianite

Evi, Rekem, Zur, Hur, Reba	Five kings who plot with Balaam to destroy Israel
Cozbi (deceitful)	King Zur's daughter, in league with Balaam
Atarah (crown)	*Midianite consort sent to King Nahari of Jericho*

Moabite

Asanath (worshipper of Neith)	*Priestess of temple of Kiriath-Huzzoth in Moab*
Balak (spoiler)	King of Moab

THE
STONES OF GILGAL
NOVELS

The *Stones of Gilgal* novels will transport you into an ancient world, a riveting era of biblical history obscured by the mists of time. The journey begins with the Children of Israel camped in the beautiful Valley of Acacias on the east bank of the Jordan River. Although human eyes see only a river separating Israel from the Promised Land, primordial powers of darkness are gathering to prevent a crossing that will change the world. As prophets, priests, and kings jostle for power and cultures collide, your heart will be touched by the sorrows and chilled by the fears of one brave Canaanite girl and six young Israelites who discover that claiming their long lost inheritance, and carving out a new life there, entails more than crossing that river.

But cross they do, at the most unlikely time—proving beyond doubt that a contest between Baal, the storm god of Canaan, and Yahweh, creator of the universe, is no contest at all for Yahweh. After a miracle crossing takes the Israelites to the other side of a river swollen to a raging torrent by spring rains, the twelve tribes of Israel commemorate the event by setting up a *gilgal,* a circle of twelve stones taken from the riverbed. It will take decades to achieve the peace implied by the term "Promised Land," but through those years of terror and triumph, the Stones of Gilgal will remain as a solid reminder that Yahweh is powerful and real. The themes presented in this gripping saga are universal, profound, and deeply moving, lingering in the mind long after the final page is turned.

THE STONES OF GILGAL
BOOK TWO

A RIVER TO CROSS

A csah sang snatches of the "Dwelling Place" as her shuttle flew.

> *Lord, you have been our dwelling place*
> *throughout all generations.*
> *Before the mountains were born*
> *or you brought forth the whole world,*
> *From everlasting to everlasting, you are God . . .* [1]

Moses had written this psalm after the appalling incident with the golden calf. Her people learned the song as they constructed the holy tent and its furnishings. They sang it during the Wanderings, sang it for forty years camped around that tabernacle, God's Dwelling Place. Acsah had known it all her life, but never had it seemed as fitting as on this bright morning. Israel was at one with her God. The war begun by the schemes of the prophet Balaam was over. Abba was home again, and he had just given her this fine Midianite loom gleaned from among the items of plunder.

---

[1] Psalm 90:1, 2 (NIV)

We are consumed by your anger
   and terrified by your indignation.
You have set our iniquities before you,
   our secret sins in the light of your presence . . .

Teach us to number our days aright,
   that we may gain a heart of wisdom . . .

Satisfy us in the morning with your unfailing love,
   that we may sing for joy and be glad all our days.[2]

Acsah's spirits soared at the mastering of a new craft—and at the surprise she was creating for Caleb. She used the small loom they carried during the Wanderings to make an occasional mat, but there had been little need for new textiles and the work on that small tool was tedious. This was pure joy.

Not only that, but today, the need and the blessing came together perfectly. As soon as she welcomed her father home the previous afternoon, she noticed the frayed condition of his robe. War and seven days of purification washings had taken their toll. At just the right time, the Lord had blessed them with many baskets of wool, and her endlessly turning spindle had spun it into yarn during the long days of the Midianite War. Today, she could not keep from singing as her eyes carefully followed the movement of the shuttle through the warp shed, laying down row after row of filling yarns. At the rate her fabric was growing, she would complete Abba's new garment before noon.

Hesitant footsteps shuffled in the sand of the walkway. Could her father be returning already? No. A quick glance at the shadowy movement on the edge of her field of vision told her it was only Jonathan.

"Shalom, Returned Warrior," she said. "That was quite the storytelling last night." She hoped her smile was appropriately hospitable since she did not take time to look up or slow the pace of her work.

---

[2] Psalm 90:7, 8, 12, 14 (NIV)

Jonathan cleared his throat with a short, nervous cough. "The best part is that I am alive to tell the story."

The silence that followed became so long and awkward that Acsah stopped the shuttle at the end of the row and looked up. His normally animated face was serious as death. "Father isn't here. You can find him down by our flocks, strengthening the new wagon we acquired. He is quite eager to cross the river now that the war is over."

"I already found him there, which is why I have come to see you."

Acsah guided the shuttle on another pass through the loom, feeling the intensity of his gaze as she waited for him to say more. She laid down two more rows. "This loom was part of Father's acquisitions from the war," she said at last, filling the silence without looking up. "What did you bring home?"

"Quite a lot, really. God truly blessed us." Jonathan began pacing.

Acsah stopped. She tucked the shuttle into the warp threads and gestured toward the cushion beside her. "Sit down, Jonathan, and take a deep breath. Why are you so anxious? You are making *me* nervous."

Ignoring her request, he thrust his hand into the bag slung over his shoulder, pulled out a gleam of gold and green, and held it out on his palm. "I brought this for you from my share of the Midianite plunder."

As she took the necklace and held it up in the sunlight, five emeralds flashed and sparkled, the very color of the sunlit meadows in this lush Jordan valley. "Beautiful!" she gasped in awe.

Jonathan's usual smile illuminated his face for the first time that morning. "But it does not come close to the beauty of your green eyes."

She laughed. "Jonathan, you flatter me. But this gift . . . it is too much. I can't take it." She held it up for him to take back.

Jonathan seized the outstretched hand with the necklace and enclosed it in both of his as he fell on his knees beside her. "In truth, it is not enough. You were named for a little ornament, that anklet you always wear, but you are a crown that would honor the head of any man who could claim you as his own. Acsah, I love you. Let me be that man. My father and I have already spoken to your father regarding marriage."

Acsah stared at him. "What did my father say?"

"He said you were very capable of deciding for yourself."

His face was so endearingly expectant at that moment, she could hardly bear to crush his hopes, but those hopes were wrongly placed. "Jonathan, I love you dearly as a friend, but marriage—"

"All I could think about while I was gone with the army was you. Every dream, every waking moment, even when I thought I was facing certain death, there was only you. I will accept no answer but 'yes.'" Jonathan leaned close to embrace her, but she pulled back.

"That answer I can't give you—now or ever. Thank you for the honor of your request, but it cannot be."

Jonathan drew back, studying her eyes for some understanding. Suddenly, he leaped to his feet and began pacing again. "Don't tell me that you love my cousin," he groaned.

"Cousin? Which cousin? What are you talking about?"

"Phinehas."

"Phinehas?" Acsah smothered a laugh. "He is a priest. He must marry a Levite girl. I can think of him in only one way—someday he will be my high priest."

"Well, it's fortunate that you don't love him." Jonathan's expression reminded her of a petulant child. "If you married my cousin, I would kill myself."

"Jonathan, stop. You are talking like a mad man."

"Well, I was almost mad with jealousy the day Phinehas was introduced as the one God had chosen to command the troops for this war. Your admiration for him was . . . was . . . well, more enthusiastic than the occasion warranted." He began to pace again. "Who then? Salmon? Ethan? Surely not Igal or Othniel."

Jonathan's possessive arrogance was making Acsah angry. "I do not have to answer that question."

"But I need to know if there is someone—"

"One man has my heart, only one," she snapped. "He is the center of my life, and I do not feel obligated to reveal his name to you."

Jonathan's face went dark with despair. He raked his hand through his hair and his whole body slumped.

Acsah felt a stab of regret. She had to finish this unpleasant conversation immediately. *Stay calm, stay calm,* she continued reminding herself as she rose to her feet. She placed her hand gently on Jonathan's arm. "My father has my heart, Jonathan. Who can measure up to Caleb in courage or kindness? In righteousness or wisdom? I am quite content to remain only his daughter."

Jonathan swayed with a sigh of relief, and his voice took on a soft, reasoning tone. "Our love and respect for your father is mutual. Next to my own grandfather, I regard Caleb above all other men, but you cannot mean to reject *me* forever because of him. I don't want to wait to claim you as my bride, but I will, if that is what you want. Like Jacob, I would wait seven years for my Rachel and it would seem but a day."

"Don't think of waiting for me, Jonathan. This will not be."

"Your father is old, Acsah. You care for him now, as he cares for you, but who will you have when he is gone? The inheritance in Canaan will go to your brothers. Where will you go then?"

Acsah gasped out her rage. "Enough! Please leave." With a flash of green and gold, she flung the necklace toward him and darted into the tent.

"Acsah, please. I did not mean to make you angry. I just want you to see reality. I *will* wait for you. I could never love anyone else."

Acsah could see his shadow on the tent wall as he leaned toward the silence. She held her breath.

"Please . . . tell me I have a chance," he cried hoarsely. Never had she heard such desperate tears choke a man's words.

She did not answer or move—even after she heard his footsteps crunching slowly away. Her head was still spinning with images of his shattered visage when she finally emerged from the tent. She picked up the shuttle with shaking fingers. *Think of something else, anything else.*

An image of aged Miriam came to her mind and she began singing Miriam's song from the Red Sea story.

Sing to the Lord,
  For he is highly exalted.
Both horse and driver
  he has hurled into the sea.[3]

As her singing grew more vigorous, her fingers fairly flew.

---

[3] Exodus 15:21

CONTACT INFORMATION

MOUNTAIN VIEW PRESS

To order additional copies of this book, please visit
www.mountainviewpress.com
Also available on Amazon.com and BarnesandNoble.com
Or by calling toll free (855) 946-2555

CPSIA information can be obtained
at www.ICGtesting.com
Printed in the USA
BVHW071434110720
583421BV00004B/363

9 781632 323712